DYED IN THE WOOL

ED JAMES

For Pat and Ginty.

OTHER BOOKS BY ED JAMES

SCOTT CULLEN MYSTERIES SERIES

1. GHOST IN THE MACHINE
2. DEVIL IN THE DETAIL
3. FIRE IN THE BLOOD
4. DYED IN THE WOOL
5. BOTTLENECK
6. WINDCHILL
7. COWBOYS & INDIANS

CRAIG HUNTER SERIES

1. MISSING
2. HUNTED

DS VICKY DODDS SERIES

1. TOOTH & CLAW

DI SIMON FENCHURCH SERIES

1. THE HOPE THAT KILLS
2. WORTH KILLING FOR
3. WHAT DOESN'T KILL YOU
4. IN FOR THE KILL
5. KILL WITH KINDNESS

DAY 1

Wednesday
3rd October 2012

1

Detective Constable Scott Cullen parked and got out. He locked the door of his Golf, checking all four buttons were down. He really should get a new car.

He crossed the road before walking up the short garden path. He knocked on the door and stepped back. The house was a post-war semi, the long street populated entirely with them, all with subtle differences — ivy, cladding, paved drives, front gardens, porches, conservatories. The street that could just as easily be advertised as any of three areas, depending on which was more in vogue at the time, Trinity holding the current edge over Granton and Newhaven.

The door opened, the noise of drunken chatter bursting out, accompanied by the tang of cigarette smoke. DS Sharon McNeill scowled as she stepped onto the porch, closing the door behind her.

"Sorry I'm late."

She raised her eyebrows. "Forty-five minutes is a lot to make up for, Scott. Your dad and my mum are both hammered."

"My counselling ran over and the traffic was a nightmare."

"This is a bloody nightmare."

Cullen rubbed his forehead. "Sorry, this is my fault. This was all my idea. Dinner with both sets of parents. What was I thinking?"

"When you suggested it I thought it was quite romantic. Now... Bloody hell."

He touched her arm. "Well, I'm here now. I'll give you some respite care."

She laughed. "You owe me for this. Big time."

"I don't need to guess your terms."

She grabbed him and kissed him. "That's just a taster."

"I can taste red wine. I suppose I'll be driving, then?"

"If you can call what that car does driving." She pulled him inside by the hand and led him down the long corridor, decorated in magnolia and pine.

He hung his suit jacket up on the coat rack halfway down, glancing at a photograph he'd never seen before. Sharon in her twenties, posing moodily for the camera. She looked thinner than was healthy, a lot lighter than her slightly voluptuous frame now. Her hair was in a sort of wedge cut — shaved up one side and flicked over. He pointed at it. "When was that?"

She closed her eyes briefly. "Mum just found that the other week. There are another five new photos of me she's put up. None of Deborah, so it must be for your parents' benefit."

Cullen laughed. "I love the look. Maybe you should go back to it."

"That was after I came back from university in Aberdeen." She prodded him in the chest with her finger. "That's the last I want to hear of it."

"So, aye, Mary found this box of old photos of Sharon when she was cleaning out the spare bedroom the other week." Brendan McNeill started handing around the first in the pile, similar to the one in the corridor. He looked over at his daughter and grinned, a mixture of pride and pleasure in making her feel awkward.

"That haircut didn't exactly suit you, did it, princess?" He playfully grabbed Sharon's cheek.

"No." She pulled away.

"There's a couple of good shots in there, though, as well." Mary McNeill was slightly slurring her words. "A lot of memories, good and bad."

"We've got some lovely shots of Scott." Liz Cullen reached down to her handbag.

"We've a lot more photos of his sister." David Cullen's thumb drumming on the dining table was irritating the shit out of Cullen already. "That's what happens, though. You get a new camera for the first born and take as many photos as you have rolls of film. By the time wee Scotty came along, we'd seen it all." He laughed. "Well, almost all. The bath times were different." He made a hook with his finger.

Mary and Brendan fell about.

"Cheers." Cullen fired daggers at his dad with his eyes.

"It was the same with our two." Sharon's mum drained her glass. "Lots of photos of Sharon and hardly any of young Deborah."

Cullen frowned. "I thought Deborah was older?"

"What makes you think that?"

"She's settled down, got married and had wee Rachel. I'd just assumed."

Sharon patted Cullen's hand. "She's two years younger, Scott."

"Right."

"It's funny how they drift apart, though." Cullen's dad handed the last of the photos on to his mother. "Scott's sister lives in Edinburgh again and how many times has he seen her?"

"I've tried." Cullen looked at Sharon. "We've tried. Michelle just doesn't seem to want to see me."

"You sure?"

Cullen raised his hands. "Yes!"

"We're both really busy." Sharon leaned in towards Cullen. "Working in CID isn't really a nine-to-five job, despite what it says on the tin. We can get called away at all hours, get kept back for any amount of time. It's not easy arranging to meet someone at the weekend."

"Sharon's right." Her dad settled forward on his forearms. "You know I was a sergeant in Lothian & Borders. I worked in CID for about a year in total. It's not easy. It's hard holding a marriage or relationship together with those hours, let alone be social." He reached over and held his wife's hand, making her giggle. "Mary was always very forgiving of the hours I worked. In some ways, I wish I'd had a more fixed working pattern but I can honestly say I made a difference to the wider world."

"Don't see why you can't make an effort to see your sister, that's all." Cullen's dad held his gaze for a moment then broke off.

Cullen took a long drink of his orange juice, wishing it was something stronger.

Sharon's mother got to her feet. "Who's for coffee?"

She took three orders then got up and collected the dinner plates.

Sharon's distinct ringtone blared out from the hall — that Texas song Cullen really hated. She smiled. "I'm leaving it."

Cullen raised his eyebrows. "On your head be it." His mind whirred through the possibilities. He quickly settled on DI Brian Bain, her boss and his until recently. He'd be stuck with the parent-sitting. Shite.

Cullen's phone rang this time. He got to his feet. "Detective Constables don't get the chance to turn down calls."

He went into the hall to take it, not recognising the number. At least it wasn't Bain. His network of contacts in West Lothian and Edinburgh got through phones and SIM cards at a ludicrous rate.

"Cullen."

"Hi, Scott." A woman's voice.

Cullen could only vaguely place it. "Who is this?"

There was a pause. "Scott, it's Alison Carnegie. We had a thing last summer."

Cullen walked further down the hall, feeling guilty at getting that sort of call at Sharon's parents'. "I thought I told you to stop calling me?"

She exhaled. "I know. Look, I've been going to a different counsellor and he says I need closure on my relationship with you."

"Look, there was no relationship."

"I need to see you."

"I appreciate you've been going through some hard stuff. Believe me, I'm sorry about what happened, but I don't think I've got anything to say that could help."

"Let me be the judge of that. I need closure on what happened. I need you to help me."

"You need to move on with your life. I'm not who you thought I was. What happened between us — what you think happened between us — just didn't happen. It was someone else using my account on Schoolbook. I know I saved you, but that's what I do for a living. I'm nobody's hero, believe me. You have to drop this."

"You're being heartless."

"I probably am." He ended the call, pocketing the phone but staying where he was.

Why hadn't he spoken about Alison to his counsellor? She was part of the past, something he didn't want to deal with any more.

Cullen felt a buzz in his trousers. He looked at the phone — Bain.

"Here, Sundance, where's your bird?" Bain was outside — wind rapping against the microphone on his mobile.

"She's with me, sir."

"How come she's not answering her phone, then?"

"Must be on silent." That was one she owed him.

"Right, well, just as well you're behaving cos I need both of you out here."

Cullen scowled. "Where's 'here'?"

"Your old patch. The bings just off the M9 by Kirkliston. Head to Winchburgh. There's a mobile Incident Room set up there. Some uniform plod will get you up here."

"What's happened?"

"Some boy's driven off the side of the bing. Looks a bit fishy."

"How fishy?"

"None of that shite, Sundance. The pair of you need to get out here. Turnbull's orders."

Cullen went back through to the dining room. His mother had disappeared — presumably to help with coffee and loading the dishwasher — leaving Sharon to listen to their dads taking a shared delight in the plight of Rangers. "Wondered how long it would be before a Hibs and Aberdeen fan got round to discussing Rangers."

Sharon's dad grinned. "Got what was coming to them, Scott."

Cullen smiled at Sharon. "We've got to get back to work."

"See what I mean?" She sighed as she looked at both fathers. "I'll better get some coffee from Mum."

2

"So what did he say?" Sharon took a sip of coffee from a travel mug.

Cullen pulled her car — a sporty Focus — onto Ferry Road and shot off to avoid the Merc bearing down on them. "Usual Bain vagueness. Someone's taken a tumble off one of the bings. Get out to Winchburgh."

"What's a bing when it's at home?"

"How long have you lived in Edinburgh for? Big piles of shale from when they used to get gas out. Huge red mounds you see from the M9."

"With you now."

Cullen shrugged. "I went up a couple when I was in uniform."

"And he's got detectives for someone taking a tumble off one?"

"Reckons it's fishy. You know what he's like. Playing it defensive before Police Scotland. He needs to make sure that everything is done to the letter, by the book. Turnbull's orders, anyway."

"He's not in a good place. Things will keep changing. And Cargill is pretty much running the show now."

"Don't I know it." Cullen pulled up at the lights by Morrisons. "She's busting Irvine's balls and he's busting mine."

"You can bust Buxton's balls, then. That's how it works."

"The only reason Bain's got this case is because Cargill's on leave, right?"

"Aye. Not due back in till tomorrow." She finished the coffee. "What else did he say?"

"Just head to Winchburgh. Mobile incident room. We'll get driven over. Blah blah blah."

"I hope he's interrupted a family dinner for something important."

"Don't tell me you're not glad to get away."

"In future, let's only do one set of parents at a time."

"Agreed." Cullen pulled off from the traffic lights. "Mad Alison phoned me again."

Sharon looked round, eyebrows arched. "What did she want?"

"To meet up. She's got a new counsellor and he said it would be good to get closure on us."

She gritted her teeth. "There was no us, was there?"

"I told her to stop calling me. Hopefully this time she'll actually listen."

"Thanks for telling me." She sounded anything but thankful.

THE POLICE RANGE Rover broke the cover of the light wood as it trundled over from Winchburgh.

"When you get up close they're actually covered with trees and bushes."

"They're still pretty red."

Cullen shrugged. "I suppose."

The Range Rover stopped at the bottom of one of the bings.

Cullen waved thanks to the uniform as they got out, watching him do a three-pointer before heading back.

Sharon led them towards the tent Scenes of Crime Officers had set up, a network of arc lights giving some detail to the pitch black.

Cullen looked up. "You can almost see the stars tonight, even though we're not that far from Edinburgh."

"I'll get you a telescope for Christmas, shall I?"

"Maybe not."

An outer cordon had been established at the base, a familiar face in full uniform stood there, clipboard in hand.

Cullen chuckled to himself. "It's Shagger."

"Shagger? Him?"

"PC Paul Green. Aye. Same way you'd call a tall guy Shorty."

"You'll get caught out with your nicknames one day, Scott."

"Yeah, probably." Cullen waved as they approached.

Green held up the clipboard. "We're all safe now that Detective Constable Scott Cullen has shown up!"

Cullen walked up and shook hands. "Been a long time, Paul."

"You've forgotten us, Scotty, now you're a big city cop."

Cullen laughed. "This is DS Sharon McNeill."

Green looked her up and down. "Paul Green."

Cullen snatched the clipboard off him and signed them both in. "PC Green and I used to work out of Bathgate."

"Back in the dim and distant."

Cullen handed him the clipboard. "You been here long?"

"Was second here. You know how it is — blue lights, yellow tape. Been here three hours and it's getting colder." Green held up the clipboard. "Some nightmare of a DI put me on crime scene management duties."

Cullen looked around. "I'd put money on knowing which DI it was. Bain?"

"Aye."

"So, what's happened? I just got a 'get your arse out here' message."

Green pointed behind them. "A Range Rover was spotted in a the field. Looks like it's rolled down the side of the bing. It's practically a munro. No chance anyone's going to survive that, no matter how good their four-by-four is."

Sharon folded her arms. "Why's CID here?"

Green gave a shrug. "You know how it is. Everybody's so scared of Police Scotland they're taking no chances. Anything that looks slightly suspicious is going to you guys first. Ask me, it's people keeping themselves in jobs."

"Couldn't Livingston have handled this?"

Green grinned. "This is just inside Edinburgh City. Half a mile that way and it's West Lothian."

Sharon smiled at Cullen. "Come on, we'd better get over."

Cullen nodded. "I'll be a few minutes."

Green watched Sharon trudge up the path to the crime scene. "That your DS?"

"Used to be."

"Wouldn't mind a go up that."

"She's my girlfriend now."

"Shite. Sorry, Scotty."

"You're not any less of a dirty bastard these days, then, Shagger?"

"Aye, well, got to live up to my nickname, somehow."

Cullen laughed.

"Evening, Cullen." James Anderson, one of the lead SOCOs, grabbed the clipboard from Green.

"Evening, James."

Anderson headed over to the group.

Cullen recognised most of them but couldn't place the uniformed male officer chatting to DS Alan Irvine, his current boss and long-term adversary. "Enough banter. Give me a blow-by-blow of what's happened here. Any eyewitnesses?"

"Nope. Local farmer called it in at about half five. Heard a big thump from over this way. We headed out and found the wreckage." Green pointed to a tent, an orange car nestling beneath the canvas.

Bain stood there, arms folded, staring at it.

"Bastard luck, though, Scotty. I was seeing some boy in Kirkliston about a drug deal when I got the call through."

"You still in Bathgate?"

"Aye, for my sins."

"I'll need to pop out." Cullen pointed at Irvine. "Any idea who that is?"

"Some wanker DS from out your way."

"That is my DS. I meant the other guy."

"Aw, man. Didn't mean anything by it."

"It's okay, he is a wanker." Cullen patted his shoulder. "Any idea who the other one is?"

"Kieron something. First Attending Officer. He's based out at Bathgate, but he covers your old patch of Ravencraig. Seems like a bit of a cock."

Cullen laughed. "So everyone's still a cock, a wanker or a bit of skirt?"

"Aye, well, can't help it if I'm perfect."

"Anything else I should know?"

"Nope."

"I'll pop in and see you sometime, maybe go for a pint?"

"Sounds good." Green looked over Cullen's shoulder at some newcomers.

Cullen headed through the light rain and mud towards the wreckage. The inner cordon was guarded by another uniformed officer. It should have been CID officers managing the process. Maybe Bain wanted continuity from when it had been established.

"Here, wait up."

Cullen looked behind him.

Irvine had finished his chat and was on his way over. He started to jog, his feet splashing in the dirty puddles. "Bain call you out?"

Cullen nodded. "We were at Sharon's parents."

"Christ, it's getting serious."

"Aye." Cullen quickened the pace.

"He caught me just as I was leaving, was going to catch up with you, but you'd already left."

"Had my counselling."

Irvine laughed. "Aye, good one. What a skive that is."

Cullen ignored him as they approached Bain and Sharon.

Bain stretched out. "Here's my dream team. Cannon and Ball."

Cullen smiled, desperate to disarm him. "I'm not going to ask who's who."

"Best leave it that way, Sundance, you don't want another nickname."

Irvine reached into his pocket and retrieved a tub of chewing gum. "I better not be Ball, by the way."

Bain laughed. "Last thing you are is on the ball."

"Speaking of which, who've Rangers got in the next round of the Glenmorangie Camanachd Cup? Is it Forres Mechanics?"

Bain rubbed his moustache. "That's a fuckin' shinty tournament for teuchters like Sundance here, you cheeky bastard."

Cullen grimaced. "We don't play shinty in Angus."

Bain glared at Irvine. "Football is off limits for the next three years, you know that. Besides, a Jambo like you shouldn't talk about the financial difficulties of another club. Paid the wages this month?"

Irvine shrugged his shoulders. "Still in the SPL, though."

"For now." Bain grinned.

Sharon put a hand on her hip. "Shall I leave you boys to talk about football all night?"

Bain held her gaze for a few seconds then smiled. "Right, I'm SIO on this case. We've got Scene of Crime here and Deeley's just been signed into the inner cordon. The pathologist isn't going to hold us up for once." He turned and faced the wreckage of the car. "From what we can tell, the Range Rover rolled off the top. The thing is totally battered."

Cullen glanced over at the car. "What about the victim?"

"No idea who he is. The science boys will be a week digging the body out at this rate. From the brief glance I've had through what's left of the windscreen, we've got an IC1 male in his early twenties. Light build, dark hair. Not much blood or brains left."

"So why are we involved?" Sharon flicked her hair over. "This feels like a pretty run-of-the-mill case. Some local ned steals a car and takes it for a run down the bing, ends up getting himself killed."

Bain creased his forehead. "Who said anything about it being stolen?"

"Is it?"

Bain got out his notebook. "Got one of the laddies to run a PNC check on the number plate, even though it was in about seven bits and scattered half across this field. Turns out it was stolen off a boy in Ravencraig."

Cullen winced. "Ravencraig used to be my beat when I was in Bathgate."

"Lovely place." Bain smiled. "Right, well there's a whole heap of bugger all going on here just now." He nodded at Cullen and Sharon. "Can you pair go and speak to this boy?"

"Are you sure, sir?"

"Be just like old times, Butch, before you let Sundance here into your knickers."

3

"I'm not living here." Cullen pulled in outside the address Bain had given them. A large, modern detached house with the barest of gardens.

"It's cheap."

"For a reason. Most other places I'll consider. I'm practically public enemy number one out here."

"We'll never afford anywhere at this rate." Sharon got out and stormed off up the drive.

Cullen followed, clocking another Range Rover as he walked, before waiting beside Sharon as she rang the bell.

Craig Smith answered the door, frowning at Sharon's warrant card. "Have you found it?"

Sharon pocketed her card. "Can we come in?"

Smith led them inside through the sprawling hall into a large living room, occupying the space of three or four rooms in a standard house. Pride of place was given to a large reclining armchair in front of a flat-screen TV that Cullen guessed must be in excess of sixty inches. A football match filled the screen, the sound muted.

Smith sat and switched off the screen then swivelled the chair round to face Cullen and Sharon on the sofa. "When can I get my car back?"

"I'm afraid it is almost certainly written off." Sharon got out her notebook. "It rolled down one of the shale bings by the M9."

"That's a bloody shame. It's a one-off." Smith's face twisted into a smile. "And not just the paintwork."

Cullen nodded. "The orange?"

"I'm a dyed-in-the-wool Rangers fan." Smith pointed at the wall behind them — a Rangers shirt from the McEwen's Lager days hung above the mantelpiece. "Signed by Mark Hately the day we beat Aberdeen to win the title in '92."

Cullen stabbed his pen into his notebook, not needing reminded of that day. "What can you tell us about the vehicle, Mr Smith?"

"That car cost me eighty grand. Custom suspension, custom body work. I won't bore you with the engine specs."

"I can see why someone would want to steal it, then."

"Aye, well, you'd think it would have been easy for you lot to find a bright orange Range Rover, but no."

"Were you at work when the car was stolen?"

"I was. I've got three Range Rovers. I use that one for the occasional weekend trip up north or something. It was just sitting on the drive outside. I should have locked it away."

Sharon cleared her throat. "What do you do for a living?"

"I own a garage in Ravencraig. Ranger Rover."

"Could the theft be in any way linked to your job?"

Smith rolled his shoulders. "You tell me."

Sharon leaned forward. "When we found the car, there was a body behind the wheel."

Smith gasped. "You're joking."

"Wish I was. A young man, white, early twenties. Any idea who it might be?"

Smith stared into space for a few seconds before shaking his head. "None at all, I'm afraid. Must be the person who stole it. I went through this with your colleague the other day. He said there'd been a spate of car thefts in West Lothian."

Cullen looked at Sharon — he had nothing further. Neither did she.

CULLEN STOPPED outside the mobile Incident Room in Winchburgh, a police caravan at the edge of a muddy football pitch. He pointed at Bain through the window, going mental at someone. "Better give it a minute."

"Who's that?"

Cullen peered in. "I think it's the First Attending Officer."

Sharon leaned back against the caravan. "What do you think of Smith, then?"

"I think he's dodgy."

She laughed. "Is that based on anything he said, or what he had hanging over his mantelpiece?"

"Aye well, never trust a car salesman, especially in Ravencraig."

"Especially a Rangers fan?"

"It's nothing to do with that. It's the fact he's selling cars."

"I can see why you don't trust them." She grinned. "It's time you got a new car."

"We need to have a proper chat about this. Am I saving for our mortgage or spending money on cars?"

The pool Range Rover appeared from the bottom of the bing.

The Edinburgh City Pathologist, Jimmy Deeley, almost dropped his bulging medical bag as he get out. He smiled at them as he approached. "Where's the prince of darkness at this hour?"

Cullen pointed in the window. "Giving some poor uniform a shoeing."

"Why change the habit of a lifetime?"

The uniformed officer hurried past, leaving the door wide open.

"Kieron!" Bain stood in the doorway. "Oh, for crying out loud."

"Another of your long string of lovers?"

"Shut your face, Cullen." Bain glowered at them in turn. "Going to get your arses in here so I don't lose all the bloody heat?"

Cullen followed them in, shutting the door behind him.

Bain stood at his usual whiteboard, already fully populated with a confused mass of doodles. He looked at Deeley then Cullen. "I see you've brought a friend, Sundance."

Deeley smiled. "Nice to see you too, Brian."

"It'd better be good news from you."

"I'll see what I can do. I left the fire service and James Anderson removing the body from the car. I did manage to perform an interim analysis, though it's pretty loose."

Bain snorted. "And?"

"There's maybe a bit too much bruising on the body."

"What's that supposed to mean?"

"Well, where you've had someone involved in a vehicular accident with a seatbelt on, I'd usually expect the body to be fairly heavily bruised. With this, though, his face is worse than I would expect." Deeley pulled out a compact camera and brought up a photo of a man's face, his finger tracing an area as he zoomed in. "All that plus there's an imprint of a ring here. I'll need to wait till I can get him on the slab back at the station, but I'd suggest someone's punched him recently."

"We're not wastin' our time with this?"

"I've never seen you spend your time properly." Deeley winked.

"I'd suggest it looks sufficiently suspicious to warrant CID investigating. I'll see if I can determine whether he got into a bar fight or whatever. All part of the service."

Bain nodded, lost in thought, before scribbling something down. "Right, Jimmy, I'll not hold you back."

Deeley grinned as he left the caravan, just as Irvine appeared through the door.

"Evening, gaffer." Irvine's jaw pounded on gum. "Got an ID for you. Alexander Aitken." He held up a leather wallet, encased in an evidence bag, before tossing it over to Bain along with another bag containing a set of house keys. "Present from Anderson."

Bain rummaged around in the wallet.

Irvine produced another bag. A high-end HTC mobile phone. He handed it to Cullen. "You arse about on your phone often enough. You have a look."

"You should get this to Tommy Smith."

"Aye, whatever. You touched it last."

Bain glowered at them. "Seems like the boy was known as Xander."

Sharon folded her arms. "Does nobody like the name Alex or Sandy any more?"

"Nobody under thirty anyway." Irvine shrugged. "There's that sheep-shagger plays for Aberdeen, Cullen's team. Zander Diamond."

"Used to play for Aberdeen."

"Aye. He's a 'z' Zander, isn't he? What makes someone choose between a 'z' and an 'x'?"

"Right." Bain put the cap back on the marker. "Where are we with this Smith boy?"

Cullen shrugged. "Lost his car one day. Seems to earn a packet. It was one of three he had, fairly souped-up model."

"Think he's involved?" Bain casually doodled a note by Smith's name.

"Not sure. Seems dodgy, but we've nothing to suspect him of so far."

"Right, I'm enthralled." Bain put the wallet on a table by the whiteboard. "There's an address on his driver's licence. Given that he's a young punter, chances are it's his current one or his parents. Christ knows what address is on mine." He chucked the keys at Cullen. "Can you and Butch head there now?"

Sharon caught the wallet. "Have you got a warrant?"

"I'll get one."

She squinted at the driver's license. "Says he lives in Ravencraig."

"Aye."

"We've just been there, Brian."

"Aye, well you're just going back, then."

CULLEN PULLED up in front of the address Bain had given them.

Sharon tossed the keys to him. "I'm sure there are Acting DCs and uniformed plod who could be doing this."

"Just think of the overtime."

"I'd rather think of my dad's shite jokes as he gets more pissed." She checked her watch. "They'll hopefully still be there by the time we're finished with this crap."

Cullen put a pair of rubber gloves on and took the keys from the evidence bag, before heading across the street to Xander Aitken's flat.

Sharon's mobile rang. "It's Bain." She answered it.

Cullen peered up at the building, an early nineties development with yellowing harling, before trying the buzzer. No answer. He gave it another twenty seconds and tried again.

"Right. Will do." Sharon pocketed the phone. "The Procurator Fiscal's office's just faxed a warrant to Bain's ice cream van."

Cullen laughed. "I'll have to remember that one."

"Said a local uniform was driving it over."

"Think we should go in?" Cullen sorted through the key chain, looking for the most likely suspects.

"Aye, we can blame it on Bain."

The first key Cullen tried worked on the communal entrance. "The address was 'flat 1', right?"

"Think so."

"Should be ground floor. The door on the left has 'Aitken / Souness' on it." Cullen tried another key and lucked out again.

Sharon entered the flat and flicked a switch inside the hall. The place lit up.

It wasn't the grandest residence Cullen had ever been in and it smelled something rotten. "Stinks in here."

"Aye, it's absolutely minging." She pointed to the two doors on the right. "I'll take these two." She headed through the first one, leaving Cullen alone.

His nose started twitching. Flies buzzed around. He went through the first of his two doors, leading into an L-shaped living room-cum-kitchen, fairly spacious and with modern fitted kitchen units. A large sofa sat around the corner in the living room space, tucked against the wall.

Cullen stopped dead. A pair of Nike Air Max. They were

connected to dark blue jeans. Someone was sitting there in the dark. He didn't know whether to go back for Sharon. Sod it, move on. "Hello?"

No reaction.

He reached for his baton, slowly extending it. "Hello. It's the police." He stepped forward, baton poised.

The jeans led up into a hooded top, lying open. Cullen almost lost his dinner.

It was a body. Eyes blank, covered in blood.

Dead.

4

"Here he is." Cullen tapped the window. "Fifteen minutes from Winchburgh to Ravencraig is Colin McRae standard. Especially at this time of night."

Bain's purple Mondeo travelled far too fast for the residential street, double-parking just by Sharon's Focus.

Cullen put the curtain back before stepping away from the window. "He's going to do his nut. We've no idea who this boy is."

"I presume it's Souness from the door."

"Bit of a leap. Nothing in either bedroom?"

"Loads on Aitken, just nothing on his pal here."

"Assuming he's his pal."

"Quite."

They stood, hands on hips, waiting for Bain.

"Sod it." Cullen leaned over and started checking the deceased's pockets. He found a wallet in the second, caked in dried blood. He put it in an evidence bag, before opening it through the membrane. He quickly found a photographic driver's license which matched the body. "Kenneth Souness."

"Any relation?"

Cullen shrugged. "They don't usually have relations to famous footballers on driver's licenses."

"Very funny." Sharon added the wallet to the pile of objects she'd already acquired from the kitchen.

"What happened here? Looks like Aitken and Souness were flatmates. One drives off the top of a bing in a stolen Range Rover, the other is dead in their flat."

She shook her head. "No idea what Bain's going to make of this. Aitken killed Souness and then killed himself, probably."

"Bit of an elaborate way to die, though."

The flat door swung open and several sets of footsteps approached. Bain appeared first, followed by Irvine, Deeley and Anderson, all wearing white Scene of Crime suits.

Bain stopped in the middle of the living room and glowered. "I told you to look around the flat, not find another body."

Sharon laughed. "We didn't put it there."

Bain pointed at the body. "Jimmy, do you want to have a shufti?"

"Glad my years of training and experience have been reduced to a 'shufti'." Deeley grinned as he moved closer, before getting some instruments out of his bag and setting about work.

"Right." Bain looked over at Cullen. "What have you pair been up to?"

"We've searched the flat. There are two separate bedrooms and a bathroom, as well as the living room-kitchen."

Sharon held up the wallet. "We've got an ID. Kenneth Souness."

"Right." Bain looked at Anderson. "You're going to need a team in here. I want this place done by morning."

"Fine." Anderson stroked his thick goatee. "We're just about done at the bing anyway."

"Good." Bain nodded at Irvine. "Alan, I want you as crime scene manager here. Nice opportunity for you to show your quality. I've got a clipboard in the car and some forms, so you can get started now. I want us six signed in straight away. The plod on their way over can handle the outer cordon downstairs."

"Cheers, gaffer." Irvine's shoulders slumped.

"What about us?" Sharon folded her arms.

Bain looked out of the front window for a few seconds then turned around. "You pair can head off. I want you back in at seven, fresh as a pair of daisies."

"Out here?"

Bain shook his head. "Leith Walk. We've nothing else to get on with, other than making sure Anderson and Deeley are doing their jobs properly. You pair have found quite enough bodies for one evening."

~

CULLEN TAPPED the driver's side window, pointing to Sharon's parents' house. "I hope they're getting on well inside."

Sharon yawned as she collected the coffee mug from the footwell. "I'm shattered."

"We really shouldn't stay long." Cullen checked his watch — quarter to eleven. "We've got to get back into work in eight hours."

"Aye, you're right, but we need to show our faces. Besides, I'm not thinking of doing that much sleeping."

Cullen smiled as they got out of the car. He'd never been out with anyone with as voracious a sexual appetite as Sharon — usually it was him that was the pest, but it was at least six times a week with her. Cullen knew officers who probably hadn't had sex that often in ten years.

She marched down the garden path and headed inside.

Their parents stood up as they entered the lounge, a small square room filled with settees.

Sharon sat on a dining room chair by the window. "Have you lot had a nice evening?"

"It's been lovely." Cullen's mum grinned.

Cullen's dad finished his can of beer. "I take it you pair have had a shite one?"

Cullen almost laughed at the scowl his dad got from his mum for the 'S' word. He sat on the other dining chair as their parents resettled themselves. "That would be a good way to describe it. Out in West Lothian. Dead bodies."

"Aye, pots of overtime." Sharon's dad rubbed his hands together. "I know how it works, Scott. You pair will have coined in a small fortune from it. Spending money for your holiday to Tenerife in January."

Cullen sighed. "Just over three months to go. I hate January in Edinburgh."

"We were there in the spring." Cullen's mum nudged his dad. "It was lovely, wasn't it?"

"You'll have a great time, son." His dad's phone rang. "That'll be the taxi. We're staying at the Holiday Inn Express at Ocean Terminal."

Cullen raised an eyebrow. "You could walk there in ten minutes."

"Walk through Leith at eleven o'clock at night? Are you mad?"

Sharon's dad raised a hand. "Hey, this isn't Leith. It's Trinity."

Cullen had to bite his lip and keep his eyes away from Sharon to stop laughing. Instead he checked his own watch again. "We'd best be going, too, seven a.m. start tomorrow."

Sharon's mother frowned. "Oh, just a fleeting visit?"

"Afraid so, mum. Got to make sure Scott doesn't sleep in again."

"We're heading back up the road tomorrow afternoon." Cullen's mother got to her feet. "Will we be seeing you?"

"I'll try and get some time." Cullen winced. "The way this case is going, though, I'm expecting to be out in West Lothian all day."

"Okay then." She looked at her feet. "Will you two be up for the weekend soon?"

"Think we're both off in a couple of weeks. Pencil it in."

Sharon shot him daggers — they had precious few weekends together, the last thing she wanted was to spend it at his parents.

CULLEN STARTED OVER AGAIN.

Ross County, Inverness Caley Thistle, Elgin, Peterhead, Aberdeen.

Sharon was on top of him, grinding away, her hands pressing down on his chest. Going through the mantra kept the wolf from the door.

Arbroath, Brechin City, Forfar, Montrose, Dundee, Dundee United.

She quickened her pace, sliding up and down.

St Johnstone, East Fife, Cowdenbeath, Raith Rovers, Dunfermline.

Her panting quickened. "I'm going to come, I'm going to come."

Cullen stopped his recital and quickened his pace, thrusting harder and faster beneath her. She leaned forward, her hard nipples pressing into his chest. His hands moved from her hips to grab her breasts, his eyes focused on the mole on her left hip, his favourite one. He closed his eyes and came, just as she buckled.

She put her head against his shoulder and bit. "Oh, fuck, oh fuck, oh, fuck."

They lay there for a minute or so, before she rolled off then snuggled into him.

"I love you." He kissed her on the head.

"I love you, too."

Cullen tied up the condom, not thinking about anything for once.

She leaned over. "You know something?"

"What?"

"You only tell me you love me just after you come."

"That'll be about ten times a day with you."

She laughed. "It took you a while the first time."

"And now I can't stop." Cullen pecked the top of her head. "Love isn't something us hairy-arsed Scotsmen are used to expressing."

"You shave yours, don't you?"

"Very funny."

"Not long before you move in, is it?"

"Three months. Just after Christmas, just before Tenerife."

"And you definitely told your flatmates?"

"Last week. Tom can't bitch too much because I've given him a fair amount of notice."

"He'll still bitch, though, right?"

"He hasn't spoken to me since." Cullen laughed. "I just hope the action doesn't stop when you've got me in your nest."

She propped herself up on his chest. "You really think that?"

He laughed. "Of course not."

"You'd better be joking."

"I can't see anything curtailing your sex drive."

She frowned. "Do you think there's something wrong with me?"

"No, I think I'm just too lovely for you to keep your hands off me."

She fell about laughing. "Aye, that's it."

He turned on his side and started stroking her. She'd lost a fair amount of weight in the fourteen months they'd been seeing each other, her slight paunch disappearing. He seemed to have taken it all — despite all the shagging, he'd put on a stone and felt slightly less than sexy. "Our parents seemed to get on well."

"Aye, almost too well. I hope they don't make a habit of it. It was excruciating at times. I'm glad poor Xander Aitken turned up when he did."

He slowly moved over to her, eventually lying on top, his cock not far from danger. "That's not a very nice thing to say."

"Maybe I'm not a very nice girl."

"Time for some discipline then."

Cullen reached over to his side of the bed and grabbed another condom.

DAY 2

Thursday
4th October 2012

5

C ullen entered the lift and sipped from the Americano, still piping hot, gasping as he felt the inside of his mouth burn. "Bloody hell."

"Oh, you poor lamb." Sharon patted him on the arm, lip pouting, as she pressed the button.

"Very funny."

"You look tired."

"I am. I couldn't stop thinking about work and this counselling."

"Even after all that exertion?"

"Feels like I've torn the foreskin."

She snorted. "Maybe you're allergic to the spermicide in the condoms?"

"Maybe. Look, it's fine. You don't want to go on the pill and I'm cool with that."

"Nothing to do with you being frightened of having children and wanting to maintain control?"

Cullen shrugged. "Maybe. It's just James I worked with in Bathgate, his girlfriend was desperate for kids and he wasn't. One day, she stopped taking the pill and hadn't told him. Too late then."

Sharon pecked him on the cheek. "I'm less desperate for kids than you are, Scott."

The doors opened and Cullen followed her through the first floor of the station to the Incident Room.

Bain stood at the front, ready to hold court, dark rings beneath red eyes as he drank from a can of Red Bull clone. There were over twenty officers in the room by Cullen's reckoning, including a few of the usual faces — DC Angela Caldwell sat off to the side, DC Chantal Jain and Irvine behind her.

Sharon sat next to Angela at the edge of the table near the back and Cullen perched alongside.

Acting DC Simon Buxton barged in next to Cullen. "Morning, Sundance."

"I've told you before, not that name."

"Know what they say, Scott, best way to lose a nickname is not to rise to the bait."

"I'll bear that in mind, Budgie."

Buxton rolled his eyes. "Less of that."

"Do you prefer Britpop?"

"Bain can bugger off with that one."

Cullen reached over and patted Buxton's hair, short on top and at the back, the fringe at the front stuck between long side lappers covering his ears. "Paul Weller called and asked for his haircut back."

"Piss off." Buxton held up his phone, an over-sized Samsung. "Just found something you'll love. Turnbull's got a Twitter account."

"You're kidding me. Has Bain got one?"

"Just the boss for now." Buxton laughed. "Think it's some new initiative, using social media to help bring the community together. It was just starting to come in a few months ago — I would have been @LeithWalkPC4 if DCI Turnbull hadn't given me this Acting DC gig." He prodded the screen, before handing the phone to Cullen. "Here you go."

Cullen took the phone and looked at the stream of messages from @LeithWalkDCI, mostly retweets from open crimes posted by PCs on the beat in Edinburgh, Dalkeith, Ravencraig, Galashiels and others.

Buxton took the phone back. "Interesting how it doesn't mention Lothian & Borders. Future proofing."

"Still a good while before we have to deal with Police Scotland."

"You say that, but you were the one moaning about Bain and Turnbull carving out their corner of the empire."

"Yeah, well they are." Cullen took another drink of coffee, cooler now.

Bain cleared his throat. "Right, then, thanks for joining us. We've got two bodies found last night out in West Lothian."

He pressed a button on a clicker and the large screen behind him filled with the image of Aitken from his passport. "First, Alexander Aitken, known as Xander, is potentially death by misadventure, but potentially not — Jimmy Deeley will confirm later on today. He was found in a Range Rover at the bottom of a shale bing near Winchburgh. The car is a clear write-off."

He clicked again — Souness' face appeared. "The other one, Kenny Souness, is clearly murder. The body has a deep knife wound to the stomach and it looks like he bled to death, despite attempts to apply a bandage."

"We know next to nothing about these two, other than they were flatmates." He took another swig from his can. "The only useful information that's come back so far is that the interior of the Range Rover has been dusted for fingerprints. Anderson's team only found the prints of Xander Aitken and Craig Smith, the owner."

Bain flicked the ring pull as he stroked his moustache. "Now, the car was reported stolen on Tuesday. Just over twenty-four hours later, it turns up at the bottom of a bing with a body in it. I want to know what happened to that car."

He looked around the room, locking eyes with a few officers, Cullen among them. "I'm mobilising several strands to the investigation. First, I want the backgrounds of Aitken and Souness checked out. DC Cullen, can you take Aitken? DS McNeill, I want you take Souness."

Both nodded as the rest of the room looked round at them.

"Next, I want this knife looked into. DS Irvine will lead the search for it. Somebody's stabbed this boy and the knife isn't in their flat, so where is it? Also, I want a team going round the flats in that street." He pointed at Jain. "Chantal, I want you to lead the investigation into the stolen Range Rover. Start with this Craig Smith boy and see where you get to."

He stared at Angela and Buxton in turn. "Batgirl, Britpop, I want you pair to help DS Holdsworth finish setting up the Incident Room and start getting the case onto HOLMES. Okay?"

Both nodded.

Bain looked round the rest of the room. "All other officers, please report to DS Holdsworth who will allocate your actions. Dismissed."

Cullen finished the coffee then turned to look at Sharon. "Here we go."

"Thought the ice queen was supposed to be back in?"

"Back shift, wasn't it? Gives Bain seven hours to arse this up before she comes in."

She laughed. "I need some breakfast. You coming?"

"Aye, could do with a roll. I wasn't hungry when I started that coffee but I am now."

6

"Here, Sundance."

Bain. Shite. What now?

Cullen put his roll down, took a deep breath and turned to face whatever nonsense Bain was going to put his way.

It was Buxton.

"Simon, would you bloody stop doing that?"

"Should have seen your face." Buxton sat down next to Cullen. He nodded at the black mobile on Cullen's desk. "Finally arrived then?"

Cullen picked up his iPhone 5. "Couple of days ago. Had to make sure my flatmate didn't nick it."

"How does it compare to the 4?"

"Better."

"Really? You look a bit disappointed with it."

"It's fine."

"I remember getting the first one. It just blew me away. I think Apple have lost the wow factor, though."

"You think?"

"Makes me think of that argument I lost when I got this." Buxton tossed his Samsung in the air and caught it. "Not a patch on this baby."

"Look at the size of it. It's a phone for the long-sighted. My dad would love it."

"Whatever." Buxton pocketed the phone. "Oh, some boy from the Complaints was after you."

"Muir?"

"Aye. What has Bain done now?"

Cullen laughed. "He's innocent for once."

"I said you'd give him a call."

"Brilliant."

"Should I have told him where to go?"

Cullen sighed. DS Simon Muir of Professional Standards and Ethics. The Complaints. "The boy's a wanker. He sent me a chaser to an email and copied in his boss and Turnbull."

Buxton took a bite of his Lorne sausage roll. "How long have you been ignoring it for?"

"A month."

Buxton laughed.

"I've been busy."

"A likely tale. What was it about?"

"Nothing, really. Just some case last year. Cop booted the shite out of a suspect."

"That's a relief. I thought it would be about that Keith Miller."

Cullen struggled for breath for a few seconds. "Why do you think that?"

"Heard Bain blaming you for his death."

"Wanker."

Angela slammed her tray down, the cup of tea and bowl of porridge bouncing with the impact. "Scott, do you need any help looking into this Aitken guy?"

Cullen shook his head. "Bain told you to work with Holdsworth. I'm not getting in the way."

"That's the problem."

"It's a nice opportunity for you to work closely with him, Angela." Sharon sat down with more grace. "Now you're a full DC, you'll be looking to impress the brass, maybe beat Scott here to a DS position."

Cullen wagged a finger. "That's not funny."

"I complained to Bain before the briefing." Angela stirred maple syrup into her porridge. "He said it's a key activity of being a DC which I worked hard to get. Then he told me to shut it."

"I can well imagine." Cullen bit into his roll.

"Were you lot out at the crime scene last night?" Angela took a mouthful of porridge.

"Yes." Cullen put the roll down and chewed. "Nothing much to see."

Buxton chuckled. "Other than finding that second body."

"Yeah, well, we shouldn't have been there." Sharon stabbed a fork into her fruit salad. "The warrant hadn't properly come through."

"What did you get up to on your day off yesterday?" Cullen looking over at Angela. "Was Bill off too?"

Angela made a face. "Don't start. We had a nice day down in Northumberland."

Buxton slurped at his coffee. "Holdsworth caught me in the corridor just before the briefing. He said they've got another DS starting today."

Sharon frowned. "Are you sure?"

Buxton nodded slowly. "Catriona Rarity. She's from Strathclyde. Paisley, I think."

"She'll fit in with Bain, then."

Cullen finished his coffee and loudly crumpled the cup. "Great."

Sharon raised an eyebrow. "Here we go again."

Cullen chewed another mouthful, catching his cheek between his teeth. "I'm being serious here. That's the second new DS in the last few months, after bloody Methven came in. Why am I not in consideration for it?"

Buxton made eyes at Angela. "We'd better get downstairs, Angela."

"Oh, right. Aye."

They got up and left them to it.

Sharon pinched her nose. "Scott, we've been over this. Did you speak to Turnbull?"

Cullen didn't say anything for a few seconds. He'd meant to, but he just hadn't managed to find the time. Or pluck up the courage. "No."

"If it's pissing you off that much then you need to speak to him. Irvine or Cargill aren't going to do it for you."

"I've meant to, I'm just shit at that sort of thing."

"Tell me about it. It doesn't stop you moaning about how nobody's making you a DS." She reached over and took his hand. "It took me years to get it, you know that. I had to go speak to DCI Whitehead every fortnight to see if there was anything opening up. I did that for nine months before he started taking it seriously."

"I've been too busy focusing on the cases."

"Scott, if you want to get on, you need to focus on your career a bit more. Community outreach, that sort of thing. I'm sure Turnbull's got some initiatives that he wouldn't mind foisting on an ambitious young DC."

"Great."

"It's good for your profile."

Cullen slouched back in the seat. "It's brown nosing."

She licked her lips. "What's up?"

"Nothing."

"No, there's something else. You keep whining to me about it. Why haven't you spoken to Jim?"

"I can't be arsed."

"That's shite, Scott. You're always going off on some little side quest to show everyone how much of an arse Bain is but you can't be bothered sorting your own career out. Why?"

"You're right." He mopped up brown sauce with the last bit of roll. "I'm maybe frightened of authority. It feels like there's so much riding on me asking that single question. What happens if he says no?"

"What happens if he says yes?"

Cullen smiled. "You're right. But the authority thing... I used to get a doing off a teacher at school. Ridiculous shit. He'd haul me in front of the class and verbally abuse me."

"Maybe he fancied you?"

Cullen struggled to not laugh. "It wasn't good. I think a lot of it comes down to why I only got an ordinary degree. When I was struggling, I didn't go and speak to anyone about it. I had the same sort of thing before I joined the police. My boss was a total wanker, used to belittle me. I didn't give a shit about the work."

"And yet you joined the police?" Sharon had an impish grin on her face.

Cullen raised an eyebrow. "There is that. Maybe I wanted to be that authority figure."

"Well, maybe you can, but you need to tackle it head on. It's no good letting it cripple you, you know that, right?"

Cullen was about to continue his rant, but he spotted a familiar face approach their table.

DI Paul Wilkinson. "Sharon, Curren. Not at all surprised that I'd find you pair here skiving off, like." He sat, taking his coffee, paper and two link-sausage rolls off his tray which he lay against the table leg. He took a huge bite from a roll and shook his head slowly.

Sharon smiled. "What brings you back here?"

"Renovations at HQ ahead of April. They had some spare office space here on the third floor, just above your lot. Supposed to be six weeks but we'll bloody see. Don't know what's wrong with the current bloody system. Why do you Jocks want a single police force, anyway?"

"Wasn't aware that we did." Cullen scrunched his roll wrapper into a ball. "I don't remember the referendum."

Wilkinson wagged his finger at him. "I forgot how much I enjoyed your cheek, Curren."

"Cullen."

"Right, lad, right, No need to get all shirty about it, like."

Cullen's nostrils flared.

Sharon beat him to it. "Is that just two months you've been gone, Wilko? Doesn't feel that long."

"It'd feel a lot longer if I'd still been your boss." Wilkinson laughed. "How's old Bain doing? Still fighting that bloody nightmare woman?"

"You know exactly what he's like. And yes, he's still up to his tricks, mainly centred around DI Cargill."

Wilkinson finished chewing his first roll, sausage fat dripping down his chin. "Always one for his games is Brian and not one to give up easily, even when he's clearly lost."

"You think he's on his way out?"

Wilkinson shook his head. "Of course he bloody is. Writing's been on the wall for almost a year. Why do you think I've been trying to sort out my detachment?"

"What's your detachment?"

"Football hooligan unit. Little bastards are playing at it again." Wilkinson took a big slurp of coffee. "It's good for me, though. It's what I did back in God's own country, investigating Leeds, Bradford and Sheffield United fans. It's why they brought me up here in the first place, but it took them so bloody long to get budget approved that I ended up stuck with Turnbull and babysitting Bain. Still, I've got where I wanted, working on the strategy. It's a long-term investigation."

He took a big bite out of the second roll, over half of it going in. "It's come down from the Home Office. It's one of the Chief Constable's biggest priorities. I'm in a good position."

"I don't get football hooliganism." Sharon folded her arms. "Why do people fight about it?"

Cullen held his hands up in defence. "I've not been in a fight about football since I was nine."

Wilkinson laughed. "Blokes will fight over anything. Cameras, cars, computers."

Cullen nodded. "Absolutely. They're not fighting about football. They're generally just arseholes trying to prove how hard they are."

"Totally. I've seen it up and down the country. There are particular hotspots — Millwall, Chelsea and West Ham in London, Leeds United and, of course, your very own Hibs, Rangers and Aberdeen."

Sharon took a sip of tea. "What about Celtic?"

"They're not really big on it." Wilkinson finished his roll. "Funnily enough, same as your Hearts boys through here. That said, they are getting worse."

"Why?"

"Sectarianism."

"I thought that was getting better?"

"It's just been driven underground, that's all."

"I really do not get sectarianism." Sharon pushed her tray over to the other side of the table. "I grew up in a Catholic family and I got dog's abuse from Protestant kids at school. I didn't even go to church."

"I'm investigating a bloody stabbing with sectarian links." Wilkinson rubbed his hand across his mouth. "There was a fight in an old quarry in West Lothian. Something stupid like Hearts and Rangers against Celtic and Hibs. Two boys got killed." He held up the newspaper, open at a page. The headline read Police appeal for witnesses in quarry stabbings.

Cullen glanced through the first paragraph and spotted the names Beveridge and Crossan, neither of which meant anything to him.

Wilkinson put the paper back down. "Never trust a bloody hooligan. Supposed to be no knives at these things. Some fucker brought one along and used it. Not that we've bloody found it, mind." He finished his coffee. "Still, it's a high profile investigation."

Cullen narrowed his eyes. "Is this connected to our case?"

"Not you and all." Wilkinson folded his arms. "I've already had Bain up my trouser legs like a ferret. We sat down with a few of my boys late last night and there's no connection. Your pair weren't involved, as far as we can tell."

Cullen wondered how thoroughly Bain and Wilkinson had actually looked, neither being the most diligent officers. "No issue then, is there?"

"None at all." Wilkinson grabbed his newspaper and got up. "Better get back to the grindstone." He waddled off towards the lift, tugging at his trousers as he walked.

Cullen looked back at Sharon. "Never even asked about the case we're working on."

Sharon laughed. "He's like that. I know you never worked with him that closely, but he's not that bad. Just a bit self-centred."

"Maybe I saw the bad side of him, but all DIs seem to only have a bad side."

"I tell you what, though, he's pretty good at spinning a story. Truth is Turnbull got fed up with him and sidelined him. Bain's worried he's next."

"And with good reason."

⁓

JUST AFTER EIGHT O'CLOCK, Cullen sat staring into space, haunted by what Buxton had said earlier.

Keith Miller. Dead in the line of duty. The reason for his counselling. The initial reason, anyway. Cullen still struggled with the guilt.

He picked up the phone and dialled Derek Miller, Keith's brother.

"What do you want?"

"Charming." Cullen leaned back in the chair. "How are you doing?"

"Fine." Derek's voice was clipped.

"What's with all the hostility?"

"Nothing. I'm at work and it's early. What do you want, Scotty?"

"I just wondered if you wanted to meet up for a pint. We've not seen each other for a few months."

"Here was me thinking you'd stopped fancying me."

Cullen rubbed his face with his free hand — Derek had a similar sense of humour to his late brother. "Do you want to meet up, then?"

"Aye, all right. I've got a spare ticket for Hibs-Dundee on Saturday. Three o'clock kick off."

"Go on, then. Windsor Buffet at two?"

"Deal. I'll warn you now, Scotty, it's twenty-five sheets."

"For Hibs playing Dundee?"

"Aye, tell me about it. Got to go, right. I'll see you at the Windsor at two, aye?"

"Aye." Cullen hung up and stared at his notepad, half-filled with scribbles.

Sharon slumped in the chair next to Cullen. "Who was that on the phone?"

"Derek Miller."

"Oh."

"Aye. Budgie mentioned Keith earlier and it made me think about him. I haven't seen Derek in months. I'm going to the football with him on Saturday."

"That's fine. I'm supposed to be at a baby shower in the afternoon."

"I know that."

"It's not like I want to go anyway." She grinned. "Where have you got to?"

"Nothing much." Cullen looked down at his pad. "Xander Aitken originally came from Ravencraig. By my reckoning, he grew up on the second roughest street in the town."

She chuckled. "What's the worst?"

"Next one over. You can see why I don't want to live there."

"Go on."

"Aitken was twenty-three when he died, three months from his next birthday." Cullen held up his crime sheet. "Had some misdemeanours in his teens, but he appears to have knuckled down from seventeen onwards. Well, nothing's been recorded."

"It could be he's just better at not getting caught."

"Right, except for the fact he worked for RBS. The banks have a strict policy on criminal records."

"More Tom info?"

"Right. Alba Bank, HBoS, RBS, they're all fairly similar." Cullen checked the pad again. "That's pretty much all I've got — age and profession."

"That's more than me." She got up and walked off.

Cullen looked at the pad. All roads lead to RBS. He called the central switchboard and asked to be put through to Alexander Aitken's desk. The phone rang for a few seconds before being answered.

"Xander Aitken's phone." The female voice was clearly out of breath.

"Can I ask who I'm speaking to?"

A gasp for breath. "This is Sheena O'Brien. I'm Xander's line manager. To whom am I speaking?"

"Ms O'Brien, this is Detective Constable Scott Cullen of Lothian & Borders. I need to speak to you concerning Mr Aitken."

There was a long pause at the other end of the line. "Is everything okay?"

"I need to speak to you. Urgently. It would be better done face-to-face."

"Okay." She paused and he heard a ruffle of papers. "I'm free until eleven."

"Where are you based?"

"Drummond House."

"I know it. See you at the back of nine."

"I'll book you a visitor space."

7

"Sorry, I've not got your number plate listed." The security guard held up a clipboard in his hut at the entrance to Drummond House.

Cullen ground his teeth. "Can you phone Sheena O'Brien, please?"

"It's not on the system, son."

Cullen held up his warrant card. "Just let us in, okay?"

The guard held up his hands. "Aye, on you go, then. But if anyone asks—"

"It wasn't you. Got it." Cullen drove off as the barrier raised. He glanced over at Angela. "What a wanker."

"Tell me about it."

Cullen found an empty parking space and pulled in. "Here we go." They got out and headed over to the front door.

A burlier security guard stood in front of the door.

Cullen flashed his warrant card again. "Police. Here to see Sheena O'Brien."

The guard pointed back towards the roundabout they'd driven across moments ago. "You'll need to go through the main entrance and get signed in, sir."

Cullen held the warrant card out for longer. "This is police business."

"Fire regulations, sir. You need to get signed in."

Cullen stared at him. Not worth getting into anything. "Fine." He stormed off across the car park, Angela having to jog to catch up. He pushed through the revolving doors and found a reception desk manned by two young women, rather than ex-forces types. He leaned against the desk. "I'm here to see a Sheena O'Brien?"

The receptionist smiled. "I'll just call her." She pointed at a pair of cream sofas. "If you'll just have a seat?"

Cullen walked over and sat down, twitching from the two coffees he'd already had. "Bloody nightmare this place."

Angela sat next to him. "Thanks, by the way."

Cullen frowned. "What for?"

"Rescuing me from Incident Room preparation duties when Bain's back was turned."

Cullen shrugged. "I'm going to have a busy morning and I need corroboration in case anything juicy comes up."

"Good to get away from Holdsworth. Pompous twat."

Cullen nodded. "I thought you'd like that."

"Have you heard about his divorce?"

Cullen raised an eyebrow. "I'm obviously a lot less well connected than you are."

She grinned. "His wife kicked him out. Caught him looking at porn on the internet. She's really taking him to the cleaners. One thing about my divorce is it was just me, Rod and a house. Mrs Holdsworth is taking him for everything, including a grand a month in school fees."

"How does he afford that?"

"Think his wife was on a decent amount of money. Worked at the university, pretty high up. Doesn't stop her stinging him for more, though."

"You're coping well."

"Aye well, Rod isn't." She'd previously referred to Rod only as him but since her infidelity had become public knowledge, her terms of reference had changed. "He's been turning up at our flat at weekends and stuff, causing a nuisance."

"Are you serious?"

"Aye. Stupid bastard. That's two police officers he's pissing off." She looked out of the window to the car park.

"How's Bill?"

"He's fine. Oh, he was wondering if you fancied a game of golf with him and Stuart Murray."

"I don't play. Pub golf, maybe."

"I'll see if they're up for it."

"Scott Cullen?"

Cullen looked over. "Yes."

"Sheena O'Brien." She shuffled her large body over to them. "I've signed you in. Do you want to follow up?"

She led them through what looked like a call centre, legions of people of different ages sitting in front of computers with headsets clamped to their skulls. Cullen soon became bewildered by the layout, the building clearly going through some sort of renovation — half of it was all-glass meeting rooms and open spaces, the other half tight corridors and small offices.

O'Brien led them to a meeting room, six red chairs around a modern pine-effect table in the renovated part of the building, large glass windows giving a view across the office.

Cullen sat, draping his coats over the backs of adjacent chairs, Angela following suit.

O'Brien smiled. "I don't know how long you plan to be here, but I've managed to book this room for the whole morning."

"Thank you." Cullen took out his notebook. "You're probably wondering why we're here."

"I'm in suspense." O'Brien grinned. She was in her mid-thirties and overweight. She was tarted up — make-up, fashionable haircut, designer glasses, designer clothes a couple of sizes too small. She leaned across the table, tossing her dyed blonde hair, her huge breasts almost popping out of her top. As heterosexual as Cullen was, it made his cock shrink into his stomach.

Cullen fixed her with his hard policeman stare. "Mr Aitken's body was found last night, just outside Winchburgh."

O'Brien held her hand to her mouth. "Oh my God." She looked down at the desk and did that irritating fan thing with her hand that Cullen had seen come into vogue over the last few years.

"Xander worked for you." Angela tapped her pen on her notebook. "Is that correct?"

O'Brien looked at her, nodding slowly. "It is."

"How would you describe him professionally?"

O'Brien stared up at the ceiling for a few seconds. "Xander wasn't the most career focused. His performance was okay. I mean, in his last annual appraisal he scored a three, which is average. I never had to think about putting him on an action contract. He was solid, always did what I asked him to but never anything more."

"What do you do here?"

O'Brien scowled. "This is a bank?"

Cullen smiled. "I meant your team?"

"Oh, right. We handle customer complaints. Back-office resolution team."

"When was the last time you saw him?"

"He didn't turn up for work on Wednesday."

Cullen scribbled it down. Something might have happened to the boy on Tuesday night. "Did you hear from him?"

"I tried phoning his home, as per company policy, but there was no reply. The next step would be visiting his house on Monday."

Angela made a note. "What else can you tell us about him?"

"He was a big Rangers fan. Most of his money went on going to see them. Every weekend he'd be through in Glasgow or travelling the country to away matches. He's been to see a few different teams this season given what's happened. He was up at Elgin last weekend and still hung-over when he came in on Monday."

"Do you have any idea who would want to harm Mr Aitken?"

O'Brien slowly shook her head. "Not that I'm aware of."

Angela smiled. "Would it be possible to speak to his colleagues?"

"That shouldn't be a problem."

O'Brien showed in the last of Aitken's colleagues, a middle-aged man. "This is Will Brown. I'll leave you to it. I've got an audio conference I'm late for." She shut the door behind her.

Cullen gestured across the table. "Please, have a seat."

Brown sat, eyes darting around, arms folded across his chest. "How can I help?"

Angela cleared her throat. "What can you tell us about Alexander Aitken?"

"Sat next to him. Didn't know the boy very well."

"Why would that be?"

"He was a bit of a loner." Brown rubbed his thinning hair, spectral wisps held back in a facsimile of the haircut he would have had as a younger man, the white of his scalp clearly visible. "None of us knew him well. We're a pretty tight team and Sheena's a good manager. We all go for lunch in the canteen, except for Alexander. He wasn't what you'd call a team player, but he got through the work reasonably well."

"Is there anything at all you can tell us about Mr Aitken?"

Brown sneezed into his white handkerchief. He pocketed it then leaned forward on the table. "The only time Alexander would engage with us, was on the few nights out that he came to. He used to get really pi— drunk. We'd see a different side to him."

"In what way?"

Brown shrugged. "He'd get all animated. I mean, most of the time Alexander was a typical Scottish hard man. Lots of grunts and glares. He was too cool for school that boy."

"So he'd get aggressive on these nights out?"

"The opposite. He'd get really hyper. Sort of dancing, like." Brown made a show of dancing, hands in the air, like at a rave or a club. "There's a few times we went to those clubs in town that start at four on a Friday, fifty pee a shot, that sort of thing. I only went along for the drink, you understand, but the lassies in the team would start dancing early. Alexander joined them."

"Did he ever make advances on any of them?"

Brown stuck his bottom lip out, looking thoughtful. "Not that I can remember. He used to bug— leave pretty early."

Angela frowned. "Could he have been getting the train home?"

"I live out that way myself. Bathgate. There are trains till midnight and buses well into the wee small hours. I've taken them many a time."

"But you've no idea where he'd go on these nights out?"

"Afraid not. He wasn't the sort to have a banter about it on the Monday morning, you know?"

"I see." Cullen smiled at him. "Could you send Ms O'Brien back in?"

Brown got up, looking relieved. "Will do, son."

Cullen was about to take him to task for the 'son' but a look from Angela made him hold back.

Brown left the room and pulled the glass door to. In another conference room directly across the corridor, a particularly heated meeting was under way, a large man with a bald head and glasses waving his arms around and stretching his suit jacket to its limits, the other attendees looking bored by the rant. Cullen could only think of Bain.

Angela shut her notebook. "You could have bothered a bit there."

"Eh?"

"I asked most of the questions in all the interviews. You've just sat looking pretty."

"I'll take that as a compliment."

"I'm serious. You're supposed to be leading, yet I'm the one asking all the questions."

"I'm taking the information in and giving you an opportunity to show how good you are."

"To show who? You're not in charge of me, you know."

"What's up with you?"

"You. I've carried you this morning."

Cullen creased his forehead, unsure where this had come from. She was in danger of becoming as resentful of him as he was of Irvine or Bain. "Angela, you've not carried me. I've let you show that you can lead an interview. I could tell Cargill how well you're developing now you're formally in the role. Not sure I can be arsed if you think I'm riding on your coattails."

"Whatever, Scott."

O'Brien waddled down the corridor, playing with her expensive haircut.

"Come on, our ticket out of here has arrived." Cullen got to his feet. "I'll get you back to Holdsworth."

8

Cullen sat at a free desk and got out his laptop, ready to write up his interview notes, with a view to getting Angela to overlay hers later.

"Mr Cullen."

Cullen recognised it. DS Colin Methven, Cargill's new deputy. He slowly turned. "Colin."

Methven narrowed his eyes, almost lost under his thick brows like billowing smoke. "I've not seen you around this morning. DI Cargill was looking for you."

"Been interviewing Xander Aitken's work colleagues. Bain's orders."

Methven leaned against the desk and put his hands in his pockets. "Tell me."

"Seems like he was a bit of a loner. Didn't mingle with the rest of the team much. Only oddity was that he got hammered pretty quickly on nights out then disappeared."

"Is that it?"

"I can only find what's there to find. Thought you were off today?"

"Yes, well, DI Cargill finally got notified by DI Bain and brought me in. I'm missing a day's training — I was going to run up Arthur's Seat this morning." Methven folded his arms across his chest. "I need to know everything you're up to from now on."

"I report to DS Irvine."

Methven sat on the edge of the desk beside Cullen. "For this case, you're working for me. This is too big a case to let the likes of Irvine and Bain mess it up. You're a good officer, Cullen, but you've got a reputation for being a bit of a sodding cowboy. I'm here to make sure you don't screw this case up."

Bain approached, eyes locked on the pair of them.

Slowly, Methven stood, putting his hands in his pockets and starting the incessant jangle — he must be top ten in pocket billiards.

"Sergeant." Bain shifted his gaze to Cullen. "Sundance, I need an update on Aitken."

Methven stood between them. "He's given the update to me, Inspector."

"Oh he has, has he?" Bain grinned. "Last time I checked, I was Senior Investigating Officer on this case and you were at home scratching your nuts, Crystal."

Methven closed his eyes as a smug grin filled his face. "You obviously haven't checked in a while, then." He reopened his eyes. "DI Cargill has been appointed SIO, you and I are Deputy SIOs."

Bain's eyes darted left to right. "Nobody's told me this."

"Do you honestly expect to be running a case like this with your reputation?"

"My reputation? While you've been up rogering sheep in Aberdeen and investigating who stole a can of Coke from wee Eck's corner shop, I've been solving big cases down here. Heard about the Schoolbook Killer, Crystal?"

"I love the nickname." Methven laughed. "Yet another example of your abuse of staff."

Bain squared up to him. "Have you heard of the Schoolbook Killer? And how I caught him?"

"I heard DC Cullen put it all together and you didn't back him up. Lost an officer, didn't you?"

Bain pointed a finger at him. "Listen, I'm not taking any of this shite from a DS."

"What's going on here?" DI Cargill was standing by the entrance to the Incident Room, hands on her sizeable hips, her forehead creased below her short fringe.

Bain thumbed at Methven. "This joker is telling me I'm no longer SIO on my own case."

"You're not." Cargill got in Bain's face. "Jim Turnbull has been trying to call you, but your phone is conveniently off."

"Conveniently? What are you trying to say?"

"He's summoned us to his office. Now."

Bain rubbed his face. "Fine. Let's go see him."

"Good." Cargill nodded at Methven. "You too." She looked at Cullen. "You shouldn't have to see that, Constable. It's not the sort of professional environment I wish to foster on one of my investigations."

Cullen raised his shoulders. "Not a problem with me."

"No, that is a problem. You shouldn't be used to it." Cargill marched out of the Incident Room, making sure Bain and Methven followed.

Cullen leaned back in his chair, trying to process what had just happened.

Sharon sat down next to him. "What was that all about?"

"Bain got his arse handed to him by Cargill. He's not SIO any more. Crystal is co-deputy with him."

"That's all we need."

Cullen gripped the edge of the desk. "Touch wood, this is the beginning of the end for Bain."

"We've said that before, Scott. Better just wait and see what happens."

"I suppose so." Cullen pointed at the door. "I feel like it's an 'out of the frying pan into the fire' thing with Methven."

"How?"

"Well, it's all this 'sodding' and 'bastarding'. At least Bain's machine gun f-bombs express something. 'Bastarding'? Really?"

Sharon chuckled as she sat next to him. "How's it going with Aitken?"

"Not another update I've got to give. First Methven, then Bain, now you. I'll just write my report up then everyone can read it."

"We're working on related parts of the investigation, so we need to work together."

"Fine." Cullen gave her his notebook.

She read it for a few seconds. "Interesting. Souness was a Rangers fan as well."

"Really? Suppose they all are in Ravencraig. There's only really Fauldhouse that's Celtic. I was going to use it as an opportunity to wind Bain up about Rangers being in the Third Division."

Sharon tutted. "You boys and your banter about football."

"Hey, I'm not that bad."

"Scott, that's just because your team's shite. Forgot to say, I got a text from my dad asking if yours was a Celtic fan."

"Why?"

"They were both moaning about Rangers last night so he thought your dad supported Celtic."

"He could've asked." Cullen laughed. "My dad's in danger of becoming an anti-Rangers fan, rather than a pro-Aberdeen fan. He's a sheep shagger through and through, just like me."

"Chip off the old block, aren't you?"

"You can talk, joining the force like your old man."

"And you wonder why Bain calls me Butch." She smoothed down her trouser leg. "I've got to head out to Ravencraig to speak to Souness's employer. He was a mechanic at Nichol's Garage. Can you help?"

"I really should get these notes typed up."

"Come on, Scott. You're my last hope. I couldn't prise Angela away from Holdsworth. No idea why, but he's in a shite mood."

Cullen winced. "That's probably my fault."

"Come on, chum me out to Ravencraig."

"I'm not hearing the magic word."

"Okay, please."

Cullen got to his feet. "Fine. It'll keep me away from whatever games are going on here."

SHARON DROVE THEM INTO RAVENCRAIG, the small town perched on top of the hills overlooking much of West Lothian. In the daylight, Cullen could clearly make out Bathgate in the foreground and Livingston in the distance.

Cullen's phone beeped — a new text message from his mother. *Aer wee e meeetngi up!* He glanced over at Sharon, focused on the driving. "Reckon there's any danger I'll get away to see my parents?"

"None."

Cullen tapped at his phone. "Sorry. Can't get away today."

The road opened out into the wide, long High Street as they passed Ranger Rover. Sharon took the turning to Souness and Aitken's flat, before entering the usual sights — a Co-op, a Greggs, a fish and chip shop, two off-licenses and several pubs. Pretty much the last building on the street before it became an A-road was Nichol's garage.

Sharon pulled into the single parking space. "Must be like coming home. Back to the wild west."

Cullen got out and leaned across the roof of the car. "Believe me, I'd much rather be out in Garleton or Wester Hailes."

She led them over the road. The sign above the door to the garage read 'Proprietor: Hugh Nichol'. It was busy and loud, at least seven cars on the go, with a gang of mechanics shouting at each other and throwing tools. No sign of any customers. Maybe it was the sort of place you left your car in the morning and collected after work.

A middle-aged man approached, rubbing his hands on an oily rag. "Can I help?"

Sharon got out her warrant card. "Can we speak to Hugh Nichol?"

"You're speaking to him. And I prefer Shug."

"Fine." Sharon put her card away. "We believe a Kenneth Souness works here?"

"You'd better come through to my office."

They followed him into the garage, even louder than when they'd been standing on the periphery. He led them through a battered wooden door, a crude hand-drawn cartoon of Wonder Woman sitting on the toilet with her spangly pants round her knees pinned to the inside.

Sharon scowled at it.

Nichol sat down at a cramped desk, his chair wedged in a small gap. He gestured at two mismatched chairs opposite. "Kenny's not been in since Monday."

Sharon sat on the more stable-looking chair. "Has he called in?"

Nichol rubbed his ear. "Afraid not. No sick call."

"Are there any friends or family you know about?"

"Not that I'm aware of. Only relations he's got is that flatmate of his, Xander. Doesn't talk about his family, doesn't have a bird that I'm aware of and he only talks about his flatmate as an afterthought, you know, when they were going to the football."

Cullen shifted on the wonkier chair. "Was Mr Souness a Rangers fan?"

"He is, aye, son. Goes through to Castle Greyskull every second week, and to most away matches and all."

"Are you a fan?"

"I'm a Jambo, one of the few out this way." Nichol suddenly frowned. "Did you say 'was'?"

"I did. Mr Souness's body was found last night in his flat."

Nichol leaned back in his chair. "Jesus Christ. I was going to head round tonight and check on him after I'd locked up here." He took a deep breath. "I take it you pair are investigating his death, then?"

"That's correct." Sharon got out her notebook. "Do you know of anyone who'd want to harm him?"

Nichol chuckled but his eyes remained cold. "I'd have put myself on that list. Kenny was a good worker when he was hard at it but it used to take a good push to get him up to speed, if you know what I mean." He picked up a document from the desk and tossed it back down immediately. "He was always late, usually only about ten minutes but sometimes half an hour or more. It was particularly bad if there was a Champions League match on."

"You can't think of anyone?"

"Only one I could even think of to speak to is that Xander boy." Nichol scowled. "Should be Alex or Sandy, not Xander. Sounds like he's in Friends or something."

Sharon rolled her eyes. "Mr Aitken was found last night as well."

Nichol screwed his eyes up. "You're kidding me, right?"

"He was in a stolen Range Rover that rolled down one of the bings by Winchburgh."

"Jesus Christ." Nichol stared at the desk.

"Mr Souness was stabbed."

Nichol rubbed his forehead. "Are you having me on here?"

"No. Any ideas who might want to do such a thing?"

Nichol let out a deep breath and thought about it for a few seconds. "I can't. And that's the truth."

"You wouldn't happen to know anything about stolen cars?"

Nichol's eyes shot up. "What are you saying?"

"It's a simple question." Sharon gently brushed her hair over. "Do you know anything about stolen cars?"

"This is just a garage, I don't sell cars."

"I didn't say anything about selling cars. You've got a lot of men, a lot of equipment. You could do anything."

"Well, I don't. I run a legitimate business here. Besides, if it was a Range Rover that Xander was found in, I wouldn't be involved. The biggest we can do here would be a Picasso or a C-Max. You need special tools for SUVs. In case you hadn't noticed, I've got competition on that front in the town. We cut our cloth to suit ourselves."

Sharon nodded while she jotted a few things down. "Okay, I think that's about all from me. Anything from you, Constable?"

Cullen almost smiled at her use of his formal title. "No, I'm fine."

9

A s they arrived back in the Incident Room, Cargill collared them. "I need to speak to the pair of you."

Sharon frowned. "Okay, what about?"

"In private." Cargill headed passed them towards the meeting room, Sharon following her.

Cullen followed, fearing an impending bollocking. What had he done this time?

Cargill stood outside a room just down the corridor. "In here."

It was one of the smallest in the station, four chairs around a circular table.

Sharon sat across from Cargill, giving Cullen no choice — he had to sit between them. He chose the seat away from the door — he could at least see who was being nosy and peering into the room through the floor-to-ceiling window.

"You're probably both already aware that DI Bain is no longer the Senior Investigating Officer on this case." Cargill shifted her chair forward. "This is a big case, we're under no illusion of that. DI Bain will operate as deputy, alongside DS Methven."

Sharon nodded. "We've heard."

"Good." Cargill licked her lips. "First, you two being paired up on an investigation is inappropriate given your relationship. I don't know why DI Bain did that, but I'm stopping it." She took a breath. "Second, everything is to go through myself primarily. Failing that, seek approval from both DI Bain and DS Methven. Nothing should go through either of them in isolation."

Cullen glanced over at Sharon, her eyes locked on Cargill.

"Third, I've got some actions for you both. Much as I hate to admit, they're in line with what DI Bain asked you to do. I want you to speak to the family of the deceased you were previously allocated. Sharon, you can have ADC Buxton to assist. Cullen, you can have DC Caldwell."

"Thanks." Sharon got out her notebook. "I'm not sure Kenny Souness has any surviving family."

"Well, if that's the case, we've got a dead end with one of the victims."

"What sort of approach are you taking to this?" Cullen folded his arms. "Are they separate cases or the same?"

Cargill smiled. "I'm treating them as both. Finding the second body in their flat is suspicious but it could just be coincidence. I'm keeping an open mind. They could be linked or they could be entirely unrelated."

"I just wanted to be clear on it."

"One final thing. Your relationship is your own. I want you to keep it that way. You're to collaborate only under strict instruction from myself or DS Methven. I need to have a clear audit trail with this and I don't want anything muddying the water. Are we clear?"

Sharon nodded. "Crystal."

Cullen had to concentrate hard to stop himself laughing. "Absolutely, ma'am."

"I DON'T KNOW where she gets off. I really don't." Sharon prodded at her salad, skewering a cherry tomato.

Angela grinned. "She's probably just jealous of you, Sharon, what with you being shacked up with a stud like Scott."

Cullen looked up from his lasagne. "Do you really want to start talking about shacking up with people? Besides, she's probably more jealous of me shacking up with Sharon."

Sharon glared at him. "What's that supposed to mean?"

"Well, she's gay, isn't she?"

Angela put a hand to her mouth. "You don't know that, do you?"

"She looks gay."

Sharon scowled. "Scott, are you being homophobic again?"

Cullen held his hands up. "I'm not being homophobic. I'm just saying, that's all."

Sharon shook her head. "You better not be away to use that 'some of my best friends are gay' line again."

"Well, they are. But besides, I'm not being homophobic. I'm just saying that she looks like a lesbian, that's all. Isn't she?"

Sharon put some mackerel in her mouth and chewed. "Well, as a matter of fact, she is."

"How do you know?"

Sharon put her knife and fork down on the plate and pushed it away, the salad half eaten. "I worked with her for a couple of years. Unless she's had some sort of epiphany, she's still gay."

Cullen clocked Methven heading over. "Change the subject. Didn't Shug Nichol say Souness had no family?"

Sharon glanced over her shoulder. "No, he told us Souness never talked about a family. Doesn't mean he didn't have one."

"Good point."

"You lot talking shop? Well I never." Methven stood by the table beside them, carrying a tray with a bowl of soup and some bread, hand jangling in his left pocket. "Got room for two more?"

Sharon frown. "Who's the other?"

A seriously thin woman appeared next to Methven. She had long dark hair and looked like she was in her early thirties.

"DS Catriona Rarity." Methven patted her shoulder. "This is her first day in Jim's team. This is DS Sharon McNeill, DC Scott Cullen and DC Angela Caldwell."

Sharon shuffled to the side. "Have a seat."

Methven sat at the end of the table, between Sharon and Angela, while Rarity sat opposite Cullen.

Cullen pushed his lasagne away. "Where have you moved from?"

"Central. I was based at HQ in Stirling."

"That's going to be the new HQ, right?"

"Maybe. It'll be Tulliallan until they decide."

"Do you know DI Cargill?"

"I worked with her on a couple of nationwide community outreach initiatives. They were pretty successful."

Methven dunked some bread in his soup. "Let the woman have some lunch, Cullen."

Cullen smiled. "Just being friendly."

"Yeah, well, your reputation precedes you."

Angela and Sharon laughed.

Cullen held up his hands. "Relax, I'm spoken for."

Methven took a spoonful of soup. "Doesn't sodding stop some people."

Angela shot daggers at him. Sharon tapped her on the wrist.

Rarity grinned at him. "Actually, I wouldn't mind having a catch up with you, Scott. DI Cargill asked me to keep an eye on how you're getting on with the Aitken investigation. I'm deputising for her in the post mortem at two, but I'll come find you after."

Cullen clenched his jaw. Someone else keeping an eye on him. "Sure."

They ate in silence for a few minutes.

Methven put his bowl back on the tray. "We'd better get back to it. DI Cargill wants a catch-up before the PM."

"I'll see you later." Rarity smiled at Sharon and Angela.

When they were out of earshot, Sharon piped up. "Where does he get off? We've not been working with him that long and I can't stand him already. Sanctimonious shit."

Angela smirked at Cullen. "Were you flirting with Rarity?"

"Hardly. I was just being friendly."

Sharon reached across and held his hand. "I don't think she was interested."

"It wasn't that. I was fishing for information." Cullen leaned back in his seat. "That's another DS that's come in. That's four. I'm screwed."

Angela rolled her eyes. "Here we go again. The career woes of Scott Cullen, detective constable for a whole eighteen months."

He scowled at her. "Is it pick on Cullen day or something?"

"Oh, come on, Scott." Angela folded her arms. "First, you get me to do your job for you this morning, then you're moaning that you're not getting promoted."

"Thanks for the sympathy."

Angela got to her feet. "Get over yourself, Scott."

"Cargill's put me in charge of you. I'll see you in the Incident Room in ten minutes."

"Great. I'll just get back to work and let you strategise." Angela walked off before throwing her tray onto the trolley.

Cullen turned to Sharon. "What's got up her?"

"DS Lamb."

Cullen grinned. "Very good." His expression darkened. "Since she got made a DC, she's been a right bloody princess. Bain was spot on with that nickname."

"Scott, she works hard. She's pretty good and she's going through a tough time, so let her get through it."

"Doesn't give her a remit to go around pissing everyone off."

Sharon shrugged her shoulders. "Maybe it does."

10

"We could do with an Incident Room out in West Lothian." Cullen kicked down to overtake a tractor, the Golf struggling to make it, the post-harvest fields around them reduced to yellow stubble. "I know this is an A Division gig, but I'm getting fed up driving out here all the time."

"I'm surprised your car's coping at all." Angela folded her arms. "Maybe you should get Shug Nichol to take a look at it."

"There's nothing wrong with it. It still works."

They drove through Ravencraig, busy with the lunchtime rush, the sun threatening to break out from behind the clouds. Greggs the baker had a queue almost round the block. A gang of school kids hung around in front of the Co-op.

Cullen indicated just before Nichol's Garage and headed down Mason Avenue, a street filled with semi-detached council houses, their harled exterior walls painted yellow. "Tina Aitken lives at the end of this one, I think."

The street was mostly empty and Cullen pulled into a space just in front of the three-storey block of flats she lived in. "Do you want to lead?"

"You owe me from earlier, I'll let you."

They walked up the path to the flat, the garden filled with dulled white pebbles and the sort of grey thistle Cullen always associated with municipal housing.

The door was eventually answered by a thin woman in her early forties.

Cullen showed his warrant card. "Mrs Aitken?"

"No, son, I'm her sister, Kerry. I'll show you through."

The house was in a state of disrepair, frayed carpet, peeling wallpaper, much worse than the flat her son had lived in — Xander Aitken had clearly gone up in the world.

The living room was small and packed with furniture — a three-piece suite in brown fabric filled the walls. A small portable TV sat in the corner, sound muted, showing an old Western.

Tina Aitken was sitting on an armchair, ignoring them as they entered, eyes focused on the floor. She was a few years older than her sister, her reddish brown hair thinning in places.

"Tina, the police want to speak to you."

She looked up, revealing sunken cheeks. Her eyes, surrounded by dark rings, barely acknowledged their presence. "Police have already been."

Kerry led them back into the hall, pushing the living room door shut behind Angela. "She's not taking this well."

"It's to be expected." Cullen loosened his tie — the flat was sweltering. "When were the police around?"

"A couple of young guys came this afternoon. I didn't catch their names. They were wearing uniforms, said they were from Ravencraig nick."

Cullen knew it should have been officers assigned to the investigation who were allocated to FLO duties — he'd have to check that out. "I need to ask her a few questions about her son."

"Okay, I'm not sure you'll get much out of it."

"I understand, but I need to try."

"I'll be in the kitchen. Give me a holler if you need me."

Cullen headed back into the living room, sitting on the settee nearest Tina with Angela perching on the other. "Mrs Aitken, I need to ask you some questions about your son."

"Xander's dead."

"I know, I'm a detective and I'm trying to find out if Xander was murdered. I need your help."

Tina looked up at Cullen, her large eyes pleading with him. "You think my Xander was murdered?"

"It's a distinct possibility. His flatmate, Kenny, was found dead in the flat not long after we found Xander's body."

"Oh my God." Tina wiped a tear from her face. "They were best pals. I can't believe they're both gone." Tears flowed down her cheeks, quickly sliding onto the cream cardigan she wore. "They used to go to the football together."

"Can you think of anyone who might want to harm your son?"

"Xander was a good son. He got into bother when he was a

teenager, but he sorted himself out. His father battered him until he stopped hanging about with the gangs he was in." Tina closed her eyes. "I shouldn't be telling you that, but it's the truth. Tommy battering him was the best thing that could have happened to the boy."

She opened her eyes again, glazed over with tears. "He got himself a good job at the Royal Bank. He was doing well, too. He should have moved away from this town. It's a bad place. I didn't want Xander getting trapped here like me."

"You mentioned Xander's father. Are you still together?"

"We split up about five year ago. Maybe four year, who knows? We didn't get divorced, couldn't be bothered with all the hassle."

"Does he still live locally?"

Tina nodded. "He does, aye. Other end of the town from here. It's still not far enough away."

"Can I ask why you separated?"

"You can ask, but I don't see why you need to know."

"Mrs Aitken, I need to know if your son was murdered. We're looking for any motive at all, any possibility. I have to understand why you split up with your husband."

"It was mainly the beatings. He used to batter Xander and he used to batter me. He likes a drink. I might have said it helped him, but there comes a point, you know? Tommy was the most charming man you'd ever meet when he was sober. Soon as he had a lager in him, this demon came out. The only good thing that came of it all was getting Xander to quit the gang."

Cullen had seen it so many times before in small towns across the Lothians — a young couple trapped by their relationship and children. Frustration and resentment turned to anger and then anger turned to violence. Those that got out did well — those that stayed were generally doomed to sire the next generation, which would repeat the same mistakes. "Did you ever go to the police about this violence?"

"At the start, but then they couldn't do much, could they?"

"How did it end?"

"He just got fed up. As soon as Xander left home, he only had me. He just got bored of it. I was cramping his style."

Cullen jotted a few things in his notebook. He looked over at Angela. "Have you got any more questions?"

Angela leaned forward on the settee. "Was Xander seeing anybody?"

Tina nodded. "He was, aye. Sweet wee lassie called Demi Baird. Lives in Queensferry Avenue, other end of the town."

Cullen noted down Demi's mobile number.

"Of course, she'll be at work the now. She works at McArthur Glen in Livvy."

THEY STRUCK LUCKY — Tommy Aitken was in.

Cullen leaned into the intercom. "Mr Aitken, it's the police."

"Ah, right."

Cullen looked back at Angela. "Can we come in?"

"I was just on my way out."

"We need to speak to you now."

"Right, come on then." The buzzer sounded and the door opened.

Cullen pushed into the dank stairwell. "Where do you think he's on his way to?"

Angela shrugged. "Probably the town's cheapest, roughest pub."

They got up to the second floor, Tommy Aitken standing in his doorway. He was a thin, wiry man with the cheeky smile of George Best in his happy drunk phase. He wore baggy denims and a hooded top. He looked mid-forties, old enough to be there for the Second Summer of Love — the Stone Roses, Acid House, Spike Island and all that. "Come on in, then."

The front door entered straight into his sparsely-furnished living room, which was tiny, even smaller than his wife's.

Cullen took one of the chairs. "Mr Aitken, we need to speak to you about your son."

"Aye, can you be quick about it?"

Cullen frowned. "Xander's dead, Mr Aitken."

"Aye, I know. No use in crying over spilt milk, you know what I mean? I was just heading out."

"Where to?"

"Wanted to meet a few of my pals. Try to process things."

"I see." Cullen unfolded his notebook. "What can you tell us about Xander?"

"The boy had a screw loose."

Cullen wasn't exactly wondering where the boy inherited the trait from. "What makes you say that?"

"Just couldn't focus on anything. When he was a laddie, he was getting into trouble with gangs and stuff. I managed to stop that behaviour, you know?"

Cullen made a show of flipping through his notebook. "When we spoke to your wife, she told us that you battered it out of him. Is that correct?"

Tommy inspected his fingernails — a couple on his right hand were long enough for finger-picking an acoustic guitar. "Suppose it is, aye."

Cullen pointed up at the Stone Roses posters on the wall above the fireplace, the only colour in the room. "Hard to reconcile the One Love stuff up there with beating your own son up."

Tommy screwed his face up. "It was tough love. The boy was going to end up in a bad place if we didn't sort his life out there and then. He ended up doing better than me. Working in a bank is such a good thing for this family to have achieved. We were both proud of the laddie."

"And yet he had a screw loose?"

"Aye, well. We could never quite stop him doing stupid things."

"Compared to your wife, you don't seem to be that upset. Why is that?"

"You know what women are like since Diana. I like to keep my cool."

Cullen wondered how much of his cool he kept when he beat the shit out of his son and wife. "Just out of interest, why did you and your wife split up?"

"None of your business."

"Xander's body has been found in suspicious circumstances. Coupled with his flatmate's body also being found, we're dealing with a major inquiry here. Any information — and I mean any — could prove useful and help us bring a killer or killers to justice."

"Did you say Kenny was dead?"

"He was discovered in their flat last night, just after Xander's body was found."

"Jesus." Tommy sat there for close to a minute, staring into space. "Jesus Christ." He rubbed his hand down his face. "Those pair were inseparable. From the age of about fifteen, they were best mates. Both of them were Rangers daft. Used to take them through to Ibrox when I was still working. Been a long time since I took them, mind you. I was proud they still went but Christ... I can't believe they're both dead."

"Can you think of anyone who might wish them dead?"

"Just a whole busload of Celtic fans." Tommy laughed.

"I'm glad your son's murder is a laughing matter."

Tommy's face straightened up. "Sorry. It's how I deal with things"

"That and beating your wife and son up?"

"What the hell is this?"

"Mr Aitken, I need to know if there are any people that would wish to cause Xander harm. I would appreciate it if you would co-operate."

"Nobody springs to mind." Tommy sat, deep in thought for a few moments. "No, nobody. One thing, though — my son was found in a stolen Range Rover, right? I can buy that the silly wee bastard would have driven it down the bing himself and smashed it up, but you're saying he was murdered, is that right?"

"It's an avenue we're investigating. It's current protocol to treat all deaths as suspicious until proven otherwise. Given Xander's flatmate was also found murdered on the same evening, this certainly fits the profile."

"Right, right. Well, as I say, there's nobody I can think of that would have hated them pair enough to kill them. The boys were well thought of in the town."

"We understand Xander had a girlfriend. Demi Baird, is that right?"

"It is, but she doesn't pronounce it like that. It's just 'Demmy', not 'De-mee'."

"Are you close to her at all?"

"Daft wee lassie." Tommy screwed his face up. "I've no idea what my boy saw in her. He could have done a lot better."

"Okay. I think that's all for me. DC Caldwell?"

She shook her head.

CULLEN TURNED RIGHT at the roundabout, McArthur Glen coming to view. "Instead of a high street, Livingston has McArthur Glen."

"Snob."

"Hardly." Cullen looked around the front of the mall. "Where did you say she worked?"

"M&S."

"Here'll do." Cullen pulled into the car park nearest to where he remembered the shop to be. "Used to come here all the time when I was based in Livvy."

"Well done you."

"Oh, come on, are you still pissed off with me?"

"Any reason why I shouldn't be?"

Cullen pulled on the handbrake. "Well, I asked every single question in both houses."

"Almost. You didn't ask about his girlfriend. If it'd been up to you, we'd never have known about her."

Cullen flared his nostrils. "What is it?"

"Nothing."

"No, that's the second time today you've gone off on one at me. I'm not aware of doing anything to deserve it."

"That's part of the problem." She took a deep breath. "I'm sorry. I'm being a bitch and you don't deserve it. Well, not all of it. I'm just tired from the commute. I suppose I was expecting to get a bit more of a lead role in this. So far, I've helped Jobsworth put the case into HOLMES then helped you speak to some people in a bank. That's hardly exciting, is it?"

"And you call me a princess?"

She laughed. "Well, we're here. Do you want me to lead?"

"Aye, go on."

Cullen got out and led them across the car park, half empty in the October late afternoon sunshine. They walked through the main entrance, past Wetherspoon's, the curry house and Pizza Express. M&S was just ahead on the right.

Angela asked for Demi at the customer service desk.

They only had to wait thirty seconds before a pretty, if surly, girl approached them, Demi on her badge. "Is it DC Caldwell?"

Angela showed her warrant card. "It is, yes. Is there somewhere private we could go to discuss matters?"

Demi turned up her lip. "What 'matters'?"

"Your boyfriend's death?"

Demi's mouth dropped open. "Are you serious?"

Nobody had told the girl Xander had died.

Angela put a hand to Demi's shoulder. "Where can we go?"

"My parents' house."

11

Demi's parents' house was a modest sixties bungalow on a quiet street on the outskirts of the town.

The Family Liaison Officer got out of a car and headed over.

Cullen wound down the window. "PC Rowley?"

"Aye." She nodded in the back and spoke in a low voice. "How is she?"

"She's been silent all the way, just staring out of the window."

Rowley shook her head. "This sounds like a disaster."

"I think you're right." Cullen looked in the rear view at Demi, hand clasped to her face. "The boy's parents were told but nobody's seen fit to tell her. She's pretty shell-shocked."

"How do you think you'd feel if you'd just been given that news?"

"We need to ask her a few questions."

Rowley tutted. "As ever. Her parents are on their way home. They both work in Edinburgh. Give me five minutes to get her inside and settled, then we'll see if you can speak to her. I'll stop the interview if she is reacting adversely. Okay?"

"Fine."

Rowley's face changed, a different mask being applied.

Cullen waited, watching her gently cajole Demi into leaving the car and heading inside. "Why didn't I think it weird that Demi was at work?"

"It's not just you, Scott. Bit of a disaster, indeed."

"Wonder whose balls will get toasted for this?"

"Yours, no doubt." Angela led him inside. "What are we looking for here?"

"Just need to get some background, nothing too aggressive."

"Sure you can manage that?"

"You lead then."

"I might just do that."

The front door was unlocked, so they walked through to the living room.

Rowley sat with Demi, hands clasped around a red can of Coke.

Cullen sat on the sofa opposite next to Angela.

Rowley put her hand on Demi's shoulder. "Demi these detectives want to speak to you about your boyfriend, okay?"

Demi shrugged Rowley's hand away. "I know who they are. They told me about Xander."

Rowley sat back. "Are you happy for them to ask questions?"

Demi nodded. "Shoot."

Angela sat forward on the settee. "So you're engaged?"

Demi held up her left hand, her ring finger raised up to show the golden ring with a small diamond. "We are." She eased the ring off. "Were."

"But you didn't live together?"

Demi shook her head, her ponytail dancing around. "No, we didn't. We'd been talking about it, but we didn't get round to it. Xander was actually quite funny about it. Didn't want to jinx anything. His parents' marriage was a mess and he didn't want to repeat that. He wanted things kept pure, not to move in together until we were married."

"Was Xander religious?"

Demi shrugged. "In a way, yes. The only church he went to was Ibrox stadium but he had certain ideas, that's for sure."

Cullen frowned at his notebook. Where did the boy develop this religious purity? It certainly wasn't from his parents. Then again, he was the product of a severely broken home. Most football fans were superstitious — sitting in the same seat on the coach on match day, wearing the same shoes — and it wasn't much of a stretch to believe that luck was a factor in marriage. Rangers fans weren't fanatical about their Protestantism, unlike their Celtic counterparts and the Catholic faith, the sectarian divide being more of a tribal thing than a point of ecclesiastical principle. Gangs. Us versus them.

Demi fiddled with the ring. "We were going to have a white wedding in a castle. I'd been planning it for months. It was going to be perfect."

Cullen made another note. Where was the money coming from? A call centre worker and an M&S till girl weren't going to have those resources. Aitken's parents wouldn't even be able to afford the bus ticket to the registry office. From the decor in the house, it didn't look like Demi's parents were loaded. Besides, the girl was seventeen if a day — surely she'd have been coerced into some form of further education if they had money.

Angela smiled at her. "Mr Aitken's flatmate, Kenneth Souness, was also found dead. Do you have any idea who would've wanted to harm them both?"

"Was Kenny in the car as well?"

"No, he was found at their flat. He died from a knife wound."

"Jesus Christ." Demi pinged the ring pull on the can of Coke for a few seconds. "Can't think of anyone. They were well thought of in Ravencraig. They had a load of pals they used to go to the football with. Ravencraig's pretty much all Rangers, so there was none of the fighting like in Bathgate."

"Is there anybody you can think of at all?"

"No."

Angela looked at Rowley. "I think that's us." She tossed her card on the table. "If you think of anything, please give me a call, okay?"

Demi swallowed. "I will."

They got up and left her with Rowley.

Cullen shut the front door behind him. "Unbelievable."

"What, her or the fact she hadn't been told?"

"Both. She's living in a fantasy world. How the hell were they going to pay for a wedding like that?"

"A girl's got to have a dream. Ours was just a registry office job, but a lot of my pals did the whole castle thing. Always ends up the same way. Why waste the money?"

"Catch the romantic cynic."

"Scott, I'm just realistic now, that's all. These days, I want to be with someone who doesn't piss me off and who wants to spend some time with me."

"I can understand that."

"Back to the Incident Room, then?"

Cullen looked at the darkening sky — it was going to rain soon. "Seeing as how we're out this way, there are a few things I want to check out."

Angela scowled. "Remember this is your decision. If Methven gives anyone a bollocking, it's you."

"My, my, Angela. You've changed."

"If I have, it's working with cowboys like you that did it."

≈

THE POLICE RANGE Rover dropped them off at the scene of the wreckage, the bing looming over them. The cordons were still in force, guarded by two PCs — Cullen wasn't sure how much longer they'd get away with the expense.

Cullen walked up to the constable managing the outer cordon, a young Asian officer, vaguely recognising his face from somewhere out west. He flashed his warrant card and signed into the crime scene.

"You DC Cullen?"

Cullen nodded. "Aye."

The officer held out a hand. "Kamal Johal. Used to be based in Bathgate with you."

Cullen pointed at him. "Thought I knew you from somewhere." He nodded towards the tent. "Is the car still here?"

Johal looked across the field. "Supposed to have been picked up this morning but it's still not been shifted. Wish they'd bloody hurry up. It's starting to get bloody cold."

"Thought the SOCOs had been over it?"

"They did a search on it here but not a full one. Still got a couple of people here."

"Anyone else been out?"

"A DS Methven paid us a visit. Asked pretty much the same things as you."

Cullen looked over to the bing — a rough path ran up the mound. "Has anyone been up to the top?"

"No, it's as it was when the accident happened." He pointed up at the sky. "It's going to piss down soon, so it won't stay like that."

"It's not rained since, has it?"

"Don't think so, besides, the SOCOs did some tyre track analysis yesterday."

Cullen nodded at Angela. "Come on."

She scowled at him. "If you think I'm walking up there."

"Only a wee bit of the way."

Cullen left Johal to his clipboard and walked over to the path, hopping over a small ford to cross a stream running down the edge of two fields. He led them up the path about twenty metres before stopping to check the tracks — there were three distinct sets of prints. "That's funny."

Angela rolled her eyes at him. "What is?"

"I need to get Anderson to look into it, but there's three sets of prints. I'd expect one if it's a car going up and rolling off the side."

"Maybe someone else went up before?"

"Maybe." Cullen looked around for a few minutes but found nothing of interest.

"Can we get back to the Incident Room?"

"I want to check something else out first."

CULLEN LED inside Souness and Aitken's block of flats, the yellow tape still flapping in the breeze outside.

An officer stood inside, having his ear bent by a middle-aged woman.

"I said, I shouldn't need to have to sign into my own house."

"I understand, madam. I'm afraid this is a murder case and we have to protect the integrity of the crime scene."

Cullen reached over and took the clipboard, signing him and Angela into the flat while he kept an eye on what was happening outside.

"Here, you." The woman clicked her fingers at him.

Cullen looked round. "What is it?"

"You look like you're in charge here. Can you get them to stop this?"

"I'm afraid I'm not in charge. I can put in a word with the Senior Investigating Officer." Cullen had no intention of mentioning it to Cargill, but he could at least buy the put-upon officer some time.

"That would be magic. Any idea when I'll hear?"

"I would expect some time tomorrow at the very earliest."

"Thank you." She scowled at the PC before heading into the flat next door.

The PC raised his eyes to the heavens. "Twenty minutes she's been like that."

Cullen grabbed a Scene of Crime suit from the stack by the door and tossed it to Angela, before putting one on himself. "Have you interviewed her in connection with the murder?"

"We have. That's probably what pissed her off."

Cullen smiled. "Well, I'll see what I can do." He entered the flat and headed straight for the living room.

Halfway down the hall, Angela tugged his arm. "Scott."

He stopped and spun round. "What?"

"Why are we here?"

"I want to have a proper look around. There was a body in the flat last time, so I was kind of distracted."

"You need to start planning this stuff out. We can't just keep on dotting around everywhere in case some of that Cullen magic dust settles in the right place."

"Will you give me a break? I'm trying to investigate what happened here."

"Well, I'll be a lot happier when you let me know what you're planning on doing. This John Wayne shite is pissing me off."

"Look who it is."

Cullen turned around to face the living room.

Charlie Kidd stood in the doorway, carrying a large cardboard box.

Cullen nodded recognition. "Long time no see, Charlie."

"Aye, well, that's a good thing for me. Keep me away from you and your cowboy antics."

Cullen screwed his eyes up. "Why does everyone think I'm a cowboy?"

"Cos you are one?"

Angela smiled. "That's what I said."

"Whatever."

"You're a wild boy." Kidd patted Cullen's shoulder with his free hand. Cullen brushed it off. "Why are you here anyway?"

Kidd held up the box. "Picking up laptops for forensic analysis. Got their Xbox, too."

"Thought you were a PC gamer?"

"Aye, I am. It's not for playing games on, it's for all that Xbox Live shite. Never know what they've been up to on there, other than getting shot to bits by fourteen year olds on Call of Duty."

"Well, nice to see you," said Cullen.

Kidd grimaced. "Always a pleasure, but every time I bump into you I get the feeling I'm going to get involved in some utter nonsense."

"Well, I'll try and keep it to myself for once."

Kidd walked over to the front door. He opened it then turned around. "Oh, your boss is in there."

Cullen closed his eyes for a few seconds. "Bain?"

Kidd smirked. "I'll see you around, Scotty." He shut the door behind him.

Angela shook her head. "This is your idea, remember."

"Come on."

"Just as well you're not on a stakeout." Methven stood with his hands on his hips. "I can hear you down the sodding street."

"Sorry, Sarge."

Methven put his hands in his trouser pockets and started jangling his keys. "Other than shouting at Charlie Kidd, what are you actually here for?"

"We went to speak to Aitken's mother and father then his girl-friend. Turns out nobody had told her Xander was dead."

"You're joking?"

"I'm not in the habit of joking about that sort of thing."

Methven's bushy eyebrows arched up again. "Have you got any clear leads from all that petrol?"

"Not yet. Need to type up our notes and do some thinking. The only new thing is that he was engaged."

"Now that is interesting." Methven reached over for an evidence bag. "We found some extra strong condoms in Aitken's top drawer. If what you're saying is true, his girlfriend likes a bit of anal."

Cullen blushed. "Or they really didn't want her to get pregnant."

"That's a possibility, we should consider it."

"She's seventeen, I doubt she's into anal."

"Some girls are." Angela shrugged. "It's a different generation, we shouldn't make any assumptions."

"I wholeheartedly agree." Methven put the bag back. "It could be nothing, but it could be something."

"Hang on." Cullen looked at Angela. "Didn't she say they were keeping themselves pure?"

Angela nodded. "She did."

Cullen chuckled. "Maybe he just liked a very safe posh wank."

Methven glared at Cullen. "I beg your pardon?"

Cullen shrugged. "I take it you've never heard the expression?"

"I'm fully aware what it sodding means, Constable, I just wish you'd keep such terminology away from the crime scene."

"It's an explanation."

Methven sighed. "I take your point."

Angela leaned against the door. "Do you want us to speak to her again?"

"Let her sodding get over her boyfriend's murder first. Give her a couple of days before we go over her sex life. It might be better for someone more sensitive than Mr Cullen to do that."

Angela smiled. "I've been an FLO, I've got the skills."

"Good. DCs need a broad skill set."

Cullen decided to leave any further backchat. "What do you want us to do, then?"

Methven checked his watch. "DI Cargill's got a briefing at six thirty. I want you two to compile your notes ahead of it."

ngela stopped at the door leading from the garage to the stairwell. "Scott, I've said I don't want to get tarred with the same brush as you, can't you just leave it at that?"

"No, I can't." Cullen put his hand against the door. "You know as well as most that I don't just leave things."

Angela glared at his hand as she stood back and folded her arms. "And that's the problem. You're always off on your own, trying to prove you're better than everyone else." She stabbed a finger in the air. "I got hit on the head with a hammer because of you."

"I got my shoulder opened as well."

"If you don't care about your own well-being then that's fine. You've had an ADC get stabbed on your watch and then I got my head battered with a hammer. And all because you couldn't wait for backup."

"Both of those were Bain's fault. I solved two murders, saved two lives."

"And cost one life and almost another two. I had to save you."

"Where's this come from?"

"Your actions mainly."

"I'm serious. Since you became a DC, you've been a nightmare."

"A nightmare? You're the one who's a nightmare, Scott. I'm your partner, which means every decision you make looks like it's supported by me."

"Is this coming from Bill?"

She laughed as she shook her head. "We don't talk shop at home."

"It's Bain, then, isn't it?"

She yawned. "So what if it is?"

"What did he say?"

She paused for a few seconds. "When I got made DC, Bain warned me off following your example too closely."

Cullen felt his blood boil.

"Can I go?"

Cullen stood back and held his hands up. "Fine. Don't want to hold your career back."

"Don't be like that, I'm just following advice."

"Well that's good for you. I'm just going to head upstairs, type up the report and make sure I'm not making any other officers go out on a limb or actually, you know, catch criminals."

"If you want to be like that, then be my guest."

And with that she was gone, leaving Cullen looking at the closing door. He really needed to sort out his reputation.

"THE USUAL, IS IT?" Barbara, Cullen's favourite canteen worker, gave him a cheeky wink, her wrinkled face screwing up.

"Aye."

She gave a laugh which quickly turned into a rattling cough. "You know, yours is the only BLT with brown sauce on."

"Is it?"

"Bad day, is it?"

"You could say." Cullen sighed. "I've been staring at a screen for hours. My eyes are starting to go."

"Your day's about to get worse." Bain appeared to Cullen's right, clutching a Müller Fruit Corner.

"Inspector." Barbara headed off to get Cullen's roll and coffee.

Cullen didn't turned to face Bain. "What have I done now?"

"Always on the defensive, Sundance, who says you've done anything?"

"You just implied my already shite day is going to get worse."

"You think you're having a shite day. That witch Cargill is treating me like a bloody' DS. Just been at both post mortems. That witch is getting right on my tits. Which are bigger than hers, by the way."

"What happened at the PM?"

"I was too angry to pay attention." Bain held up a document. "Came up here to read through the report."

"Anything else making you angry?"

"Turnbull is treating me like shite as well. Prick."

"I'm not sure you should be saying that in public."

"I'll say it where I fuckin' like."

Barbara appeared with Cullen's roll and coffee. She scowled at Bain. "Language!"

"Sorry." Bain lowered his head. "Haggis, bacon and tattie scone, please."

"If you promise not to swear in here again."

"Aye, okay."

Barbara gave him a stern smile. "Good."

Cullen handed her a fiver and she gave him his change. "Better head back down."

"Aye, I'll see you, Sundance."

"THE POST MORTEM for Kenny Souness is complete." Cargill held up a report as she stood at the front of the room, full for the briefing, officers having been dragged back from the investigation in Ravencraig and wider West Lothian. "We believe Souness was stabbed in the stomach with a serrated knife at least twenty-four hours before he was found by DS McNeill and DC Cullen. The cause of death was almost certainly blood loss. According to Dr Deeley, he would most likely have survived if he'd received hospital treatment."

She picked up another report from the table at her side. "His flatmate, Alexander Aitken, died as a result of his injuries in the crash after the Range Rover descended from the top of the earth mound where the car was found. While we've no eyewitnesses so far, we've enough forensic evidence to confirm the car plummeted from the top."

She paused and looked around. "Now, Deeley believes the wounds Aitken received are only partially consistent with the stolen car rolling down the hill. The upshot is that we believe Aitken may have incurred injuries by some other means."

"What 'means' would those be?" Irvine's mouth pounded on chewing gum.

"Deeley's performing a follow-on activity to identify that." Cargill's cold eyes stared at him. "He may have been beaten, but we can't confirm that just now. The seatbelt's cut into his chest and severely bruised him. However, we've confirmed the ring imprint belonged to what's unfortunately the second-most popular sovereign design in West Lothian."

"Who do you think beat him up?"

Cargill held her hand up. "Please let me finish. I want to progress this investigation in an efficient and clean manner. We will look for the experts to complete their analysis, draw the conclusions we need and then complete the activity. Am I clear?"

"Crystal."

Bain, standing alongside Cargill, gave a quick smirk before his face settled back.

Cargill set down the second report. "The specialists in James Anderson's team are going through the forensic analysis now. The investigation at the flat Souness and Aitken shared is drawing to a close. The car has now been moved to the investigation hub downstairs and there's a full forensic analysis underway."

She picked up a sheet of notepaper, reading it for a few seconds, her lips moving as she read. "We have another four streams underway. First, DS Rarity is leading the door-to-door investigation in Ravencraig on the victims' street. Whilst it may be early days in the investigation, we have a couple of avenues to explore. I don't want to go into explicit details at this point. Our prevailing theory is Souness was stabbed in the flat. There's sufficient forensic residue to point to that, but we don't have a murder weapon."

She looked at Cullen. "The other three streams are key information gathering exercises, led by DS McNeill and DC Cullen, with DS Methven giving oversight. DS McNeill is looking into Kenny Souness's history, while Cullen is doing a similar activity with Alexander Aitken."

She gestured at Methven, standing on the other side from Bain. "DI Methven's activities relate to tying the various pieces up and pulling together a picture of these young men's lives." She paused for a few seconds. "This is a highly suspicious case. A man is found in a car at the bottom of a bing, with injuries more severe than they should be. His flatmate is found the same night dead from stab wounds."

Irvine readied himself to interrupt again, but the expression on Cargill's face clearly made him change his mind.

"From the very first moment on the Aitken case, we've treated it as murder. We view these cases as potentially linked. I want to make sure that we're all on the same page and our activities are focused. The majority of you are on the door-to-door. Don't treat that as anything but the most important part of the investigation. Write everything down, no matter how insignificant it seems at the time. Please report to DS Rarity and DS Irvine for revised actions. I want DC Cullen and DS McNeill to stay behind with myself, DI Bain and DS Methven."

Cullen shared a look with Sharon, unable to work out if he was heading into a doing or not.

13

"You were all there for my briefing." Cargill folded her arms and leaned across the desk. "You know where we are with this case, so I shouldn't have to spell it out for you. Nonetheless, in the interests of clarity, I will. I can't help but think that these are connected. Somebody has murdered Kenny Souness, that much is clear. The evidence is starting to point to Alexander Aitken having been murdered. We need to get a list of potential suspects."

She got to her feet and went over to the flip chart in the corner of the room, presently showing an anonymous structure chart. She flipped it over and uncapped a pen, then wrote Souness and Aitken on the board. "What are the connections between them?"

Sharon raised a hand. "They're both from Ravencraig."

Cargill wrote it down, joining the arrows from the victims. "Good, what else?"

Cullen cleared his throat. "They were Rangers fans."

Rangers went up on the sheet.

Cullen flipped through his notebook. "From what I've been told about Aitken, they were both season ticket holders and they'd also travel to away games."

Methven got to his feet and joined Cargill at the board. "Could they be hooligans?"

"Worth looking into." Cullen shrugged. "They're young and Ravencraig is a rough town."

Cargill looked at Sharon. "DS McNeill, can you check if they were involved in hooliganism, please?"

"Will do." Sharon scribbled it down. "DI Wilkinson may have some useful information."

"For once." Bain grinned.

Cargill shot him a look. "Anything else?"

"If you're just looking for connections, I've not got any more." Bain rubbed his moustache. "There are a few things we could look at independently, though."

"Connections for now." Cargill folded her arms. "Any more?"

"They were flatmates." Methven tapped at the flipchart. "I know it's obvious but it should be put down."

Cargill added it. "Okay, anything else?"

Cullen frowned. "How about Aitken stabbed Souness before killing himself?"

Bain tutted. "Jumping to conclusions, Sundance."

Cargill scowled. "Let him continue."

"It's a possibility." Cullen licked his lips. "They might've had a fight or something. The evidence we've got could point to Aitken stabbing Souness, leaving the flat, stealing a car and then killing himself. The post mortem report said Souness had been dead for at least twenty-four hours before we found him. Say it's a couple of days and in that time Aitken is so wracked with guilt, he kills himself."

"Why, though?" Methven frowned. "Are you suggesting an argument about the sodding washing up?"

"Make a joke of it if you like." Cullen folded his arms. "I'm saying it fits, that's all. What about the bruising on Aitken? They could've had a fight at the flat, he stabbed Souness, but he's been beaten black and blue. He goes mad, steals the car on Tuesday afternoon and then kills himself on Wednesday."

"No forensics in the flat." Bain scratched his head. "Souness was definitely not slotted there, unless Aitken's got the old bin bags out, done him and then pissed off. Anderson found a trail of blood going inside the flat from outside. Difficult to spot but it's there. Souness was stabbed elsewhere and got home somehow, either with or without Aitken's help."

Cargill glared. "DI Bain, why have you not shared this information with the rest of the team?"

Bain grinned. "Let me know when I get an audience with you which isn't you undermining my position."

Cargill put her hands on her hips. "I just stood in front of thirty officers to say it looked like Souness could have been stabbed in the flat."

"Best check your facts in future."

"I did. I spoke to James Anderson and he didn't give that same story."

"Mustn't have asked in the right way. He just needs tickling under the chin." Bain waved a document in front of her. "He gave me a copy of the draft report."

Cargill snorted. "Let's keep it as a possibility, but it's an outside bet."

Bain grinned. "It's hardly the three ten from Chepstow. It's there in black and white."

"Until this report of yours is published, it's an outside bet. Okay?"

Bain beamed to himself. "Fine."

Cargill looked back at the board for a few seconds. "Next, let's focus on Aitken. Cullen?"

"His girlfriend, Demi Baird. He disappeared on nights out. Worked at RBS. His parents are both a bit dodgy and they're not divorced."

"Doesn't feel like a lot."

Cullen's ears burned. "Tell me what else I could have done?"

"Sorry, Scott, I'm not having a go at you. I'm just saying there doesn't seem to be a lot to go on with this young man." Cargill rubbed the back of her head. "Sharon, what have you got on Souness?"

"Parents both dead, Mum had cancer, dad from a heart attack. Both in the last three years." Sharon flipped through her notebook. "He worked at Nichol's Garage in Ravencraig as a mechanic. That's it. Not a lot to show for a day's work, I'm afraid."

Cargill screwed her eyes up. "No girlfriend?"

"No."

"No boyfriend?"

"No anybody. Other than his flatmate, he didn't have any close friends. Neither has a criminal record, other than Aitken's early career."

"Let's focus on finding out more about these two. We need to get the street team on this, try to get people in Ravencraig to open up here." Cargill scribbled a few more notes on the chart. "Has anyone got anything else to add?"

Nobody had.

"Okay, in that case I want us to cast our net wide. This is a mystery and we need to get to the bottom of it. DS McNeill and DC Cullen will lead on the ground, but I want DI Bain and DS Methven to oversee and make sure we're covering everything in a holistic manner." Cargill stared at Bain. "And until documents are formally published, I do not wish for their contents to be discussed." She checked her watch. "Briefing is at seven a.m. tomorrow. Make sure the paperwork is up to date before you leave tonight."

~

CULLEN WALKED through Technical Investigation Unit floor, realising he'd not been up there in some months.

Charlie Kidd was still at his desk at half past eight. Most of the civilians the force employed worked a standard nine-to-five but Kidd was a notorious night owl, happier in the hours of darkness than getting into the station when Cullen did. He had huge black headphones on, the sort that Premiership footballers would wear in post-match interviews, his head nodding to a beat.

Cullen crept up to him and tapped him on the shoulder.

No reaction.

Kidd tapped a mirror to the side of his monitor. "I put this little beauty in to stop you and Bain doing that." He turned around and folded his arms. "What can I do you for?"

"Just wanted to see how you were getting on with Aitken and Souness's laptops."

"Aye, well you're not very joined up downstairs. Had your bird up here an hour ago pestering me about them."

"Anything?"

"Just games, emails and tax returns. The boy was self-employed, subcontracting from Nichol's Garage, so there's a load of paperwork for Mrs Cullen to get through."

"Sharon isn't Mrs Cullen."

Kidd laughed while he played with his ponytail. "Aye, whatever, that's what we call her up here."

"Well, you can stop calling her that."

"What about calling you Mrs McNeill?"

"Very funny. Did you get anything out of Aitken's laptop or the Xbox?"

"Nothing much on the Xbox, just played games off disk, nothing online really." Kidd tapped a cream Alienware laptop, a good few kilograms of gaming machine. "Did get a good load of stuff on this, though."

"Can't imagine that's the most portable of laptops." Cullen picked it up — it was even heavier than he thought.

"It's an impressive beast, Scott. These boys were into their games. Shooters mainly. Call of Duty, Gears of War, stuff like that. Fifa, too. Didn't even have Portal." Kidd opened up a screen on his computer. "Aitken had a slightly more interesting internet history. Nothing too juicy, mind. Got a check going with their broadband provider to compare what he's got on the laptop with what they've been sending him, just in case they've been trying to go off-grid."

"Feels like you're avoiding something. What sites had Aitken been on?"

"Gmail, BBC Sport, couple of Rangers forums, couple of football sites. But also a lot of time on Schoolbook."

Cullen rolled his eyes. "No way."

"Way." Kidd avoided Cullen's eyes.

"What sort of stuff has he been up to on there?"

"There's absolutely no chance I'm going back, even if you paid me."

"We do pay you."

"Aye, well, I'd need warrants and all sorts again."

Cullen could just picture Bain's face at the prospect of them going back into Schoolbook.

≈

CULLEN PICKED up his mobile and dialled a contact from his list. He put his feet up on his own desk, away from the hubbub of the Incident Room, and looked across the floor, spotting only a few bodies.

"DI Davenport."

"Ally, it's Scott Cullen."

"Long time, no speak, I'd expect you to be a DCI by now."

"Really?"

"No. How's my favourite detective constable?"

"I'm adequate."

"Still got the same lines, Cullen." Davenport bellowed with laughter down the line. "I was just talking about you the other day."

"Oh?"

"Young DC by the name of Eva Law. Just brought her in from Haddington in the summer after she got her fixed tenure in CID. Sounds like she was another of your conquests."

"She wasn't." Cullen swapped hands as he put his foot up on the desk. "Besides, I'm settled down now. I've had a serious girlfriend for fourteen months."

"Fourteen minutes is a record for you, isn't it?"

"Aye, very good."

"What can I do for you?"

"I'm fishing. Wondered if you had any DS jobs going."

"Same old Cullen, obsessed with the number of stripes on your sleeve."

"Well?"

"There might be. You'd need to have been an Acting DS for three to six months before we'd consider it, though."

"I've pretty much been Acting DS."

"What do you mean by 'pretty much'?"

"Well, my DS is a twat and I've been doing his job for him."

Davenport laughed again. "So if I called up Jim Turnbull, he'd say the same?"

"He might. He said I'm one of his rising stars."

"Might isn't good enough, Cullen. I need a proven DS to even consider bringing them in." Davenport paused for a few seconds. "I seriously don't think that's you yet."

"Oh, come on, we worked well together."

"We did, I'm just saying that I don't think it's you yet. Give yourself another year, get that Acting DS activity formally on your CV and then we can talk."

"Right."

"Besides, all these changes that are happening in April, who knows — you might be my new boss by then."

"Cheers."

"We should have a chat in a few months, okay? And get the Acting DS experience."

"Will do." Cullen ended the call, before staring into space for a few minutes. His options were shrinking around him, restricting him to surviving in the current environment.

SHARON RETURNED TO THE TABLE — a glass of Rioja for her and a pint of Staropramen for him. "Here you go."

Cullen held up his glass in mock toast. "As my gran would say, your face is tripping you."

The corner of Sharon's mouth turned up ever so slightly. "It's been a shite day."

"You've barely said a word to me since we left the station."

She took a big drink of her wine. "That's better." She drummed her fingers on the table, looking distracted. "Having Cargill as my boss again hasn't exactly been a great experience."

Cullen took a sip of lager. "It's just for this case, though."

"Even so, any meetings that I'm in with her, I just want to smash her face in."

"Why is she so bad?"

Sharon shrugged her shoulders. "Who knows? Maybe she had a DI like Bain."

Cullen smiled. "I meant why do you find her so bad?"

"It's just the way she carries herself. She's a nightmare. Her attitude is so tunnel vision. She's ignorant of how people feel or what they're thinking."

"What happened between you two?"

Sharon took another drink of wine. "We were pretty close to start with, then one day she just threw me under the bus. I can't even remember what it was now, but she made me take blame for some mess she'd made. I was a DC and she was a DS. It wasn't right. She should have owned up for it."

"Aren't you worried about all these new DSs she's bringing in?"

"In a way, yes. Methven's clearly going to get a DI post before I do. She's supposed to be bringing a few new DCs in as well."

"That's all I need. More competition."

"Tell me about it. Methven's been auditing my work all day."

Cullen took a big drink of lager, the alcohol starting to hit his bloodstream. "I phoned Davenport earlier."

"What for?"

"To see if there are any DS jobs going in St Leonard's. He said I need to get some experience. Like that's going to be possible with all these full DSs kicking around."

"That was brave of you."

Cullen took the pint below halfway. "How hard would it be to get an Acting DS gig?"

"Hard. The only sitting duck is Irvine but it would take a disaster of monumental proportions to unseat him."

"Here's hoping."

DAY 3

Friday
5th October 2012

14

———

"I just don't see what that briefing achieved." Cullen yawned as he collected his breakfast from Barbara. "Could've done with some more sleep."

"Yeah, me too." Sharon shrugged. "I suppose it made sure we're here at seven."

"The only thing I took from that was how bad Bain has fallen. Leading the investigation into the stolen car."

"I agree."

"Don't know if you noticed." Cullen handed over a tenner to Barbara. "I managed to avoid getting any actions other than 'find out a bit more about Aitken'."

"Don't take the p— mick, Scott." Sharon smiled at Barbara as she paid for her porridge and latte before moving off. "Can't believe I've got to look into this hooligan nonsense."

"The privilege of rank. Besides, you'll be able to catch up with Wilkinson again."

She winced before sitting at a quiet table by the window.

Cullen watched Leith Walk come to life below them as they ate in silence, early morning traffic progressing through the wet darkness, the sun struggling to get up.

"Barrel of fun you pair are."

Cullen looked round, still chewing. Irvine.

"Mind if I have a seat?" Irvine sat at their table, a milky coffee and a full fry-up on his tray.

Sharon smirked. "You're welcome to join us, Alan."

"Less of that." Irvine ate with his mouth open, the mush of

sausage, beans and egg in danger of unsettling Cullen's stomach. "Us long-timers need to stick together, what with all these new DSs. Won't recognise half the team soon."

"You've noticed, then?"

"Course I've noticed." Irvine's lips slapped together as he chewed. "There's a whole army of them." He made a sandwich with fried bread, beans and bacon, swallowing the lot in two bites. "That Methven boy's a total fud. Thinks he's it, doesn't he? Running around telling the gaffer what to do. Total prick. He's world class at pocket billiards, too." The two sausages disappeared as quickly as the sandwich. He took a big slurp of coffee. "They're not taking care of the long-serving members of the team, though, eh, Sharon?"

"Doesn't feel like it."

"Course it doesn't." Irvine put a whole haggis slice in his mouth, barely chewing. "Methven's got a DI job lined up for himself, that much is bloody obvious. They've got to replace Wilko now his new role has been confirmed. That's a bloody shoo-in there. Maybe I should go to HR about it."

Cullen knew Irvine's kind well. He'd memorised every line of every HR policy and determined how to milk the system — sensible policies quickly became distorted by Irvine's actions.

"They'll have to go through due process." Sharon set her cup down. "Maybe they won't replace Wilko. Cargill's come in as DI and Turnbull's had three DIs on his headcount for almost a year. With the big changes afoot next year, who knows if they'll bother."

"Aye, well, it's a bloody nuisance if you or I don't get it. That's all I'm saying." Irvine finished his coffee, burped, then took a big fistful of gum out of the drum he carried with him. "Right, I'm off out to Ravencraig to see what Rarity has been up to."

Sharon gave a mock salute. "See you later."

Irvine glanced at Cullen, got up and headed for the canteen exit, just as Turnbull entered, Irvine stopping the DCI for a brief chat.

Sharon tapped Cullen on the hand. "You know you didn't speak to him?"

"I might be forced to work with him, but I'll be buggered if I have to listen to his rancid chat on my own time."

"Well, here comes somebody a bit more important, so make sure you open your mouth this time."

Turnbull headed their way, clutching a coffee in one hand and his Blackberry in the other. He sat down in the seat Irvine had just vacated and tore the lid off the coffee. "Good morning, Sharon. Morning, Cullen."

"Morning, sir." Cullen disgusted himself at how slimy he sounded.

"Just wanted to check a few things with you both."

"Fire away."

"Has DI Wilkinson been speaking to either of you?"

Sharon shook her head. "No."

Cullen took a bit longer, pretending to think it through. "No."

"Keep it that way. I know what he's like. Make sure he's using his own resource for his investigation. It's not to come out of my budget."

"Will do."

"He and DI Bain will be the death of me." Turnbull slurped at his coffee. "Shouldn't really be saying this to you both, but I think I'm finally squaring the circle with regards to team profile. We could do with more solid officers like you two, particularly yourself, Sharon."

"Thank you, Jim."

Turnbull's Blackberry chirruped. "Infernal thing." He stabbed his stubby fingers at the device. "Can't get these bloody tweets to stop popping up. Need to take it to Charlie Kidd and see if he can fix it."

"Are you on Twitter?"

Turnbull nodded. "Mandated by my betters. They want to make sure CID has an open door with the public, as well as those officers on the beat. All I do is retweet the drivel that's out there. I've got six people following me so I don't see what endgame I'm achieving here. I'll give it another month and then I'm stopping it."

"I'm sure it's in a good cause." Sharon smiled. "You never know — one of your six followers might come forward with something useful in a case."

"That's if they're not all Lothian & Borders officers having a good laugh at my expense." Turnbull put the phone down with a sigh before turning his focus to Cullen. "You know Bill Lamb, don't you?"

"I've worked with him on a couple of cases this year."

"Ah, yes, that's right. I'm looking at seeing if I can bring him into A Division. What do you think the chances are?"

"I think Bill's pretty settled out in Garleton, sir."

"Disappointing. I'll give him a call nonetheless. Need to tighten my ship in this place." Turnbull put the lid back on his coffee. "Needs must." He got to his feet and left them.

Cullen finished his coffee. "Well, that's one less DS job going then."

"What was that Twitter stuff about?"

"Budgie showed me it the other day." Cullen got his phone out and showed her. "See, there's a retweet of a message from @RavencraigPC about that stolen Range Rover. It's absolute nonsense."

"Don't get caught."

"Relax. I've subscribed to his feed by a back door means."

"Well, you made another good impression there. Don't arse it up by taking the piss out of him."

"Maybe all these brownie points I'm saving up will get me a DS position when I'm fifty." He checked his watch. "I'm going to head out west and see what I can find."

"Are you taking Caldwell with you?"

"This is a solo album."

"Scott, seriously, you better not be mucking about."

15

"Come on, Barry, I know you're in there." Cullen hammered again at the door of Barry Skinner, one of the few remaining active snouts he still had in West Lothian and the only one in Ravencraig.

Cullen caught an eye at the spyglass. He battered the door again. "Come on, Barry."

The door opened onto the chain. "Is that you, Cullen?"

Cullen showed his face. "Yes, it is."

The door closed then opened fully again. "Come in."

Cullen walked through the door, pulling it shut behind him.

Skinner locked it, two bolts, a Yale and a mortice. "Come on through, then."

Cullen followed him into the barely-furnished living room, standing by one of the large picture windows. He looked across the back yard, a patch of cracked concrete with a couple of dead tyres.

Skinner sat on an armchair, his short and skinny frame receding into the chair. He rubbed his neck, just where a large black snake tattoo coiled around, emerging at his left ear. "What can I do you for, my man?"

"I need some information about some Ravencraig locals. You might know them. Alexander Aitken and Kenneth Souness."

Skinner smiled. "I know those boys. Heard they both died. Is that right?"

"It's been in the press."

"Spoken like a true professional. You're all grown up now. Like a proper policeman."

"I've always been a proper policeman."

"If you see it that way. But anyway, I know those boys." Skinner nodded slowly, before pausing for a few moments. "I could do with a wee hand with something, though."

Cullen had expected this. He focused on the broad grin, the lines stretched around the eyes. "What is it this time, Barry?"

"No need to be like that, Cullen. See, the thing is, I've got myself into a spot of bother in Bathgate."

"What have you done?"

"You know the drill, you just sort it out for me and I'll give you some gen on those boys."

"There are limits."

"Given you're here so early in the case, I must be the only lead you've got."

Cullen leaned back against the window frame, folding his arms. "What sort of trouble is it?"

"Your old colleagues in Bathgate have got me in the frame for something."

"What?"

Skinner held up a hand. "Just fix it."

Cullen leaned forward. "I need to know two things. First, what have you done? Second, why should I help you?"

Skinner smiled. "Let's just say I've got something I think could prove useful to your case. I'll let you work out whether you can find it in your heart to help me out."

"What have you done?"

Skinner looked away. "The usual."

"Flashing old ladies?"

"Aye."

"And you've been caught?"

"Aye."

"Me making charges disappear or whatever is a big ask. This better be worth it."

"It is."

"Then tell me."

"No chance." Skinner wagged a finger. "I've got some leverage here."

"How solid is it?"

Skinner rubbed the stubble on his chin. "Let's just say one of your suspects might have done something to warrant whatever's happened to him."

"Who?"

Skinner nodded. "Okay, I'll give you this one little titbit. It's Kenny Souness."

"Right." Cullen stared up at the ceiling and thought it through. He was already going out on a limb and he wasn't sure his gamble was going to pay off. Eventually, he nodded. "I'll see what I can do."

Skinner licked his lips. "You won't regret it."

"I've got a feeling I will."

WALKING into the public reception room in Bathgate police station, Cullen felt like he'd gone back in time a few years. Nothing had changed — it still had the same smell, the same acrid taste in the air.

Sally Meldrum, the desk sergeant, looked up from her computer. "Long time no see."

Cullen gave his best smile. "Hi Sally. Wondering if you could help me."

She raised her eyebrows. "Oh aye, still asking favours?"

"Always." Cullen grinned. "Have you had Barry Skinner in for anything?"

"Him?" She tilted her head back, staring at the ceiling. "Yes, we've had him in. Lewd behaviour. Again."

Cullen winced. "Who's leading the case?"

"Duncan West. And you're in luck, he's upstairs."

"Thanks, I know my way up." Cullen signed the ledger.

She buzzed him through and he made his way upstairs to the main office area.

PC Duncan West was sifting through a case file. He looked up and caught Cullen approaching. He shook his head and nudged the officer next to him — PC Green. "Here, Shagger, it's a papal visit."

Green turned round. "Bet you're here to see me, right?"

"I'm here to see Duncan, actually."

"Oh."

West leaned back in his seat. "I'm putting money on Barry Skinner."

"Glad I didn't take the bet, then. Got it in one."

West nodded slowly. "Let's get a room. The walls have ears in this place."

Green scowled. "What you saying?"

"Not you. Just can't be too careful." West got to his feet, towering over Cullen at six foot seven, enough to make even Angela look small. He led them into the interview suite, looking through the small windows in the doors until he found an empty one. "Here we go."

Cullen followed him in, sitting opposite. "This room still stinks of mushrooms."

"Nothing much changes in this place." West put his feet up on the table. "What's Barry got you doing then, Cullen?"

"He's got some information I might need."

"Doesn't he always? If information on Ravencraig scumbags was a currency, he'd be a millionaire."

"Quite. Thing is, I'm working a double murder just down the road and the victims are both from Ravencraig. We know next to nothing about them and Skinner does."

West leaned across the table. "Okay. He's been caught flashing again. Whipping his willie out to little old ladies is one thing but doing it outside a primary school is another. He says he's flashing the mothers after the kids have gone in but they don't quite see it that way."

Cullen rubbed his forehead. "Jesus Christ."

"I don't think even the good Lord can save that boy. He's already appeared in court. He's out awaiting trial. We've got officers around the schools in the town plus a patrol down his street making sure he keeps himself to himself."

"Is there anything we can do?"

"Like what?"

"Well, this is a murder inquiry. If there's anything he comes up with that can help us, is there any chance of leniency?"

"Are you serious?" West held his hand up. "Wait, I know. You are. This is a major collar we've got here. Dirty little bastard could go down for years for this and you're asking if we can go for some leniency?"

"I know it's a bit morally dubious, Duncan, but this is a major murder."

West leaned back in his chair. "You're quite the big shot these days, aren't you?"

"If you want to see it that way. I still get paid pretty much the same."

"Is the information worth it?"

"I need to dangle a carrot in front of his face to find out what he's got. If it's useful then I want to make it happen pretty quickly."

West drummed his fingers on the table and for a few seconds. "What's in it for us? This is a conviction we'd be giving up. You know how it is, we're under serious pressure here ahead of Police Scotland."

Cullen took a deep breath. "Is this a personal gripe you've got, or a professional one?"

"Professional, of course."

"Pity."

West frowned. "Why?"

"Well, if you were after personal glory, I might be able to see what I could get coming your way."

"Are you trying to bribe me, Cullen?"

"I'm trying to solve a murder and I'm using whatever tricks I can to get there. I can make this difficult. We've worked together long enough for you to know I don't take no for an answer. My DCI could have a word with the inspector here."

"So you're trying to take the decision away from me, right?"

Cullen shook his head. "I'm trying to save us both hassle. Besides, if Skinner is talking shite, I'm more than happy to do him with wasting police time and any other charges we could drop on him."

"He's your CHIS, though."

Cullen shrugged. "I don't work out here any more. More than happy to drop him, especially if he's been doing what he's supposed to have been."

West sat in silence for practically a full minute. "I'll see what I can do. It's possible we could alter some of the charges. You'd be due me a huge favour, though."

Cullen raised his hands. "Just say the word."

"Oh, don't worry, Scott. I will."

"WHAT DID HE SAY AGAIN?" Skinner leaned forward, making a steeple with his hands.

Cullen sighed — this was the third attempt to get the message through. "PC West said he might be able to get the charges altered so they relate to a lesser offence. I'd imagine you'll get community service."

"See that's the bit I'm struggling to get. I thought the charges were going to go away."

"I'm not a miracle worker. You've committed a serious crime, Barry. In fact, I doubt we'd be having this conversation now if I'd known what you'd actually done when I left here first thing. You were flashing at a primary school."

"I was tempted by the mothers. They were asking to see my willie!"

Cullen screwed his eyes up, doubting whether he did have anything useful — Skinner's world only occasionally intersected with reality. "I've done my bit, Barry. You need to give me your side."

"Fine." Skinner took a deep breath. "As I said, it's about Kenny Souness. This never went to the cops, right, but he kicked the shite out of a guy called Gavin Tait."

"Who's he?"

"He lives in Ravencraig, likes. You know that Little Britain?"

Cullen couldn't stand the programme. "I know it."

"Well, that sketch, 'only gay in the village', that's Gavin Tait. Only gay in Ravencraig."

"Kenny Souness beat him up because he was gay?"

"That's what I heard a couple year ago."

"Why did it not go to the police?"

"No idea. It just didn't."

Cullen made a note. "Where does Tait live?"

Skinner got a sheet of paper and wrote an address down. "Here you go."

Cullen knew the street, just two over from Skinner's flat. He got to his feet and snatched the sheet of paper. "I'll be in touch if this doesn't go well."

"Just remember your side of the deal."

Cullen left the flat. As he hurried back to his car, he got out his phone and called West.

"You get anything useful?"

"We'll see. It's a possible. Did you guys ever hear of Kenny Souness beating up a Gavin Tait?"

"News to me. Is this Skinner's amazing revelation?"

"It is."

"Good luck with it."

"Listen, Duncan, I need to honour my end of the bargain either way."

"You owe me big time, Scott. Big time."

"Don't I know it."

He ended the call, unlocked his car and got in. As he drove, his heart raced. He was really in the shit if this didn't go well. Sharon had warned him about letting his cowboy antics get the better of him and here he was up to his waist in muck.

He pulled up outside Tait's flat, a seventies concrete tenement. He checked the sheet — flat two. Ground floor.

He got out and entered the building. The nameplate above the door on the right read 'TAIT'. He knocked and waited. Nothing.

He knelt down and shouted through the letterbox. "Gavin, this is the police."

No answer.

"Gavin. This is DC Scott Cullen of Lothian & Borders. I need to speak to you."

Cullen got up, sweat beading in his armpits. He'd gone out on a limb to get Skinner off a serious charge and he'd fallen into a trap,

Skinner knowing exactly how to snare a desperate and ambitious Cullen.

He kicked his boot against the door but there was still no answer. He headed across the landing and knocked on the door.

An old man answered, blinking in the light. "Can I help you, son?"

"I'm looking for Gavin Tait."

The man nodded slowly. "Ah, young Gavin. You'll be lucky. Moved to Stirling a few weeks ago."

"Do you have an address?"

"Aye, I do. As a matter of fact, I've got a big bundle of post for him." He looked Cullen up and down. "You a debt collector or something?"

Cullen got out his warrant card. "Police."

"Right you are." He reached over to the sideboard and retrieved a pile of post, wrapped in a sheet of paper. "Here you go, son. The address is on there, I think it's up by the castle."

16

As he drove through the city, Cullen realised he didn't really know Stirling that well, but he knew where the castle was. Sandwiched between streets filled with beautiful Georgian and Victorian houses and some of the worst housing estates in Scotland, was a smaller version of Edinburgh's Royal Mile, old tenement buildings leading uphill to the castle, hotels and arts centres sitting amongst low-rent housing. Gavin Tait lived halfway up the hill, just past a large hotel displaying adverts for a Scottish crime fiction festival.

He got out and checked the sheet wrapped around Tait's mail. Nineteen was a tall building, looking like a sixties facsimile of the seventeenth century. 2F1 — flat one, second floor. Cullen pressed the buzzer and the door opened without a word. He headed up, carrying the stack of letters under one arm.

Tait stood leaning against the doorframe. He was young and thin, a dressing gown open almost to the waist. "You're early. Come on in." He turned and sauntered inside.

Cullen frowned before following him. He swallowed as he worked out what was going on — Tait was a rent boy and he clearly thought Cullen was his john. He followed Tait into the living room, wondering how far he should play along.

Tait sprawled on the settee.

Cullen sat on the edge of an adjacent sofa and looked around the bohemian room, wooden cabinets in the kitchen area, lots of pot plants and unlit candles in empty wine bottles. "Mr Tait."

"Yes." Tait fidgeted with the lining on the dressing gown. "It's Paul, isn't it?"

"It's Scott, actually." Cullen got his warrant card out. "Detective Constable Scott Cullen, in fact."

"Oh my God." Tait started to panic, his leg twitching.

"You can relax. I'm not vice and I don't work in Central Division."

Tait reached over to a side table and got a pair of glasses. He looked at Cullen's warrant card, then put his hand over his mouth. He handed the card back before crossing his legs. "Why are you here, then?"

Cullen got out his notebook. "I believe you are acquainted with one Kenneth Souness."

Tait gulped, his large Adam's apple bobbing up and down. "I know Kenny."

"Mr Souness was found dead on Wednesday night."

"I see." Tait frowned. "Why would that have anything to do with me?"

"I gather you were once beaten up by Mr Souness on account of your sexuality."

Tait pouted. His mouth began to twitch. "That's true. There were a few of them, really, but Kenny's the only one I recognised."

"Why did they do it?"

"Because he couldn't stand how lovely I am."

"Okay. And in truth?"

Tait sighed. "We were at school together. The same year. One day... One day, I came on to Kenny. I hadn't actually come out myself at that point. I knew what I was gay — God did I know — but it's not something you want people in a town like Ravencraig knowing, let me tell you."

"Why Kenny?"

"Are you kidding?" Tait laughed. "He was a beauty at school. Film star looks. Like Brad Pitt with maybe a bit of David Beckham."

Cullen tried to recall the photos plastered all over the Incident Room — Pitt and Beckham weren't the sort of names that came to mind when he thought of Souness, a Scottish hard man. "What happened when you tried it on with Kenny?"

"This was when we were seventeen. It was at a party, we were sharing a pack of Marlboro Lights in someone's parents' back garden. We had a real moment. When I tried to kiss him, he punched me and ran away. I didn't really see him again after that."

Cullen made a note of it. "Didn't really?"

Tait's eyebrows twitched. "I don't know what you mean."

"You were at school with him. You both lived in Ravencraig. You said yourself, it's not the sort of town you want people to know you're gay. When you say 'didn't really', that means you did."

Tait nodded. "After that, I kept myself to myself. I left school at sixteen. Went to college, got a job as a hairdresser. Typical Scottish poof."

"I tried to find you in Ravencraig."

"I moved up here to get away. I'm much more of a city boy."

"I can sympathise with that. Did you see Mr Souness after that incident?"

"Just a couple of times. Once in the street, once in the pub. The night in the pub." Tait bit his lip. "I hadn't wanted to go but one of my pals from college made me. It was with her and her friends. It wasn't one of the pubs in town I would go to, let me tell you that. Kenny was there with his friend, Xander. Now, he was a hunk at school. Was always into the younger girls, though."

Cullen jotted that down — if Aitken had a thing for younger girls then maybe he'd got caught by an angry father. Demi Baird was seven or eight years younger at a rough guess. "Go on."

"Okay, so they're in there, drinking, and I'm with Kelly-Marie and four other girls. I went to the toilet and I saw Souness stood at the urinal. He was pretty drunk. I mean, he was pretty and drunk. He said something like 'Keep your poofy eyes off of my cock' as I passed him."

"And he beat you up?"

"No." Tait avoided Cullen's eyes. "It was about four weeks later. I'd been out in Edinburgh and got the last bus home, gets into Ravencraig at three. I'd been in CC's all night, had a wonderful time and I was walking home from the bus stop. Kenny jumped me. He hit me on the side of the head then pushed me over. A couple of other gorillas held me down as he kicked me."

"How did they know you'd be there?"

"Xander was on the night bus. He must have called ahead."

Cullen frowned as he made a note of it. He flicked back a few pages, finding the statement from Xander's workmate, the supposition that he'd get the bus back to Ravencraig. "And this was at three a.m.?"

"Yes."

"Okay, then, so what happened after they attacked you?"

"They left me in the street, covered head to toe in bruises. I probably cracked a rib — it still hurts. I somehow managed to crawl home. I didn't leave the house for weeks. Kelly-Marie was a saint, she nursed me and got me back to full health."

"So what happened?"

"I'd had enough of that place. It was like a bomb waiting to go off. I'd get killed if I stayed there. I'd had abuse in the street, don't get me wrong, but nothing like that. Now that those boys knew what I was, they'd not stop until either I left or they killed me."

"So you left the town?"

Tait nodded. "I had friends up here. My landlord's a good man. He helps me out. I really should have moved earlier."

Cullen tapped his finger on his notebook. He'd nailed another one. Still needed some shoe leather, but he reckoned he almost had Tait for Souness. Hopefully, the murder of Xander Aitken would quickly follow. "Okay, let me just ask you straight out. Did you kill Kenny Souness?"

Tait narrowed his eyes. "No. No way."

"Mr Tait, you've a motive. We can always find means and opportunity. We're very resourceful like that. I want to know your whereabouts from Monday morning to Thursday morning."

"I was in Edinburgh."

"That's very convenient."

Tait leaned forward on the settee. "I was. I work Thursday to Monday here, then I go and play. Mostly in Stirling, sometimes Glasgow, sometimes London but quite often in Edinburgh."

"And what do you do for a living?"

"I'd incriminate myself if I told you that."

"I'm here on my own, Gavin. I've no means of corroboration. I'd need to get you on the record in front of your lawyer."

Tait laughed. "Are you trying to buy my trust or something?"

"I'm trying to get you to talk. I don't care what you do. I'd imagine it involves meeting married businessmen here and lying on your front a lot."

"You'd not be a million miles away."

"Edinburgh. Where were you? I want names, addresses, places."

"I stayed with Tim and Colin, two very good friends of mine. They live just off Broughton Street."

Cullen knew it well — it was one of Edinburgh's two gay streets. "And what did you get up to?"

Tait smirked. "What didn't we get up to?"

"Mr Tait, you're a suspect in a murder enquiry. The only suspect. You better make sure you're keeping me onside here."

"Right, so you're threatening me now?"

"Places."

"Fine. We'd mainly been in CC Blooms but we went to Planet Out, Cafe Habana and some bars on Broughton Street I can't remember the names of."

"Were you with them all the time?"

"All the time. We weren't apart the whole three days. Even at night."

"Thank you." Cullen tried to avoid thinking what three consenting adults could get up to. "I'm going to verify your story. If I find anything out of place, you'll be giving a formal statement and probably facing charges."

"I've nothing to worry about then." Tait grinned. "I'll see you around."

Cullen glared at him. "I'd advise you don't leave the country. We'll be monitoring your movements."

"Good. I hope you'll help me avoid another kicking."

Cullen got up and left the flat. He walked back to his car, certain Tait had done it. A revenge killing — he'd killed Souness because of the beating. He'd been with his friends all the time, never a moment apart. Convenient.

At some point, he'd have to log it in the case file with Holdsworth. First he needed to visit Tim and Colin, either at home or at work, then go to each of the bars to look for holes in the story Tait had spun.

He turned the ignition just as his phone rang. Bain. Shite. "Where the hell are you, Sundance?"

"Stirling."

"Stirling?"

"I'm working a lead."

"Right. Anything I should know about?"

"Not yet."

"Well, I need you in Ravencraig. I want to speak to this Craig Smith boy whose car was pinched. You spoke to him earlier, I want us back there."

"Why me? I thought Chantal Jain was looking into that."

"Aye, well, Cargill's pulled her off it."

"Has my time been approved?"

"Quit with the games. Yes, it's been approved."

"I've got my car up here."

"Right, I'll meet you at Bathgate station, okay?"

Cullen felt Tait disappear from his grasp.

17

"Fuckin' Chelsea tractors." Bain got out of his car and zapped the central locking. "Don't know when proper cars went out of fashion."

"Is a Mondeo a proper car?"

"You of all people shouldn't be commenting on another man's car, Sundance."

"What's the drill here, then?"

"Just sit there and look pretty. Sure you can manage it?"

Bain led over, the glass front giving way to a large room filled with Range Rovers and Land Rovers of varying styles. There were a few customers inside, though Cullen couldn't work out why anyone would spend their lunch hour in a Range Rover showroom.

Craig Smith was in the middle of the showroom, talking to a customer beside an orange Evoque, a carbon copy of the vehicle Xander Aitken was found in.

Cullen wave over. "That's him."

"Let's give him a minute."

They waited beside another car, Bain leaning against it and folding his arms.

Cullen copied Bain's pose. "What are you thinking about DI Cargill then?"

Bain glared at him. "Swanning in here and stealing my investigation like that. And she can take that twat Methven with her — useless arse. Sometimes I wonder what I did to Jim Turnbull to upset him so much. Then I remember the fact I keep solving cases and showing him up. He's jealous."

Cullen didn't quite follow the logic. "DCI Turnbull asked what I thought of Bill Lamb."

Bain scowled. "Are you fuckin' kidding me?"

"Damn straight."

"That giant-shagging twat?"

"I wouldn't put it that way but Angela's boyfriend, aye."

"That's all I fuckin' need. If it's not him, it'll be Methven trying for my job. Got to watch your back in this game, Sundance, I'll tell you that for nothing."

Smith walked over, hand casually in a trouser pocket of his three-piece pinstripe suit. "Cullen, isn't it?"

Cullen held up his warrant card. "This is Detective Inspector Bain."

Bain flashed his own card.

Cullen pointed at the orange Range Rover. "I see you've replaced it already."

"Oh, that's not a patch on my previous car."

Bain grunted at him. "Have you got an office?"

"Certainly." Smith grinned before leading them across the show-room to a glass-fronted office, the heels on his polished brogues clicking all the way. He gestured for them to take the seats in front of his clear glass desk, largely empty except for a Moleskine notebook and a preposterously large Apple iMac. He made a bridge with his hands and looked across the desk at them. "Now, how can I help?"

Bain got out his notebooks, loudly clicking his pen. "Mr Smith, your car was found at the bottom of a shale bing near Winchburgh. Inside the car was the body of a young man from Ravencraig, an Alexander Aitken."

"Your colleagues have been over this with me already."

"Were you acquainted with Mr Aitken?"

Smith leaned back in his chair. "We've been through this."

"Right, you have no idea who Mr Aitken is?"

"None whatsoever. I probably passed him in the street or saw him in the Tesco but I've never knowingly met him."

"And you're sure about that?"

Smith leaned forward. "Inspector, if you've got some evidence to suggest I knew Mr Aitken, then please share it with me. Until your colleague and DS McNeill appeared the other night, I'd no idea he even existed."

"What about Kenny Souness?"

"Never heard of him either. Sorry."

Bain scribbled something down. "Have you started the insurance claim yet?"

Smith leaned back in the chair and crossed his legs. "My insurer wrote it off and a claim's now in progress."

"I see. How much is the car worth?"

"That particular beast cost me eighty grand." Smith reached into a desk drawer to retrieve a paper folder. "A like-for-like replacement will be in the region of ninety. The custom engine's risen significantly since." He tossed the folder onto the desktop. "Have a look, if you want. In case you think I may benefit in any way, I won't. That car was personally tuned by my mechanic here and ran like clockwork. I'm going to have to go through it all again, which will be a royal pain in the arse."

Bain flicked through the file. "Take me through the events surrounding the theft."

Smith smiled at Cullen. "I can get my assistant to make you a coffee if you want to sit this one out again."

Bain tossed the file on the desk, sending a few sheets spilling out. "Mr Smith, I want a detailed statement of what happened. We can do that at the station if you'd prefer but I don't imagine a busy man like yourself can spare the time."

"I'm just mindful of how many times I've told this story." Smith put the folder away. "There was DC Cullen and DS McNeill the other night. Before that, there was the young constable who took the initial call."

"I'm not in the mood." Bain folded his arms. "Here or the station?"

"Fine." Smith threw his hands up in the air. "It was stolen on Tuesday. I took the Defender into work — I do that every Tuesday just to keep it roadworthy. I've got a problem with collecting cars, you see."

"Not a problem I've got." Bain scribbled a note down. "When did you notice that car was missing?"

"We were pretty quiet on Tuesday, so I left Alistair in charge and went home early. There were football internationals on the telly and I had some legal documents to get through. The car wasn't there when I got home. It usually occupies pride of place in the drive. That's when I called the police in."

"Fine." Bain scribbled something down in his pad then pocketed his notebook. "That's all from me."

Cullen frowned — he'd been expecting another twenty minutes or so of grilling.

Bain got to his feet. "Thanks for your time." He handed him a card. "Give me a shout if anything else comes up."

≈

"WHAT WAS THAT ALL ABOUT?" Cullen gripped the grab handle above the door.

"All what about?" Bain hit the national speed limit sign already at sixty as they left Ravencraig, heading back towards Bathgate.

"You were giving him a doing and then you just stopped."

"He's not our boy."

"Are you sure?"

"Of course. Cargill just had me running a little insurance policy. Only people who'd spoken to this boy were you and your bird, before we found out about Souness. She just wanted to make sure there's nothing dodgy about him. Only fingerprints we've got in that motor are his and Aitken's. As far as I'm aware, that's him out of our enquiry."

"And you needed me for it?"

"Continuity of investigation." Bain passed over two roundabouts at reckless speed. "Doubt Craig Smith's involved. What have you been up to, anyway, Sundance?"

"This and that."

"What?"

"Been speaking to some snouts, if you must know."

"Oh aye," said Bain, suddenly sounding interested. "What about?"

"Nothing. Background."

They entered Bathgate from the north, past rows of new-build housing, all erected in the last fifteen years.

"That's a hell of a lot of background. Nobody's got any idea what you've been doing."

"I'm digging into Xander Aitken as Cargill asked."

"So it's not just me you don't tell anything to?"

"No comment."

Bain looked over at him as they stopped at a set of traffic lights. "Don't hold anything back from me, Cullen."

"As if I would."

"You've got previous." Bain winced. "You bastard, you."

"You okay?"

"I'm bursting for a shite." The lights changed and Bain floored it, heading into the forest of new builds.

"Can't you go at the station?"

"I've got better bog roll at home."

Bain pulled into the drive of a two-storey semi-detached house, getting out before the handbrake was even on. "Get us a coffee while I do this?"

"I wonder if the amount of caffeine you consume has anything to do with the state your guts are in."

"Just get me one, Sundance." Bain trotted off up his drive, legs dancing as he struggled with his keys.

Cullen followed him, retrieving the keys still hanging from the lock. He went inside, surprised at the decor in the hall — white walls with sensitive artworks in strong colours.

He tried a door. Living room. Same paint job, huge TV, stack of DVDs.

He tried another door. Kitchen. A large Batman poster on the wall — Cullen recognised it from his flatmate Tom's collection, the cover to The Dark Knight Returns graphic novel. He took a photo on his phone and sent it to Angela. Bain's house — the root of all his shit Batman + Robin jokes.

On the black granite counter sat a Nespresso coffee maker. Cullen didn't know what he was doing but he hoped it worked. He got a mug off the tree and put it under the nozzle. He pushed a cartridge in and pressed the button for Americano. The silver machine clicked and started rattling, before hissing for a few seconds. It flashed up 'Enjoy your drink!'

Cullen opened a few of the matte black cabinets, eventually finding the fridge. He reached down and took out a pint of milk. He sniffed it, trying to work out if it was still okay.

"Who the fuck are you?"

Cullen spun round. It was the First Attending Officer from the bings, the one speaking to Irvine.

Cullen whipped out his warrant card. "DC Scott Cullen. The owner of the house instructed me to make coffee. Who are you?"

"That's better. Feel like I've lost a fuckin' stone." Bain stormed in, tucking his shirt into his trousers. He looked at the other man, eyes almost popped out on stalks. "Jesus, what are you doing here?"

Cullen grinned. "Is this your boyfriend?"

"No, Sundance, this is my son."

18

C ullen stood in stunned silence for a few seconds. "Sorry, what did you just say?"

Bain avoided Cullen's eyes. "I said, this is my son, Kieron."

"Dad, who's this?"

"He's one of my officers." Bain stroked his moustache. "What are you doing here, Kieron?"

Kieron nodded in the direction of the next room.

Bain followed him, closing the glass panelled door behind them.

Cullen heard every word — the walls were paper thin.

"Mum kicked me out again. She found out I'd been gambling. It was just a tenner on the horses but she started nipping my head about going to the football whenever I've got a minute off work."

"Right. Why don't you leave us in peace for a few minutes?"

Kieron grunted. "Right."

Bain came back into the kitchen.

"I didn't know you had a son." Cullen held out Bain's mug. "Didn't even know you were married."

"Well, I like to keep my private life private." Bain took it and slurped some coffee. "When you get to my position, Sundance, you've put a lot of guys away and you don't want them going after your family."

Cullen almost laughed. "There's keeping things private and there's keeping secrets."

"Aye, well, let's just say I don't trust a lot of people. Didn't know he'd be here, otherwise I'd not have brought you in."

"You're going to have to tell me what's going on now the cat's out of the bag. He's involved with this case and that's got to be logged. You know the rules on nepotism."

"Nepotism? Eh?"

"Whatever you want to call it, we need to log it. We can do it secretly if you want, but we need to make sure the paperwork is done. Or I can go to Turnbull and Cargill."

"Fine." Bain sat on a tall stool at the breakfast bar and held his head in his hands. "Fuckin' mess this is." He rubbed his moustache again, flattening it down. "Not a lot of people know this, but my marriage has been fairly rocky for years. Total cliché, but the divorced inspector, well, that's me. She kept on her folks' place in Dalkeith after her old boy died eight years ago. She kept running away to there, taking my boy with her. We broke up eighteen months ago. She's taking me to the cleaners."

"That must be tough."

"You don't know the half of it, Sundance."

"Try me."

Bain looked at Cullen, his eyes screwed up. They gradually released and then he closed them with a sigh. "Kieron's nineteen, but it feels like he's lived with her on her own as long as he's lived with me. He's based in Ravencraig but he lives with her in Dalkeith. Looks like the stupid mare kicked the boy out, so he's come here, tail between his legs. Could have warned me." He leaned forward on the stool. "You need to keep this a secret."

"I think Turnbull might already know. He's asked me a few things over the last few months."

"All the same, Jim's one thing. I don't want that witch Cargill knowing."

Cullen sat and thought it through. It put Bain's behaviour in context — contending with a disintegrating marriage alongside the tough day job. He didn't have any sympathy for Bain — or for his wife, for that matter — but he thought silence might be the best thing. "Okay. I'll keep it from Turnbull."

"Cheers."

Cullen held up a finger. "On two conditions."

"Go on."

"First, we log it in the case file, somewhere near the back where nobody will check. Second, Kieron has nothing to do with the case. He's taken off it."

"Fine." Bain finished his coffee. "Thanks."

Cullen was in no doubt as to who caused the marriage to break up.

≈

"So he's divorced?" Sharon held her hand over her mouth. "I didn't even know he was married."

Cullen's code of silence lasted all of fifty minutes. He pushed his plate of lasagne away before nodding at Angela. "Has to be said you've handled your divorce slightly better."

"Yeah, well, no kids involved. Makes it easier. Not that it's exactly easy." Angela took a swig of Diet Pepsi. "You just know, if push came to shove, Bain would use this as an excuse for all the behaviour he's subjected us to over the last few years."

Cullen nodded. "Tell me about it."

"So his son is the FAO from out at the bing?" Sharon took a sip of water.

"That's him. Kieron Bain."

"Now you mention it, there was a certain family resemblance."

Angela laughed. "Need to get him to call you Sundance and use a form of the F-word ten times per sentence."

"I was thinking about the initials all the way back. There was a Rangers player from Kilmarnock called Kris Boyd. I couldn't work out why they'd used the English spelling. Then I found out the boy's father, a dyed-in-the-wool Rangers fan, had used the initials KB for both his children."

Sharon shrugged. "I don't follow."

"KB. King Billy."

"Bloody hell."

Angela scowled. "Who's King Billy?"

"William of Orange." Sharon crushed her can. "The Dutch prince so celebrated amongst Scottish and Northern Ireland Protestants for some ridiculously loose reason I can't remember."

"I think most of them think he scored the winner against Celtic in the 1688 Scottish Cup final."

Angela laughed. "I wondered what you were doing there when you sent me that Batman photo."

"Aye, he was bursting for a shite." Cullen finished his drink. "Keep this to yourselves. I'm the only one who knows and if this gets out, I'll get a proper doing."

Sharon made a zip sign across her mouth. "Does Cargill know?"

"Bain didn't want me to tell her. It's logged in the case file, but that's it."

"Just watch it, Scott, I don't know why you're doing it, but he's not worth protecting."

Cullen clocked Wilkinson approaching. "Remember to keep it to yourselves."

"Curran." Wilkinson stood at the head of the table, hands in his pockets. "Finally found you. Need to speak to you."

Charlie Kidd was next to him, tossing his ponytail about in the way he did when he was nervous.

Cullen looked at Sharon and Angela. "I'll see you back downstairs." He got to his feet, his brain whirring with the possibilities — him plus Kidd multiplied by Wilkinson equalled Schoolbook.

"This way." Wilkinson led them over to bollocking corner, sufficiently far away from the rest of the canteen to prevent other officers overhearing. He sat down in the seat facing the wall, away from the canteen itself.

Cullen sat on the opposite side from Kidd. "What is it, sir?"

"You two are our experts on Schoolbook, right?"

"In a way. We looked into the website when we caught the Schoolbook Killer. Charlie did most of the work, though."

Kidd's eyes shot daggers at him. "Under Cullen's supervision."

Wilkinson lay his palms flat on the table. "This case I'm working on, these hooligans seem to use this Schoolbook site to arrange their meetings. I want you pair to help me out."

Cullen frowned. "Have you cleared my time with Cargill?"

"Curran, I'll plough through any bollocks you try and spin, okay?" Wilkinson got a sheet of paper out of his suit jacket. "Four hours maximum, including travel."

Just what Cullen didn't want — getting waylaid on some stupid errand for Wilkinson, while his own shot at glory managed to cover over its own trail. "Have you got a RIPSA?"

"Not yet. It's a formality, anyway."

Cullen raised his eyebrows. "Didn't they tighten up the operational procedures after the last time? I think it has to be completed by a DCI and approved by the Chief Constable."

"You're kidding me?"

"It's true." Kidd nodded. "Came from the top."

"But we caught the bloody killer!"

"Even so." Cullen shrugged. "They wanted to make sure the process was transparent. Don't you read your memos?"

"Haven't got the bloody time." Wilkinson folded his arms and sat in a huff for a few seconds. "Don't you piss off anywhere, like. I'm going to grab you two later, all right?"

Cullen got to his feet, free to clear up on convicting Gavin Tait.

19

C C Blooms was jumping, even at four p.m. on a Friday. It was at the top of Leith Walk, two blocks from the police station, and was notorious as the gay bar in the city. Cullen had walked past many times but had never been in.

The DJ played a selection of slightly more obscure Abba songs — currently "Does Your Mother Know?" — and he had a couple of middle-aged men grinding on the dance floor, shaven salt-and-pepper heads kissing up to each other. The song blended into Rick Astley's Never Gonna Give You Up, causing more fury.

Cullen flashed his warrant card at the barman.

The barman sniffed. "How can I help, officer?"

Cullen handed over a photo. "Do you recognise this man?"

The barman looked at it for a few seconds. "Is this Gavin?"

"Gavin Tait." Cullen nodded. "He says he was in here every night from Monday to Wednesday this week. Is that correct?"

The barman smiled. "It's true. He was in with two regulars. Tim and Colin. Six p.m. till closing on Monday, then eight p.m. till closing on Tuesday and Wednesday."

"Do you know the arrival times of all of your patrons?"

"I'd remember you." The barman held Cullen's stare for a few seconds. "Tim and Colin are regulars and I'd never seen this Gavin before. Very unusual character. Bit rough on the tongue, but then you can't have everything, I suppose."

"He was definitely in here all that time?"

"I know everything that's going on in here."

"He didn't nip outside for a fag?"

The barman grinned. "Not a word you should use in this place."

Cullen blushed. "Sorry. I meant a cigarette."

The barman took the bar towel from his shoulder and dried his hands with it as he thought. "Actually, now you mention it, I don't really remember seeing him that much on Tuesday night."

"Where else could he have gone?"

"Lots of gay bars around here, especially for a young lad like that. Habana, Planet Out or somewhere down Broughton Street, maybe."

"Is the Outhouse a gay bar?"

"No, it's not." The barman went back to washing glasses.

"Can I get your CCTV tapes?"

"Is this for personal use?"

"Very funny. Don't make me arrest you."

"Fine, I'll get them delivered to you."

"Can't I just have them?"

"No. A company in Bonnyrigg handles it all. They're not stored on the premises."

"Fine." Cullen put a card on the bar. "I'm based just down the road at Leith Walk."

"This you giving me your number, sunshine?"

"Only if your memory's jogged."

Cullen left the bar, having to cross the dance floor as Salt 'n' Pepa blared out, pleased he'd found a gap in Tait's movements.

CULLEN WAITED in the reception area of McLintock, Williams & Partners, looking across George Street to Waterstones. His phone beeped.

Text from Angela — *"Briefing at half five. Where are you?"*

He tapped out a reply. "Meeting some people."

The phone buzzed with her response. "Cowboy shit?"

"Yeehah."

"Mr Cullen?"

He looked up. "Yes?"

A tall man in his mid-fifties wearing a sharp business suit stood there, hands clasped in front of him. "Tim Jeffers. How exactly can I help?"

Cullen got to his feet and nodded to the front desk. "I explained to the receptionist. I need to speak to you about Gavin Tait."

Tim swallowed hard. "I see."

"Is Colin Grainger about?"

Tim tipped his head up. "I think there's a Mr Grainger works here."

"I thought you were—"

Tim held up a hand. "Let me see if I can find Mr Grainger." He showed Cullen into a large meeting room off the reception area. "If you'll just wait here a few seconds?"

Cullen sat and got his notebook and pen out, wondering what the hell was going on. Tim and Colin. They barely seemed to know each other.

The door opened again and Tim walked through, closing it behind him. "Mr Grainger will be along presently. Now, how can I help?"

"Mr Jeffers, I believe you're acquainted with one Gavin Tait."

Tim narrowed his eyes. "The name doesn't really ring any bells, I'm afraid."

The door burst open, a man barging through, looking roughly the same age as Tim, though heavier and bald. He thrust out a hand after he sat down. "Colin Grainger."

Cullen nodded. "As I said to your partner here, I'm looking to talk to you about a Gavin Tait."

They exchanged a look.

Colin cleared his throat. "I'm sorry?"

"Gavin Tait, Mr Grainger." Cullen scowled. "I spoke to him in Stirling this morning. Said he'd had a lot of fun with you two this week."

"I see." Colin brushed some dust off his suit jacket. "What allegations are these?"

"Allegations? I don't think they're allegations. Mr Tait said he'd been with you two from early on Monday through to Thursday. Drinking, sharing a bed."

Colin held up his hands. "Stop right there. I suggest you get a lawyer in here yourself. These are libellous claims here."

"Libel?"

"You're insinuating we're in some sort of relationship?" Colin pinched his face tight.

"Aren't you?"

Neither spoke.

Cullen leaned forward in his chair. "The barman in CC Blooms seems to know you."

Colin gulped. "What we choose to do with our own time is none of your concern."

"No, it's not."

"This is harassment."

"This is a murder inquiry. Mr Tait is using you two as an alibi."

Tim patted Colin's shoulder. "It's okay, Colin." He smiled at Cullen. "Yes. We're a couple. We've chosen to keep it secret from our work colleagues. That's a private matter."

"I see." Cullen flicked back a couple of pages in his notebook. "Can you confirm Mr Tait's alibi? He says you were with him from early on Monday evening through to Thursday morning."

"That's true." Tim nodded. "You don't need to wonder what we saw in young Gavin, do you?"

"I can imagine."

"We'd taken some time off work to relax with him. We'd been out drinking in bars and clubs then we... had fun with him before we collapsed at dawn."

"Three nights in a row?"

Tim grinned. "Viagra's a wonderful thing."

CULLEN SLUMPED in a chair near the front as the Incident Room filled up for Cargill's briefing.

Angela sat next to him. "What's up with you?"

Cullen looked up. "Nothing."

"Yeah, right. You look like you've been told you're working with Irvine again."

"I resent that." Irvine glanced over, mouth pounding on chewing gum.

Angela leaned in close. "Seriously, what's up?"

"Do you honestly think I'd want to tar you with whatever brush I've been tarred with?"

"Look, I said I'm sorry. I was in a bad mood and I shouldn't have reacted like that."

"Okay, apology accepted."

"Tell me, then."

Cullen slouched back. "I've spent a fun afternoon visiting CC Blooms, Cafe Habana and Planet Out. At least I now know the Outhouse isn't a gay bar."

"What were you doing?"

"Checking an alibi."

"I see what you meant about your cowboy stuff, Scott. Christ."

"Yeah, yee-ha."

"Did you confirm it?"

"Aye." Cullen sighed. "CCTV backed up the story this rent boy gave me. Some lawyers who work for Campbell McLintock were buggering him all week."

"Were you picking on homosexuals?"

"No. I swear."

Angela shook her head, albeit with a smile on her face. "Typical

Cullen. Off trying to solve the case on your own and prove to everyone how much of a hero you are."

"That's not what I was doing." Cullen felt his ears burn.

Angela laughed. "Of course it is. You wanted to do exactly what you did in the summer in that distillery and prove to the powers that only Scott Cullen was right. Everyone else was wrong."

Cullen shrugged his shoulders. "There might be a bit of that."

"More than a bit." Angela folded her arms.

Cargill called the room to order, the assembled officers quickly settling down.

Sharon arrived just after Cargill started, giving him a little wave from the back of the room.

Cargill led them through updates on the major strands of investigation — to Cullen, it looked like the rest of them had experienced the same sort of day he had. Nobody had come up with any new information, no new leads. Sharon's investigation into the Rangers connection proved it was just innocent football club supporting.

Cargill looked at him. "The only update I haven't got is yours, DC Cullen. Would you care to pass it on to the assembled officers?"

Cullen cleared his throat. "I have been in Ravencraig, checking out local background on the victims. As some of you know, I used to be based in Bathgate and know Ravencraig pretty well. I've retained a snou— sorry, CHIS in the town who passed on a lead, which I then investigated. It initially looked promising but unfortunately proved ultimately fruitless."

Cullen was embarrassed he'd almost used the word 'snout', like he was in The Bill. Covert Human Intelligence Source sounded much more modern, even if it's the sort of phrase Cullen would mark Turnbull down for using in a briefing.

Cargill smiled. "Can you give us some more detail, please?"

"Certainly." Cullen had to think things through for a few seconds, trying to work out exactly how much to reveal. He didn't want Irvine or Bain getting too much ammunition with which to wind him up, especially as he'd spent a couple of hours going round gay bars. "My CHIS gave me the name of a Gavin Tait, a former resident of Ravencraig, who now lives in Stirling."

Cargill wrote the name up on the white board. "And who is he?"

"Mr Tait is a former acquaintance of Souness. It turns out Souness once beat Tait up in the street, almost hospitalising him. The matter wasn't reported to the police, as Mr Tait didn't want his homosexuality to be common knowledge in the town. Tait had allegedly come on to Souness at a party a few years ago."

"This sounds like good work." Cargill nodded. "Is he a suspect?"

"Well, that's the thing. His alibi checks out. I validated it for the three nights in question. Mr Tait was at a series of gay bars in Edinburgh."

Irvine piped up. "Have you spent all afternoon talking to poofters?"

There was uproar in the room.

Cullen closed his eyes — he could have died of embarrassment.

"DS Irvine!" Cargill stabbed a finger in the air. The room fell into silence. "I will not tolerate homophobic comments like that."

"Who says I'm homophobic? I've just always wondered about DC Cullen's sexuality."

More laughter.

"Enough!" Cargill's eyes shot around the room. "DS Irvine, I want a word with you once this is finished." She looked back at Cullen. "Anything further, DC Cullen?"

"Just that Gavin Tait isn't a suspect any more."

"Okay, I think we're done here."

Cullen slumped back in the chair. "What a mess."

Angela leaned over. "Yee-ha."

"I've just given that twat a whole new set of jokes, haven't I?"

"Nightmare."

"Tell me about it. I should have briefed Angela before, but I couldn't find her."

Sharon sat down next to him. "Irvine was right out of order there."

Cullen spotted Irvine chatting to someone, looking like he was in no hurry to speak to Cargill. "I'll get him back, don't worry."

"Just don't go and throttle him."

"I'd never try to do that." Cullen winked.

"He was off being Bruce Willis again." Angela thumbed at Cullen. "Trying to show everyone how good he was. Hadn't told anybody what he was investigating."

"Oh, Scott." Sharon shook her head. "Is that true?"

"I wanted to make sure it was sound before I presented it to the brass, that's all." He caught Irvine walking over. "Here we go."

"Didn't mean anything there, Scott." Irvine play punched his shoulder. "Just having a laugh, you know?"

Cullen ignored him.

Sharon pointed her finger at Irvine. "That sort of behaviour might be fine in the canteen but it's pretty stupid in a briefing."

Irvine's lips smacked together as he chewed. "Who cares? It was good for morale."

"Was it? Racism, sexism and homophobia have gone out of the

window now. I've worked with you for years and, if anything, you've got worse."

"More's the pity."

"What's that supposed to mean?"

"Whatever you say about sexism and homophobia, it's certainly benefited the likes of DI Cargill." Irvine grinned as he glanced at Cullen. "Or should I say, Sharon, your ex-girlfriend?"

20

C ullen shot to his feet, hands reaching for Irvine. "I've told you."

Irvine stepped back, a smug grin on his face. "It's true!"

"What's he talking about?" Cullen turned to Sharon. "Ex-girlfriend?"

Sharon couldn't look at him.

Irvine laughed. "He doesn't even know!"

Cullen stabbed his finger at Irvine. "Will you shut your face before I kick the shit out of you?"

Irvine swallowed and backed off a bit.

Sharon reached for Cullen's shoulder. "Scott, it was a long time ago."

"What was?" Cullen frowned — he didn't know what the hell was going on. He felt dizzy. Blood was rushing to his head.

Sharon took a deep breath. "I used to go out with Alison Cargill."

Cullen tasted blood at the back of his throat. He had to blink tears away.

He felt lost as he stared at Sharon — she'd lied to him. How could she? Why hadn't she told him? Was she really in love with him or was she messing him about?

Irvine poured more chewing gum in his mouth.

Shame burnt Cullen's face. Irvine had known for a long time and he was going to spread it around. Here's Scott Cullen and his dyke girlfriend!

Cullen bit his lip and tried to breathe. The Incident Room was slowly clearing. He glowered at Sharon. "I'll see you on Monday."

~

CULLEN SANK the rest of his third pint of Staropramen.

He couldn't believe it. Could not believe it.

Sitting in the window booth of the Elm, he looked across Leith Walk at the station, watching the rush hour.

How could she?

She'd lied to him. He knew there had been a falling out, but she'd never gone into any detail about it. She'd told him they'd fallen out because Cargill threw her under the bus over something. That was most likely a load of shite. Now he knew it was much more than that — they'd been an item.

Cullen thought back to Sharon's parents' house — the photo of her with short hair. She didn't tell him she'd had a lesbian phase. Quite a lot of people experiment in their teens, not their twenties.

Their whole relationship was a lie. She was gay. She'd been stringing him along. All that sex — her on top of him grinding away — he might as well have been some female rugby player with a strap-on.

The Butch nickname — had Bain been in on it? Were they all laughing at him?

In January, he'd grabbed Irvine by the throat in a car park in Haddington because he'd called Sharon a dyke.

What a mess.

He went and ordered another pint.

The barman put the fizzing pint on the bar top. "Rough day?"

"Something like that." Cullen handed over the money.

"Every day's like that for me, pal."

Cullen collected his change and headed back to his seat in the window. It had started raining.

"Thought I'd find you here." Sharon sat down across from him. "I'm sorry."

"Are you?" Cullen avoiding looking anywhere near her.

"I'm sorry, Scott. I really am."

"Seems like everybody knew except me."

"What do you want me to say?"

Cullen took a big drink. "Just tell me what happened."

"Look, Scott, I was young and confused."

Cullen finally looked at her.

Her make-up was streaked with tears and a poor patch-up job had been attempted.

He looked away. "Not that young."

She sighed. "I'd... dabbled at university. With men and women. I think I'm bisexual but it's been a long time since I've been with a woman."

"Was Cargill the last?"

She nodded. "Yes."

"Is that the truth?"

"Yes."

"I'm struggling to believe anything you say right now."

She took a deep breath. "We went out for a few months, Scott, that's it. I just realised I wasn't interested in the whole lesbian scene. That's why I asked to work for Bain when Wilko moved on."

"So Turnbull knew before I did?"

She reached over to grab his hand. He pulled it away. "Scott, come on."

"Come on, what?" He took another drink and slammed the glass down. "I've been lied to, Sharon. Irvine and Turnbull and God knows who else knew before I did. You've kept things from me. I can't trust you any more."

She took a deep breath. "I understand."

"You told me she made you take the blame for something you didn't do and that's why you fell out. Is that true?"

"It is true." She brushed the tears away from her eye. "She made a mess of her statement on a case. She made me take the blame for it."

"Made you?"

"I told our DI I'd made the error. It tore us apart. That's why we fell out. She didn't care about me, she was just after her own career."

"If she hadn't done that, you'd have still been together, right?"

"No. There were other things. Besides, I was getting fed up with her. I needed a man not a woman."

Cullen slumped back, unsure what to believe. He felt the acid in his stomach burn. As the tears came back, his nose started running. He felt another surge of anger rise up. "All that shite I went through about Alison, you just wouldn't let it lie. And now I find this out?"

"Scott, that was different."

"How? How was it different? I shagged a girl before we started going out. You might not have been happy about it and I wasn't proud of it, but I let you know that."

"Are you sure you're not homophobic?"

"I can't believe I'm hearing this. It's nothing to do with it being a woman. It's because you lied to me. It could've been Irvine and it would've been exactly the same." He sunk the rest of the pint and put his jacket on. "It's over, Sharon."

He got up and left her there, sobbing into her hand.

21

"That's pretty fucked up." Rich shook his head. "Worse than even my private life."

Cullen tried to laugh. "I suppose I'll be staying in the flat."

"That not a bit soon?"

Cullen shrugged — he couldn't see himself moving out of the flat, or going to Tenerife. He took a long drink of St Mungo Lager, burping afterwards. "I just can't believe this is happening."

Cullen's mobile sat next to Rich's Samsung Galaxy S3, ringing on the table, the volume muted. The display flashed up Sharon's name and number. He let it ring out.

Rich nudged the phone. "Is that her?"

"Eleventh call."

"You should speak to her, you know."

"She should've spoken to me. She should've told me the truth."

It rang again — he let it ring out again.

Rich waved his hand in front of Cullen's face. "I said, do you know a Keith Miller?"

"Aye. Why?"

"That's the copper who was killed by the Schoolbook Killer, right?"

"Aye."

"Someone at the Argus is writing a book about him."

Cullen looked up. "Who?"

"Just some bloke in features. He was trying to get a hold of that Alison girl you shagged."

"Alison Carnegie. Keep him away from her."

"Don't worry, Skinky, I will."

Cullen folded his arms. "Have you heard anything about these stabbings out in West Lothian?"

"Not my bag. I'm covering the Parliament just now. West Lothian's a different desk."

Cullen finished his pint. "Another?"

"Mm?" Rich was leching again, at a tall bloke walking past, mainly at his arse.

"Stop it."

"Homophobe." Rich grinned.

Cullen flared his nostrils. "Don't. I'm not in the mood."

Rich held up his hands. "Okay, tonight you have permission to be a redneck homophobe. I'd prefer it if you didn't veer into sexism or racism at the same time."

Cullen picked up his glass and mobile and headed to the bar, waiting a while before he could order. He got another two calls from Sharon which he let ring out. He stabbed the decline button on the second call, making him feel slightly better.

The display lit up again — Tom. "You on your way?"

"Aye. Get us a St Mungo."

"Will do."

Cullen took the three stein-style glasses back to their booth.

Rich was sitting in the middle of the arc, finishing off his last pint, staring in the direction of the arse he'd spotted earlier.

A rough-looking ned had planted himself at the far edge from Cullen, carrying a Sainsbury's orange plastic carrier bag, eyes darting around the bar.

Rich took his pint. "The things I would do to that arse."

Cullen leaned over to Rich. "Who's that?" He pointed at the end of the booth.

Rich glanced over at the ned. "Didn't spot him." He called over. "Excuse me?"

The ned nodded. "What you saying, pal?"

"Could you go and sit elsewhere, please?"

The ned shifted round the booth. "What you saying?"

Rich rolled his eyes. "My friend's just broken up with his girlfriend and he's not in the mood. Could you just go and irritate someone else?"

"I'm not hurting anybody, pal. Just resting my pegs here. Had a busy day."

"Can you go and rest them elsewhere?"

The ned stared at him. "Are you saying I can't sit here? It's a free country, pal."

"You've not got a drink, so I'll get the barman to chuck you out."

The ned leaned over and looked Rich up and down. "Think you're something, pal?"

"No, I don't. Just kindly fuck off and leave us."

The ned raised his hands in the air. He shook his head then collected his bag and headed off. He slinked over to the bar, where he stood next to a woman sitting on a stool. Her handbag sat on the bar top, just out of her line of sight as she talked to a friend. He inched closer to the bag.

"Sod it." Cullen walked over to the bar manager he'd clocked earlier. "Excuse me!"

The manager was pulling a pint. "What is it?"

Cullen whipped out his warrant card. "There's a man over there." He pointed to the ned, the bar manager's eyes following the line of his hand. "He looks like he's going to steal from your customers. If you don't chuck him out, I'll nick him. Not going to look good for you."

"Cheers, son." He put the half-poured pint aside and headed through the hatch in the bar.

Cullen walked back to the booth and sat down.

The bar manager threw the ned out, protesting his innocence before eventually giving up. He turned left at the front door and walked down the lane, flicking the v's at them as he passed.

Rich held up his pint. "Good effort."

"Not sure they want that sort of punter in here, anyway." Cullen took another sip of lager.

They sat in silence for a few minutes. Cullen couldn't even bring himself to think about how he felt.

"Where's my phone?" Rich patted his jacket pocket and ran his hands all over the table. "That little fucker stole it!"

RICH POINTED DOWN THE LANE. "You go that way!"

Cullen headed past the Voodoo Rooms down towards the Penny Black. He felt the booze hit as he ran, almost stumbling into a bin. He came to the crossroads. Left was the Guildford and Princes Street, right was a dead end.

Right.

He ran along and looked up and down. No trace. He doubled back towards the Guildford Arms. Two bouncers on the front door.

He flashed his warrant card. "Have either of you seen a wee ned run this way?"

They shook their heads. "Sorry, sir. Just you."

Cullen ran back down the lane to where he'd left Rich. He took a left along West Register Street, coming out onto South St Andrew Street.

He looked around. No sign of either of them.

Sod it. He needed beer.

He walked back along the lane, past the shut Greggs, and went back inside the Cafe Royal. Their table was already taken — a man and a woman. "Excuse me. That's my table."

A man in tweeds scowled at him. "It was empty."

"We were at the toilet." Cullen pointed at the three fresh pints. "Those are our drinks."

"You can squidge up at the end over there."

"Sorry, mate, clear off. I'm not having the best of nights."

He got to his feet and raised his chin. "I shall report you to the bar manager."

Cullen watched them trudge over to the bar as he sat down. He took a long draught of his pint.

The barman shook his head.

Cullen tipped his glass in toast.

"What are you up to, Skinky?"

Cullen looked up — Tom. "You wouldn't believe it."

"Cheers." Tom sat down, pulling over one of the pints. "Try me."

"Fine. Rich just had his mobile nicked."

"All those little black book numbers." Tom shook his head. "Where's Sharon?"

Cullen stared into his pint glass. "She's not here."

"I can see that. Where is she?"

Rich collapsed into the far end of the booth, heavily out of breath. "Little bastard got away."

Tom pushed a pint over. "The ned who stole your phone?"

"Aye. Shite!"

Cullen still focused on the surface of the lager, the bubbles popping as they reached it. He needed to get home, get some sleep then think about what the hell he was going to do.

Tom clapped their shoulders. "You boys up for the Liquid Lounge?"

Cullen looked up from his glass. "No."

"Seriously? I've got half of my department out."

"I need to get back, Tom."

"I've got two hundred quid of bar vouchers on me."

≈

CULLEN THREW the Jaegerbomb down his throat. "That's how it's done."

"Good effort, Skinky." Tom slapped his back. "That's your tenth, right?"

"Right." Cullen got up and staggered to the toilet, having to take it really slowly. He glanced at his watch. Half one. He pushed the door open. For some reason, there was a man sitting by the sinks with a selection of aftershaves.

He leaned his head against the wall above the urinal and pissed straight into the hole, causing the yellow cubes to spin around.

"Seen Rich?"

He looked over as Tom staggered in, undoing his flies. "No. He was dancing with that guy, can't remember his name."

Tom snorted. "He's welcome to him."

"Why, were you thinking of firing into him?"

"Hardly, just not seen him for the last twenty minutes."

"He does that." Cullen finished pissing then zipped up and washed his hands. He made his way back to the table, using the wall to brace himself.

Someone had filled their table with Red Bull and double vodkas.

Rich pointed at Cullen. "Come on, Skinky."

Cullen shook his head and downed the one nearest.

One of Tom's pretty colleagues turned her seat round to face him. "You're the policeman, right?"

"That's me. Detective constable. Useless idiot who doesn't catch the criminal."

"I'm sure that's not true." She held out her hand. "It's Becky."

"Pleased to meet you. Scott." Cullen picked up another drink, tipping it in this time. "So what do you do?"

"I work for Tom."

"Right. Is he your boss?"

"Hardly."

"Isn't he senior there?"

"No, it's just a different part of the project, that's all."

"Okay." Cullen took a sip, inspecting Becky as she looked over the dance floor. Tight legs, thin arms, pretty.

"Whooo! I love this song!"

Cullen strained to hear it — he was so pissed it wasn't quite working. Something about a waterfall. "What is it?"

"Feel So Close by Calvin Harris." Becky grabbed Cullen by the hand and led him onto the dance floor.

DAY 4

Saturday
6th October 2012

22

Cullen squinted in the early morning sunshine, so incongruous in October, as he unlocked the front door. Buses belched out fumes behind him on Portobello High Street. He put his keys into his suit trouser pocket, still worn from the previous day.

Cullen went inside and slowly walked up the stairwell, head thudding from too much booze and far too little sleep.

A flashback hit him, a song about waterfalls. And a girl, dancing with him, jumping on him.

As he entered the flat, he felt a haze around his head, as if every movement was through an invisible body of water. There was nobody up yet. He slumped down in a chair and tossed the newspaper on the table, along with the bag of morning rolls he'd bought. The way his stomach felt, he had no idea when he'd actually be able to get around to eating any of them.

He got out his phone — his battery down to three per cent. The little green calls icon had the number six inset in a red circle, all from Sharon.

It flooded back to him — the alcohol had only temporarily cushioned the blow. He'd have to face up to it sooner or later.

"Morning."

Cullen turned around.

Tom tied up the belt of his dressing gown.

He grunted acknowledgement.

"You had a good night last night, Skinky. How was Becky's flat?"

Cullen screwed his eyes up. "Who's Becky?"

"That girl you were dancing with. She dragged you up to the dance floor at about one and you didn't stop until the lights came up."

Cullen put his head in his hands. All he could remember was waking up dressed in his suit in the flat and feeling like he'd died. He'd no idea how he'd got home, if it was with Tom or twenty minutes earlier. "Shite. What happened?"

Tom laughed. "You were wasted and she started unbuttoning your shirt on the dance floor."

"Did I do anything?" Much as he hated Sharon right then, Cullen simply didn't want to be a hypocrite.

Tom smiled. "What do you think?"

"I honestly have no idea. I was buckled."

"True, I've not seen you that bad in a long time."

"What happened?"

Tom let the silence grow. "Nothing happened."

Cullen breathed a sigh of relief.

"I got in there and split the pair of you up just as the lights came on. Your tongue was hanging out of your mouth, though. Pretty young girl like that. Twenty-five, just split up with her boyfriend."

"Cheers, mate."

"Hey, it's what friends are for. Besides, the bouncer made me bundle you into a taxi. You were muttering about Sharon all the way home."

"Yeah, well, it's pretty fucked up."

"Not as messed up as some of the stuff you were saying. Who's Gavin?"

Gavin Tait? Cullen swallowed. "Somebody on the case I'm working."

Tom raised his eyebrows. "Interesting. You were going to stab him."

"Ignore me, I was pissed." Cullen rearranged the rolls and paper on the table. "Is Rich back yet?"

"His door's wide open. Guess he got lucky."

"He disappeared about half midnight, didn't he?"

"Aye, after the free booze ran out." Tom looked inside the rolls bag. "He's doing my head in. Never does the dishes, never cleans the bog. In a way, I'm glad you and Sharon have broken up, cos it won't just be me and him left."

Cullen got up and headed to the bathroom. He sat down on the pan, head in his hands. That song was stuck in his head — it had a line about being a big deal. Like he thought he was. He couldn't get the image of the girl dancing with him out of his mind.

The smell of cooking bacon wafted through, making his stomach lurch. He got on his knees, head over the toilet pan. Nothing happened. He swallowed hard, trying to ignore the aroma from the kitchen.

His world was collapsing in on itself. His girlfriend was gone, he was the laughing stock at work and he was stuck in this flat again. He had about fifteen grand saved up for a deposit but that wouldn't cut the mustard, maybe a one-bedroom flat in the arse end of Gorgie.

He tried to make himself sick to purge the booze and Red Bull. Nothing happened. He threw cold water over his face and left the bathroom.

No sign of Tom, but the hall stank and smoke fogged the kitchen. He went in and switched on the extractor.

In his bedroom, he took off his suit. The bed looked tempting.

Shit.

He ran back to the bathroom, just managing to catch his sick in the pan. He sat on the floor, head on the porcelain, waiting for the second wave. It didn't come.

He struggled to his feet and went back into the hall, standing in just his pants, shivering despite the heating being up full blast.

The flat door opened.

Rich hurried in. He stopped and looked Cullen up and down. "Not bad, but nothing compared to what I've just left behind."

Blushing, Cullen reached into his bedroom for his dressing gown and put it on. "You pulled, then?"

Rich sat down at the table and grinned. "Yep. Went to CC's with one of Tom's work mates. Danced to Abba and Hot Chip then went back to his flat down on the Shore. Twenty-four years old. I can show that wee laddie a thing or two. Not that he was wee."

Cullen thought about Gavin Tait again — bumping and grinding to Abba in CC's with Tim and Colin. He wondered if Rich and Tait's paths had ever crossed. "Tom had to wrestle some girl he worked with off me."

"Nice work, Skinky. Not long after you break up with Sharon and you're getting in someone else's knickers."

"Hardly, I was totally locked."

Rich laughed. "Scots are like Eskimos with snow. As well as having fifty words for rain, we've got fifty words for being pissed."

Cullen sat down alongside him. The newspaper was still there — this morning's copy of the Argus. The headlines had moved on to some MSPs' expenses but there were a couple of paragraphs at the bottom about the Aitken and Souness case.

Rich tapped the paper. "Who cares about two neds in West Lothian?"

"I have to care."

"They pretty much stab each other all the time anyway."

"Nothing to do with it pushing the story with your byline onto page two?"

Rich grinned. "You're working that case, aren't you?"

"I'm not telling you anything."

"You did ask me if I knew anything about it last night."

"Beer talk." Cullen's belly rumbled — a sure sign the hangover was passing. He scanned the table — the morning rolls had disappeared. Tom. There was no sign of them in the kitchen. A tub of Lurpak sat on the counter, a fork stuck in the middle. On the counter, the grill pan was swimming in bacon fat.

Cullen returned to the table. "Why does he have to line the grill pan with tinfoil?"

"He's a barbarian." Rich laughed. "I had a go at him about it as well. It saves on washing up, supposedly. Wastes a load of tinfoil is what it does."

"The barbarian has eaten all four morning rolls I bought."

"That's not much of a challenge. They're just air."

"He used a fork to spread them."

"He's not done the dishes since Tuesday and I'm not helping him out."

"Did you get your phone back?"

"No, couldn't even get Daniel's mobile number, had to give him Tom's. Hate having the ball in someone else's court."

Cullen checked his watch. He was supposed to meet Derek Miller at two — the way he was feeling, he needed to give himself extra time to get there. "I'm going for a shower."

"Well, I'm not joining you."

~

THE HANGOVER DIDN'T ABATE until Cullen got hold of his first pint of the day, an ice cold Stella in the Windsor Buffet. He sunk half of it pretty much straight away, feeling the ache in his joints abate slightly and his head start to clear. There wasn't much he could do about the fuzzy vision.

He looked around. The pub was pretty busy, the navy jerseys giving away the fact it was a rugby weekend, autumn internationals or some other fruitless activity.

Still no sign of Derek Miller. He'd give him till quarter past before calling him.

He headed back to the bar to get another pint.

His phone rang. He looked at the display, hoping it was Derek. Sharon. He let it ring out again. He wasn't ready to think about that yet.

"Get us a Peroni, Scotty."

Cullen looked over.

Derek was grinning at him. He was wearing smart clothes for once — shirt and trousers with a decent jacket — and looked almost presentable.

The barman handed over the Stella, already pouring the Peroni.

"I like this place." Derek loosened off his jacket, untying his Hibs scarf. "Nice atmosphere and it never gets busy without you still being able to get a seat." He also had a black eye.

"It's not bad." Cullen didn't want to know where he got the black eye from. Scratch that — he did. "What's up with the eye?"

"Got mugged. This double-dip recession, man."

"Did you report it to the police?"

"They only got twenty quid, didn't seem worth it."

Cullen paid for their beer then headed back to his table. "You've obviously still got that job, then?"

Derek cleared his throat. "Aye. Got a proper job now. The old man got us into sales at Standard Life. Earn a decent wedge. Got myself a room in a flat on Easter Road."

"Well done." Cullen tilted the second pint.

"You're looking a bit rough there, Scotty. Out last night?"

"Something like that. Had a few after work." Telling Derek Miller about his break-up from Sharon didn't seem like a great idea.

"Got a big sesh tonight. Meeting up with some boys on George Street after the game. Wonder what time the bouncers will chuck me out of Tiger Lily, eh?"

Cullen chuckled. "Rather you than me."

"You're welcome to come along."

"We'll see, I'm feeling a bit tender."

LEIGH GRIFFITHS STEPPED up and battered the penalty home. Two nil to Hibs.

Cullen sat still while everyone around him exploded to their feet.

They had decent seats in front of the goal Hibs traditionally attacked after the break. Cullen couldn't remember if it had been up or down the slope back in the day, but he figured they'd play uphill against a tired opposition.

Cullen checked his phone as the crowd still stood — Aberdeen had just equalised away to Kilmarnock. He'd been glancing at the BBC Sport website every minute or two, hoping for it.

He got a notification as he was watching the scores — Jim Turnbull had sent another tweet. Looking to obtain buy-in from public stakeholders at this evening's Community Interlock session. Cullen made a note to add 'interlock' to buzzword bingo.

"You not watching?" said Derek.

"Sorry. Bad habit." Cullen pocketed his phone. "When I used to go to Aberdeen matches with my old man, there was always some guy with a radio nearby who knew if Rangers had gone ahead or United had a man sent off. Nowadays, everybody's got their mobiles out."

"You tweeting, Scotty?"

"A bit."

"Who follows you?"

"No idea." Seventeen followers. Tom, Rich, Buxton and a few other coppers. A local crime author, though the book he was spamming hadn't interested Cullen. Aside from the annual Rankin, he wasn't much of a reader and, besides, he wasn't likely to buy a Kindle. "What about you?"

"Not really. Not my bag."

Cullen cleared his throat. "Decent match, though I don't think much of Dundee."

"First Division team. Wouldn't be here if it weren't for the Hun getting nailed."

"True." Cullen nodded. "Still, you lot will be top of the league till Celtic play."

"Aye, there's that. Got the Jambos, haven't they? Should be a walkover for them, Hearts are as fucked as the other cousins of William."

Cullen laughed. "I love that phrase."

Derek pointed to the pitch. "We'll keep it up till Christmas then you just watch us plummet."

Cullen watched him, eyes following the ball as it was hoofed from one end of the pitch to the other, before Hibs suddenly started passing it up the left channel. The black eye looked severe to Cullen. "You sure you got that from a mugging?"

"Still sure." Derek briefly stood up then sat down again.

"I'm happy to listen."

"I'll bear that in mind."

"Does that mean you didn't get mugged?"

"No, it means the next time someone batters me, I've got a friendly policeman to go to."

Cullen raised his eyebrows. "I believe you." He didn't.

A crunching tackle brought the Hibs physio on, stopping play for a few minutes.

Derek glanced at his phone then at Cullen. "You fancy coming out with us tonight?"

Cullen was torn — he didn't exactly have much on. He clearly wasn't going to the cinema with Sharon. "Who are you meeting?"

"Few guys from work. Maybe my flatmate Dean."

"Dean and Derek? You sound like a sixties folk band."

Derek laughed. "I tell you, I'll be folking some bird tonight." He gave a leery grin. "Got two hundred quid in my wallet and I'm getting ripped before I rip into some cheeky bit of skirt."

Cullen chuckled. "I'll leave it for another time."

"Who says I'll invite you again?"

"I'll take my chances."

"Come on, Scotty, even just for a couple."

"I need to get home."

The match restarted and Hibs immediately had a break down the right. The ball ping-ponged back and forth before breaking to one of their midfielders who hit a curving shot into the far corner. The fans around them got to their feet and even Cullen had to stand up and applaud.

Derek nudged him with his elbow. "There will be birds there."

"No."

"You might just stop me from getting mugged again."

"All right. I'll come out for a couple." Cullen pointed to his jeans and trainers. "I'm not dressed for a night on George Street, mind."

"RECKON THEY START POURING them at half time?" Cullen pointed at the bar, completely filled with pints of lager and the occasional Guinness.

"Probably, aye." Derek got two from the barman. "Be lucky if these have any fizz left."

Cullen took a long draught, his hangover disappearing into the middle distance as they tanned their pints in the crowded pub. "Decent match."

"Always decent when the Leith boys batter someone. Four nil. Man." Derek checked his watch before making another large dent in his pint. "You ever work the football?"

"A few times. Mostly the Almondvale in Livvy and Tynecastle but occasionally Easter Road." Cullen took a big drink, instantly regretting it. The two pies he'd wolfed down before the match had mated with the third he'd added at halftime and they were seriously repeating on him. "Easter Road was always the worst. Especially against Rangers."

"Hun bastards."

"You could put it that way, but the Hibs casuals were really bad."

"We're still really bad." Derek grinned.

Cullen pointed at the black eye. "That's not from a football fight, is it?"

"It's a mugging." Derek pointed at Cullen's pint. "Come on." He zipped up his jacket while Cullen struggled through the rest of his pint.

They left the busy pub, Derek smiling and waving at a few people.

Seeing him in his element really brought home how well-connected Derek was.

They walked away from the stadium down Albion Terrace towards Easter Road itself. The tenements on both sides quickly gave way to an open expanse and they crossed a railway bridge. The street was solid with rubbish — burger cartons, bottles of cider and Buckfast, cans of lager.

"Gettin' quite cold." Derek tied his thick scarf in Hibs green and purple over in a loop.

"Nice Take That scarf."

"Eh?"

"That's the sort of scarf Take That wore when they did their comeback."

"Piss off."

"It is. Still, it's quite a difference from the ned clothes you wore when I first met you."

"I've got cash now." Derek uncoiled the scarf. "Better take this off before we head into George Street, anyway."

As they crossed the railway line, Cullen realised he'd no idea where the rails went. "Is this still a live station?"

"Think so, aye. Freight. The station in Leith was knocked down years ago."

"Right?"

"Fancy getting a cheeky one in at Pivo by the Waverley?"

"Aye, that would be good. I like it in there."

Derek led them down a side street towards Easter Road.

Cullen heard heavy footsteps from behind them. He spun around as quickly as he could.

Four men in tracksuits approached them. Cullen relaxed — they were just out for a jog. He turned back and kept walking.

He was hit on the back of the head and sent sprawling.

"You Hibs cunts!"

Cullen tried to get up. He was kicked from behind and fell forward, before taking another kick in the side, then in the shoulder. He groaned then rolled over, lashing out with his foot.

He connected with someone. A voice screamed out and a body tumbled to the ground.

Cullen struggled to his feet and headed over to the man he'd knocked down. A swift kick from behind caught him and sent him falling forward again.

He was winded. His stomach ached. He pulled himself into a ball, wary of any more kicks. He heard footsteps again.

"We'll get you again, Miller!"

Cullen looked around.

Derek was in a similar pose on the opposite pavement.

Their assailants were gone.

Cullen got to his feet and walked over to Derek. He crouched down and placed a hand on his head. Derek flinched.

"They've gone, Derek."

Derek spun round quickly. His jacket had been ripped open. He lay on his back, breathing quickly.

"Was that your muggers?"

"Christ knows."

"They seem to know you."

"Think one of them knew my flatmate." Derek sat up, breath misting in the air.

"Charming."

"Don't worry, I'll shove his toothbrush up my arse."

"I'm going to have to report this."

"There's no need for that, it's just harmless fun."

"It's assault. My shoulder's shite at the best of times."

"The one who hit you wasn't Dean's mate, anyway."

"Still, Dean or his mate will know who did it."

Cullen helped Derek to his feet.

"Still fancy that pint?" Derek dusted his jacket.

"Sod it, I'm going home. I suggest you do the same."

They walked up Easter Road, Cullen intent on heading to the bus stops at the top, just on London Road.

"Might take your advice, Scotty. This is my flat here." Derek had stopped outside a tenement. "You serious about reporting it"

"I'll think about it. I don't know if I can be arsed with the admin."

DAY 5

Sunday
7th October 2012

"Thought you were off today, Curran." Wilkinson folded his arms and put his feet up on his office desk.

"I am." Cullen sat opposite him. "Meeting someone, but I wanted to check something out."

Wilkinson looked away. "Still haven't got approval to go to School-book, if that's what you're thinking."

"Nothing like that. You're looking into football hooligans, right?"

"Right."

"I've got a CHIS I'm concerned is in a gang and isn't one hundred per cent reliable. He could be feeding me false information."

"We've got all that stuff on HOLMES, I'll have a look for you. What's the name?"

"Can I look at it myself?"

"No chance, Curran. This is top secret stuff. I shouldn't be looking for you, but I suspect I'll want to have a favour in my pocket."

"The name is Derek Miller."

Wilkinson frowned. "Isn't that Keith Miller's brother?"

"It is."

Wilkinson exhaled. "Better make that two favours, then, cos I don't believe he's a CHIS."

"He is and he isn't."

"Well, I don't even need to look. I put him on there myself. Last week. The boy's involved in a Hibs casuals group."

Cullen bit his lip. "Thanks."

"What are you going to do with it, like?"

"I don't know, but I doubt I'll confront him about it, if that's what's worrying you."

"If you do, then it goes through me, understand?"

"Understood." Cullen got to his feet. "Cheers."

"Not so fast." Wilkinson stood up and grabbed the sleeve of Cullen's polo shirt. "Bain's been in my bloody ear asking about the press release you put out. Reckons he's been trying to get hold of you all day."

Cullen looked at his phone's display. Four missed calls from Bain. "Must have come in when I was out for a jog. What was it about?"

"Something to do with a sighting of a car in Ravencraig. Wanted you to head out there."

"Can you get him to speak to ADC Buxton about it?"

"Right, I'll get Britpop onto it." Wilkinson grabbed a bunch of his top. "Remember, if you speak to the Miller boy, you go through me, right?"

"Fine." Cullen headed off, not really knowing what he was going to do about it.

"Here you go." Dawn returned to the table carrying a tray with two large Americanos. "You going to register a note of interest in that flat?"

"The Gorgie one?" Cullen blew on the coffee. "I don't know if I can be bothered."

"Typical Scott."

"How's Johnny doing?" Cullen took an exploratory sip.

"He's good. Away on a stag do this weekend, hence me being so happy to get out of the flat and watch you depress yourself in a series of shoeboxes. Surprised you boys haven't been out more."

"You know how it is, out of sight, out of mind. I've been really busy. And I've spent a lot of time with Sharon."

Dawn smiled. "That's the first time you've mentioned her."

"Is it?"

"I wondered why you were looking for a flat on your own. You've split up, haven't you?"

Cullen took a deep breath. "She lied to me."

"What about?"

"She's bisexual." Saying it out loud made it feel real. The jolt of pain hit Cullen in the heart again.

"Is that a crime?"

"She had an affair with the woman who's now our DI."

"Recently?"

Cullen shook his head. "Ten or eleven years ago."

"How did you find out?"

"The arsehole sergeant I work for blurted it out. Turns out half the bloody station knows."

"And she didn't tell you?"

"No. She didn't."

"How do you feel?"

Cullen looked around the busy cafe, full of young professional couples drinking coffee over the Sunday papers. That would have been him and Sharon. Could have been. Should have been. "I feel let down. Betrayed. Humiliated."

He took a big gulp of coffee, almost burning his mouth. "Our parents met up the other night, you know? I was ready to commit my future to her. I don't mean get married, or any shit like that. I just wanted to be with her."

"Did you tell her how you felt about what she'd done?"

"She got it both barrels, put it that way."

"I meant how you felt, not shouting at her."

He'd told her it was over. He'd shouted at her. Told her he was angry. He hadn't explained. "Not really."

"Maybe you should call her."

CULLEN SAT on the reclining chair in his bedroom, tossing his phone in the air. Seven p.m. on Sunday. Monday morning weighed heavily on his mind. Mostly the first meeting with Sharon.

He'd call in sick. The worst thing was he couldn't — everyone would know why he wasn't in and he'd find it too hard to come back. How long would he leave it? He could be a right coward at times. Tackle it head on.

He'd deleted her from his contacts and deleted all her texts. He had to dial voicemail and write down her number. A lump formed in his throat as he listened to the first snatch of the very first message on Friday. He pressed dial.

"You've finally decided to answer my calls?"

"It's over, Sharon."

"How can you say it's over?"

"Because you lied to me. You were shacked up with Cargill and you never told me." Cullen sighed. "As it stands, I've no trust left in you and I'm the laughing stock in the station."

"That's what it's all about, then? How the great Scott Cullen can stand in the queue in the canteen and not get jeered at about his girlfriend?"

"What makes you think I'm like that?"

"All this shit about why you're not getting promoted, why Turnbull doesn't rate you. It's all the Scott Cullen show."

"I just want to get what I deserve. I'm pretty much doing DS duties and I'm not getting paid for it. I'm making clowns like Bain look good and he's taking all the glory."

"Whatever. If they don't see you as DS, who will?"

"I've got other irons in the fire."

"I doubt it."

Cullen took a deep breath. "It's over. I can't trust anything you say. All that shit I took over Alison. At least I'm honest. At least I say how I feel."

"Me and Cargill happened when you were still at university. Besides, I didn't lie, I just didn't tell you. Have you told me every girl you've had sex with?"

"I'll get my stuff from your flat next weekend."

A long pause. "That's it? Fourteen months of the best relationship either of us has had and you end it just like that?"

"I had to find out about your love-in with Cargill from Alan Irvine."

"Fine." She sounded ready to hang up.

Cullen looked around his bedroom, his prison for the foreseeable future. The Aberdeen scarf hanging up, the swiped nightclub posters, the view out of the back across the Forth to East Lothian. "We need to act professionally at work. We have to be cordial."

"I'll see what I can do." Sharon ended the call.

Cullen leaned back in his IKEA chair. That went as well as he'd hoped. It was over and she recognised that. They both just needed to move on.

Tears slipped down his face. He rubbed his eyes, trying to stop them flowing. He gave up and gave in to it.

He saw his future disappear — the years he'd planned with her were now gone. He didn't want kids and neither did she. They were a perfect match.

Lying was the worst. Anything else Cullen could bring himself to forgive — if she'd told him, they could have worked it out.

He'd mentioned the shit he'd had to put up with about Alison as a way of scoring more points but it dug into him. All that hassle for nothing in the end.

She'd called him the other day, needing to get things sorted out. He'd acted like such a dick. His brain flooded with the times they'd met up — flirting in his ex-girlfriend's kitchen, going on a date, her turning up at his flat convinced they were an item, finding her in the Schoolbook Killer's bedroom.

Shit.

She wouldn't have been caught up in the case if he hadn't flirted with her and pulled her into his messed-up life.

He called her.

"Alison Carnegie."

"Alison, it's Scott Cullen."

"Why are you calling me?"

He bit his lip. "I was a bit short with you the other day. I was totally out of order. Because of me, you went through hell and you're lucky to be alive. I just wanted to say I'm truly sorry for what happened."

"Okay." She paused. "I'd still like to meet up with you. I need to hear it from you face to face."

He should keep her at arm's length. "Okay."

"How about Tuesday night at six?"

"See you there."

He put the phone down on the bed. Shite.

DAY 6

Monday
8th October 2012

24

Monday morning, seven a.m.

Back to the new reality.

Cullen stood in the Incident Room, arms folded, one of roughly forty officers in the early briefing.

Cargill was holding court, though it sounded like nothing much had happened over the weekend. "The street team has put in hundreds of man hours over the weekend. So far, we've identified only ten acquaintances of Souness or Aitken. Nobody has seen anything relating to either of their murders."

Across the busy room, Cullen couldn't help but make eye contact with Sharon. She smiled. Cullen looked away.

"Key activity in the Aitken search is for DC Cullen to dig into what happened with the Range Rover theft. That's still a glaring hole in the investigation." Cargill narrowed her eyes as a thin smile spread across her lips. "I hope you're sufficiently refreshed to pick it up and deliver. Everyone else, please report to DS Methven or DS Rarity for actions. Dismissed."

Cullen took a deep breath. Taking a weekend off during a major inquiry hadn't gone down well with the brass. The room burst into action, queues starting to form around the named DSs as they awaited their allocation of tasks.

Cullen found a desk and called Giles Naismith from the CCTV office on the Royal Mile to chase him up for the CCTV records. No answer.

DS Holdsworth headed his way. "DC Cullen, I know you're busy with this case but the Procurator Fiscal's office has been ringing me. Your paperwork on that stabbing in Pilton is overdue."

"Bryan, I gave you the paperwork last week. I don't know what you've done with it since then."

Holdsworth frowned at him. "It's not logged on the system."

"Well, that's not my fault. Papers were given to you on Monday last week. I can certainly try to keep it secret from DCI Turnbull if you've lost them."

Cullen hadn't given him the files. He'd have to look the documentation out and finalise it for submission to Holdsworth and his labyrinthine admin processes.

"I'll have to check through my inbox to make sure the papers were appropriately lodged." Holdsworth waddled off, clipboard in hand.

"Scott, I've been thinking."

Cullen turned around.

Sharon.

He took a deep breath. "What about?"

"I think it would be more appropriate if we swapped Angela for Simon. That way, a DS can have a DC, and a DC can have an ADC."

"Whatever. If you've got a thing for Angela, you just need to say. Of course, you don't like telling me about your lesbian relationships."

"Scott, if you can't be civil, then keep your mouth shut. Do you disagree with swapping them?"

"Sorry. You're probably right. Fine, I'll take Budgie, you have Angela. She's been a bloody nightmare anyway."

"Good." Sharon turned around and left the Incident Room.

Cullen counted to ten. He logged onto the laptop on the desk and found the overdue paperwork. It had been sent. He sent it again, pointing out the error and CCing Turnbull. Ram it, Holdsworth.

Buxton sat down next to him. "Your bird says you've swapped me for Caldwell. That right?"

"It is. You had breakfast?"

"No."

"Come on." Cullen led them out of the emptying room, taking the stairs two at a time. "Good weekend?"

"In here, wasn't I?"

"Desperate to get your full DC stripes, aren't you?" Cullen pushed open the door to the canteen. "Was it busy?"

"Yeah, mate it was. Crystal shoved me out to West Lothian all day yesterday. Bloody nightmare."

Barbara nodded as Cullen joined the queue, only three officers in it.

Buxton picked up a fruit scone and two butter portions. "Why weren't you in?"

"I'll tell you when we sit down."

"Secret bloody squirrel, you."

Cullen paid for his breakfast and went over to bollocking corner, getting stuck into his standard BLT with brown sauce.

"That's unnatural." Buxton pointed at Cullen's roll as he sat, face screwed up. "Brown sauce has no business going anywhere near a tomato."

"What about bacon?"

"Yeah, I'll give you that but it's still a freaky sandwich."

"We call them rolls up here."

"Yeah, whatever." Buxton tucked into his scone. "Don't even start on how I pronounce one of these."

"Truce." Cullen put his roll down, a half-eaten slice of tomato flopping out and smearing the plate with brown. "Sharon and I broke up."

"Bad luck."

"I broke up with her, Budgie."

"Don't call me that, Sundance."

"Fine, fine, I was the one doing the breaking up."

"Not cos you couldn't get it up?"

Cullen laughed. "That was the least of our problems. Twice a night, at least."

"What happened, then?"

"I found out she had an affair with DI Cargill."

Buxton almost fell off his chair. "What, recently?"

"Ten years ago."

"I don't get it, mate."

"The trouble is she didn't tell me."

"Nightmare."

Cullen's phone rang.

"It's Mr Naismith, I've got your tapes."

"That was quick."

"We've got an increased service level agreement. Have to turn things around for the police in minutes these days."

"Glad to hear it."

Naismith sniffed. "I'll leave them at reception."

"Thanks." Cullen ended the call. He looked at Buxton, tucking into his scone. "Got a great errand to run."

"What is it?"

Cullen couldn't bring himself to ask Buxton to get the tapes. He glanced at the serving area and caught Irvine heading over with his usual fry-up. "Great." He munched the rest of his roll and put the lid on his coffee.

Irvine sat down alongside them. "Good result for your boys at the weekend there, Cullen. Three one away to Killie isn't bad."

Cullen grabbed his coffee and got to his feet.

Irvine frowned. "Was it something I said?"

"It was, aye."

CULLEN ENTERED the Incident Room to fetch his jacket for the walk to the Royal Mile and immediately regretted it.

"DC Curran, not so fast." Wilkinson was in the middle of the room, standing beside Bain.

Cullen grabbed his coat.

"Curran!" Wilkinson walked over, arms folded.

"What is it? I've got an urgent task for DI Cargill."

"I bet you do, lad. It's about your buddy, Derek Miller."

"What about him?"

"Well, since you spoke to me yesterday, I did a bit of digging. Turns out he's involved in my case. One of the few witnesses that we do have reckons young Miller was at the quarry for the fight. I'm sure I bloody mentioned it to you the other day."

Cullen tried to look mystified.

Wilkinson sighed. "There was a hooligan fight in West Lothian, at a place called Ginty's Quarry. Two deaths. If I can crack this one, then I'm a bloody DCI."

Cullen nodded. Two and two together. Derek Miller's black eye was definitely not from a mugging, but the result of a hooligan fight. "Thanks for letting me know. Do you want me to have a chat with him about it?"

Wilkinson laughed. "I told you, I want you to keep away from him. Besides, that's not why I came here, lad. I've got me RIPSA form approved. I need you and that lad with the ponytail to head out to Schoolbook in Livingston."

"Haven't you got your own team to do this?"

"None of my boys are familiar with the inner workings of Schoolbook. You are."

"You really need to clear it with DI Cargill."

"Why do I need to do that?"

"Because I'm doing a priority investigation for her. Normally, I'd love to help out, but I've got to watch."

"I've got four hours of your time. I bloody agreed it with her last week!"

"Priorities change."

Wilkinson glowered at Cullen. "Any idea where she is?"

Cullen pointed behind Wilkinson. "DI Bain might know."

As soon as Wilkinson turned around, Cullen was off through the door.

25

"You called?" Buxton leaned against the wall, arms folded.

"Yeah." Cullen opened the door to the CCTV review suite. "In here." The room was cold and empty and Cullen had to turn on the lights. What looked like a three-day-old prawn sandwich sat in its plastic wrapper on the table. He put it in the bin.

Buxton sat in the next seat. "Methven's got me reviewing the calls received into Bilston."

"Well, you're my resource, so I'm prioritising this. He shouldn't have done that."

Buxton folded his arms. "Your funeral."

"You met that Naismith guy?"

Buxton frowned. "Think so. Bit of a wanker?"

"Aye." Cullen held up the packet of DVDs. "He called these 'tapes'."

"Cracking. What have I got to do?"

"Just go through the disks. Half each. We're trying to work out where the Range Rover went after it was stolen."

"This is linked to that other wild goose chase Wilkinson had me do, isn't it? Made me go out to Ravencraig to speak to some mad woman about a sighting of the car." Buxton took out a DVD. "He bloody called me Britpop as well. I hate that."

"Worse than Budgie?"

"Definitely."

"If you got a proper haircut, maybe it would stop."

"Ha ha."

Cullen took a deep breath and stuck the disk in the machine. He waited for it to spin up. Back to pure DC duties — sitting in front of a computer, ploughing through a stack of discs, the modern equivalent of old-fashioned shoe-leather work.

The first tape was of Craig Smith's street. The camera was around the corner from his house with a view to the cul de sac's entrance. He let the footage run, while digging out a map of the town on the neighbouring computer. He flipped the footage into fast forward, watching cars appear every ten minutes or so.

Almost exactly an hour before the theft was called in, the orange four-by-four drove out of the cul de sac. "Got you."

"What?" Buxton look over.

"Here he is." Cullen slowed the video right down to an eighth speed and wound it back. It looked like a snapshot taken every second, presumably for cost reasons, so there were very few shots of the car approaching the camera. "Buggery."

"What?"

Cullen tapped the screen. "The camera's calibrated for standard cars. The drivers of SUVs are shielded from sight."

"Chelsea tractors."

"Don't. Bain called it that the other day."

Cullen took screen grabs of the few inconclusive shots he had, before putting the next disk in.

His phone rang. Methven. "Sarge."

"Constable. Where are you?"

"In the CCTV room with Buxton. Why?"

"I thought he was reviewing call logs?"

"He was allocated to me."

"Very well. I'll meet you in the garage in two minutes."

"Why?"

"Tommy Aitken just tried to assault someone."

"REMEMBER YOU STILL OWE ME, CULLEN." PC Duncan West got up from his desk in the admin area at Bathgate station.

Methven frowned. "What's this about?"

Cullen glared at West. "Personal stuff, Sarge. I lost a game of pool."

Methven's large eyebrows briefly flashed up. "Fine." He looked at West. "What's Aitken done, then?"

"He's assaulted Hugh Nichol."

"The mechanic?"

"Aye, him. He pitched up there this morning, absolutely out of his tree. Looked like he'd been on a three-day bender. Squared up to him, shouting the odds and they went at it. Aitken threw the first punch. Nichol threw the last. Couple of Nichol's lads pulled them apart. Both of them look like they've been dragged through a hedge backwards."

Cullen rubbed his forehead as he thought. "Kenny Souness worked for Nichol, right?"

"Aye." West nodded.

Methven put his hand in his pocket. "You think this means something?"

"Could mean something, then again, could just be an angry father lashing out."

Methven focused the eyebrows on West. "Has his lawyer turned up yet?"

"Not yet, no. You guys want to go in anyway?"

Methven spluttered. "I've no idea what sort of arrangement you run out here, but this is a major murder enquiry. It's all over the papers. My DI has to spend an hour a day speaking to sodding journalists. We're not cutting any corners here."

West looked ready to argue the toss but he backed down. "Okay. Let's wait."

The desk sergeant, Sally, walked into the admin area accompanied by a plump woman in her late forties. Sally pointed at West.

The woman nodded before heading over. "I believe you've got one Tommy Aitken in here?"

"We have." West sat on the edge of his desk. "Are you his lawyer?"

"Just the duty solicitor." She held out her hand. "Audrey Mitchell."

West shook hands. "This is DC Cullen and DS Methven. They're investigating Mr Aitken's son's murder."

"I see."

"I take it you've been briefed on what your new client has been up to?"

"I'm aware of the situation. My soon-to-be client was under the influence when the alleged attack happened. Is he sober enough to be interviewed?"

"He's had enough coffee to keep a detective inspector going."

Mitchell laughed. "Very well, I think we just need to get down to it. I'll make sure my client isn't over-stretching himself legally but it's all down to you."

West led them down the corridor towards the interview room, opening the door to the first one and gesturing for them to go inside.

Mitchell went in first. "Where is he?"

West leaned into the room. "Eh?"

"My client's not here."

PC Green appeared down the corridor, carrying a steaming plastic cup of coffee.

West jogged over. "Shagger, have you seen Aitken?"

Green frowned. "He's just in the room, isn't he?"

West rubbed his temples. "Christ's sake."

Cullen looked around for a Policy Custody and Security Officer. "Where's the PCSO?"

Green shrugged. "It's me."

Cullen pointed a finger at West. "This equalises the favour."

26

G reen opened the back door to the station. "You pair head out on foot. We've got five officers from Broxburn on their way over."

Cullen followed Methven as he jogged out of the police station, heading onto the wide high street. To the right, the road led out of town. "Which way?"

Local officers ran out behind them — six in all. One pair crossed the road to the town library, another headed right, while the third bombed into the area behind the station. A police car emerged from the side entrance, carrying another two — West and Green.

"No choice now." Methven started a jog towards the Farmfoods across the road. "What a sodding mess this is."

Cullen struggled to keep up with the aggressive pace Methven set, catching up as they passed bus stops on either side of the road. "I hope he's not got on a bus."

"He's not got any cash. You know what bus drivers are like these days."

Cullen would have laughed had he not been struggling to breathe. His fitness run on Sunday morning started catching up with him.

They ran past a row of charity shops, coming to the wide, modern concrete town square.

A police car running blues and twos bombed past them in the opposite direction.

"I hope they've got him." Methven radioed the control room on his Airwave. "It's just support from Broxburn."

Cullen gasped for breath, his lungs burning as they ran full tilt across the square. He stopped and took stock. "Which way?"

Methven had his hands on his hips, barely out of breath. He looked around then jogged over to a middle-aged woman sitting on a bench. "Police. We're looking for a man with long hair, probably running."

She looked him up and down. Cullen couldn't guess which class A drug she was on. She raised her arm slowly and pointed behind them, across the road, to a lane running between an estate agent and a print cartridge shop. "That way."

"Come on." Methven sprinted off again, speaking into his Airwave as they ran.

Cullen struggled to keep up. They headed up Union Road, Methven turning the corner and sprinting up the hill through the houses.

Cullen spotted someone run along a raised platform leading away from the second floor of the curry house. The man scrabbled up the steep verge before launching himself over a beech hedge.

Tommy Aitken.

"This way!" Cullen pointed up.

Methven headed back, shouting into his Airwave.

Cullen clambered up the wooden stairs after the man, before crawling up the verge. He tumbled over the hedge into the garden, brown beech leaves coming with him. Methven vaulted over seconds later, effortlessly flowing into a forward roll.

Aitken ran around the side of the bungalow. They set off, Methven quickly outstripping Cullen.

Aitken went over another hedge into the back garden of a row of flats.

Cullen followed, watching Aitken bouncing off the walls at the side as Methven accelerated.

He caught Aitken by the bins, rugby-tackling him into the steel railings. "You are under arrest!"

Cullen slowed to a walk as he headed over, desperately out of breath, relieved Methven was in control. He really needed to get into shape.

Aitken spun around. He flipped Methven over onto his back. He kicked, catching Methven square in the testicles.

Methven screamed out.

Aitken got up, sprinting off across the wide patch of grass.

Cullen followed.

A siren sounded from behind.

Aitken headed into a corner between the blocks of flats, putting further distance between them as he weaved his way into the garden.

"Tommy!"

Aitken spun around to face him before bombing back into the second garden.

Cullen saw sirens on the high street coming towards them.

Aitken glanced over, before twisting in the other direction, heading away from Cullen.

Cullen tried to speed up again, tasting the burn in the back of his throat. He turned the corner, catching himself on the harled wall, ripping his suit jacket open.

A shout came from in front, round the corner.

Cullen sped up, careering round.

Methven lay on top of Aitken.

Cullen slowed to a halt. "What happened?"

"Silly bastard tried to jump over me. I caught him."

CULLEN SAT opposite Tommy Aitken and his solicitor. Green stood guard by the interview room door, having made sure Aitken was properly handcuffed to the table this time.

Methven came into the room.

Cullen checked his watch — he had spent over twenty minutes in the gents', putting cold water on his testicles, all other officers avoiding the room while he was in there.

Methven started the interview, before nodding to Cullen to continue.

"Mr Aitken, can I ask why you visited the business premises of one Hugh Nichol this morning?"

"It's his fault." Aiken glowered through hair hanging down his face, sweat-soaked from the chase. "Xander's death. His fault."

"Why would that be?"

"Isn't it bloody obvious? He used to take Xander and Kenny and a few other boys rally driving up in the countryside. They drove his four-by-fours up the bings and the hills."

"And you blame Mr Nichol for encouraging your son's interest in off-road driving?"

"Aye. If he hadn't stoked the boy's interest, he'd never have nicked that motor and gone up there. Stupid bugger was mad for it, like."

"Do you think that Mr Nichol may have murdered your son?"

"Murdered?" Aitken face screwed his up.

Cullen nodded. "We suspect your son was murdered."

Aitken looked around the room at each of them. "Is this on the level?"

Methven winced as he produced a sheet of paper. "Here's an extract from your son's autopsy. There's evidence suggesting Mr Aitken was severely beaten prior to the fall down the bing. Coupled with the fact the car he was in was stolen during the day, when we know for a fact he was at work, it's pretty clear this isn't mere death by misadventure."

A vein started throbbing in Aitken's forehead. "Why didn't you tell me?"

"We tried." Methven looked at another sheet of paper. "Your wife was informed on Saturday afternoon. The Family Liaison Officer tried to get in touch with yourself but couldn't, for one reason or another. Until you assaulted Mr Nichol, you were off our radar."

Aitken stroked his hair with his free hand. "You told me it was a murder when you came around, but I didn't believe you. I know my son. He was a bloody idiot. Always taking risks."

Cullen leaned forward. "You should've listened to me."

"You should've found me and made me listen. I needed to hear that again. You said it was just something you were treating as a possibility. I had it in my head he'd accidentally killed himself." Aitken shook his head, slowly. "Jesus Christ."

"Mr Aitken, did you beat your son up?"

"You what?"

"You have admitted to beating him up in the past. Did you this time?"

"What the hell is this?"

"The last sighting we have of your son was on Tuesday evening. What were your movements that night?"

"I was in the pub, playing pool."

"And you'd have people that could back this up?"

"I might."

Cullen looked at the solicitor. "We'll get statements from these men." He faced Aitken. "You're in deep trouble."

27

C ullen put his tray down on the table, macaroni cheese and chips plus a large coffee.

Buxton mashed the second half of his baked potato, stirring beans and cheese into the buttery gloop. "Ah, you're back. You missed a fun morning."

Cullen chewed cheesy pasta. "Aitken's dad went mental."

"You serious?"

Cullen nodded. "Aye. He threatened that Hugh Nichol guy who runs the garage in Ravencraig. The idiots I used to work with in Bathgate let him escape. We chased him. Methven caught him but got battered in the balls for his trouble."

"Bet you're enjoying that."

"Hardly. It's been a total waste of time. We've got nowhere with it."

"Must beat what you've had me doing."

"How's it gone?"

"Got through nine of the twelve disks."

"Not bad for, what, three and a bit hours?"

"Yeah, whatever. I've got a trail of the vehicle heading out of town, but I've lost it on the last disk. One of the remaining disks might have it."

"Does it show anything?"

"Not really." Buxton put a mouthful of potato mush in his mouth. "There is a potential sighting heading back through town which we need to validate."

"I'll give you a hand."

"Thanks. I feel honoured, by the way."

"Why?" Cullen frowned.

"You spending two meals with me in one day. Feels like a royal visit or something."

"You wish." Cullen slumped back in the chair and took a sip of burning hot coffee. "You lot love the royal family where you come from."

"Gawd bless you, ma'am."

"It's Tottenham you support, isn't it?"

"I'm QPR, man. Don't ever make that mistake again."

Cullen was keen to keep talking and stretch out to the full lunch hour, before they went back to the CCTV room.

Angela sat down next to them. "Here they are, the golden boys."

"You sound more and more like Bain every day." Cullen took a sip of coffee.

"You act more like him."

"I need to get back downstairs." Buxton got up and he left them to it.

Cullen looked over. "Have you just come here to be nasty, Angela?"

"I actually wanted to see how you were doing. I heard about what happened with Sharon. It's a real shame, you were good together."

"Didn't stop her lying to me."

"And you've never lied in your puff?"

"There are various levels of lying. White lies and the stuff I say to Bain are pretty much fine. What she did just wasn't on."

"Sounds like you're saying it's okay for you but not for her."

"Hardly, this is long-term deceit."

"She's torn apart, Scott. She might not show it, but she's really upset."

"Well, she should've told me the truth. Maybe her next boyfriend or girlfriend will benefit from the experience."

"That's harsh."

"Has she got a thing for you?"

"Are you serious?" Angela looked over his shoulder.

Cullen turned around.

Wilkinson was heading their way. "There you bloody are. Had to ask Britpop."

Angela frowned. "Who's Britpop?"

"Buxton." Cullen smiled at Wilkinson. "How can I help?"

"You're coming with me." Wilkinson grabbed Cullen by the shoulder and tugged him to his feet, tearing his suit jacket further.

"Can't I finish my lunch?"

"No."

Wilkinson led them out of the canteen. "I'm not happy with you and your game playing, Curran."

"What's this about?"

"I caught up with DI Cargill, after I finally found her." Wilkinson pushed through a swing door into the main stairwell and started trotting down the stairs. "We've agreed I can have your time."

"Are you sure?"

"Yes." Wilkinson stopped at the top of the stairs and took a sheet of paper from his trouser pocket. "To stop you bloody wriggling out of my grasp, I've got her to sign another form." He handed it to Cullen. "So no more nonsense, all right?"

Cullen inspected it — Cargill giving permission to use him until the investigation at Schoolbook was closed. He trotted down the stairs, Wilkinson almost a flight below him. "Where are you taking me?"

"I'm driving you and Charlie Kidd out to Livingston to get to the bottom of this nonsense." Wilkinson entered the car park and headed towards his C-Max.

Charlie Kidd leaned against it, arms folded.

Wilkinson glanced around. "Besides, it might do you good to be apart from your ex-bird. Heard she's been sniffing around young Caldwell."

~

WILKINSON PULLED AWAY from the Hermiston Gate roundabout, putting his foot down as they came onto the first stretch of the M8 towards Livingston.

"What are you looking to achieve at Schoolbook?" Cullen shifted in his seat to face Wilkinson.

Wilkinson took a deep breath. "I told you about this hooligan fight I'm looking into, right?"

"You did."

"We've got an undercover operative on the Celtic side. One of his ringleaders let slip the fact the fight was organised on Schoolbook. I want you pair to see if it was and, if so, who organised it."

"Just wanted to make sure this is solid intelligence."

"Well, I've spoken to the Procurator Fiscal and my superintendent, we're comfortable this won't be a waste of resources."

"Your funeral."

Kidd leaned between the seats. "What is it we're looking for?"

"I've told you. Whoever organised this fight."

"I know that. Schoolbook's a big site. Based on what we had to do before, this isn't going to be quick, easy or cheap."

"Not my problem. I've been given the name of the chatroom. The rest is over to you two."

Wilkinson turned off the dual carriageway to join the road to McArthur Glen.

As they passed the outlet park, Cullen wondered how Demi Baird was coping with her fiancé's death. "Have you been looking into connections to the English or Scottish Defence Leagues?"

Wilkinson powered on, heading towards the business park where Schoolbook was based. "I'm afraid so. It's not just bloody sectarianism these boys are up to. Islamophobia's where it's at nowadays. Half the time these fights are training for kicking in clerics in Luton or somewhere like that. The Rangers and Hibs fans are the worst. I had to go down to Bedfordshire last month to share some of our intelligence after a few lads from up here got arrested."

Cullen spotted a security guard at the entrance to the car park. "Look, Charlie, they've got security."

"Aye. Physical security. Bet their network security's still a joke."

Wilkinson glanced over, his forehead creased. "Are you telling me you walked into the building?"

"Aye."

"This should be easy."

"Not sure about that." Cullen grimaced. "Have you called ahead?"

"Aye. Got some boy called Aitchison meeting us in reception." Wilkinson checked his watch. "Said we'd be there at half past one but it's bloody nearer two."

The guard at the parking barrier let them through.

Wilkinson parked in a visitor's space near the front entrance and led them across the car park. "Quit dawdling, you two. All right?"

Inside, a grizzled old security guard sat behind a desk, flicking through The Sun. He looked at Wilkinson's warrant card, muttered to himself then made a phone call.

Cullen looked around — the previous open plan area had now been boxed off, large security doors with card readers leading off in both directions.

A man appeared through a door and nodded their way.

Cullen frowned before it dawned on him. Gregor Aitchison. He'd lost his beard and was wearing business casual — dress trousers and a striped shirt open to the neck. His eyes avoided Cullen and Kidd. "DI Wilkinson, is it?"

Wilkinson shook his hand, while showing his warrant card. "I presume you know my colleagues?"

Aitchison grunted. "I do, aye. Come on through." He led them into a large room, rows and rows of servers surrounding banks of desks with noticeably more people than fourteen months previously.

Cullen pulled across a couple of seats.

Aitchison settled down at his desk. "How can I help?"

Wilkinson got out his notebook. "I explained the case in detail on the phone but specifically, I need to get a list of usernames for a chat room on your site."

"Which one is it?"

"It's called CentralBelter, all one word."

"Okay." Aitchison tapped his keyboard, flicking through several screens and pages. "Bad news, I'm afraid."

"What is it?"

"That's an old Intarwubs chat room. We bought the technology from them last Christmas and integrated it in March, don't know if you saw the announcements?"

"No. Spell it out for us."

"The integration wasn't perfect. It was rushed to make sure we avoided paying a default as part of the contract. There's a second release going in soon which will be a bit tighter."

Kidd let his ponytail drop. "So what are you saying?"

"Well, it's got a separate user database. We're working on that for the next release, but I can't link people on Schoolbook to people on the chat room."

"You must be able to."

"I can't. It's all aliases and nicknames and they don't enforce any integrity. Here, look at this one. It's got names like gorgie_billy, dubliner1916 and blackburnteddy. They're the biggest users of the chat room."

Cullen scribbled them down in his own notebook. "What does this mean, Charlie?"

Kidd sat tossing his ponytail for a few seconds. "If he's right, then we're snookered. I can have a fiddle, see what I can do."

"Okay." Wilkinson pointed at the screen. "These names here, are they the ones that organised this meeting?"

"Hold on a minute." Aitchison brought up a screen with some message trails.

Cullen didn't have to read between any lines or pixels, it was pretty clear they were organising a mass fight, no code words or anything. "And you just let this happen?"

"What can we do? There's over twenty-seven thousand chat rooms. We can't afford to police them."

"You've taken an unsecured chat room and added it to your site." Cullen dug his nails into his palms. "Haven't you learned anything?"

Wilkinson held his hand out warning Cullen to calm down. "I think we've got something here. These users were the ones that arranged the fight. While Charlie works with Mr Aitchison, I can do some digging in the real world."

Cullen couldn't believe it — he wanted to tear the servers apart and shut the place down.

Wilkinson got to his feet. "Charlie, stay here and work on linking these back to users?"

"I've not got my car."

"I'll get someone to pick you up. This is important." Wilkinson nodded at Cullen. "I need to get you back to your lord and master." He shook Aitchison's hand before leading Cullen back to the reception area.

Cullen waited until they were out of earshot of any employees. "Why the hell have you got me out here?"

"Weight of numbers. Plus, all the stuff with the Schoolbook Killer last year, I thought a friendly face such as yours would put the frighteners up him. Seemed to work."

Cullen bit his lip. "Any idea who these people are?"

"The first two, I've no idea." Wilkinson grimaced. "Blackburn Teddy, though, I think I've got a possibility."

"Go on."

"Tommy Aitken."

"Xander's father?"

"Aye, lad. He's from Blackburn, you know, the West Lothian one. Moved to Ravencraig when he was a teenager. He's a Rangers fan that we've had under investigation by my lads for a few months."

"Why didn't you mention it before?"

Wilkinson stopped to open the security door. "The minute Cargill hears anything about how my case might be linked to hers, you watch it disappear out of my hands."

"That's not right."

"That's the way this thing works. Now, I've got to get a couple of lads to bring him and his computer in."

"He's in Bathgate nick. Just interviewed him."

WILKINSON KNOCKED on the interview room door. "A word?"

Methven looked up. He narrowed his eyes before leaning across the table. "Interview paused at fifteen seventeen." He screeched the chair on the lino as he got to his feet, smiling at Aitken's solicitor. "I'll be back in a few seconds." He left the room, pulling the door shut behind him. "What?"

Wilkinson folded his arms. "Need to have a word with your suspect in there."

"I'm deep in an interview. His alibis haven't checked out."

"Let me remind you who has rank here, Sergeant."

"I can get DI Cargill on the phone."

"Go grassing to teacher, lad? Very big of you."

Cullen's phone rang. Buxton. Stepping away, he answered it down the corridor, a safe distance from the cock fight. "Britpop, how can I help?"

"Bloody freezing in here and bloody boring, too."

"You can come out here to Bathgate, if you want."

"I'll pass. Anyway, I think I've got something. Check your phone."

Cullen held his phone away from his head — he'd five messages from Buxton. He put the call on speaker and opened the first one. The shot covered the entrances to Ravencraig from the north, giving a good angle right down the street, showing the Range Rover, its right-turn indicator on. While the angle was perfect for viewing the car, it was next to useless for showing its occupants. "What is this?"

"What do you think? The Range Rover went into that street."

Cullen flicked onto the next image, a map. He tilted the phone to get his bearings. The way the Range Rover was indicating, there was only one side road, which headed to a set of lock-ups. He squinted at the screen, pinching to zoom in — a couple of the garage doors were just about visible through the haze of pixels. He looked at the map again — there were another four garages circled in red.

Cullen tried to work through his options. Keeping things from Cargill and Methven — as he'd done earlier with the Gavin Tait investigation — had been a bit stupid. Much as he wanted to be the hero, he was starting to think working with these officers, playing the team game, was a better strategy than merely doing the opposite of whatever Bain told him. "Who knows about this?"

"Well, I put a call out to uniform in West Lothian. Boy called Green."

"Right, good. Tell Cargill." Cullen ended the call and made his way over to Methven and Wilkinson. He got between them, angling his body to face Methven. "We've got something."

Methven finally acknowledged him. "What is it?"

Cullen held up his phone, showing the black and white image of the Range Rover. "Buxton's just finished the CCTV review of Smith's car. Looks like it visited a lock-up in Ravencraig before it went to the top of the bing. Uniform are already on their way over."

"This is good work." Methven scowled at Wilkinson. "Inspector, you can have the witness."

Wilkinson let his folded arms go. "After all that bloody nonsense from you?"

"Take it up with DI Cargill." Methven turned to Cullen. "Come on. Let's go" He raced off down the corridor.

As Methven unlocked his car, Cullen's phone rang. PC Green.

"Scott, where are you?"

"Still at Bathgate station. Why?"

"Hurry up. The garages are on fire."

28

M ethven bombed into the outskirts of Ravencraig. "Why the sodding hell did some bugger set them on fire?"

"Might be innocent."

"I doubt it." Methven turned the sharp bend. "Nice to see you finally playing the same game as the rest of us. Your reputation precedes you. You're a loose cannon. You're not a team player."

"Is this coming from Bain?"

Methven glared at him. "Not just from DI sodding Bain. I've spoken to a number of officers about you. I know what happened between you and DS Irvine. I know you didn't toe the line in three major cases."

"I think you'll find in all those cases, I got results."

"DI Cargill doesn't sodding like cowboys." Methven focused more on Cullen than the road. "You might think you've got results, but you've undermined the police service. We need to make sure we're above board, that everything has an audit trail and the PF has a clear path to prosecution." His hands tightened on the steering wheel. "We don't want Acting DCs being stabbed or hit with hammers."

"I didn't get back up in either case."

"Then you should have waited."

"I would've had two extra victims."

"This isn't a game, Constable. Two wrongs don't make a right. You can't equate saving two members of the public with losing an Acting DC. You need to do things in a safe and controlled manner."

Cullen slouched back in his seat. "I'll bear that in mind."

They pulled up alongside a Lothian & Borders Volvo, twenty

metres away from the burning lock-ups. Twenty-foot high flames burst out of the roofs.

Green was speaking into his Airwave.

Cullen got out of the car and jogged over.

"What the sodding hell happened here?"

"Fire service is on its way from Bathgate." Green reattached his Airwave to his vest. "It was burning when we arrived."

"And when the sodding hell did you get here?"

"We just arrived, Sarge."

"Where were you? ADC Buxton called this in ages ago."

Kieron Bain got out of the car. "We needed to get approval from our sergeant."

Methven spun round to focus on him. "No, you sodding didn't. You're both allocated to this investigation."

"We're not. Our inspector unassigned us first thing this morning."

Methven stood there, nostrils flaring. "This is not good form. I'm going to speak to your inspector about this."

"We've got to follow protocol." Green folded his arms. "We've got two major murder investigations to support as well as actually doing our day jobs."

"What's the other investigation?"

"We're allocated to DI Wilkinson."

"Bloody hell." Methven rubbed his eyebrows. "What happened when you finally turned up here?"

"It was well alight. Looked like it had been burning for about twenty minutes, maybe longer."

"Was there anybody around?"

Kieron shook his head. "Nobody."

"Hmm." Methven got out his notebook before pointing at Green and Kieron. "You two stay here and support the fire service." He looked at Cullen. "Get ADC Buxton to investigate the ownership of the garages."

"Will do." Cullen scribbled it down. "What about me?"

"Can you get the latest CCTV tapes of this place and see who was here in the last hour?"

"WHAT IS IT?" Methven was sitting in the corner of the Incident Room, tapping on a laptop, not even looking up at Cullen.

He held up a wad of photographs. "Finished the CCTV search just before the fire. Got a very loose lead."

Methven grabbed the photos, spending a few seconds looking through them. "Doesn't show a great deal, does it?"

"We could get those four boys in hoodies brought in." Cullen pointed to a few shots showing kids running away from the garages, across the adjacent waste ground.

"Good shout." Methven sighed as he put them down before shutting the lid on the laptop. "It feels a bit of a coincidence, that's all. You find out the car was taken there and within an hour the whole lot's up in flames."

"I thought that as well. The only people who knew were you, me, Buxton, DI Cargill and PC Green."

"Plus Green's sergeant and half that bloody station. Who was that kid with him? Looked familiar."

Cullen hesitated. He hadn't told anyone Bain's son was even on the force, let alone the same case. "It's Kieron Bain, works out of Ravencraig."

"Any relation?"

Cullen rubbed his forehead. "His son."

Methven slammed his fist down on the desk. "You know the sodding rules around this. He was the First Attending Officer at the bing, wasn't he?"

"He was."

"Why haven't you told me this before?"

"It's in the file. He's supposed to be off the case."

Methven spoke with his eyes shut. "Don't you think DI Cargill or I should've been informed?"

"I'm not hiding anything."

"Like hell you are." Methven opened his eyes. "You know I've been brought in here to stop this sort of nonsense. You and Bain and Irvine, you're all the same. Bloody cowboys."

"With all due respect, we're not the same."

Methven sneered at Cullen. "Get out of my sodding sight. I'll take this up with DI Cargill."

Cullen checked his watch — twenty past six. "I'm going home."

"Fine by me." Methven opened his laptop. "Might solve this case if we've not got you making a mess of it."

29

The flat was empty when Cullen got home. He sat at the dining table and switched on the TV. The One Show — the worst concept for a TV programme ever, which seemed to be "don't have a concept". Sharon loved it. Maybe that was why he hated it.

He went through the other channels. Nothing.

He gave a deep sigh. How did people fill evenings watching TV? He'd never had a problem finding stuff to do, but he was at a loose end now.

He was hungry. Maybe he should go to the Co-op for something healthy, rather than the usual pizza or curry. A shish kebab wasn't too unhealthy — vegetables and protein.

The front door opened and Rich walked in, wearing his black work suit with grey shirt and black tie.

"You look very nineties there, Rich."

Rich scowled. "Whatever."

Cullen turned off the TV. "Bad day?"

"Insurance company are being dicks about my phone. It's my life in there. Only good thing is it's cancelled and everything's backed up, so I can just get a new one." He sat next to Cullen. "You're home early."

"Had a shite day myself."

"Sharon?"

"That's only part of it. The DS I'm working with just now is a total fanny and he's got it in for me."

"They're all like that, aren't they?" Rich grinned. "What have you done this time?"

Cullen threw his hands in the air. "Nothing. I've worked my arse off today. He's just picking on me."

"I believe you. Pint?"

≈

THE BELL RANG. "LAST ORDERS!"

Rich swirled his pint glass. "One for the road?"

Cullen checked the time — just after eleven. They were pretty much the only ones left. "Aye, sod it. One more pint isn't going to make it that much worse tomorrow."

Rich headed to the bar.

Cullen looked across the Dalriada, a gastropub in an old Victorian mansion at the far end of the promenade in Portobello. Their plates were still on the table — steak and chips for Cullen, tomato pasta for Rich — alongside several empty pint glasses.

He couldn't believe he'd spent his first working night as a single man getting pissed with Rich. What had Sharon done?

Rich put the two pints on the table. "Here you go. Better drink up — the barman wasn't impressed. Poor guy looks like he just wants to go home."

"Fine."

"What's up?"

"Don't know. Sharon, probably."

"Right, so you do miss her?"

"I think so. It's only been a weekend. Can't believe it's been so short a space of time. I must look like a total pussy."

Rich held his hands up. "Hey, I'm all for guys showing their sensitive side. I'm not Tom, you know?"

Cullen smiled. "Thanks. It's just I feel she's taken our future away. I was going to move in with her. We had a holiday booked. I can't bloody believe it."

"Must hurt, right?"

"Like you'd know."

"Just try me."

"Spit it out."

"Look, Scott, the reason I moved back up here was this guy I'd been seeing in London. Andrew. Third generation Greek. Real Adonis type, you know?" Rich took a big gulp of his beer. "Thing was, he'd been shagging guys at the gym. He'd been lying to me all that time. It was going on for months, must've been about twenty blokes."

"You've never told me this."

"I preferred my return north to be shrouded in mystery."

"So, basically, you know what it's like being lied to?"

Rich looked away. "It's not just that. Sharon's lie was kind of safe, in a way."

Cullen pointed a finger at him. "Watch where you're going with this."

Rich held his hands up. "Stop being such a bloody princess. I'm serious. Andrew was shagging loads of blokes in a gay gym. Just think about that. Those guys could have had anything. He was bringing that into our home."

Cullen slowly nodded. "Oh shit. Are you... you know?"

"Am I what?" Rich folded his arms.

"HIV positive."

"I've had a test, if that's what you mean. Had three, in fact, just to be sure." Rich took another swig of beer before looking away. "Relax, I've not got AIDS."

Cullen breathed a sigh of relief. "I suppose Sharon's betrayal's nothing compared to that."

"Aye. She used to go out with a woman. Big deal. I know a few blokes who'd be turned on by that sort of thing, or at least say they were."

Cullen glowered. "Not me."

"I suppose you're quite traditional." Rich nodded at his eyebrow. "Where did you get that scratch from?"

Cullen tugged his hair down. "I got into a fight on Saturday."

"What sort of a fight?"

"I went to the Hibs match with a mate. We were going for a pint when we got jumped by some neds in tracksuits."

Rich smirked. "Really? Local hero cop assaulted by neds?"

"Aye, very good. They almost opened the wound in my shoulder."

"What are you going to do about it?"

"Still haven't decided."

"Which pretty much means do nothing, right?"

"Yeah."

Cullen sat in silence, thinking through his options. He didn't like getting battered by casuals. He didn't like the fact they knew Derek Miller. "I can't make my mind up about how to deal with it."

"How do you mean?"

"I'm enough of a laughing stock at the station because of Sharon. Being jumped by some neds wouldn't be great."

"Still, you can't like those wankers getting away with it, can you?"

"No." Cullen needed to speak to Derek again.

Rich leaned forward. "You in early tomorrow?"

"Usual time. Why?"

"You fancy going to a club?"

~

THE MUSIC WAS loud and the Liquid Lounge was busy for a Tuesday. Rich and Cullen worked the dance floor, prowling it like a pair of panthers, at least in Cullen's head.

As they danced, Rich had his eyes on a tall, athletic guy wearing a suit, vaguely reminiscent of a young Ewan McGregor.

Above the thumping beats of a Fatboy Slim track, Rich shouted in his ear. "More shots?"

"Thought you had your eyes on that bloke?"

"It's not him I'm worried about. It's her again." Rich gestured in the opposite direction — a girl in her mid-twenties had been staring at Cullen since they arrived.

Cullen quickly formulated a plan. "More Jaegerbombs?"

"Slag bombs."

Cullen grinned. "Back in a minute." As he left the thud of the dance floor, he clocked the girl again — not bad. Not bad at all.

Rich made his move, reminding him of a nature documentary where a lion attacks a wildebeest.

He made for the bar, a long dark room with booths opposite, leaning against it with a twenty pound note out, like some mid-nineties City trader.

"Aye?"

"Two slag bombs." Cullen waited while the barman poured the booze and squeezed the can.

"Hey there."

Cullen spun round. The girl from the dance floor, definitely after him. "Hey."

"You can really dance." She was absolutely banjaxed.

"Thanks. I try my best."

She stood there, eyes wide. He held out his hand. "Scott."

"Katie."

Cullen tried to smile. He'd loved that name until a girl with it totally destroyed his heart.

She leaned close. "Pretty busy for a Monday night."

"Yeah. Why are you here tonight?"

"I'm a nurse. Tomorrow's my day off."

"Right." Cullen nodded.

"What about you?"

"Oh, I'm just a piss head."

She laughed hard, perhaps too hard.

Cullen could feel the old magic coming back. He looked at her again — she was mid-to-late twenties. Dark hair hanging loose. She was curvy with a slim waist. Tall. His type.

A couple in a booth opposite were grabbed by a bouncer, pushing them towards the exit. The guy struggled to do his flies up, the girl adjusting her skirt.

Katie giggled. "What do you think they were up to?"

"No idea."

The barman put the drinks on the bar top, along with the change.

Cullen nodded towards the booth. "Want a seat?"

Katie grinned mischievously as she pounced on the bench.

Cullen sat alongside her rather than opposite. Avoid eye contact. He put the drinks on the table.

"Is that for me?"

"Sure," He pushed one of the drinks over.

She leaned forward, cleavage pushed up by her arms. She put her hands around the glass and raised an eyebrow. "After three, then... one, two, three."

Cullen tipped the drink up, the shots and the Red Bull mixing when they hit his mouth, before slamming the glass down on the table at the same time as Katie. "That was good."

"Yeah. Was that a Jaegerbomb."

"A slag bomb."

She laughed. "Never heard of that before."

"Where are you based, Katie?"

"The Royal Infirmary."

"Right."

"You've not said what you do."

"I'm a police officer." He'd been tempted to lie but sod it.

"Oh, are you off tomorrow?"

"No. Like I told you earlier, I'm a piss head."

She laughed again. "My round. Jaegerbomb this time?"

"Go for it."

She sashayed to the bar.

Cullen admired the wiggle. Her legs were pretty well toned — must be all the walking she did in the hospital.

He felt a hand on his shoulder. "Skinky, we need to go."

Rich stood there, face bloody, dabbing at his nose with some toilet paper, his white shirt stained red.

Cullen jerked backwards. "What happened?"

"That Ewan McGregor boy nutted me."

"Are you all right?"

"No, I'm not all right. Turns out he wasn't gay after all."

Cullen raised an eyebrow. "Could've fooled me."

"Aye, well, he did fool me."

Katie reappeared, holding two tumblers with shot glasses inside. She smiled at Cullen then stared at Rich, open-mouthed. "Oh my God! What happened?"

"Got head-butted."

"I'm a nurse, I can sort this out." She put the glasses down on the table. "Let me have a look."

Rich let his hand go.

Katie prodded around with his nose, causing him to squeal twice.

Rich motioned his head towards Cullen then Katie then the Jaegerbombs, a frown etched on his forehead.

Cullen looked away.

Katie patted his shoulder. "I don't think there's any lasting damage. You'd better go to the doctor, though. I'd be tempted to recommend A&E but I don't want you to take this hunk away from me."

"This hunk is my flatmate and he's going to take me home." Rich's legs buckled and he had to support himself. "I'm in no fit state."

Katie's eyebrows arched up. "I could come with you."

Rich smiled. "I hope Scott hasn't been leading you on. He's just broken up with his long-term girlfriend and I wouldn't want him giving you any ideas."

She turned to face Cullen. "Is this true?"

Cullen rolled his shoulders. "I wasn't leading you on. I was just talking to you."

"*Men.*" Katie downed her shot. "If you're a policeman then I suggest you arrest the guy who attacked your pal. As for me, I'm going. Nice speaking to you, Scott." She took Cullen's drink with her.

"Bloody hell." Cullen looked up at Rich. "I'm lucky to have got away without a slap, right?"

Rich slumped down in the booth across from him, tentatively rubbing his nose. "Where's my drink?"

"Are you kidding? We should go."

Rich's eyes danced around the bar. "The night's still young."

"Aye, well, you're not going to trap any blokes looking like that."

Rich looked down at his shirt. "I can wash it."

"You said we need to go. You were right." Cullen led out of the bar, making for the cloakroom to retrieve Rich's overcoat.

While they waited, Ewan McGregor headed their way, accompanied by a guy who looked like a young John Hannah.

Cullen nudged Rich. "There's your boyfriend."

"Piss off."

"His mate looks like John Hannah."

"He looks bugger all like him." Rich grabbed his jacket. "Maybe the eyebrows."

The two men were smoking outside. Ewan McGregor squared up to Rich. "Here's that poof."

"I'm a police officer and I'm not above arresting you for assault."

"Just try it. I can get the CCTV tapes of what your boyfriend was trying to do to me in there."

"Let's just leave it. We've all had a fair amount to drink."

Rich pointed a finger at him. "I don't think I'm finished with this one. I don't know whether to kick the shit out of him or shag him."

Cullen grabbed him by the shoulder and pulled him away. "Come on." He led him up Hanover Street, towards George Street and hopefully some taxis.

Rich shrugged away from Cullen. He turned to face back down Hanover Street and grabbed his crotch. "I'm going to fuck you, pal! Right up your tight, little arsehole!"

The Ewan McGregor lookalike tossed his cigarette aside and started up the street towards them.

Cullen flagged down the first available taxi.

DAY 7

Tuesday
9th October 2012

30

C ullen lay in bed, bursting for a piss, sunlight penetrating his eyelids. His head was thumping, his mouth bone dry.

His dream still lingered. He'd starred in a film with John Hannah and Ewan McGregor, a cross between The Mummy and Trainspotting.

Rich was in it as well, kissing Ewan.

John Hannah laughing at Cullen.

Occasionally, the other Katie would appear — Cullen's ex — but she acted like Sharon, kissed Angela and got off with Ewan McGregor.

He opened his eyes. The sunlight had crept from the open curtains right up to his bed. He glanced at the alarm clock.

9.03.

Shite.

≈

CULLEN STAGGERED into the Incident Room having broken at least two laws on his way in.

He sniffed his armpits — the quick blast of Lynx in the car at the traffic lights on Leith Walk would sort him out.

He spotted Buxton swearing at a laptop and made a beeline for him. "Seen Methven?"

"Not since the briefing. He was looking for you, though. What did you think of it? You seemed to get off without that many actions."

"Well, I'll be in the CCTV suite if he's looking for me."

"Awake or asleep? You stink of booze, mate."

"Must be the new aftershave."

"You haven't shaved, you cheeky wanker."

Cullen left the Incident Room and headed to the canteen. He was tempted to try Bain's hangover cure again but he couldn't honestly say it had any effect on Saturday. The only thing that would help would be more lager. He made eye contact with Barbara and picked up a stick of chewing gum.

A hand grabbed his shoulder. Methven. He tugged Cullen off towards bollocking corner. "You can forget about getting a sodding bacon butty." He pushed Cullen to sit opposite him. "Why weren't you at the briefing this morning?"

"I was out in West Lothian speaking to a CHIS."

"At seven in the morning?" Methven's hands jangled away in his pocket. He held Cullen's gaze for ten or so seconds before Cullen had to break off. "I can sodding smell the booze off you from here, Cullen. You were out drinking last night, weren't you?"

Cullen looked away then gave a slight nod. "Yes."

Methven shook his head. "When did you get home?"

"After one. I slept in. The alarm didn't go off."

"Cullen, can I just sodding remind you we're working a double murder investigation here. You get to go drinking when we've brought someone in and charged them, not when we're in the middle of it. Especially when you've just taken two days off."

"They were after nine days back-to-back."

"You look like crap."

"I just broke up with my girlfriend. It goes with the territory."

"DS McNeill?"

Cullen nodded.

Methven gripped the edge of the table. "I really don't like it when officers get involved with each other. It always ends up like this. It's no excuse, you know? DC Caldwell's going through a divorce. I don't see her out on the town in sodding nightclubs or what have you."

Cullen looked away, across the canteen. "I'm sorry."

Methven closed his eyes, hand jangling. "Before I took you on, I'd heard a lot about you. You were promising, you got results, but you might be out of control. Well, I've confirmed it now. I don't think DI Cargill or DCI Turnbull realise how out of control you are, Cullen."

"I'm not out of control, I'm just going through a rough patch."

"Alcohol abuse isn't the best way to deal with rough patches."

"I'm not an alcoholic."

Methven's large eyebrows furrowed. "Did I say you were?"

"No." Cullen grimaced.

"We all like a drink, don't get me wrong, but there's a time and a place for everything. Don't let it dominate you."

"Okay."

Methven pointed a finger at him. "I covered for you at the briefing this morning. It'll be the first and only time, okay? If you don't buck your ideas up, DI Cargill and DCI Turnbull will be told about this. It's all documented."

"This will be the last time."

"It better be. Given the state you're in, I assume you're not fit for normal duties."

"I can do my job. Besides, I think I need something to take my mind off it. I'll be fine once I've got a coffee in me."

Methven looked him up and down. "You might want to wash your face and brush your hair while you're at it." He got out his notebook and flipped back a couple of pages. "Your actions for the day, assuming you're actually capable of working, are as follows. The door-to-door in the street came in and it looks like Aitken didn't return home on Tuesday night. We've backed that up with the forensics."

"So he was abducted?"

"We don't know that. What I need is for you and Buxton to do some digging. Find out if he disappeared or ran away. The last sighting was at work on Tuesday."

Cullen jotted it down in his notebook. "I'll get onto it."

Methven pointed at him. "I'm serious about this, this is the last sodding time I ever cover for you. You'll be dropped in the muck so sodding fast, you won't know what's hit you."

31

Cullen filled up his desk with prints of phone records over the previous fortnight — Aitken on the left and Souness on the right.

He cross-traced their contact, noticing they'd made a number of calls to each other, mainly Aitken to Souness. There was a spike in frequency on Tuesday, starting about ten a.m., but which came to a sudden stop just after five. He looked through the previous weeks that he had in a loose pile and noticed their regular phone contact was two or three times a day.

There were two mobile numbers he couldn't square off against contacts. He called Tommy Smith in the Phone Squad, an old acquaintance.

"All right, buddy? How can I help?"

"Morning, Tommy. How do you know I'm looking for help?"

"I don't think you're interested in my Lothian & Borders poetry club."

"No, you've got me." Cullen laughed.

"You sound a bit rough. Been hitting the whisky?"

"Jaegermeister and Red Bull."

"Oh dear. My youngest is a fiend for the old Jaegerbomb."

"Tommy, I've got some phone numbers I need to trace. I've come up empty on my own searches, so I was wondering if you could help."

"Sure thing, buddy."

Cullen read out the two numbers.

"Give me a minute there, I need to stick this on mute, all right?"

Cullen leaned back on his chair. His eyes were stinging. His head was throbbing. He still felt pissed. He knew well enough 'never again' meant 'until the weekend', but this time he might actually mean it.

"All right, buddy? Got something back. They're Pay As You Go SIM cards, delivered to a shop in Ravencraig, imaginatively enough called Ravencraig News."

Cullen sat forward in the seat. "Both of them were?"

"That's right. Consecutive serial numbers, but they only acquire the network number when they connect first time. Definitely bought at the same time, though."

≈

"You shouldn't be working if you're too pissed to drive." Buxton pulled into the kerb outside the shop, just off the main drag in Ravencraig.

"Relax, Budgie."

"Would you stop it with that? You're becoming a right bloody hypocrite, mate. You're pissed off with Bain calling you Sundance, but you've got a million and one names for people. Budgie, Britpop, Shagger, God knows what else."

"Sorry. I must seem like a dick."

"You do. I'm sorry but that's the God's honest truth."

"Okay."

"Now, are you sure you're okay to do this?"

"Relax, I'm fine." Cullen felt anything but.

"Don't think Methven thought that way. He was still raging when he came back to the Incident Room."

"Was he?" Cullen stared out of the window. "Let's go and see what this shop's got to say."

Cullen hadn't phoned ahead for fear of warning the proprietor. They trudged into the shop and joined a queue.

The guy behind the till looked Polish — he had dark hair and the classic Slavic look. He screwed his eyes up at an old lady at the front. "That's the seventh time in the last month my paper's not turned up."

Cullen grabbed a bottle of Lucozade as they waited.

The next two customers quickly bought stuff with exact change.

Cullen paid for the Lucozade then held out his warrant card. His hand was shaking, so he put it back in his pocket.

"How I help, Officers?"

"You can start by giving your name."

"Sure, it is Marcin Wdowski."

"We've got two phone numbers we've traced to Pay As You Go SIM cards delivered to this address. Do you keep a record of sales?"

"I not." Wdowski tapped his head. "I have steel trap mind."

"How many do you sell each month?"

"Maybe five."

"Do you ever sell more than one at a time?"

Wdowski nodded. "It happen. Time to time."

Cullen got out his notebook, flipping through to the notes he'd taken on the call records. The first phone was calling Aitken three weeks previously — he could assume the card was bought that week. "What about around about the eighteenth of September?"

Wdowski laughed. "You funny man. How I suppose remember that long ago?"

Buxton looked around the shop. "Do you have CCTV?"

"No I not. Too much money."

"Thought you had a steel trap mind?"

Wdowski laughed again. "You very funny man. You should be on stage like that John Bishop. He very funny."

Cullen folded his arms. "I'm serious. Do you remember anyone in that week?"

"Lot of people. Give me minute." Wdowski cradled his hands, holding them up to his nose. He stood like that for some time.

Cullen looked around — the queue behind them was ten deep now. A couple of people left the shop, shaking their heads and swearing.

"I remember now." Wdowski stabbed a finger in the air. "Was boy with, how you say, hat that is part of jumper?"

"A hoodie?"

Wdowski smiled. "Yes, that it. Man with hood bought two card. Was middle of afternoon, so I not busy. I remember him."

"What did he look like?"

"Hood was low. I not see he face too good. He white, that all I say."

"What accent did he have?" Cullen frowned. "Was it like mine or like yours?"

Wdowski shook his head. "He not speak to me. He pay cash then go."

Buxton pointed to the shelf behind Wdowski. "Did he not ask for them?"

Wdowski smiled, exposing gappy teeth. "He point like you. He grunt. Say 'card'. I ask him if phone card. He shake head. I ask him if SIM card. He nod. I give him card."

Cullen handed Wdowski a card. "Give me a phone if anything else comes to you or the man in the hood comes back."

Wdowski nodded. "I do that."

Cullen led them back out, stopping by the car. He opened the

Lucozade and downed half of the bottle in one go. "What do you think?"

"It could be the same guys that set fire to the lock-ups. Worth looking into."

"Hoodies torching the garage and hoodies buying disposable mobile phones. Methven's going to kill me for this."

"You reckon? He seems like a proper geezer to me."

"He's got it in for me."

"That hangover's making you paranoid."

"It's making my day shite."

"What next?"

"What we're supposed to be doing. Let's try and pick up the trail from when Aitken went missing after his work on Tuesday."

"WHAT'S THE PLAN, THEN, MORSE?" Buxton switched off the ignition.

Cullen laughed. "You're hardly Lewis, are you?" He watched the lunchtime crowds walk about, some heading to a coffee shop on the corner, some to a burger van and others into Drummond House, where Aitken had worked.

"This ain't Oxford, that's for sure."

"Have you been there?"

"I went to university there."

Cullen scowled. "Shut up."

"God's honest truth, did PPE at Hertford College."

"Didn't know you could do PE at Oxford."

Buxton laughed. "PPE is Politics, Philosophy and Economics."

"Thought you'd be working in the City with a degree from Oxford?"

"Moved up here after I graduated. The bird I was seeing was from Edinburgh, wanted to move back, so I came with her. I was in a band for a few years. Both things broke up at the same time. Tell you, the band was a harder break-up than the girl."

"And you joined the police then?"

"Yeah, I was just working in a shitty office, selling pensions. Decided to do something with my life."

"Why not go back south and work in the City?"

"Cos it's full of wankers. I'm from London, I know what goes on there. I'm keeping as far away as possible."

"It's very noble, if I actually believed it."

"Believe what you like. It's the truth."

"What did you play?"

"Bass."

"Brilliant. You'll need to show me it some time."

"'64 Fender Precision. Worth a mint, I tell you. Should really sell it, but I just can't bring myself to."

"So you didn't get signed?"

"Just about did. Couple of labels were interested in us but it never came to nothing."

"I still don't believe it." Cullen opened his door. "Come on, let's speak to the security guard."

They trudged over the road, the cutting wind carrying a few falling leaves, heading to the security barrier.

Cullen rapped on the glass.

The guard looked up. "You again?"

"Afraid so. We're investigating the murder of an Alexander Aitken who worked in this building."

The guard's face contorted in concentration. "The name rings a bell."

"Does he have a parking space?"

The guard gave a nod. "That'll be it." He rummaged around in a clipboard on the desk. "Aye, his motor's been left here for the last few days."

"In the car park?"

"Aye, son, in the car park. A blue Subaru Impreza WRX. Lovely motor. Been left overnight since Tuesday. We normally report them after a week."

Cullen whipped out his mobile and called Methven, ready to break some good news for once.

～

CULLEN STOOD in the canteen putting milk into his and Buxton's builder's teas, using a small wooden stirrer to mash the teabag against the side of the paper cup.

"Scott."

Cullen looked up.

Sharon. "How are you?"

"Fine."

"There's no need to be like that."

"Really?" He put the lids on the cups, noticing Angela lurking in the distance. He started off towards the stairs.

Sharon grabbed his arm. "We need to talk this through properly."

He looked down at her hand then up at her face. "No, we don't."

"Come on."

"Is that another conquest you've got?"

Sharon glanced at Angela. "You're one to talk. We need to sit down and discuss this."

"I've said all I'm going to say. I'll collect my stuff on Saturday. That's it."

Sharon slowly loosened her grip on his arm then shook her head.

Cullen walked out of the canteen, feeling a pang of guilt. She knew it was over and yet she still persisted.

He needed to get out. He just needed a sideways move to a place with more opportunities. It'd be better in the long run. Maybe St Leonard's. He knew how it worked, knew the faces and the area they covered. That was the only way to get away from her.

Cullen entered the CCTV room, handing Buxton his tea.

Methven folded his arms. "You've not got me one again?"

Cullen smiled. "I'm not psychic."

"You need the gift of foresight."

Cullen almost laughed. "How can I help, Sarge?"

"I was just asking Simon how it was going down here. I hope you've not been sleeping off that sodding hangover."

"Hardly. We've been over the CCTV footage from the Gyle. Might be on to something."

"Go on."

"We need to verify it from the other footage, but we think we've got Aitken leaving work at quarter past four and getting into a Land Rover Discovery." Cullen nodded at Buxton. "Show him."

Buxton pressed play on the machine. Xander Aitken walked through the revolving doors at the front of Drummond House, a tiny figure in a grey landscape of cars, concrete and tarmac.

Aitken walked through the car park, out through the pedestrian entrance by the parking barrier. He then vanished off the screen. Buxton switched to a camera looking down South Gyle Crescent.

Aitken leaned into the passenger window of an old Land Rover before getting in.

"This is excellent work, boys. Do you have a license plate?"

"Just away to process it now." Buxton flipped to another view — the camera facing across the roundabout towards the Gyle Centre. He put a freeze-frame image on screen of the dark grey Land Rover. "It's a bit of an odd one, though. Just a string of five numbers."

Methven got to his feet. "Don't let me hold you back."

"Just be a second." Buxton switched to the Police National Computer and entered the license number. "Says it was scrapped in 2005."

Methven collapsed into a desk chair. "What? Can you contact the owner?"

"Will do." Buxton went through another couple of screens. "It's nobody we know, if that's what you were hoping."

"This is still good, guys."

"We can get an ANPR search done on it." Cullen blew on his tea. "It'll trace where this car's gone after here."

"Cracking idea. Get onto it."

"Knowing them, it'll be an overnight return."

"That's fine." Methven fixed his eyes on Cullen. "I'm starting to see why Turnbull might think you're a rising star."

Cullen tried to ignore the sarcasm in his voice.

32

J ust after five, Cullen's phone chirruped — a reminder to meet up with Alison Carnegie that evening, just after six. Shite. He could really do with going to bed. He got to his feet and stretched out. "Think that's me done."

Buxton scowled at him. "Really?"

"Aye. I've got the Automatic Number Plate Recognition search kicked off. Naismith reckons it's an overnight turnaround time."

"Okay. See you tomorrow."

Cullen left the CCTV room, making for the stairwell, hearing footsteps in front of him.

As he got out into the car park, he saw Angela unlocking her car. He jogged and caught up with her. "Is this you going back to your love nest with Bill?"

She stopped and glared at him. "Stop it, Scott. I'm going home, yes. To Bill, yes. You don't need to be so nasty. I'm not Sharon."

"That's harsh."

"Is it? You're being outrageous. You've no idea how upset you're making her."

"I'm not making her feel anything."

"Really? What you said earlier was below the belt as well. Are you saying I look like a lesbian because I'm so tall? Well, newsflash for you, Captain Caveman, I know lots of short lesbians."

"I'm not a homophobe."

"I keep hearing that from you. Your behaviour stinks."

"I don't like being lied to."

Angela laughed. "Scott, you're the biggest liar I know." She turned, got in her car and drove off.

∿

CULLEN WAS EARLY FOR ONCE. He checked his watch — Alison was running ten minutes late already. He had a lemon and lime drink, which he'd almost finished. He took the last mouthful of a meatball melt, sating his hunger.

The cafe was bright and airy and they were playing some chilled techno which helped Cullen's mood slightly.

"Hey, Scott."

He looked up, stunned at how much she'd aged in just fourteen months. She looked ten years older, her hair streaked with grey, skin pale and lined. Her eyes darted around the room, surrounded by deep rings.

He got up and offered her his hand. "Can I get you anything?"

"Cup of tea would be nice." She slowly took off her coat and sat down. "Just black, thanks."

He went over to the counter to order her tea and get himself another drink. He checked her out. Her dress revealed a very skinny frame. When they'd been intimate, she'd been reasonably buxom — full chest, muscular physique. That had all gone.

He paid for the drinks then took them back to the table.

"Thanks."

Cullen finished his drink. "How are you doing?"

She looked at him for twenty or so seconds, eyes burning into him. "I look like shit. If I hadn't slept with you this wouldn't have happened to me."

His stomach lurched — this was his fault. All the harm she'd done to herself, by neglect, all stemmed back to Cullen, his libido and his inability to say no to available women.

Cullen nodded. "I'm sorry about what happened. I acted badly, I'll be the first to admit that."

"That's a start, I suppose." She fished out the teabag. "I need closure on this. I reached out to you for help the other day and you shunned me."

"I shouldn't have done that." Cullen looked away. "It wasn't the right thing to do. You needed help from me and I didn't give it to you. I'm sorry."

"Thank you. That's the probably first time you've been honest with me."

"A lot of what you thought was me wasn't actually me. You know that, right?"

"I know that."

"How've you been?"

"I had been better. When I spoke to you and you treated me like shit... I haven't been so good the last few days."

"What can I do to help?"

"I'm trying to get closure on what happened between us. I know a lot of the time it was..." She paused for a few seconds, her eyes moistening. "I know it was him most of the time, but I need to know what was actually you."

"Hardly any of it was me and that's the honest truth. We met at that party, we... we had sex. Just a one night thing. I'm a shallow bastard, I know that and I'm sorry. We met up again and I got called away. Then you came to my flat and that's literally it. Everything else wasn't me."

She nodded. "Thanks."

"Are you back at work?"

"I was. I went back a few months ago. I've been off the last few days, I've not been feeling too good."

Cullen took taking a drink. "How's it been?"

"It's been okay. People at work are frightened of me. Even working in HR, there are people who can't accept I've got issues. They call me the mental girl." A tear rolled down her cheek. "I'm getting through it a day at a time." She took a sip of tea. "I've been trying to deal with a lot of the problems and move on. I've put half a stone back on in the last three months. That's progress."

"That's good."

She laughed. "I used to wish I was thinner, you know? Katie thin. I was the skinniest one at her wedding."

Cullen widened his eyes. "When did she get married?"

"In August. The bank holiday weekend. It was a lovely day."

"I didn't know."

"Well, she's not likely to tell you, is she?"

"I guess not."

"I got a phone call from someone at the Argus today. He wanted to do an article on my experiences. It's almost a year since he got sentenced, you know?"

"I can sort that out, if you want. I've got friends who work there. I could put some police frighteners on them."

She smiled. "Thank you. The guy's name is Frank."

"I'll have a word."

"There's talk of a film."

"You should maybe think about doing it."

"Really? Why?"

"I'm serious. It might help you." Cullen poured his drink over the ice in the cup. "Is there anything I can do?"

"Just knowing exactly what happened will be a start. I can work things out now." She reached into her bag and pulled out a sheaf of papers. She tossed them across the table to him.

Cullen looked through them — print-outs of Schoolbook messages between his account and hers. "I didn't send any of these."

"I know." Alison took them back. "I was such a naive little bitch. There was always this discrepancy between what you'd say in your messages and what you'd say when we spoke on the phone or in person. I can't believe I fell for it."

"Don't beat yourself up. Another four women fell for his tricks."

"I'm the lucky one. Left to survive and rot while they're all dead."

"You've got a second chance." He reached over and grabbed her hand. "You know he'd been hacking into all your messages, right? That's how he did it. He knew what you were saying to people, he could second guess you. It's not your fault."

She took a sip of tea. "Most days I wish I hadn't been saved. This just tore me apart."

Cullen's nostrils flared. "One of my colleagues died saving you. You should be grateful."

"Grateful? I should be grateful?"

"Keith died saving you."

"His brother says it was you who saved me, not him."

She knew Derek? "What do you mean?"

"Ever since I started with this new counsellor, I've been meeting up with Derek every couple of weeks. It's helped me."

Why had Derek kept this from him? "But you're feeling better, right?"

"Scott, my life's a living hell. I'll forever be the one who got away from the Schoolbook Killer. I keep getting phone calls from people, asking for titbits for articles or books on my story. I hate living through that."

"I understand."

"Do you? Every night I wake up screaming. He's about to kill me." She finished her tea. "I just want to be held by someone during the night, told it's all right."

∽

CULLEN PARKED ON EASTER ROAD. He looked up at Derek Miller's flat. Lying shit.

He got out. The front door was open. He entered and climbed the stairs, clocking the fact there was a light on inside flat four. He rapped on the door.

Derek opened the door a sliver. "Scotty?"

"Got a couple of things I wouldn't mind talking to you about."

"I've not done nothing."

"Relax, this is personal." Mostly personal.

Derek eased a little. "Have you reported the fight to the pigs?"

"We're called police officers."

"Aye, whatever. Have you?"

"Not yet. Can I come in?"

Derek widened the door. "Aye, all right. Dean and Kyle are out."

The flat was even worse than any Cullen had stayed in as a student. Giant posters decorated the wall in the hall — Hibs, Trainspotting, Taxi Driver, a band called The Enemy.

Derek led him into the cramped kitchen area, basically a few decaying units and doors. They sat on a pair of tatty grey sofas at right angles to a forty-two inch TV, Playstation controllers resting on the scarred wooden coffee table. The room stank of cigarette smoke.

Cullen pointed at the TV. "Sticks out like a sore thumb."

"It's mine. Got it from my parents for Christmas."

"So I wouldn't find it matching any burglary reports?"

"Look, what is this?"

"I want to talk about a couple of things. Alison Carnegie for starters."

"Fine." Derek stood up again. "You want a coffee?"

"Got anything sweet?"

"Got a big bottle of Irn Bru in the fridge I've not opened yet. Kyle drinks out of the bottle too."

"Irn Bru would be good." Cullen settled into the settee. The TV showed the latest FIFA game on it, paused. Hibs vs Barcelona. "I don't have to guess which team you're playing as."

"Aye. Getting spanked four one, though."

"Surely the one is a miracle."

"Aye, probably just my natural flair showing through." Derek came over with two pint glasses of Irn Bru.

"Classy." Cullen took a sip.

"I'd give you a Stella but you're on duty."

"I'm off duty."

"Whatever, here's cheers." Derek took a big drink.

Cullen followed suit — the ice cold drink took another layer off the hangover.

Derek put his glass down and switched off the TV. "You going to report that wee skirmish?"

"I might."

"Been a couple of days now. That not a bit suspicious?"

"I've been busy."

"You look like shite."

"Had a bit too much to drink last night."

Derek laughed. "Drinking isn't the answer."

Cullen took a drink of Irn Bru. "Okay, tell me about Alison Carnegie?"

Derek frowned. "Alison? What's she been saying?"

"That you met up with her to discuss Keith's death."

"Aye." Derek's eyes shifted about. "I'm not a poofter or anything but I thought it would help to talk about... Keith."

"I'm not saying you are. How have you found it?"

"Not bad." Derek avoided Cullen's eyes. "Talking with you was kind of useful but speaking to that lassie was good. She's pretty messed up by what happened."

"You should have told me."

"Why?"

"Because."

"She told me you porked her once." Derek grinned. "Couldn't get out of her if it touched both sides at the same time, but I guess she must've been pissed."

"Very good." Cullen took a sip. "I know about the gang."

"What gang?"

"You were spotted in a quarry in West Lothian last Monday night. There was a big fight."

Derek took another big gulp of Irn Bru. "So? I wasn't there."

"Did you really get mugged?"

"Got into a fight. Didn't want you to go running to your mates."

"Lying about it is much more likely to make me dig into it, Derek. What happened?"

"Just a wee pagger on Leith Walk."

"Like Saturday?"

"Kind of. I punched some boy, he socked us one back, so I booted the shite out of him. All good fun."

"When was this?"

"Last Monday night."

"Not in West Lothian on Tuesday?"

"I swear I wasn't there, Scotty."

"Two people died in that quarry."

"Aye. So I heard." Derek drummed his fingers against the glass. "Saw it in the paper."

"Really?"

"I know people, Scotty. A lot of people are a bit worried about it. I wasn't there."

"I don't believe you. If you know anything, you should really tell me. Who are these people, Derek?"

"I'm not telling you that."

The flat door opened. Footsteps came through the hall into the kitchen. "All right, Derek?"

"All right, Dean. This is my pal, Scotty."

Cullen looked round. It was the ned who stole Rich's phone.

33

C ullen got to his feet. "See you, Derek."

Dean narrowed his eyes at him. "Do I know you, pal?"

"Don't think so." Cullen left the flat, hurrying down the stairs, mobile clamped to his ear.

"Sundance." Buxton yawned. "What do you want?"

"You still in the station?"

"Aye."

"Can you get over to Easter Road. Number twelve."

"What have you done now?"

"Got a suspect. Bring as many uniform as you can find."

"Like how many? Ten?"

"Two will do."

"Be there in five."

Cullen pocketed his phone. He checked there wasn't a back entrance. It was locked. He walked over to the front door and leaned against it, heart thumping.

Dean. That little shit. Getting the bastard might make something good happen today.

A squad car pulled up on the double yellow line.

Cullen jogged towards them. He heard the door slam behind him and footsteps race off. Spinning round, he saw Dean running down Easter Road towards Leith.

"Shite."

Cullen set off after him, hearing the others behind him take off.

Dean ran across the street, almost being hit by a car.

Cullen followed him, watching as he bolted down a side street by a Polish shop, quickly losing sight of him.

At the end, the street forked. Cullen looked around.

Dean had gone left.

Cullen crossed the road, running past a pub before turning left again, doubling back towards the Hibs stadium.

Dean crossed the footbridge over the railway line.

Buxton and one of the uniforms crossed the bridge from the other side.

Dean stopped in the middle. "I'll jump!"

"Go ahead." Buxton held out his baton. "I doubt there'll be a train there for another fifty years."

Cullen started sneaking up behind him.

"This is police brutality, man!"

Cullen stepped forward and grabbed hold of Dean, pulled his right arm up behind his back. He put a choke hold on. "I'm arresting you on suspicion of mobile phone theft."

"This is a joke." Cullen stood in Leith Walk station, watching Dean Richardson make his phone call in the secure room.

Buxton nodded. "Tell me about it."

"That bloody Cadder's arsed everything up. Used to be able to just bung them in a room and interview them, now it's worse than your system."

"I might be English but I'm not responsible for the English judicial system. Is the Scottish one your fault?"

"I suppose not." Cullen laughed. "This is such a pain in the arse. Having to watch the suspect making the call but not listen to what they say."

"You still haven't told me what he's done."

"Nicked my mate's phone."

"Taking the law into your own hands."

Cullen grinned. "If I was doing that, I'd not have called."

"That's some progress, I suppose."

"Don't you start."

Richardson hung up the call and sauntered over to Cullen. "Lawyer's on his way."

Cullen tugged him by the arm and led him back to the cells.

"WHAT CHARGES ARE you levelling at my client?" Alistair Reynolds looked barely out of high school, let alone a qualified lawyer. His face was covered in acne, but he carried himself with an assured manner.

"Mobile phone theft." Cullen sat opposite him in the interview room. "I'd like to get Mr Richardson on tape. We've gone to the hassle of getting you in, so I'd appreciate if you'd get him to speak."

"My client's not in a fit state to communicate."

"Bollocks."

"He's been subject to police brutality."

"He was evading arrest. He was out of that flat as soon as the squad car arrived. Didn't even have the lights on." Cullen spun the file he had over and pointed at the charge sheet. "This is the crime he committed. We've already retrieved the mobile phone from his bedroom. I just need to get a statement from him and I'd appreciate it if we could have it documented on tape."

"Fine, fine."

"Good. I'll get him in." Cullen got to his feet and wrapped on the door. "We're ready."

Cullen's least favourite PCSO showed Dean Richardson in before standing at the back of the room.

Cullen waited until he was settling before leaning over and starting the interview. "Mr Richardson, can you please confirm your whereabouts on Friday night?"

"No comment."

Cullen looked at the lawyer. "Mr Reynolds, can I inform you and your client that silence doesn't imply innocence, especially when the phone in question was discovered in his possession?"

Richardson slouched back in the chair, a smug grin on his face. "I know my rights and I'm saying nothing."

"I was there when you stole the phone."

"Mr Cullen, while my client's been accused of a crime, he will not partake in further discussion on this subject with yourself or any other officer."

"Fine. I've charged him and he's in court tomorrow morning." Cullen picked up Richardson's report. "Not a first time offender, either. Judges are going pretty heavy on mobile theft just now. Just wondered if you fancied clarifying your statement. Maybe save the taxpayer some time and money?"

"I'm saying nothing."

Cullen ended the interview and got to his feet. He nodded for the PCSO to take Richardson back down to the custody suite before leaving the room himself.

Buxton followed. "I see what you mean. It's getting like London."

"Tell me about it. No comment this, no comment that. Fed up with it. I saw him steal the phone, it was in his bedroom. He's going down for this."

"Thought you'd foxtrot oscared for the evening?"

"I had. Then I found that little scumbag. I've just given myself a shitload more paperwork to do."

Buxton grinned. "Methven will love that when he hears about it."

CULLEN GOT home at quarter to ten, totally broken. He barrelled into the kitchen and dumped his twelve inch pizza on the counter.

Rich was cooking an omelette. "That stinks."

Cullen opened the lid. "Jalapeños, spicy mince, onion and extra mozzarella."

"That'll really settle your stomach." Rich swirled the egg round in the pan. "Captain Swordsman."

Cullen laughed. "You can talk." He picked up a slice. "Last time I saw you, you were trying to shag Renton out of Trainspotting."

Rich flipped the omelette over and threw cheese, peppers and mushrooms on the top. "Let's call it a score draw." He folded the omelette in half.

"I've got your phone."

"What?"

"Your S3. Managed to retrieve it."

Rich rolled his eyes. "I've just ordered an iPhone 5."

Cullen laughed. "Thought the S3 was a much better phone?"

Rich took the omelette off the heat and slid it on a plate. "Yeah, well, the Samsung was getting on my tits. It's just too big."

"Never thought I'd hear you say those words."

"Whatever." Rich got cutlery out of the drawer then led Cullen through to the dining table in the hall, pizza box in hand. "So, what happened?"

"Funny story. You know the brother of the guy I worked with that died? Well, his flatmate stole it. Guy called Dean Richardson."

"Good work." Rich took a mouthful of egg.

"It's a coincidence, that's all. Stroke of luck. Besides, you can cancel the iPhone."

Rich chewed another mouthful. "Do I need to report it?"

"Aye. I've got a crime on the system but if you could pop into a station tomorrow, I'd appreciate it." Cullen took another bite, feeling the chilli heat build up. "You know you said someone at your paper's doing a book on the Schoolbook Killer?"

Rich raised his eyebrows. "Aye?"

"Is his name Frank?"

"It might be."

"Well, could you get him to stop stalking Alison Carnegie?"

"The Survivor?"

"Is that what you're calling her?"

"I'll see what I can do." Rich nodded. "It's interesting you've been speaking to her, though. How's she doing?"

"She looks like shit."

"So does every bird you shag."

Cullen laughed. "I'll take that as a compliment."

"Seriously, though, how is she?"

"She's back at work, though she's clearly haunted by what happened."

"How do you cope?"

"Who says I do? I'm a total mess behind this suave exterior."

"Be serious."

"I don't know. Seeing a counsellor has helped. Other than that, alcohol abuse and a voracious sexual appetite."

"That's not exactly healthy."

Cullen put down the crust of the seventh wedge. "Think Tom will want that?"

"Bound to. Just leave it in the kitchen, it'll soon disappear."

"Where is he?"

"No idea, he's been in late the last few weeks. You've not really noticed, have you?"

"What, cos I've been at Sharon's? Thanks for reminding me." Cullen got to his feet and stretched, his gut aching. "Time for bed."

DAY 8

Wednesday
10th October 2012

34

"You look happy for once." Buxton pushed open the door to the canteen.

"Proper night's sleep, no drinking." Cullen joined the back of the queue.

"Nothing to do with getting the lightest of all actions at the briefing?"

Cullen shrugged. "Write up the CCTV searches. Pure tedium."

He noticed DC Chantal Jain was in front of them in the queue. She turned around and glared.

Cullen held up his hands. "What?"

Jain folded her arms. "What do you think? You're acting like a total fud, Scott. Sharon's torn to pieces by what you've done."

The red mist began to descend and Cullen fought hard to keep himself under control. "I'm sorry to hear that, but it's her doing."

"Are you honestly trying to tell me you've never told a lie?"

"Of course I've told lies, but not really any big ones."

"Not really?"

"Okay, not at all. I'm not overreacting. Why does nobody think how badly it's upsetting me?"

"This you finding a new bird, Sundance?" Bain slapped him on the back.

Cullen turned to look at him. "Very funny."

Wilkinson appeared alongside Bain. "You missed the briefing."

"Did I?" Cullen shrugged. "What did I miss?"

Wilkinson winced. "We just got a bollocking off Turnbull. The case review unit are in and they're looking at the paperwork for the Schoolbook case, like."

Cullen frowned as they stepped forward in the queue. "Seriously? Thought that was all sorted?"

"Aye. I need words with you and Batgirl about who fucked up over those death threats."

"LANGUAGE!" Barbara glowered from behind her counter.

Bain looked over, like a scolded schoolboy. "Sorry."

She held out a finger. "Any more of that and you'll be barred."

Bain held up his hands up. "Sorry."

Barbara went back to serving Jain.

Bain muttered under his breath.

Cullen cleared his throat. "What were you saying apart from the F-words?"

"I was saying we'd have caught the killer earlier if it wasn't for you and Caldwell mucking about with the death threats."

"If it wasn't for me, you would have convicted the wrong man."

Bain scowled. "Fuck this shite." He left them to it.

Barbara shook her head at the retreating figure.

Cullen turned back to see Jain collecting her scrambled eggs and toast. He paid for his usual coffee and BLT, watching her head off towards Sharon and Angela. He'd seen the pair of them together a lot.

Wilkinson spoke in Cullen's ear. "Can't believe you broke up with her, Curran. Wouldn't mind getting up it myself."

Cullen collected his breakfast from the server them. "I'll see you around."

"Not so fast, Curran, I've got a bloody bone to pick with you."

"What?"

"Find a table. I'll be over in a minute."

"I'll see you downstairs, Simon."

Buxton nodded. "Laters."

Cullen wandered over to bollocking corner, which had just been vacated. He sat and tucked into his roll, bacon fat dribbling down his chin. What was Wilkinson after? Another trip to Schoolbook?

"Champion." Wilkinson sat down, a doubled-up fry-up on his plate. He sprayed it with tomato ketchup before piling his fork with a black pudding slice heaped with beans.

Cullen took a drink of coffee. "What is it you wanted?"

"I saw the charge sheet. Why do you have Dean Richardson in?"

Cullen put his roll down. "He stole my flatmate's mobile. I caught him at a friend's flat. Pure fluke."

"Well, he's been under surveillance for bloody weeks. We had two lads on him for hooliganism."

"Are you serious?"

"Of course I'm bloody serious. He was supposed to be at this quarry fight."

"With Derek Miller?"

Wilkinson frowned. "Aye. Why do you ask?"

"It was his flatmate."

"You're having me on." Wilkinson dropped his cutlery to the plate.

"I'm not. Has it arsed up your case?"

"Hopefully not. You've managed to get him on a charge, which is more than we bloody did. Might be able to get something out of him now we've got some leverage."

"What about Derek Miller?"

"Let's you and me have a word with him. I've got some uniform bringing him in."

DEREK MILLER LOOKED unrecognisable in his business suit, having been picked up from his work in the sprawling Standard Life office at the bottom of Dundas Street.

Wilkinson leaned back in his chair and burped into his hand. He nodded for Cullen to lead.

Cullen started the interview. "Mr Miller, can you please confirm how you know Dean Richardson?"

"He's my flatmate."

"You just moved into that flat and there he was?"

Derek smiled. "Hardly. He's a mate of my pal, Jambo."

"I take it Jambo supports Hearts?"

"Aye. Only boy in my class at school that did."

"What can you tell us about Mr Richardson?"

"Nothing."

"Derek, I don't think you realise the magnitude of this situation."

"Don't I?"

Wilkinson leaned across the table. "We're investigating a football hooligan fight out in West Lothian. Two young men were killed. Our intelligence suggests you were there."

"That's bollocks. I was at my flat."

Derek's lawyer narrowed her eyes. "Could I receive a copy of this intelligence?"

Wilkinson nodded. "I'll make it available."

The lawyer grimaced. "That would be appreciated."

Cullen folded his arms. "Was Mr Richardson out there?"

"Have you not got any intelligence on that?" Derek grinned.

"Okay, we know he was." Cullen held Derek's gaze for a few seconds. "Was Mr Richardson involved?"

"How do you mean involved? You're saying he was there, so you tell me."

"Derek, we want to know if he was instrumental in arranging the fight."

"What makes you say that?"

"Intelligence. Was he?"

The lawyer leaned over and whispered in Derek's ear. Derek sniffed. "Aye, he was. He's one of the ringleaders."

Cullen exchanged a look with Wilkinson, grinning from ear to ear. "Where's Mr Richardson from?"

"From out West Lothian way."

"Where?"

"Think the place is called Ravencraig. Never heard of it till I met the punter, likes."

"Where does he work?"

Derek smiled. "He doesn't. Says he's between jobs but he's always been like that. He never struggles to pay the rent."

Cullen scribbled it down. "How did he arrange the fight?"

"I don't know the specifics. Dean's in some Rangers firm out that way, like I'm involved with the Hibs casuals, as I suppose your intelligence will tell you."

"Did you say Rangers?"

"Aye."

"You weren't involved in arranging this?"

"Hardly." Derek laughed. "I'm a low-level boy in our gang. So low I wasn't even invited." He wagged a finger in the air. "No names from me about how I got involved in this, mind. I wasn't there. I just know things."

Cullen noted it. "I'll accept that for now if you give us some more information on Dean or this Rangers group he's involved in."

"I know there were some jambos and some huns. It was Hibs on our side, plus some Celtic boys but mostly us." Derek took a deep breath. "Heard some stuff from Dean, some nonsense about the boss of their firm raging about something. One of the boys in the gang being bent."

"Is that bent as in corrupt or as in homosexual?"

"Poofter." Derek smiled.

"And you definitely weren't there? Last chance to change your mind."

"Just prove I was."

Wilkinson got to his feet. "Off you go."

"I'm free to go?"

"Aye. You're walking yourself back to Standard Life, mind."

"Happy days."

"The PCSO will show you out." Wilkinson left the room and set off down the corridor. "He's up to his nuts in this. There's no way he wasn't there."

"He had a shiner when I saw him at the weekend." Cullen pointed to his eye. "Tried to sell me a story about getting into a fight with some guy on Leith Walk."

"So he's bloody lying, right?"

"Much as I hate to say it, I think so. It pisses me off. I thought he'd turned the corner but clearly not."

Wilkinson held open the door to the stairwell. "I'll ask around on my side. If we can place him at that bloody quarry last week then we've got ourselves something." He stroked his chin. "You used to be based out there, right?"

"West Lothian, aye."

"Can you go and do some digging?"

"If you clear it with Cargill."

"Don't bloody worry about that, Curran, I'm ordering you out there."

Cullen stared at the table, knowing he had no real choice but to tell Methven and then just get on with it.

35

"I must thank you, Mr Cullen. I got off with a caution." Skinner's voice was almost lost to the din in the background.

Cullen put the phone to his other ear. "Where are you?"

"I'm just making coffee."

"Can you turn the kettle off?"

"Done." Skinner was clearer now. "I was saying I got off with a caution."

"Well, let's just say you still owe me one. That lead you gave went nowhere."

"It's always good to be in debt to a police officer."

"Isn't it the other way round?"

Skinner grinned. "Not with you. You'll want that debt repaid. I can be useful, then."

"Next time, I probably won't help. There are limits to what I can let pass."

"Point noted, Mr Cullen. How can I help?"

"Dean Richardson. You know him?"

"I do."

"Spill."

"He's from Ravencraig. Given you're calling me, I suspect you already know that."

"Very insightful."

"He's got himself into bother a few times."

Cullen leaned forward on the seat. "Barry, I need some concrete stuff. How do you know him?"

"He was in the same year at school as my wee sister."

"I didn't know you had a sister."

"She lives in Glasgow now."

"Does she know about your specialist interests?"

"I tell you, they're all gagging for it. I had to stop a woman in the Co-op from putting her hands down my pants yesterday."

"This wouldn't be a security guard and you wouldn't have been stealing something?"

"God's honest truth."

"So, your sister and Dean Richardson."

"They were in the same class. He was always in trouble at school. Fighting, bullying, you name it. He was good at football. Played left back for the school team. I heard he had a trial at Rangers. Would have been 2003 or 2004, maybe?"

Cullen frowned as he wrote it down. That would make Richardson only twenty-three or twenty-four. He looked a lot older. "What age is he?"

"Twenty-three."

Cullen raised an eyebrow. "No way."

"Paper round in Basra. Anyway, this trial with Rangers wasn't a success. From what I gather, he took it personally and just sort of fell apart."

Something twigged at the back of Cullen's mind. Keith Miller once told him Derek had trials with Hibs and Rangers in his youth. Was there a connection there? It felt like too big a coincidence to rule out. "Okay, what else can you tell me?"

"Nothing much, I'm afraid. He's a member of the Ravencraig Rangers Supporters' Club. Used to go to all the home matches and most of the away ones."

"How did he afford it?"

"Don't ask, don't tell."

"Thanks. I'll let you know if that's you off the hook."

"Goodbye, Mr Cu—"

Cullen pocketed his phone as he looked across the Incident Room. Wilkinson was just finishing a call. He got up and slapped him on the back. "Got something."

Wilkinson looked up with a scowl. "What is it?"

"Bit of a long shot but I think Dean Richardson might have had a trial with Derek Miller back in the day."

"That it? We've already connected them. They shared a flat."

"The trial was with Rangers. That might be behind this fight in the quarry."

Wilkinson checked his watch. "Richardson's just come back from court about your mobile phone. Let's see what else he's got to say about this."

∾

"Mr Richardson, we know you were there. So, please can you confirm it for the record?" Wilkinson sat back and folded his arms.

Richardson grinned. "Where exactly are we talking about?"

"Ginty's Quarry near Livingston. Hearts and Rangers fans fought Hibs and Celtic fans. We have witness statements placing you there."

"Fine, if you've got witness statements then surely you don't need me to confirm anything?"

"Mr Reynolds, need I remind you of the serious charges your client is facing."

Richardson leaned over and pointed a finger at Wilkinson. "I've just been up to court. The sheriff said the trial will be in the next six weeks. I don't think stealing a phone from your pal's boyfriend is a serious crime."

"I never said it was. Being involved in a fight that resulted in two deaths would be."

"Eh?"

"We're very short on suspects just now and you certainly fit the bill." Wilkinson got out a sheet of paper and traced down it with his finger. "Your police record shows a history of violence. I'd imagine we don't have to dig too deep to link you to this."

Reynolds swallowed.

"Now, I'll ask you again." Wilkinson smiled. "Were you at Ginty's Quarry last week?"

Richardson looked at his solicitor then rubbed his cheek. "I was."

"Now we're getting somewhere. You know two people were killed there, cos I just told you. Do you know anything about their deaths?"

"What were they called?"

Wilkinson turned to another sheet of paper, showing autopsy photographs of both — skinny boys in their early twenties, skin now white. "Liam Crossan, Gordon Beveridge." He glared at Richardson. "Celtic and Hibs."

"I know Gogs Beveridge."

Wilkinson frowned. "How?"

"Through these sorts of things."

"Are you admitting to being a hooligan?"

"I don't think I've much choice. You've got witnesses. Might as well be honest, hopefully you'll go easy on me." Richardson winked.

"You'll face the full force of the law."

"I will, will I?" Richardson sneered and looked round at Reynolds. "Hear that, Ally? Says I'll face the full force of the law."

Wilkinson screwed up his eyes. "What's bloody going on here?"

"If you're prepared to listen to what my client has to offer, perhaps some sort of deal may be reached."

Cullen folded his arms. "Not for the phone."

Reynolds shrugged. "Fine, not for the phone but certainly for anything relating to hooliganism."

"I'll have to have a word with the PF." Wilkinson sniffed. "What I can do is promise I'll look into it once we hear your side."

"What I've got to offer is the murder weapon."

"Have you really?" Wilkinson narrowed his eyes. "We need the murderer."

Richardson shrugged. "Wish I knew who killed those two. I just saw a knife on the ground, covered in blood and picked it up. It's in a plastic bag."

"You're in the habit of just picking knives up?"

"I nicked your boyfriend's mobile, didn't I? Besides, you never know when you might need something useful like that."

Cullen leaned over to Wilkinson. "Can I have a word?"

They got up and went into the corridor.

Wilkinson slammed the door shut. "What is it, Curran?"

"Think he's on the level?"

"Only one way to find out." Wilkinson got out his mobile. "Give me a minute." He turned around as the phone rang. "Hiya, Kate, it's Paul Wilkinson. You good for a chat just now about Operation Housebrick? It'll literally be just five minutes."

Wilkinson slowly walked down the corridor, Cullen unable to make out much of what was being discussed.

He leaned back against the wall and tried to focus on the case. His natural instinct with Richardson was not to trust him. He felt he was offering the information up far too easily. Then again, his police record was longer than most Cullen had ever seen, so maybe he just knew how to play the system.

Wilkinson reappeared, grinning. "That was the PF. She's buying it."

"So we've got a deal with Richardson?"

"That we do, lad, that we do."

36

Richardson struggled with the handcuffs as he unlocked the door to his flat. "Just in here."

Wilkinson gestured for the two uniformed officers to wait outside. "Come on, Curran, let's get this over with."

Richardson led them into a bedroom decorated in mid grey paint. The walls were covered with Rangers posters and memorabilia. He nodded at a tall, old chest of drawers beside the bed. He held up his hands. "Going to be a bugger with these on."

"I'll do it." Cullen put gloves on before kneeling down and opening the bottom drawer. He rummaged around through pairs of Calvin Klein pants. "It's just your pants. I take it you've got receipts for these Calvin Kleins?"

"They're knock-offs from the Ravencraig Sunday market."

Cullen stopped sorting through the drawer's contents. "Where's the knife?"

"Underneath."

"Eh?"

"Take the drawer out. Unless you actually want to fumble about with my grundies."

"You need to change your detergent, I can still see the skid marks on these."

Richardson grinned. "They're not washed yet."

Wilkinson laughed.

Cullen screwed his face up. "Jesus Christ." He yanked the drawer out, shoving it on the floor. He leaned inside and fished out a Tesco carrier bag. "This it?"

"You're on the money."

Cullen opened the bag and peered inside.

The serrated blade was covered in dried blood and what looked like chunks of flesh.

"WHAT'S THIS?" Anderson peered inside the bag.

"A knife." Wilkinson playfully slapped him on the shoulder. "Get it looked at quick smart, will you?"

"You do know we're up against it, don't you?"

"Like I care." Wilkinson shrugged. "Can you get a couple of your SOCO bodies round to Richardson's flat for further investigation?"

"Fine." Anderson shook his head before walking off. "I'll get the prints started now."

"How long will that be?"

Anderson rolled his eyes. "If I drop everything, I can get the prints back to you after lunchtime."

"Perfect." Wilkinson led them back into the central stairwell. "Come on, Curran. Let's get some lunch. I'm starving."

They walked up in silence, Cullen trying to stitch things together in his mind. Nothing seemed to quite knit.

The canteen was dead so they managed to walk straight up to the servery, steam wafting up from the soup bowl.

Cullen nodded at Barbara. "I'll have some soup, thanks."

She started ladling it out. "And for you?"

Wilkinson smiled. "Burger and chips please, Babs."

Cullen paid for his soup and went over to a table by the window. He tore off some bread and dunked it in the soup. It was disgusting.

"Has someone shat in it, lad?" Wilkinson sat down and started squeezing tomato ketchup all over the plate.

"It's burnt soup and it tastes of black pepper." Cullen dropped the bread on the plate with a thud. "And the bread's stale."

"Complain."

Cullen looked over. Still no queue. "I just might." He took his tray back over. "Can I get something else?"

Barbara frowned. "What's the matter?"

"Taste it."

"I made it."

"Did you taste it?"

"I was in a bit of a hurry." She took a sip of the soup. "Right, what else can I get you?"

"The usual."

She turned around and waved her arms. "The soup's off. Ray, can you make some lentil?" She threw his roll together and handed the bag over. "No charge."

"Thanks." Cullen walked back to Wilkinson, who now had tomato ketchup smeared over his chin.

"You're doing a bloody good job, Curran."

"Thanks."

"I'll put in a good word for you with Cargill. I know you've been locking horns with that Crystal Methven."

Cullen paused from taking a bite. "Who told you that?"

"He did, himself. Says you were absolutely hammered the other morning."

"He's right." Cullen took a bite and chewed. "You know I'm going through some personal stuff. I'm just not finding it easy."

"Tell me about it."

Cullen glanced at Wilkinson's left hand — there wasn't a wedding ring there and he couldn't remember ever seeing one before. "Have you gone through this yourself?"

Wilkinson chuckled. "Never got involved. One of my first sergeants in West Yorkshire was going through a bloody messy divorce when I was just starting out. Taught me a solid lesson. Cops and happy marriages don't go together, lad."

"Unless it's with another cop. Then it's a double nightmare."

"As I think you're finding out now, it'll always end up in disaster. Never shit where you eat." Wilkinson took another big bite of his burger, swallowing it quickly. "I haven't had many dealings with you over the last two years. I thought you were another useless git like that Irvine boy."

"Thought you got on with him?"

"Public appearances, lad. Can't stand him. Never seen him do a day's work in the three years I've been here." Wilkinson picked up a couple of chips and practically inhaled them. "I'm permanently off Turnbull's payroll now." He finished the burger in one final mouthful. "I've had a pretty bloody dark period here in the last few years. Turnbull doesn't rate the likes of me and Bain. Never gave us a bloody chance."

"Why was that?"

"I've been to hell and back over this bloody Schoolbook nonsense. I had one lapse and I'm bloody hearing about it forever." Wilkinson picked his teeth. "Those bloody Complaints lads will be sniffing around soon enough, you mark my words. That meeting me and Bain had with the Case Review Unit is the starter for that."

Cullen recalled the email from the Complaints in his Inbox. He felt a cold sweat — had he replied to it? "What do you think will happen?"

Wilkinson shrugged his shoulders. "Who knows? It won't be good for you, me or Bain. Bet your bottom dollar Turnbull will come out of it as if he'd caught the killer himself. We all bloody know it was DI Bain."

"It was me."

"What?"

"I caught him."

"Did you? I didn't know that." Wilkinson took a big drink from his Diet Coke, the dark liquid fizzing up. "Either way, I'm glad to be out of there. That twat Methven will get my job, you mark my words. Can only be a matter of time before Bain's out on his ear too."

∻

"AND HERE HE IS, Bain's Sundance Kid, trying to bend the laws of physics just like his master." Anderson folded his arms. "It's always the same with CID. Auditing our work, never enough to do yourselves."

Cullen grinned. "Okay, well tell us fat, lazy coppers how your genius-level intellect is getting on solving this for us, then."

"Solving it quickly as it happens." Anderson rubbed his goatee before tapping on a machine beside him. "I've got the blood type matches underway from the blood and flesh on the blade. Luckily for you, we've got the technique down to an hour these days. Not much longer now."

"What about prints?"

"I'm looking at the prints analysis on the handle as well. I've got three sets, though one is only a partial so it's going to take time to match." Anderson tapped his monitor. "The other two are running just now."

"What can I do to speed this up?"

"Stopping asking me stupid questions and slowing me down." Anderson put some goggles on and started messing about with test tubes. "Not brought a grown-up with you?"

"Just me. Wilkinson's got some other stuff to look into."

"Small mercies, I suppose."

Cullen looked around at the hulking machinery. "That's some pretty fancy technology you've got here."

"All part of the new station build. We're supposed to be a centre of excellence but I can see that all getting taken away next summer and punted through to Glasgow when Police Scotland hits the fan." The computer nearest Anderson beeped. He frowned at it. "Looks like you're in luck. Time to see some magic happening. Or at the very least, some proper work."

The screen filled with garbled information and some zoomed in photos of blood cells.

Cullen scowled. "Is that it?"

"It's all about the interpretation, Cullen."

"So interpret for me."

"Looks like your Crossan boy got slotted last." Anderson's hand traced out an area of the screen. "Got a definite blood type match on this knife with Crossan and Beveridge." He frowned. "Oh, this is a doozer."

"What is?"

Anderson beamed. "You've got a third stabbing here. Got some DNA traces on it, too, from the serrations on the knife edge."

"You're loving this, aren't you?"

"Do you need subtitles for the hard of understanding?"

"It'd help."

"There are three distinct fingerprints and three distinct DNA traces." Anderson sighed. "The DNA will be a while. The fingerprint matches are mostly complete now."

"Mostly?"

"Aye. Gordon Beveridge for definite. There's a partial, which is going to be a while."

"You said three, right?" Cullen frowned. "Are Richardson's prints on the knife?"

Anderson grinned. "The third set of prints belongs to one Alexander Aitken."

37

"Say that again." Wilkinson shut the door behind him.

Anderson rolled his eyes. "I said the third set of prints is definitely Alexander Aitken."

Cullen scowled — that didn't make any sense. "But we found Aitken in a Range Rover at the bottom of a bing."

"That's not my problem." Anderson shrugged. "The boy's prints are on record and he definitely used that knife."

"You said the other print is a partial, right?" Wilkinson folded his arms and leaned against the door. "How long till you resolve that?"

"A good few hours. It's a much harder search. More to eliminate. Actually requires thought and analysis, rather than point and click."

Wilkinson nodded slowly. "And the other print is Gordon Beveridge?"

"That's right."

"So, it looks like Aitken's bloody stabbed someone. As well as the fingerprints, you've got three blood matches, right?"

Anderson nodded. "Aye."

"Can you check them against Liam Crossan and Gordon Beveridge?"

"Doing that anyway."

"Who the bloody hell is the third one?"

"Is that rhetorical?" Anderson grinned.

"Of course it bloody is."

Cullen held up his hand. "Can you give me a minute to think this through?"

Wilkinson scowled. "You had at least two while I ran down the bloody stairs."

"Let me get this straight. Your case has two victims from the quarry — Liam Crossan and Gordon Beveridge. Correct?"

"Correct."

"Anderson has found two fingerprint matches — Gordon Beveridge and Xander Aitken. Right?"

"Go on."

"We've also just discovered that Crossan was killed last."

Anderson raised a finger. "Not necessarily killed but attacked with this knife, the last of the three."

"Okay." Cullen scratched the stubble on his neck. He nodded at Anderson. "Have you got a timeline for the use of the weapon?"

"Just about, aye. Gordon Beveridge's prints are the oldest, meaning he was first to use the weapon."

"Aye."

"And most likely to have brought the knife, right?"

"Right."

"Who did he use it on?"

"Don't know the first victim."

Cullen sighed. "Who used it next? Aitken or the partial?"

"Aitken."

"And the second victim?"

"Looks like Beveridge's DNA is the second and Crossan's is the third."

"So, Aitken must have killed Beveridge. Why?"

Anderson shrugged. "Not my department."

Wilkinson frowned. "Repeat for me, Curran. Slowly."

"We've got Gordon Beveridge stabbing someone unknown. Next, it looks like Aitken stabs Beveridge. Then our partial killed Liam Crossan."

"With you now."

"Good." Cullen stroked his chin. "Why was Aitken even there?"

Wilkinson shrugged. "No idea."

Cullen put it together. He clicked his finger and pointed at Wilkinson. "We've now got evidence proving Aitken was there. Could Souness have been as well?"

"Hang on, lad." Wilkinson held up his hands. "What are you saying?"

"You've got two known victims plus a third unknown one. Souness died of stab wounds."

"This is my case, Curran."

Cullen folded his arms. "It could be the same one."

"No chance." Wilkinson wagged a finger. "I'm not letting this slip."

Cullen looked over at Anderson. "Can you run a DNA match against Kenny Souness?"

Wilkinson screwed his face up. "He died in his flat, Curran."

"He might have died there, but he could have been stabbed at the quarry."

Wilkinson crumpled back against the door, rubbing his eyes. "How bloody long is a DNA check going to take?"

"Depends on the server load. It can be bloody temperamental." Anderson clicked and tapped his keyboard, filling in forms and selecting values from a couple of pop-up lists. "All the DNA's in the system now. I've had a bloody week to prep all this stuff while you lot have done a circle jerk."

Wilkinson shook his head. "Do it."

Anderson clicked the mouse. The progress bar jolted to the right.

Wilkinson leaned against the desk. "This is quick."

"It just does that to start with." Anderson made a circular motion with the mouse pointer, circling round the progress bar. "I've asked them to try and even the time out. After a while, you just get used to it."

"How long's this going to take?"

"Not much longer."

The bar leapt ten per cent.

"Should I go and get a coffee?" Wilkinson narrowed his eyes.

"Soya latte, cheers." Anderson sat down at the desk.

Wilkinson sniffed before leaving the room.

Anderson looked around at Cullen. "You going to just loiter there? Not sure Wilko can manage to get three coffees all on his own."

"I've seen monkeys do amazing things at the zoo."

Anderson grinned as the progress bar jumped to just over halfway. "Is there some political angle I'm not getting here?"

Cullen nodded. "He thinks Cargill's trying to take over his case?"

"Makes a difference from Bain being his enemy, I suppose." Anderson stroked his beard. "Is there any truth in it?"

"Of course there is. They're all playing games."

The door burst open and Wilkinson entered, carrying a tray with three coffees. "You like a chai latte, don't you, Curran?"

"Are you kidding me?"

"Of course. Black Americano."

"Cheers, Paul." Anderson took a sip through the lid. The machine beeped as the bar reached full. "Here we go."

Wilkinson leaned forward. "Have you got something?"

"There's a positive DNA match." Anderson tapped the screen. "The same knife was used to kill Crossan, Beveridge and Souness."

Cullen turned to Wilkinson. "We're working the same case."

"CLEAR OUT." Wilkinson marched into the meeting room occupied by some of his DCs. "Go on."

They left.

Cullen sat at the opposite end of the oval table from Wilkinson. Methven, Cargill, Bain and Sharon spread themselves around it.

"Thanks for joining us at such short notice." Wilkinson took a sip of coffee. "Curran, can you take us through this?"

"Sure." Cullen cleared his throat. "Right. We've completed the DNA analysis and most of the fingerprints."

Sharon folded her arms. "Most of?"

"There's a partial." Cullen licked his lips. "Anderson's going to take some time confirming that."

"Okay."

"It looks like Souness was killed using the same knife as DI Wilkinson's victims."

"Jesus Christ." Cargill pinched her nose. "How?"

"There's more, ma'am. Aitken's prints were all over it, too."

"So we're working the same case, then?"

Wilkinson nodded. "It'd appear so, aye."

Sharon frowned. "DI Wilkinson, when I spoke to you about this last Thursday, you told us there was no link between what happened in the quarry and the stabbings."

"That's true. Neither Kenneth Souness nor Alexander Aitken had any overt links with football hooligan groups."

"Let me get this straight." Cargill folded her arms. "The knife was used for three murders, namely Liam Crossan, Gordon Beveridge and Kenny Souness?"

"Correct."

"And there are two distinct prints on the handle of the knife, namely Gordon Beveridge and Alexander Aitken?"

"Plus a partial which doesn't match the patterns of the other two."

"Okay." Cargill bit her lip. "The initial priority is to establish a clear chain of command. We can't go on running these as two cases."

"I own this." Wilkinson took a sip of coffee.

Cargill leaned back in her chair. "I think we need to formally discuss this with DCI Turnbull and whoever you report to. I'm conscious of the fact that it won't be a quick activity. That said, we absolutely need clear guidance on the ground now."

"The initial priority is to determine whose prints are on that knife." Wilkinson glared at her. "That's going to take some bloody time. I don't think you and I arguing about who owns this bloody case is getting us anywhere."

"Agreed." Cargill smiled, revealing yellow teeth. "However, the only officer you've brought to the table is one of mine, namely DC Cullen. While the gears of bureaucracy grind away, let's agree amongst ourselves that you'll join my management team and we'll merge this into a single case. Okay?"

Cullen expected to hear further argument — I'm not working for a bloody DI.

Wilkinson ground his teeth. "Fine."

Cargill's thin tongue licked her top lip. "Good. Now that's settled, let's focus on realigning priorities across the piece. Effectively, we have some disjointed strands we need to tie together."

Cullen glanced at Sharon. What on earth had she seen in Cargill?

Cargill looked at Cullen — he looked away long enough for her to shift her gaze. "For instance, what happened to Alexander Aitken between his fingerprints getting onto the knife and him being found by the shale bing?"

She looked over at Sharon. "What happened to Kenny Souness between being stabbed and DS McNeill and DC Cullen finding him last Wednesday night? Whose is the third fingerprint on the knife?"

She paused. "We need to tie the chain of events at Ginty's Quarry together — who killed Beveridge and Crossan and why? I want us to mobilise with five strands to the investigation." She pointed at Holdsworth. "Paul, can you get DS Holdsworth to merge the cases on HOLMES?"

Wilkinson winced. "That's not easy. It'll need two full-time officers for two whole days to do that."

"It needs to be done today, I'll give you three."

"That's not how it works."

"I don't care. We need to pool resources on this and we need it centralised and done by the book. I'm sure you'll appreciate I'm not trying to pull a fast one here and instil some cowboy alternative process."

"Fine." Wilkinson furiously scribbled notes on his A4 pad.

Cargill nodded. "Now, in terms of the investigation priorities, we've four major streams. First, DI Wilkinson, can you progress with the investigation at the quarry? I want a clear timeline of events by close of play and I want your staff to relocate there."

"Okay." Wilkinson sat back in his seat and finished his coffee, crumpling the cup in his meaty fist. "One thing to bear in mind is this fight was organised. We need to trap that. I've got Charlie Kidd investigating on Schoolbook."

Bain frowned. "Did you just say Schoolbook?"

Wilkinson grinned. "You're welcome to go back there."

"Wouldn't touch it with a fuckin' bargepole."

Cargill gave Holdsworth a stern look. "We clearly need to look at resource allocation, but I want us to plough on as quickly as possible. I don't want to lose any momentum. Paul, I assume you've got a deputy who can take on operational management of this?"

Wilkinson looked at Cullen. "Well, there's DC Curran."

"Apart from DC Cullen." Cargill stressed the L's.

"Aye, I'll look into it."

"Good. Next, I want a clear timeline from before Aitken arrived at the quarry right through to when he was murdered. There are huge gaps — we haven't even placed him at the quarry, for instance. I want every single hole plugged." Cargill looked at Methven. "Can I ask you to lead this?"

"Sure thing." Methven raised his eyebrows and smiled.

"Excellent." Cargill looked at Bain. "DI Bain, can you take the lead on Souness? We need a similar timeline from before the quarry to Souness dying and then to him being found. DS McNeill has been leading this, but I want you to formally take over."

"Will do." Bain stroked at his moustache. "It is pretty much just a case of him getting stabbed then dying at home, though."

"Still needs to be closed off." Cargill tapped her fingers on the desk. "Which leaves us with the forensic search. Brian, can you and DS Irvine lead on that?"

"Aye, will do."

"Okay." Cargill got to her feet. "Let's get back to work. I want the four leads to stay with me and we can allocate resource accordingly. I'll need DS Holdsworth as well."

Cullen frowned. "What about me?"

"First, you could get DS Holdsworth in here." Cargill smiled. "You can work with DS Irvine."

Cullen sighed. "Yes, ma'am." He'd be lucky to get away without another complaint. At least he'd avoided Sharon.

38

C ullen typed the last words of his interview notes from the sessions with Miller and Richardson. He emailed the copy to Holdsworth for inclusion in the case files and printed out two copies. The clock in the bottom right corner of the screen read 15.04.

He shut the lid on the laptop and looked across the Incident Room, far busier than he'd seen for days.

Wilkinson was nearby, sitting with one of his officers, a woman in her late twenties. He caught Cullen's eye and headed over, sitting at the adjacent desk. "I hope most of the energy isn't being expended on merging the cases, rather than catching the murderers."

"Tell me about it." Cullen nodded. "Did that go as you hoped?"

"Hardly." Wilkinson checked his watch. "Got a catch-up with my DCI in half an hour. Hopefully he'll extricate me from this."

"Best of luck."

"I'll need it." Wilkinson patted Cullen's shoulder. "How's the forensics going?"

"We're waiting on Anderson." Cullen nodded over at Irvine, deep in conversation with Bain. "Need to spend time with DS Irvine to work out what he's planning to do."

Wilkinson looked over. "He's going to get to second base with Bain by the looks of things."

Cullen laughed. "I've thought of going over and giving them some abuse, but I just couldn't be arsed with it."

"Good idea."

"How's the Aitken timeline going?"

Wilkinson sighed. "Still don't know anything about how the lad ended up there. The trail from his office last Tuesday to his body being found at the bottom of a shale bing is colder than an Edinburgh winter."

"It's just the wind, sir. It's not that bad really."

"I'll remind you of that in January."

"Did they get anything on the lock-up in Ravencraig?"

"I've got that DS Rarity going round the owners and users of the garages, but nobody's come up with anything. Or, if they have, they're not telling me."

"All comes down to the forensics, I suppose."

Wilkinson nodded. "Always does. We've got four victims, two potential killers and an unidentified third suspect. We need to connect the bloody dots."

"It's all just guesswork at the moment."

"We need a witness. One who'll talk. Dean Richardson was there. Derek Miller too, no matter how much the little shit denies it."

"You been in with them again?"

"Chance would be a fine thing."

Cullen's mobile rang — unknown number. "Sorry, better take this."

"Cullen, it's James Anderson."

"How can I help?"

"Can't get hold of DS Irvine. Tried his moby but no dice. Could you get your arse down here?"

"I've got about three arses I could bring down."

"Irvine, Bain and Wilkinson?" Anderson paused. "That's not me saying you're not an arse, by the way."

Cullen laughed. "What have you got for us?"

"Just got to ninety per cent on the match for that partial fingerprint. By the time the four arsemen of the apocalypse get down here, it should be finished."

"Be there in a minute." Cullen ended the call and nodded at Wilkinson. "We're up. Come on." He headed over to Irvine and Bain. "Fingerprints are back."

Bain frowned. "Right. Good."

Cullen led them out into the stairwell before clattering down the steps.

By the time they'd got to the Scenes of Crime office, Bain was in the lead. He held the door open for Cullen, the others nowhere to be seen, before scowling at Anderson. "This better be good."

"It's all part of the magic of Crime Scene Investigation." Anderson tapped at his screen. "Ninety-eight per cent."

Bain pulled over a chair. "Thought you'd have some fuckin' whizz-bang thing showing it flicking through fingerprints as it went."

Anderson scowled. "Like in a film?"

"Aye, or in CSI."

"This is reality, unfortunately. Besides, that shit takes up stacks of processing time to display. It's much quicker to just let it do its business in private. Much like what you need to do with me."

Bain smiled. "You need supervision."

The progress bar ticked up to ninety-nine per cent.

Wilkinson appeared, looking flustered. "You bloody got anything yet?"

"He's keeping us in suspense." Bain looked Wilkinson up and down. "You're not looking your usual self, Wilko."

"Try not being SIO on your own case."

"Don't have to imagine, Paul, it's my life just now."

"You'll get something soon, gaffer." Irvine sat on the edge of a desk, mouth pounding on gum.

"There's a trend forming here, Irvine, and it's all about stuff slipping through my fingers."

Anderson crouched in front of the machine, frantically wagging the mouse.

Wilkinson groaned. "This better not have broken."

"Just give me a sec." Anderson's eyes darted over the screen, his brow creasing further as time progressed. He turned around, eyes blinking. "Holy shite."

Wilkinson got to his feet. "Bloody spit it out."

"We've got a match." Anderson's eyes locked on Bain. "It's Kieron Bain."

39

"Let me fuckin' see that!" Bain pushed past Cullen and Wilkinson to look at the screen. "How's my fuckin' son even on there?"

"We all are." Anderson tried to block him. "For crime scene elimination. How else do you think we do that?"

"My boy hasn't got his prints on that fuckin' knife. No fuckin' way."

"Brian, you need to leave. Now." Wilkinson grabbed Bain by the shoulders. "You shouldn't be here."

"I'm not fuckin' leaving! Anderson's fucked it up again. It's just a partial!"

Cullen went to help Wilkinson. "You need to leave, sir."

"This is a fuckin' partial!"

Anderson peered at the screen. "Brian, it's just part of the thumb and index finger of the right hand but it's a one hundred per cent match. Your son handled that knife."

"That's not enough to convict. There could be a fuckin' innocent explanation for this." Bain glared at Anderson. "Some boys got slotted in a quarry. The knife's in some ned's flat. How the fuck could his prints be on it?"

"We'll find out." Cullen let go of Bain. He nodded at Wilkinson, trying to get him to take over. "DS Irvine and I are responsible for this. You two need to speak to Cargill or Turnbull."

Wilkinson grabbed Bain by the arm. "Come on."

Bain swiped his hand away. "Get the fuck off me."

"I don't want to have to use force."

"Fine." Bain ran his hand over his shaved scalp. "We're going to Jim Turnbull about this, not fuckin' Cargill."

"Come on, then." Wilkinson led Bain out of the room.

Cullen let out a sigh. "What a mess."

Irvine slumped back against the desk. "What do you want to do next?"

"Eh? You're in charge here, Sarge. What do you want to do?"

"Aye, right. Just been thinking. Once the gaffer's been to see the powers that be, we need to speak to Cargill."

"We need to tell her now."

"We need to check whether Kieron was actually there." Irvine turned to look at Anderson. "Could the print have been placed after the event?"

"You've watched too many Bourne films. You'd need to be a professional in the secret service. CIA, MI6, shite like that. We're talking about a bunch of neds battering each other in a quarry. Besides, the blood pattern on his print's consistent with him using the knife."

"Right." Irvine looked to Cullen. "Let's you and me go and review Wilko's case file just now."

"We need to tell Cargill."

"She put me in charge, Cullen, not you. We need to prove Kieron Bain there."

Cullen folded his arms. "We've got a couple of people we know were there."

"Who?"

"Derek Miller and Dean Richardson."

"Maybe." Irvine put some more gum in his mouth. "We go through their files then we speak to Cargill."

∼

"Seen Irvine?"

Cullen looked up from the file. Wilkinson. "Not for a bit, why?"

"Need to speak to him about Bain. Bloody hell." Wilkinson frowned as he looked at the file in front of Cullen. "What the hell's that?"

"Irvine's got me going through the case file for the quarry fight."

"My files?"

"Aye."

"Come on." Wilkinson grabbed Cullen by the arm and took him out into the corridor. "Why does he think he can go over my bloody team's work?"

"Don't shoot the messenger." Cullen wriggled free of his grip and started rubbing his arm.

"I'm ordering you to stop doing this." Wilkinson punched the wall. "I bloody knew this would happen soon as Cargill took this over."

"Calm down. You're being paranoid."

Wilkinson stabbed a finger in Cullen's chest. "Don't tell me to calm down."

"This is Irvine's idea, I'm only following his instruction."

"That's not like you, Curran."

"Yeah, well, I got a toasting off Methven, so I'm keeping myself to myself, if you know what I mean."

"What did Cargill say about it?"

Cullen looked away. "We've not been."

"You're joking, aren't you?"

"No. Haven't you?"

"I took Bain to see Turnbull. He's not off the case, but he's to go nowhere near the quarry investigation. Just focus on Souness's background."

"Thought he'd use it to get shot of him?"

"He may yet." Wilkinson scowled. "I need to brief Cargill. Better it comes from one of us than Turnbull."

Cullen stopped him leaving. "We need to prove whether Kieron was there or not."

"We've got his fingerprints."

"We need to back it up."

"How?"

"Miller and Richardson were at the quarry. One of them might place Kieron Bain at the scene of the crime. We should speak to them."

Wilkinson screwed his eyes up. "Or they can clear him."

"Either way, we need to figure out if they know anything. Irvine had me going through the file to see if there were any other people you've already spoken to."

Wilkinson thought it through for a few seconds. "Richardson's still in, right?"

40

The door opened and Richardson was brought into the interview room, wearing handcuffs and standard custody attire, an unflattering one-piece. He sat down as if he owned the place.

The brick shithouse PCSO stayed by the door, eyes fixed on Richardson.

Alistair Reynolds followed them in, sitting next to his client before unzipping an A4 folio case. He took some sheets of paper and a black fountain pen out, arranging them neatly on the table.

Wilkinson grinned at the lawyer. "You ready?"

"Yes."

Wilkinson started the interview. "Mr Richardson, when we last spoke to you, you told us you retrieved a knife you found at Ginty's Quarry near Livingston in West Lothian. You showed us to your flat and we now have the knife in evidence."

He got a sheet of paper from the file sitting in front of him and handed it to Reynolds. "For the record, I'm passing a copy of the summary page of the forensics report to Mr Reynolds. A full copy of the detailed report will be made available after this interview."

Reynolds tossed it back on the table. "What am I supposed to be seeing here?"

"You'll note the analysis confirmed three people were stabbed with the knife." Wilkinson took out another copy of the sheet and read from it. "Liam Crossan, Gordon Beveridge and Kenneth Souness."

Richardson's eyes widened slightly but he kept quiet.

Reynolds lined the sheet up with the report. "And?"

"And we've therefore connected this inquiry with another ongoing investigation. Four murders."

"If you are implying my client was at all involved in any of the murders, I seriously hope you've got solid evidence to back this up and it's not merely police conjecture."

"What do you mean by police conjecture?"

"I mean you should really watch your words, Inspector." Reynolds pointed at the recorder. "We're on the record here."

"Perhaps you want to continue with the summary, sir?" Cullen tapped the sheet, trying to establish his good cop role.

"Okay, let's push on, then." Wilkinson held the sheet up. "In addition to the three victims, we've identified three distinct prints on the knife."

"Are any from my client? Because I assure you that—"

Wilkinson cut him off. "Your client's prints aren't on the knife." He smiled. "We've had more than enough opportunities to get a sample of your client's fingerprints and DNA over the years."

"Please continue."

"The three prints were those of Gordon Beveridge, Alexander Aitken and Kieron Bain, a serving police officer."

"Then why are you interviewing my client?"

"I want to understand what happened between the last user of the knife discarding it and Mr Richardson handing us the evidence."

Richardson sniffed. "We've been over this before."

Cullen smiled. "Then it won't harm your case to give us it again."

Wilkinson sat back, grinning. "Providing he tells us it the same again."

"Just let him speak, sir."

Wilkinson held up his hands. "Fire away."

Richardson looked at Reynolds, who shrugged. "I picked the knife up at the quarry. I had a plastic bag on us."

Wilkinson rolled his eyes. "That's convenient."

"I'd bought a sausage roll and a pint of milk from Tesco for my dinner." Richardson grinned. "I'm not in the habit of chucking bags away."

"That's very community spirited of you." Wilkinson smirked. "You must save a lot of badgers and seagulls every year."

"I got a lift home after the fight, back to Easter Road."

Wilkinson scowled. "Who from?"

"A mate."

"Who?"

Cullen held up a hand. "It's not important, sir." He looked at Richardson. "You don't have to name names but you do need to tell us if whoever gave you a lift knew of the knife or had it in his or her possession."

Richardson shook his head. "No. I stuck it in my jacket. Got a big pocket it fits in perfectly."

"Is this the jacket you were wearing when we brought you in?"

"It was, aye."

"We'll get some forensic analysis done on the jacket to confirm your story." Cullen scribbled in his notebook. "What happened when you got back to the flat?"

"I shoved it under my drawer."

"You didn't touch the knife?"

"No."

"Why did you take it?"

Richardson snorted. "Never know when it might come in handy."

"So you meant to use it?"

"No, pal." Richardson laughed. "In case anyone in the gang needed it. As ammo, likes. If any of this shite came up. Looks like it was smart of me to do it."

"And instead you gave it to us."

"Not that you gave us much choice."

Wilkinson leaned forward. "Mr Richardson, did you tamper with the knife in any way?"

"Did I what?"

"By, say, putting fingerprints on it?"

Reynolds pointed the nib of his fountain pen at Wilkinson. "Are you saying my client added fingerprints on that knife?"

"Me?" Richardson looked at Reynolds. "I'd be a bit sceptical about a wee bam from Ravencraig like me having technology like that, but not these boys."

Wilkinson hit the desk. "Mr Richardson, did you put those fingerprints on the knife?"

"No."

"Did you see who held the knife last?"

"No."

Cullen cut in. "I think you've asked enough questions."

"Do you?" Wilkinson glowered at Cullen. "I've got one more." He licked his lips. "What I'm wondering is whether Mr Richardson put the carrier bag on the knife handle then used it to stab someone."

Richardson looked over at Reynolds, eyebrows raised.

Reynolds glowered at Wilkinson. "Inspector, do you have any evidence which suggests that this might have happened?"

Wilkinson looked down at the sheet of paper. "Nothing that

contradicts it. The knife has traces of the specific plastic the bag is made from. I can try to read the name out, if you're interested?"

Reynolds gave a tart smile. "That won't be necessary. Do you have any witness statements or other forensic evidence you could use to attribute my client with such an act?"

"I'm afraid not." Wilkinson scribbled a line on a notepad. "Does your client have any evidence suggesting he didn't do this? I'm sure someone as community spirited as Mr Richardson would present us with some evidence, so we don't waste man hours."

Richardson whispered something in his lawyer's ear.

Reynolds slowly put the lid back on his pen before nodding.

Richardson inspected his fingernails, heavily chewed. "There's someone that could confirm I didn't do it. One of my mates was with me pretty much all the time."

"Who?"

"Sketchy. Lives in Restalrig."

"Sketchy?"

"All right, Ian Archibald. Used to go to art college, so we called him Sketchy."

Cullen had heard a lot of shit nicknames over the years but that took the biscuit. "You said 'pretty much'?"

Richardson leaned forward. "Aye. There was a period where we weren't together."

"Convenient. We need it to be complete."

"Right." Richardson nibbled a nail. "I've got another witness I could use."

"And who might that be?"

"Derek Miller."

"Can't believe you've brought me in here again." Derek Miller looked around the interview room. "Came down to my work again."

Wilkinson folded his arms. "Derek, we need you to confirm you were at Ginty's Quarry."

"Where?" Derek smirked. "Never heard of it, man."

"You know exactly where I'm talking about. It's between Livingston and Bathgate. We've got you on bloody tape telling us all about the fight there."

Derek ran his hand over his head, tugging the gelled spikes backwards. "Look, I told you before, I wasn't there."

"We believe you were."

Derek leaned forward. "Something's changed since last time. Can't quite put my finger on it."

Wilkinson pointed a finger at him. "Cut the shit, lad. We know you were there."

"Then why are you asking me? If you know I was there, you should be charging me or something, right?"

"Bloody central heating is up full blast." Wilkinson undid the second top button.

Cullen took up the cue. "Derek, you've admitted on the record that you were at the scene of this gang fight. It's a serious offence and would involve time in prison. You've managed to get your life on the right track so it would be a shame to see all that hard work go down the tubes."

Derek switched his gaze from the tabletop to Cullen's eyes. "What are you saying?"

"If it helped our investigation we'd potentially be prepared not to charge you."

Derek tapped his finger on the table before he looked at his lawyer. "What do you think?"

She smiled at Wilkinson. "Can we have a minute?"

"No." Wilkinson slammed a folder down on the table. "We know you were at the quarry on the night in question."

"Who says I was there?"

"An eyewitness."

"Who?"

"Dean Richardson."

Derek's mouth hung open. "He said that?"

Wilkinson opened the folder and got out a sheet before passing it across the table. "He did. This is from his statement. You were apparently with him a fair amount of the time that night. I'd expect you to be on different sides. You're Hibs, he's Rangers."

"Right."

"Is that you admitting it, Derek?"

Derek ran his hand through his hair. "What you've got to understand is these things are quite friendly. We're battering the shite out of each other, aye, but it's organised. We're just doing it for kicks. There are jambos and teddy bears I'd go for a scoop with, likewise there are Celtic and Hibs fans who I think are total cunts. We're not like the red-faced fannies you get at matches who get all incensed by the other lot. Bank managers and that, happy to shout the odds in the middle of a crowd. We're proper hard. It's a respect thing."

Cullen nodded. "This explains the black eye."

Derek looked away for a few seconds. "Aye."

Wilkinson folded his arms. "Derek, you're in a lot of trouble. There's a nationwide crackdown on this sort of thing and you've just got yourself into the middle of it."

Derek leaned against the table. "What can I do to get out of this?"

"I don't know, I'm just trying to work out what to charge you with."

"We were just having some fun, like I said, then it got out of hand. Some twat brought a knife. That's not on."

Cullen leaned across the table. "Derek, this is some serious stuff you've got yourself caught up in. You could go to prison just for being involved. We'd be prepared to be lenient on that charge if you were able to give away the group leaders."

Tears formed in Derek's eyes. He blinked them back, his hands tightly gripping the edge of the table. "It's not like I can just give you their names. I don't know them. They're just made-up names on Schoolbook."

"What about one Ian Archibald, also known as Sketchy?"

Derek looked away. "What about him?"

"Do you know him?"

Derek focused on Cullen. "I do, aye. Mate of Dean's."

Cullen narrowed his eyes. One of the guys who attacked them on Saturday was a mate of Dean's. "Was Sketchy there on Saturday?"

Derek looked away again. "He was, aye."

Cullen leaned over to Wilkinson. "I need a word."

Wilkinson paused the interview, leaving Derek and his solicitor with the PCSO. He slammed the door behind them. "What the bloody hell are you up to in there, Curran? What happened on Saturday?"

"Derek and I went to the Hibs match." Cullen folded his arms. "We were attacked afterwards."

"You bloody what? Are you telling me you were involved in a hooliganism incident and didn't report it?"

"I didn't know what to do."

"This out of control." Wilkinson prodded a finger at Cullen's chest, missing the hammer scar by centimetres. "I want this Sketchy boy brought in. I want you to report the attack as a crime. Get it on the books. We'll get him."

Cullen stood in silence. "Where are we going with this?"

Wilkinson grinned. "I've got someone I can prosecute. Two people in fact."

"Don't you want the ringleaders? Those two are barely pawns in this game of fuckwit chess."

Wilkinson bellowed with laughter. "Fuckwit chess. I love that."

Cullen shrugged. "Forget it. We need to get the killers of those three men. You have to get the ringleaders. Prosecuting those two is just going to put them underground."

Wilkinson grinned. "That's a potential strategy. Get some of the lower level minions and we put the fear of bloody God into the rest of them. Either way, we stop what these fuckwits are up to."

Cullen held up his hands. "I'd see where you can get him to bend."

"Fine. Let's get back inside."

Cullen put a hand on the door. "Get him to give us a list of people he knows were there. Pretend we'll consider prosecuting a lesser charge."

"Bloody hell. Fine. Let's do it. You lead."

They went back in, Derek Miller and his lawyer breaking off from a deep conversation.

Wilkinson restarted the interview.

Cullen smiled. "Derek, we know you were at Ginty's Quarry last Monday. We know you're involved in the fighting. What we need from you is a list of people who were there, including the ringleaders."

"What do I get in return?"

"Potential leniency. If you're seen to co-operate and your assistance leads to further arrests and convictions, the Procurator Fiscal can potentially go easy on you."

"There's a lot of potentials there." The lawyer tossed her hair. "Define 'easy'."

"That's not for us to say." Cullen folded his arms. "I'd imagine something along the lines of a suspended sentence instead of a custodial one." He turned to Wilkinson. "Would that fit with your expectation?"

"That's about the size of it."

Derek looked at the lawyer and she gave a slight nod. He turned back. "Give us a sheet of paper and a pen."

Wilkinson flipped over to a fresh sheet in his notepad and handed it over along with his chewed Bic.

Derek stared at it, then took his lawyer's Parker and started writing.

Cullen cleared his throat. "Please read out the names as you write them down."

"Ally McKay. John McGazz. Pete Marshall. Scotty Cuthbertson. Gary don't know his surname. John Thomson. Barry Nicholls. Kieron something or other."

"Say that last one again."

"Kieron."

"What's his surname?"

"Don't know."

Wilkinson leafed through his papers, eventually finding one of Kieron Bain dressed in full uniform for an official photograph. He tossed it on the table. "Is this him? For the record, I'm showing Mr Miller a photograph of Kieron Bain, which will be submitted into evidence."

Derek picked up the photo.

Wilkinson rapidly tapped the table with his thumb. "Is that him?"

"Didn't know he was a copper."

42

"We've got an urgent update." Wilkinson barged into the meeting room.

Irvine, Methven, Sharon and Rarity were seated around the table, not exactly looking enthralled by the session.

Cargill stood by a flipchart and glowered at him. "We're in the middle of an important agenda point here, Paul."

"Trust me, Alison, you want to hear this."

Cargill sighed. "Fine, fire away."

Wilkinson nodded at Bain. "Not sure DI Bain should be here."

"I've been briefed. He stays."

"Fine." Wilkinson sat next to Angela. "Curran, do you want to go?"

"Aye." Cullen was forced to sit next to Sharon. He stood. "We've been in with Richardson."

Irvine put up a hand. "You were supposed to be working for me."

"I'd finished. DI Wilkinson asked me to accompany him."

"Cullen, you need to sta—"

"DS Irvine, let him finish." Cargill scowled.

Cullen nodded thanks. "Richardson told us Derek Miller was at the quarry. We got him brought in. He told us Kieron Bain was there."

Bain got to his feet. "This is fuckin' bollocks!"

"DI Bain, calm down." Cargill pointed at him.

"I'll stay as calm as I want. This is utter bullshit. You've got the word of a scumbag against the word of a serving officer."

"With all due respect." Cullen took a step back. "We've got his print on the murder weapon."

"This is shite!"

"Kieron was instructed to go home." Cargill tossed her pen on the meeting room table. "I want him brought in."

"You can't do that!" Bain's face had gone a deep shade of purple.

"I can and I will."

"You're out of order."

Cargill put a hand to his arm. "You and I are going back to see DCI Turnbull after this." She looked at Cullen. "DC Cullen, can you arrange for uniformed officers to bring Kieron in?"

"Already on his way."

"DS Methven, can you speak to Professional Standards and Ethics?"

"You're bringing the Complaints in against my boy?"

Cargill nodded. "This is getting messy, Brian. A DI who's Deputy SIO on a murder case where his PC son's now a suspect."

"You have to stop this."

Cargill yanked the door open. "DI Bain, you need to come with me to see Jim. You're on thin enough ice as it is."

"Are you fuckin' kidding me?"

"No, I suggest that you calm yourself down." She led Bain out of the room.

The rest of the officers sat in stunned silence.

Methven got to his feet. "Better go and see Superintendent Fletcher."

Cullen's mobile buzzed. A text from Buxton. "Kieron Bain downstairs."

43

"Listen to what my client's saying." Alistair Reynolds was Kieron Bain's lawyer. No such thing as conflict of interest with these guys.

Cullen sat across the interview room table from them. "Mr Bain, we have a signed witness statement placing you at Ginty's Quarry between the hours of seven and ten p.m. on Monday the first of October. Can you confirm this?"

Kieron looked away. He had dark rings around his eyes and his face had taken on the grey pallor of his father. "No comment."

"I see. Do you have an alibi for that period of time?"

"No comment."

"Mr Bain, did you kill Kenneth Souness, Gordon Beveridge and Liam Crossan?"

"No comment."

"Did you kill Kenneth Souness, Gordon Beveridge or Liam Crossan?"

"No comment."

Reynolds waved his fountain pen in the air. "You clearly have very little evidence pointing to my client being responsible for any crime."

Wilkinson cleared his throat. "We have his fingerprint on the knife used to kill those three people. We have a witness statement placing your client at the scene of a football hooligan fight. That is a criminal offence, as I'm sure you are aware."

"We're well aware."

Cullen looked at his sheet of questions. "Kieron, did you see who killed Liam Crossan?"

"No comment."

"Did you see who killed Kenneth Souness?"

"No comment."

"Did you see who killed Gordon Beveridge?"

Kieron looked across at Reynolds for a few seconds. "No comment."

Wilkinson smiled. "I've got you there. You saw who killed Gordon Beveridge, didn't you?"

Kieron sat in silence for a few seconds. "I did, aye."

"Who was it?"

"Right, I saw Souness get stabbed by Beveridge."

Wilkinson leaned forward. "What happened next?"

"Xander Aitken picked up the knife and stabbed Beveridge."

"Why are your prints on the knife?"

Kieron closed his eyes. "No comment."

Cullen looked at Wilkinson, who nodded back. He ended the interview.

$\approx$

"Excellent." Cargill beamed as she wrote it on the whiteboard. "We're getting somewhere with this."

"This is a good result." Methven jangled his pocket. "It's taken us a while but that's two deaths fully accounted for now."

Wilkinson did up the top button of his shirt. "We'll get back in there tomorrow and get something out of Kieron."

"Let him stew." Cargill folded her arms. "Think it'll stand up in court?"

Wilkinson grinned. "Of course it will. We'll have to get some additional evidence here or there, but we've got a fair amount. At least it's only a Fatal Accident Inquiry."

Cullen frowned. "We still need to get Kieron's statement corroborated."

Wilkinson nodded. "Of course, but I'd certainly say we're home and hosed on Souness and Beveridge. With Crossan, I'm pretty much certain it's Kieron Bain."

"Good effort, team." Cargill looked at Wilkinson and Methven. "Rarity and Buxton are over in the Elm, if you want to join them. I'm buying."

Wilkinson grinned. "Sounds like a plan."

Methven raised his eyebrows as he focused on Cullen. "I'll be there."

"Just the one." Cullen got to his feet. "Got stuff to do later."

"I'll see you over there." Cargill turned back to the whiteboard, already lost in it.

Methven led them out of the Incident Room, heading to the stairwell. "I've not seen you much, Cullen."

"Been busy."

Wilkinson patted his arm. "Did you report that assault?"

"Aye. I've got a crime number and everything."

Methven frowned. "What's this?"

"Cullen was assaulted by some hooligans on Saturday."

Methven scowled. "I've got a real sodding axe to grind with these football hooligans. From my time at school in Edinburgh. I bloody hate football."

"It's the beautiful game, Colin."

"Really? Some Hibs fans kicked the crap out of me when I was fourteen. They thought I was a Hearts fan, just because I was wearing a sodding burgundy tracksuit at PE. They waited behind after school and kicked the living shit out of me on the way home."

"Can't stand Scottish football."

"I can't stand any form of it. Anything where people kick lumps out of each other because of which team they support can't be good."

They left the station, waiting to cross at the lights.

Wilkinson pressed the button a few times. "What about you, Curran?"

Cullen spotted Methven's eyebrows twitch at the incorrect use of his name. "I'm fed up with Scottish football."

Wilkinson laughed. "No, I meant do you have any horror stories?"

"I've never met a nice Rangers fan."

"What about Bain?"

"Point proven."

Wilkinson laughed. "Reminds me of a Spitting Image song. I've never met a nice South African."

Methven scowled. "Another world class racist country."

Wilkinson frowned. "You think Scotland's that bad?"

"Of course. You've got small-minded idiots kicking lumps out of each other in quarries and singing songs in soccer stadiums just because they have a slightly different Bible. That's racism at its finest."

"It's not racism." Cullen shrugged as they crossed the road. "I mean, I agree it's stupid, but we're not that racist."

Methven held the pub door open. "Tell that to the Indian guy that got stabbed in Wester Hailes last weekend."

"Was that football hooliganism?"

"No, it was some Scottish Defence League idiots. They thought, because he was Indian, that he was in league with Al Qaeda or something. The lad's parents were born in Bradford, he was born in Edinburgh, grew up here. He was doing a PhD in Philosophy at Edinburgh University, writing a thesis on the death of God. You couldn't get a more atheist person. He had written several articles online about how Islam was a broken religion."

"That's pretty messed up."

"Care to retract your statement?" Methven leaned against the bar.

"Fine. This is a racist country. We're not all racist is my point."

"Nobody ever is." Methven waved at Rarity and Buxton, sitting together in the corner. "What's your poison, Cullen?"

"Staropramen."

"Same for me."

"Have a seat, lads. I'll bring them over."

Cullen smiled and headed to the seats. "He's being my pal today."

"No idea why." Wilkinson frowned. "Why do people call you Cullen?"

"It's my name."

"Not Curran?"

"No."

"Why didn't you tell me?"

Cullen shrugged as he sat down. "I did. After the third time you ignored me it just felt futile."

Wilkinson shook his head. "Grow a pair, Cullen."

"Heard you've nailed Kieron." Buxton took a sip before his eyes bulged. "In a policing sense, that is."

Wilkinson laughed. "Don't let his old man hear you say that."

"His old man's not here."

"He's still on the case."

Buxton screwed his face up. "How the hell has he managed that?"

Methven put their pints down on the table. "You need to discuss that with Cargill and Turnbull, Constable."

"Don't tell me you think that's okay?"

"I think it's a bit much. That said, he's just to focus on Souness."

"We've bloody solved Souness." Wilkinson took a sip. "He was slotted by Beveridge. What more is there to do with it?"

Rarity shrugged. "Gather evidence?"

Wilkinson prodded his finger at her. "Bain should be nowhere near this case. He should be given no opportunity to get his son off the hook."

Cullen smirked. "Didn't know you felt that way about him."

"DI Bain and I were in the same bloody situation a year ago, right, but that's it." Wilkinson shook his head. "We had a lot in common in that sense but I don't rate him and I doubt he rates me."

Methven swirled his pint of ale. "What situation is that?"

"Never you mind."

"No, go on, I'm interested."

Wilkinson sat back. "We were both here when Turnbull got his current job. He didn't like either of us, so he brought Cargill in. She seems a good officer, nothing against her, but I want to be somewhere I'm bloody wanted, right?"

"I wasn't aware there was so much history in this team."

"It's like the bloody Bible." Wilkinson scowled.

Buxton got his phone out and started fiddling with it.

Rarity smiled. "Sharon McNeill seems like a good officer."

Buxton looked up from his phone and nodded at Cullen.

"She's heading to the bloody top." Wilkinson took a big drink. "Top officer."

"I asked her if she wanted to join us, but she knocked me back. Said she was going somewhere with DC Caldwell. Should I take it personally?"

Wilkinson bellowed with laughter. "It's because of him." He pointed at Cullen.

Rarity frowned. "What have you done, Scott?"

Wilkinson wagged his finger. "Scott and Sharon were an item."

Cullen downed the rest of his pint. "I'm off."

Wilkinson didn't even look up.

DAY 9

Thursday
11th October 2012

44

"Early for once." Wilkinson folded his phone up and pocketed it, as he leaned against the wall outside the Incident Room.

"I'm trying my hardest." Cullen shrugged. "Stay out late last night?"

"Not much after you left."

"On track for the seven a.m. briefing?"

"Think so. Got a couple of good ones for you, though. This Sketchy character got picked up by uniform last night. They've charged him with assaulting you and Derek Miller."

"Did he give anyone up?"

"Nope. Not giving up any of his co-conspirators."

"Still, good to get him under lock and key."

"Sure is."

"Morning, boys." Bain sauntered into the Incident Room, paper rolled up under his arm.

Cullen waited till he was out of earshot. "Can't believe he's still on the case."

"Tell me about it." Wilkinson shook his head. "Reminds me of a top flight football manager too proud to accept failure and resign after a series of shit results."

"Nothing to do with clinging on for a compensation payment?"

"There is that, I suppose."

Cargill called them into the room.

Cullen found a desk to lean against.

Cargill waited for the room to settle. "First things first, the merging of the cases has been completed in record time. We've got DS Holdsworth to thank for that."

Wilkinson leaned over. "Sad bugger was in all night doing it. His wife kicked him out, you know?"

"I heard."

"Onto the main part of the briefing." Cargill read from a sheet of paper. "A witness statement places PC Kieron Bain at the scene of the fight. In a subsequent statement, he claims Alexander Aitken killed Gordon Beveridge, in retaliation for the death of Kenny Souness. That ties up some loose ends on the case, but we still have gaps regarding the deaths of Liam Crossan at the quarry and of Alexander Aitken. It should be pointed out that PC Bain has fingerprints on the murder weapon and is being treated as a suspect in the murder of Liam Crossan."

Bain picked at his teeth, narrowed eyes scanning the room.

Cargill took a deep breath. "That leaves us with a question mark over Alexander Aitken. Was he murdered in revenge for the death of Beveridge? We have a gap in his and Souness's movements between the fight and Aitken turning up at work on Tuesday morning. It appears Aitken disappeared on Tuesday night and we currently don't know why. Aitken potentially took Souness home to their shared flat to avoid hospital. Given Souness died from loss of blood, it's possible Mr Aitken's disappearance was unexpected."

She read from a sheet of paper. "I've four key strands of investigation now. First, DS Methven and DS Irvine to ascertain what happened to Aitken between the fight and his disappearance and then after. DS Methven, can you please lead?"

Methven nodded, his eyes closed. Smug git.

"Next, I want DS McNeill and DS Rarity to investigate Derek Miller and Dean Richardson's statements. We need corroboration from other members of the gangs at the quarry. We need everything backed up. DI Wilkinson has made two of his DCs available to support you."

The two officers next to Wilkinson had shaven heads and looked like they'd done a fair amount of time under cover.

"DI Wilkinson, I want you to update your interview notes. They need to be shipshape. I plan on formally meeting the PF at some point over the next twenty-four hours. Additionally, we'll be joined by colleagues from Professional Standards and Ethics and I want you and DC Cullen to join me when we meet with Superintendent Fletcher at nine a.m."

She looked around the room, listening to the whispers about 'the Complaints'. "We've done almost everything above board on this case and, for those items that we haven't, I've given full disclosure to Super-intendent Fletcher's team. We've nothing to be afraid of. We're doing everything by the book and we're getting results."

She glanced over at Bain. "DI Bain will support me and work with DS Holdsworth in getting the paperwork on this case up to the required standard. Dismissed."

"I'M afraid DCI Turnbull is busy." Turnbull's PA, a middle-aged battleaxe, didn't look up from her screen. "I'm sure you're aware his time is fully occupied with the force reorganisation and with the ongoing investigation."

"I can well imagine, but I do need to see him."

Turnbull sneaked his head around the corner of his office. "Liz, has the expense report come through yet?"

"Not yet, I'll get on to them."

"I need it for the one o'clock with DCS Whitehead, if you could print it with a few hours to spare, I'd appreciate it." Turnbull nodded at Cullen. "Scott, how can I help?"

"I need to speak with you."

"I'm kind of tied up just now."

"Thought your door was always open?"

Turnbull winked. "I need to watch my mouth where you're concerned. I can maybe squeeze five minutes if you want to give an elevator pitch while I get a coffee."

"That'd be great."

"I'm buying." Turnbull marched off towards the lifts at a great pace, Cullen having to jog to keep up. He stopped and waited with his arms folded. "How can I help, Scott?"

Cullen felt the butterflies flap. "I don't feel I'm getting on well with the new regime."

"What new regime?"

"DI Cargill and DS Methven."

The bell chimed and they got in the lift.

"I see." Turnbull hammered his thick finger against the button for the fifth floor. "That's more augmentation than regime change."

"I don't think they appreciate how good I am, sir."

"That's very forward of you, Scott."

"You've always said I'm a rising star. I don't think DI Cargill shares that particular view."

The door opened and they got out of the lift.

Turnbull started walking to the canteen. "Does she not?"

"No, she doesn't."

Turnbull walked straight to Barbara. "A latte, please. Scott?"

"Americano, sir."

"Are you raising this because it's having a material impact on the case?"

"Not really."

"Are you sure this is the right time to be addressing this?"

"It's a problem and I always think the best time to solve a problem is there and then."

"Indeed." Turnbull passed Cullen his coffee before handing over a tenner. "You know the office culture I've tried to instil here — don't come to me with problems..."

"Come to you with solutions, I know. I just feel I've got a lot to add to this case, but I'm being marginalised."

Turnbull collected his change and his latte before leading back to the lifts, taking sips through the hole in the lid as they walked. "Marginalised in what sense?"

"I know I'm only a DC, but I like to think I'm operating at a level higher."

"You do, do you?" Turnbull smiled. "I suppose there's a case for that."

"I'm looking to move up a level at some point in the next few years. I need that experience. I need to be leading investigations."

"Aren't you? DI Cargill says you're doing well. She also told me she's tried to put you in a stretch role. Isn't that true?"

Cullen thought about it as they waited for the lift to return. "In a way."

Turnbull smiled. "What I'll do is discuss it with DI Cargill and see if she can express her appreciation more openly. She shares my opinion of you."

"Thanks. Are there any Acting DS roles likely to come up?"

The lift arrived.

Turnbull chuckled. "Something's clearly got into you today, Cullen. There's nothing in my headcount, I'm afraid."

"I see."

Cargill jogged up the stairs, Wilkinson following her. She tapped her watch.

Cullen glanced at his — he was late.

Turnbull got in the lift. "That's not to say it's impossible, just unlikely."

"Thanks, sir. I've got a meeting. I'll catch you later, sir."

∾

"THIS IS the room they'd use if the Chief Constable popped in, right?" Cullen sat between Wilkinson and Cargill, evenly spaced themselves around the table.

"I think so." Cargill closed her notebook. "DS Muir sent me an email about you."

Cullen looked up at the ceiling. "I see."

"You need to get on top of your emails, Scott."

"I will. Sorry."

"We've had him sniffing around us." Wilkinson looked up from his notebook. "We usually use the C word that doesn't stand for Complaints."

"You're both on your best behaviour, okay?"

Wilkinson nodded. "Of course."

Cargill took a sip from a glass of water. "What were you discussing with DCI Turnbull, Scott?"

"It's private."

"Of course."

The door flew open and a tall man in his early fifties burst in. "Alison."

"Michael." Cargill got to her feet. "Thanks for joining us."

"The pleasure's ours." Superintendent Fletcher sat at the head of the table, nearest Cullen. He had a slight air of the accountant about him, wearing full dress uniform. "Simon will be along soon."

Cargill stayed standing. "We'll wait."

The door opened again.

"Sorry I'm late." DS Muir was an athletic man of medium height, in his late twenties, wearing a sharp designer suit. He sat next to Cullen, his nose starting to twitch from the stench of expensive aftershave.

Cargill sat down. "This is DC Scott Cullen and this is DI Paul Wilkinson. They were both instrumental in obtaining the salient information."

Fletcher nodded as he got out a pad of paper. "I see."

Muir focused on Cullen. "I'm still awaiting a reply to my email."

"Sorry, I've been working a murder case. Given you copied my DCI in, I'd take that as proof that he's comfortable with my prioritisation."

Muir got out a folio case. "Make sure you get on to it when you've got a minute."

"I'd like to get down to the matter in hand." Fletcher leaned on his elbows. "We've reviewed the summary files you have kindly sent over and we've a number of concerns it's probably beneficial to raise at the outset."

Cargill sniffed. "What would they be?"

"First, we have an active officer under suspicion of murder. I want him in custody."

"We've got him downstairs."

"Fine, I want to speak with him, lawyers and force Federation reps present. I've had a dialogue with the Chief Constable and I can reassure you he wants this carefully managed. The political situation is somewhat delicate just now and we must insist this is treated with the utmost sensitivity."

"Would this sensitivity have anything to do with the regional commander positions not being announced yet?"

Fletcher smiled. "It may do. We've known each other a long time, Alison, and I'm sure we both know how to play around this."

"Okay, I'm happy for you to have an interview with the suspect. I want one of my senior officers attending all meetings." Cargill nodded at Wilkinson. "Can you sit in with them, Paul?"

Wilkinson raised his eyebrows. "Certainly."

Fletcher scribbled it down. "Second, I want Detective Inspector Bain taken off the case. I'll admit I'm somewhat flabbergasted that he's still even on active duties."

"And we hope it appears that way."

"Excuse me?"

"There's something not quite right about this situation." Cargill licked her lips. "We'd hoped to keep DI Bain on the case to trap him into giving away information pertaining to the active investigation."

Cullen raised his eyebrows. They were trying to trap Bain? An underhand investigation against a fellow officer... Whatever anyone thought of the Complaints, at least they were blatant about it.

"Regardless, Alison, I want DI Bain removed from the case, forthwith. It's not the responsibility of operational officers to investigate police officers. That is the remit of Professional Standards and Ethics. I'm happy to escalate to the Chief Constable if I don't get your acquiescence on the matter."

"Are we in agreement that suspension is appropriate, rather than full house arrest?"

"That's acceptable. For now." Fletcher nodded curtly. "Third, I want to have operational control of this case." Fletcher rubbed his fingers together slowly. "As the head of Professional Standards and Ethics, a case where a fellow officer is a murder suspect is clearly part of our remit."

"I disagree. This is an active murder investigation which I'm leading on behalf of the Detective Chief Inspector, who has been briefed and updated on progress with the situation at hand. Also, with all due respect, Professional Standards and Ethics aren't equipped to handle a murder investigation."

Muir raised a hand. "I've got two years as a detective sergeant."

Cargill winked at him. "I've ten as a DI and five as a DS before that. Paul Wilkinson here has eleven as a DI and is leading the Lothian & Borders aspects of Operation Housebrick, which I'm sure you'll both have been briefed on."

Fletcher raised a finger to stop Muir jumping in.

"In addition, I've got four detective sergeants, eighteen detective constables and a number of uniformed officers of sergeant and constable grade on temporary detachments." Cargill clasped her hands. "This isn't up for debate. This is a specialist case and requires a specialist team. Once we've closed out the investigation, I can assure you I'll parcel up the aspects of the case relating to your terms of reference."

Fletcher sighed. "Very well. I insist DS Muir is seconded to the investigation to ensure our specialist needs are met. While you may be experienced catching crooks, you need a certain set of skills to catch a fellow officer who's fallen foul of the law." He tightened his tie. "DS Muir will sit in on all interviews with PC Kieron Bain and DI Brian Bain, and we want first refusal of all other interviews pertaining to the investigation."

"That's absolutely fine." Cargill reached her hand over to Muir. "Welcome to the team."

Muir shook it, avoiding eye contact. "Thanks."

"Very well." Fletcher got to his feet. "I want to arrange an interview with PC Bain at the earliest convenience. Could you organise for a solicitor and a representative from the Scottish Police Federation to be present?"

"We will."

"Meanwhile, DS Muir and I will familiarise ourselves with the detailed case file."

They got up and left, Wilkinson following them out.

Cargill collapsed back in her seat. "He always gets to me."

Cullen frowned. "Have you got previous?"

"We worked together at St Leonard's for a few years. He was an inspector on the uniform side and I was a DS. We never quite agreed on anything, put it that way, but I learned how to play him." Cargill got to her feet. "I want you to inform DI Bain that he's now formally off the case."

What? A DC sacking a DI? "I'm not su—"

"Are you telling me you're not up to the task?"

"No."

45

Cullen went into the cubicle and smashed his fist into the wall above the toilet. He did it again. And again.

Blood on his knuckles. Blood pumping.

He walked over to the sink and splashed water over his face. She was seriously asking a DC to tell a DI he was off the case?

He counted to ten as he walked back to the Incident Room.

Sacking Bain.

Shite.

He inhaled deeply through his nostrils and entered the room. It was half empty — most officers must be out looking for further evidence.

Holdsworth was sitting at a laptop, furiously typing.

"Bryan." Cullen hovered by this desk.

Holdsworth slowly turned around. "What is it? I'm flat out here pulling together a dashboard for DCI Turnbull's weekly status meeting."

"Have you seen DI Bain?"

"Yes, he went down to the forensics lab with DS Irvine."

"Cheers."

Cullen heart thudded harder as he headed to the stairs, descending to the Scenes of Crime office on the ground floor of the station. A lump in his throat — the confrontation getting closer.

Anderson sat in the SOCO's office, staring at a computer screen. "Brian, just accept it."

Bain scowled. "It doesn't make sense."

Cullen frowned. "What doesn't?"

"Ah, Sundance, knew you'd fuckin' pitch up."

"We've got five tyre tracks." Irvine flashed up a photo. "We were bloody lucky. It pissed down all afternoon on Thursday, washing the tracks away. Anderson got his plaster of Paris out and did a big stretch of the path."

Cullen took the photo and checked it, unable to determine anything. "Impressive."

"I'm not just some tube that turns up at crime scenes to dust for fingerprints. I've got more qualifications than you three put together."

Bain scowled. "If you've got a single Higher you're doing better than us."

"I've got an Ordinary Degree." Cullen folded his arms.

"Ooooh." Irvine minced. "Been back to CC Bloom's again?"

Cullen scowled at him. "I never tire of that. Keep doing it."

"We reckon there's three vehicles going up and down." Irvine put another bit of gum in his mouth. "Obviously the one Aitken was in only went up."

"Right." Cullen tried to put the facts together in his head. "Could it be one going up and down twice?"

Anderson turned the monitor back and peered at it. "I've got different wear patterns on the sets of tyres. Looks like two separate vehicles."

Kieron Bain was First Attending Officer. Cullen clicked his fingers. "One of them was Kieron's police Range Rover, right?"

"We know this, Sundance." Bain rubbed his face. "The silly sod drove up to the top of the bing when he got there before realising the car was at the bottom."

Cullen scribbled it down in his notebook.

"What are you doing?"

"Writing that down. It's called a note. It helps you remember something that might be useful later."

"Cheeky little bastard." Bain scowled.

Cullen looked at Anderson. "What you're saying is there's a mystery third Range Rover, correct?"

Anderson nodded. "Could be that, aye. Can't tell from this."

"This is going to be another CCTV job, right?"

Irvine laughed. "Aye and I hope it's you that has to do it."

Cullen frowned. "The alternative is Kieron went up and down twice."

Bain got in Cullen's face. "Shut the fuck up, Sundance."

"We need to take this to Cargill."

"Grassing to teacher, eh?" Bain rested his forehead against Cullen's.

Cullen swallowed hard, the butterflies in his stomach flapping again. "I need to speak to you."

"There's no secrets here. Out with it."

"In private."

Bain stepped back and laughed. He grinned at Anderson and Irvine. "He does this every so often. He's got to take me aside and tell me how much he loves me."

"Come on." Cullen led him out into the long corridor and took a look around. It was quiet for once. He took a deep breath and decided just to spit it out. "You're on suspension."

Bain stared at him. "You fuckin' what?"

"DI Cargill has placed you on suspension. She asked me to tell you."

"You got a fuckin' camera recording this? Send it to Jeremy Beadle?"

"No, it's the truth."

Bain shook his head. "Why?"

"I must have impressed her or something."

"No, you fuckin' tube! Why am I suspended?"

"Your son's the prime suspect in one of the murders."

Bain flared his nostrils. "Fuck this and fuck you. My boy's innocent. Turnbull's getting a visit."

"You should get home."

"Fuck off, Sundance."

Cullen held up his hands. "I've done my bit."

"Aye, a million fuckin' times over."

"SAY THAT AGAIN?" Cargill looked up from the paperwork in front of her, head resting on her hand, her mouth muffled by the heel.

"Bain's going to speak to DCI Turnbull." Cullen sat alongside her. "He was complaining about being told by a DC."

"Thanks for doing that." Cargill sat back in her chair and stretched out. "How was Bain?"

"The usual. I've managed to desensitise myself to his swearing."

Cargill laughed. "I don't get what he's up to."

"You know his marriage broke up, right?"

"I'd heard whispers, Jim thought something was amiss."

Cullen nodded. "I've got some information on the forensics."

"Tell DS Methven."

"You want to hear this."

Cargill sighed. "Okay, go ahead."

"Last Thursday, when we were at the bing, I had a look at the tyre tracks leading up the mound. Anderson tells me the wear marks most likely point to three individual vehicles, but he's only matched one of them."

"Which one?"

"The car Xander Aitken drove up in." Cullen showed her the tyre analysis. "Kieron Bain drove up in a police Range Rover as FAO."

"This doesn't sound good." Cargill rubbed her eyebrows. "Which leaves us with a third Range Rover that we need to trace?"

"That or Kieron went up and down twice."

"Is that possible?"

"It's not been ruled out."

"Okay. This is good stuff, Cullen. I can see why Jim calls you a rising star."

Cullen blushed. "Thanks."

Cargill raised an eyebrow. "You just need to eliminate that little cowboy streak of yours."

"Believe me, I'm trying to."

"What do you want to do?"

"Have we done footprint analysis at the top of the bing?"

Cullen frowned. "I don't know. I can check, if you want?"

"No, it's fine, I'll allocate Sharon McNeill to it."

"What about me?"

Cargill looked across the Incident Room — Muir and Fletcher had a table in the far corner and were poring over their copy of the case file. "I want you to man mark Muir. He's done nothing so far, but he's interviewing Kieron Bain at eleven. I've been summoned to DCS Whitehead's office in Fettes with Fletcher and Turnbull, so I won't be able to attend."

"Will do."

There was a commotion from the entrance of the Incident Room. James Anderson was having a shouting match with DS Holdsworth.

Anderson looked into the room. "Where is he?"

Holdsworth pointed over at Cullen. "With DI Cargill."

Anderson marched over. "Where've you put it?"

"Put what?"

"The knife. It's gone."

Cullen raised his eyebrows. "I've got absolutely nothing to do with it. I came straight here to brief DI Cargill."

"Well somebody's pinched it. I need to run some other checks on the thing."

Cullen put his head in his hands. "Irvine and Bain were in there with you."

46

"We've got this eleven o'clock interview, haven't we?" Muir stood over Cullen.

Cullen shook his head, looking across the busy Incident Room. "Cargill's called an emergency briefing."

"What about?"

"You'll find out." Cullen tapped his nose.

"I'm not in the mood for games here."

Cargill entered the Incident Room. "Come on, can you all gather round please?"

Fletcher and Turnbull joined her at the front.

Cargill waited for a semblance of order before starting. "This is not an easy announcement so I'll just get on with it. You'll all be aware that PC Kieron Bain is the prime suspect in the murder of Liam Crossan. As you'll know, PC Bain is the son of DI Brian Bain, the Deputy SIO on this case. DI Bain appears to have tampered with evidence. The murder weapon has disappeared from the Scenes of Crime lab downstairs. DI Bain and DS Irvine were both in attendance when the knife is believed to have gone missing." Her eyes flicked around the room. "Both officers have been placed under house arrest."

The noise level cut to zero. The faces were utterly shocked. Cullen could hear the traffic outside.

Cargill cast her gaze across the room. "They may be acting together or independently. There's a distinct possibility they've hampered other aspects of this investigation. To that end, Superintendent Fletcher will be leading a thorough review of the case. I appreciate this is frustrating, especially as we're so close to solving it, but we need to make sure this is a clean conviction."

Cargill left the room, Turnbull and Fletcher following.

Cullen looked around, noticing a few familiar faces covered with looks of bewilderment.

Wilkinson tapped him on the shoulder. "None of my bloody Blackburn links came through."

Cullen frowned. "Blackburn Teddy, right?"

"Right. Had six of my lads going through contacts. Nobody knows anything about it. That's a shithole by the way, even worse than the one in bloody Lancashire."

Cullen smiled. "I thought Yorkshiremen were supposed to spit when you said that."

"I bloody feel like it." Wilkinson bellowed with laughter. "I need to speak to Charlie Kidd."

"I'm not stopping you."

"That's the thing. I don't understand that stuff half as well as you. Come upstairs with me."

"Much as I'd love to, I've got to man mark Muir. We're supposed to interview PC Bain."

"Wait here." Wilkinson dragged him over to Muir, sitting with Holdsworth. "Can you wait for Cullen to get back before you interview Kieron?"

Muir sighed. "I suppose I can."

"Excellent." Wilkinson tugged at Cullen's jacket. "Come on." He led upstairs. "I think that's Bain finally got his comeuppance."

"You think?"

"I've thought it before but he's always manages to wriggle out of it. House arrest is pretty bloody serious."

"I suppose so."

Wilkinson pushed open the door to the Forensic Investigations floor and marched over to Kidd's desk. "What are you doing here?"

Buxton looked up from his phone. "Crys— sorry, DS Methven asked me to help."

"And are you?"

"Not really." Kidd folded his arms.

"Put your phone away, Constable." Wilkinson pulled up a seat. "How's it going, Charlie?"

Kidd stretched out and yawned. "Getting there."

Cullen sat on the edge of the desk. "Where's there?"

Kidd sat back and started playing with his ponytail. "We've finally managed to get a link between the chat room and the core database."

"Thought this was supposed to be a piece of piss, Charlie? You've been at it for days."

"It's not easy. I've tried about a hundred different things and I've finally just managed to find a couple of tables hidden behind a firewall which might fix it."

Wilkinson shook his head. "I can't believe this site is legal."

"Me neither. Aitchison says they comply with all information security laws, but it sounds like bollocks."

"There could be anything going on in this chat room." Wilkinson scowled. "Football hooligans are the tip of the iceberg. Paedophiles, people trafficking, you name it."

"They regularly scan for that sort of activity using a set of keywords. I've been looking into it for that Tony boy who works for you."

"Right. We've not got any convictions yet." Wilkinson pointed at the screen. "So what are you pair actually doing?"

"Executing the join."

"It's taking this amount of time?"

"There's five hundred million users on there. You're lucky it's at all possible. I've had to nick about ten per cent of their data centre's resources to do it."

Wilkinson looked over at Buxton. "What were you up to on your phone?"

"Nothing."

"Come on."

Buxton shrugged. "Just looking at Twitter. Joey Barton was getting into a stupid argument with someone."

"Figures." Wilkinson frowned. "Who does he play for now?"

"Marseille. He's on loan from QPR. It was a dodge to get out of the three-month ban he got, I think."

Cullen pointed at Buxton's phone. "What's Turnbull been up to?"

Wilkinson glared at him. "What are you talking about?"

"He's been forced to tweet. Show him, Simon."

Buxton laughed. "He's been talking about how senior officers need to 'drink from the fire hydrant'."

"What does that even mean?" Wilkinson laughed.

"Me neither."

Kidd's machine beeped. He sat bolt upright. "Here we go."

Cullen leaned forward. "What is it?"

"That query's just returned. We've had to join across eight different systems and recreate their surrogate keys. Been a total nightmare."

"What can you tell me?"

Kidd tapped the screen. "We don't have a match for Blackburn Teddy."

"All this bloody time for nothing?" Wilkinson smacked his hand off the desk. "How come?"

"Blackburn Teddy hasn't got an account on Schoolbook."

Cullen frowned. "You said you thought it was Tommy Aitken."

Wilkinson looked away. "Believe me, we've pressed him hard on this. He's not even got a mobile, let alone a computer. It's not him."

"So he's not being held in connection with this any more?"

"Correct. He's still going to get done for assaulting Hugh Nichol. He's not going to drop the charges, even though Aitken was clearly under distress. Lot of bad blood there."

"Right, so we know nothing, then?"

"Not quite." Kidd tapped at the screen. "We've found Gorgie Billy."

"Who is it?"

"Someone called Kieron Bain."

47

Cullen opened the door to the interview room.

Methven was in full flow. "I wish you'd lose this 'no comment' nonsense. It's getting both of us nowhere."

Kieron smirked. "No comment."

Cullen waved over. "Sarge, a word?"

"Very well." Methven narrowed his eyes as he paused the interview. He led DS Muir outside into the corridor, slamming the door behind him. "What is it?"

Cullen nodded at the door. "Kieron Bain organised the fight at Ginty's Quarry."

"Sodding hell."

"That's a good thing, isn't it?"

"Yes, I suppose so." Methven rubbed his forehead. "What do you want to do?"

"Let me in there."

Muir held up his hands. "I'm staying."

Methven looked over at Wilkinson. "Does Alison know?"

Wilkinson shook his head. "Haven't seen her."

Methven took a deep breath. "Let's you and I go and speak to her while Cullen and Muir interview Kieron."

Wilkinson folded his arms. "Why?"

"We need to manage upwards, Paul. That's why."

Wilkinson grinned. "Right, but I'm pulling rank here, okay?"

"Very well."

Cullen put his hand on the interview room door. "We okay to progress?"

"Go for it." Methven led Wilkinson away.

Cullen sat down at the table and pressed started the recorder. "Interview recommenced. Present are DC Scott Cullen, DS Simon Muir, PC Kieron Bain and Alistair Reynolds. For the record, Mr Bain has foregone the right to a Police Federation rep."

Muir gestured for Cullen to lead.

Cullen leaned across the table. "Kieron, DS Muir here represents the Professional Standards and Ethics department. Do you know what they do?"

"I know what they do."

"Then you'll know you're in deep trouble."

Kieron shrugged. "Okay."

"There are a couple of other things DS Muir's helping us investigate. First, some of the evidence against you has disappeared from the Forensics Lab."

"I've no idea what you are talking about."

"The knife with your fingerprints on was misappropriated this morning. Do you know who stole it?"

"No."

"Was it your father?"

Kieron's eyes shot up again. "I've no idea. If it was him, he hasn't told me. I've no idea who stole it."

Cullen stared at him for a few seconds. "Second, did you have anything to do with the disappearance and murder of Alexander Aitken?"

"You know I was FAO when the car turned up."

"I know. You were also involved when we traced the car to the lock-ups on the outskirts of Ravencraig. They were conveniently on fire."

"What are you saying?"

"That's a lot of coincidences. You were involved when the car was stolen and when the body was found."

"So?"

"On Monday afternoon, you had the opportunity to report to your co-conspirators that the garage was going to be investigated. It gave them time to get the place torched and destroy any evidence."

"No comment."

"It's a pretty locked in conviction, Kieron. You killed Liam Crossan."

"No comment."

Cullen rolled his eyes. "Okay, so we're still playing this game, are we?"

"It's not a game. I'm not commenting on speculation."

"We know you arranged the fight on an internet chat room."

"I'm sorry?"

"Does Gorgie Billy mean anything to you?"

Kieron stared at the table. "No comment."

"It is you, though, isn't it?"

"Where do you get that from?"

Cullen cracked his knuckles. "Kieron, you used the same IP address to log on to your Schoolbook account."

"It could have been my old man. I was staying at his house."

Cullen held up a sheet of paper Charlie Kidd had given him. "Kieron, it was a mobile IP address, from an Android smartphone."

"My phone was stolen."

"Do you have any proof of this?"

"Not got around to reporting it yet."

"Is that true?"

Kieron sat in silence, eyes focused on Reynolds. "Okay, it was me."

"You're Gorgie Billy?"

"I am. I helped arrange the fight."

"Helped? Who was the ringleader?"

"No comment."

Cullen sighed. "Kieron, who was Blackburn Teddy?"

Kieron frowned. "I don't know what you mean. I led it."

"You were Blackburn Teddy?"

Kieron swallowed. "Aye, I was."

"Let me get this clear." Cullen paused for a few seconds, watching Kieron twitch. "You managed to use the same IP address for the main Schoolbook site, chat room as you did for the user name Gorgie Billy. Correct?"

Kieron shrugged. "I suppose."

"You suppose so?"

"Okay, it's true."

"Now, at the same time, you also had another handle on the chat room — Blackburn Teddy. You managed to use a different IP address for that one, though. Is that true?"

"Aye."

"It's not, is it?"

"I was working alone."

"Why were you so careful with Blackburn Teddy but not with Gorgie Billy?"

"Just one of those things."

Cullen stared at him, trying to psyche him out.

Kieron was Gorgie Billy. He'd been in online chats with Blackburn Teddy. They weren't the same person.

Who was Blackburn Teddy?

Focus on Teddy.

Teddy Bear — Rangers fans called themselves the Teddy Bears.

Blackburn Ranger. Blackburn Rangers.

Nothing.

Start again.

Blackburn Rangers. Blackburn, Lancashire. Blackburn Rovers.

Teddy Bear.

Ranger.

Ranger Rover.

Shite.

Cullen looked up. "Is Blackburn Teddy Craig Smith?"

Kieron leaned back in his chair. "Craig who?"

Cullen looked at Muir. "DS Muir, what sort of sentence would you expect Mr Bain to receive on conviction."

"I'd need to think." Muir exhaled. "There's at least four or five crimes Mr Bain will be charged with, which may rise to another two or three. Murder's obviously the main one."

Kieron's eyes darted between them. "Murder?"

"Liam Crossan." Cullen smiled. "We've already discussed this."

Kieron sat back. "No comment."

Muir folded his arms. "All in, we're probably talking a minimum of thirty years."

"I can only imagine what they do to ex-police officers inside, but you've convicted a fair few."

"Well, first they'd lose their pension. That's probably the least of Mr Bain's worries." Muir straightened his jacket sleeve. "Ex-officers aren't the most popular inmates. The prisoners don't like them and the officers don't like them."

"What does 'don't like' mean?"

Muir grinned, mischief in his eyes. "If you're lucky it involves knives fashioned from other objects."

Kieron tapped his fingers on the table top. "What do you want me to say?"

Cullen looked at Reynolds. "For the record, I'm not trying to ensure certain words come out of your client's mouth. I just want the truth, no matter how messy it is."

Reynolds reached over and whispered into his client's ear.

Cullen glared at the lawyer. "Could you repeat what you just told your client?"

"That's not a matter for the record."

"Okay. Do you wish to state anything further, Kieron?"

"No."

Cullen looked at Muir. "Where does that leave us?"

"Prison, I think."

Cullen nodded slowly and emphatically. "Well, not us. That certainly looks like where you are heading, Kieron."

"Mr Cullen, I'd suggest you refrain from bullying my client. At the moment, he's under the presumption of innocence. There's no clear path to a conviction."

"We think there is."

"'Think' isn't good enough."

Cullen grinned. "You know Kieron's employment history will be a matter of public record if this goes to full trial."

"I'm sorry?"

"A case like this will be all over the papers. TV too. If Mr Bain doesn't plead guilty then it'll be a lengthy hearing. I wouldn't like to be in his shoes."

Reynolds whispered in Kieron's ear, waiting for him to nod. "My client wishes to make a statement."

Kieron took a deep breath then rubbed his hands together slowly, his eyes were focused on the table top. "I'm not going to comment on this Liam Crossan boy. Whatever I give you, I'm not talking about that. I'll talk about Blackburn Teddy."

"Who is Blackburn Teddy?"

"Craig Smith."

48

"You sure it's Craig Smith?" Cullen licked his lips.

"Aye. It's him."

"How do you know him?"

"I knew his son, Kyle. We both went to school in Bathgate. We stayed in touch when I moved to Dalkeith. I used to go round to his dad's house all the time. We watched the football on Sky — Dad wouldn't let us have it at home. We used to play on his Playstation. He was a good lad."

"Was Kyle at the fight?"

"He moved to Aberdeen." Kieron laughed. "Studying to be a lawyer, would you believe?"

"Go on."

"Kyle's parents split up a few years ago. His old man used to have cards nights round his house. When me and Kyle turned sixteen, he let us in on them. That's when I started getting into gambling."

"Gambling? That's why your mother kicked you out of her house, wasn't it?"

"Aye."

"What happened?"

"It got out of hand, and pretty quickly, too. I worked in the Tesco in Bathgate when I was sixteen, I joined the force when I was seventeen. Had some cash put aside. I started getting cocky with it — I cleaned up at one of Kyle's old man's cards nights, took in about thirty grand. That didn't make me popular." He took a deep breath. "The next few nights we played, I was taken to the cleaners. I lost my thirty grand in two nights. After a couple of months, I was down a hundred grand."

"How did you expect to pay that debt off?"

"It didn't feel real." Kieron rubbed a tear from his eye. "I couldn't go to anyone with it. I'd lose my job if it came out. I told mum about it. Not how much I'd lost. She made me stop gambling. I told my old boy I'd lost a few hundred quid in a casino. He called me a silly bugger and that was that."

"What happened to the debt?"

Kieron gripped the table edge. "Kyle's dad gave me a loan. Craig Smith."

"How much are we talking here?"

"One hundred and four thousand plus change. He said there were things I could help out with that would get the debt cleared quicker."

"How much is left outstanding?"

"Just over seventy."

"And how much of that was repaid by cash?"

"Five grand."

"What have you been doing for him?"

"No comment."

Cullen sighed. It had been going so well, too. "We're back playing that game, are we?"

"No comment."

"Have you any idea why Alexander Aitken was killed?"

Kieron shook his head. "No."

"No comment or no idea?"

"No idea."

"Are you saying Craig Smith killed Alexander Aitken?"

"No comment."

"Kieron, was it you or Craig who pushed the Range Rover?"

"No comment."

"You were FAO, weren't you? If it was you, then you've perverted the course of justice. That's another serious crime to add to the list."

Kieron swallowed. "No comment."

Cullen stared up at the ceiling. Switch it around. "Who stole the knife from downstairs, Kieron?"

"No comment."

"Was it your dad?"

"No comment."

Cargill appeared at the door. She nodded at Cullen.

Cullen leaned over. "Interview terminated." He stopped the recorder. "I'm sure you understand this won't be the last time we speak to you, Mr Bain."

Kieron avoided eye contact. "I can, but you're not getting anything else from me."

49

"Here we are." Cullen pulled into the kerb, just outside Ranger Rover.

"You're doing well." Methven opened the door.

Cullen looked round. Patronising git. "Thanks."

"I mean it. You could've taken our chat the other day entirely the wrong way, but you haven't."

"You've not seen the best of me."

"I'm sure of it. I'm here to help you get the best out. There's a changing of the guard and you need to make sure you're on the right shift."

"Is that a threat?"

"No. Just be mindful of it."

Another car pulled in just ahead of them, filled with a squad from Bathgate.

"Thought there was supposed to be three cars?"

"We're arresting a car salesman, Cullen. How hard can it be?"

"This is a car salesman who organises football hooligan meets." Cullen got out and headed over to the car, leaning in the window. "Is he here?"

Green wound the window down. "How do you want to play this?"

Methven raised his bushy eyebrows and thought for a few seconds. "Let's go and get him. Cuff him and take him back to Leith Walk."

Cullen nodded at the two in the back seat. "You two with us." He pointed at Green. "Stay here. Cover him if he makes a run for it."

"Sure."

Cullen looked inside the garage. Smith was facing away from them, flirting with the receptionist.

"Come on, Cullen." Methven set off at a quick pace, flanked by the Bathgate uniforms.

They walked across the car park at the front of the building, full of second-hand SUVs and Minis.

Cullen felt butterflies again — there was nothing like the thrill of an arrest.

Cullen opened the door, causing a chime to sound.

Smith turned to face them, focusing on Cullen. "Have you found out who stole my car?"

Cullen smiled. "Mr Smith, we're arresting you on suspicion of organising a football hooligan meet."

"Excuse me?" Smith frowned.

The uniforms grabbed Smith by the wrist.

"You were involved in the fight at Ginty's Quarry, were you not?"

"Nothing to do with me." Smith tried to shrug them off. "Never heard of the place."

"You need to come with us."

Smith waved towards his staff. "I need to get those two to shut this place at the end of the day, okay?"

Methven. "Fine."

Smith turned away. He quickly delivered an elbow into the face of one of the officers before headbutting the other.

Cullen started towards him.

Smith stepped into Methven's run, blocking him. He kneed him in the groin, sending the DS crumpling to the floor, grabbing his testicles.

Cullen slowed his approach, trying to goad Smith into attacking.

He lunged forward, his fist shooting towards Cullen's face.

Cullen ducked. Smith's fist ploughed into his shoulder.

Cullen fell to his knees, pain screaming all over his body.

Out of the corner of his eye, he caught Smith jumping into a display Range Rover. It growled into life before jolting forward and smashing through the glass front of the showroom.

Cullen got to his feet, clutching his shoulder.

Methven staggered to his knees. "Never wanted to sodding have bastarding kids, anyway."

"We need to get after him."

Methven vomited.

Cullen put a hand to his back. "Are you okay?"

"I'll be fine." Methven pointed to the ruined shopfront. "Go after him, I'll catch up."

The uniformed officers were both unconscious.

Cullen grabbed an Airwave from the nearest. "DC Cullen to Control. Over."

"Receiving. Over."

"Need urgent back-up to Ravencraig. Ranger Rover. Repeat, Ranger Rover."

Green rushed towards them.

Cullen pointed down the road. "Where did he go?"

"He headed into town."

"Get after him, then!" Cullen started sprinting, turning to see Methven hobbling along behind.

Cullen got to their Saab and turned the ignition.

Methven got in. "Go!"

Cullen shot off, leaving the Volvo in his wake. He switched the lights and sirens on as he hit sixty on the busy high street, weaving in and out of traffic.

A long queue loomed ahead at the Co-op, so he cut into the oncoming lane, making three cars pull in, his speed dipping to thirty.

As they passed Nichol's Garage on the way out of town, Cullen spotted Smith's car. "There he is!"

He cleared ninety, the houses and other buildings giving way to countryside, damp fields under a grey sky.

He chucked the Airwave to Methven. "Are you sure you're okay?"

Methven winced — his skin had gone white. "I'll live."

"I've called Control. Can you get a roadblock set up? He's heading for Linlithgow."

"Doubt they'll be able to manage."

"Make them."

"I'll try."

Cullen overtook a bus and a slow-moving tractor in quick succession, powering down a long straight into the Ravencraig hills. As he started the descent towards Linlithgow, he saw Smith's Range Rover in the distance, darting between traffic. "There he is!"

Methven looked up. "Don't want him to get to the motorway."

"You getting any joy?"

"There's a couple of cars heading our way." Methven grimaced through the pain. "Should be able to see them soon."

Cullen spotted the flashing blue lights in the distance.

It was clear Smith had too — he swerved left, slicing through a thick hedge into the harvested field beyond, full of wheat stubble and ready for ploughing.

Cullen traced the perimeter — it ran for hundreds of yards,

looking like it abutted the M9 a few fields along, heading towards Falkirk and Stirling.

Smith was on the opposite side, heading straight for a thick forest.

Methven tapped the dashboard. "Is this thing a four-by-four?"

"Think so." Cullen felt the four wheel drive kick in as he traced Smith's arc and followed him through the hedge. One of the side mirrors got caught, knocking it back against the car.

They were thrown around inside.

Cullen braced himself as he floored it, relieved to feel the car accelerate as it made up ground on Smith.

Smith's car changed direction away from the woods, heading towards the dual carriageway.

"He's aiming for the motorway." Cullen hauled the wheel round.

Methven clicked the Airwave. "Target is heading for M9, repeat, heading for M9."

Smith struggled up the verge at the edge of the motorway. Cullen had closed the gap to twenty metres.

The Range Rover burst through the crash barrier, continuing straight across both lanes and hitting the central reservation before bouncing back and spinning.

"Thank God the traffic's light." Cullen slowed to twenty as he squeezed through the gap Smith had created, driving over the destroyed barrier.

Smith was turning his car around.

Cullen floored it, letting the clutch spring up. The Saab shot forwards Smith, smashing into the side of the Range Rover, sending it rocking.

The front of the Saab buckled, the engine grinding.

The Range Rover crawled down the motorway, groaning almost as badly.

Cullen pumped the accelerator, getting the Saab going. It started to pick up some speed.

Smith swerved across both lanes every few seconds, his head turning back to look at them.

Cullen kept a reasonable distance, then sped through on the outside, catching Smith as he switched lanes.

Cullen shifted the wheel out and then back again, pushing Smith left. He put his foot to the floor. The wheels squealed. The momentum was with him — he forced Smith off the road.

The Range Rover rolled down the hill.

Cullen slammed the brakes on. He reversed before pulling onto the hard shoulder. He got out of the car and looked down the hill. The

Range Rover was lying on its side. "There he is." He jogged down the side of the hill, almost losing his footing.

Methven was down first, ducking low to inspect the car's interior. "He's not here!"

Cullen looked around. "Where is he?"

Methven pointed behind the Range Rover. "There!"

Cullen sprinted off across the field, his shoes struggling to grip the stubble. "Stop!"

Smith turned around just as Cullen rugby-tackled him to the ground.

Smith lashed out with his elbow, connecting with Cullen's cheek.

Methven kicked Smith in the face.

Cullen reached over and put handcuffs on Smith, his face seared with pain. "You're not getting away this time!"

50

"Here we are then." Wilkinson came over to the whiteboard, carrying a cardboard tray of coffees from the canteen.

Methven winced as he reached over to take his Americano. "Thanks."

Wilkinson slurped at his coffee. "What's up with you?"

"Got kneed in the bollocks." Methven grimaced. "It fucking hurts. Second time this week."

Wilkinson bellowed with laughter. "That's the first time I've heard you properly swear, lad."

"Well, I sodding wish it wasn't."

"Let's get on with this." Cargill sipped her latte.

Wilkinson frowned. "Get on with what?"

"Proving this case."

"We've got Smith on some charges. He'll go away for a couple of years."

"We need more concrete evidence, Paul. You and I both know that Kieron Bain or Dean Richardson are going to change their minds and recant their statements"

"Aye, that or contradict each other in court."

"Correct. We need more." Cargill turned to the whiteboard. In the centre she wrote Alexander Aitken then drew three main arrows away from it leading to Disappearance, Craig Smith and Kieron Bain. She tapped on Disappearance. "What do we know about Aitken vanishing?"

Cullen put his cup down. "He was picked up by a Land Rover Discovery we later found to have been scrapped."

Methven frowned. "Did that ANPR search ever come back?"

"Came back negative — no sightings of it."

"How could it have collected Aitken in South Gyle Crescent but wasn't picked up by any cameras until Ravencraig?"

Cullen shrugged. "There are a few ways to go if you want to avoid main roads. Plus something like that could head across fields with ease."

"Basically, we've got nothing on the car?"

"Nothing."

Cargill sucked her coffee. "What about Kieron Bain?"

"We know he's Gorgie Billy. We think he killed Liam Crossan."

"And he gave us Craig Smith." Cargill drew an arrow between Kieron and each of Crossan and Smith. She tapped the pen on Smith. "Other than stopping DS Methven from having any children, what else do we have on Craig Smith?"

"He's leading this hooligan firm." Wilkinson walked over and stood alongside her. "Soon as you lot are done with him, me and a few of my boys are going to give him a right going over about the network he's involved in."

"Anything specific?"

Wilkinson smiled. "Charlie Kidd's found another three fights on that chat room. Chelsea, Millwall and my Leeds boys. Makes me proud to be a Yorkshireman. Not."

"We really need to shut Schoolbook down." Cargill shook her head. "How is Smith's group organised in the real world?"

"We think they use Rangers supporters clubs as a front. They organise buses through to Ibrox every other week, perfect front for these hooligan meets."

"Do you know anyone else in this firm?"

"Nothing springs to mind. We might have something in the files."

Cullen stared at the board, his mind dancing between the boxes. "What about Aitken and Souness? They were from Ravencraig. Used to go to every Rangers game and they were at the quarry, too."

Wilkinson frowned. "You think they're in this group?"

"Maybe."

"Let's put it down." Cargill added Aitken and Souness, linking both to Smith. "Who else?"

"Dean Richardson."

Methven jangled his change. "The guy who stole your friend's mobile phone?"

"Right. He's a flatmate of Derek Miller, brother of the late Keith Miller."

Cargill wrote the names down, an arrow joining Derek to Richardson. She stared at the board for a few seconds before turning back to face the group. "We still don't know why Aitken was killed."

Cullen focused on the board, unable to keep his eyes away from Derek. He shouldn't be up there — he was Hibs, not Rangers.

Something tickled at the back of his brain, sent his synapses sparking. Something Derek had told him. "There were two homosexuals in Aitken's firm."

"Watch it with the homophobia." Cargill arched her eyebrows. "We've had quite enough already from DS Irvine."

"Who says I'm being homophobic? It's a possible lead. Derek told me the leader of the group found out he had gay members and wasn't impressed. Smith was ashamed two of his team were gay — you know what football is like, right? There aren't any openly gay footballers and those that come out end up having to retire."

Cargill nodded. "If the leader was Smith, you're saying the gays were Aitken and Souness?"

"They shared a flat." Methven clicked his fingers. "There were extra strong condoms in one of their drawers."

Methven frowned. "Didn't Souness attack someone as part of some homophobic assault?"

Cargill folded her arms. "Where did that come from?"

"Gavin Tait. He'd tried it on with Souness back in the day."

Cargill went back to the board. "We know Souness was stabbed by Gordon Beveridge at the quarry." She drew a line. "According to Kieron Bain, Aitken grabbed the knife from Beveridge then stabbed him. Souness bled to death in their flat. Aitken must have tried to care for him."

"He went to work, though."

Cargill shrugged. "Got to keep up appearances, I suppose." She tapped the board over Aitken. "Aitken has a girlfriend, right?"

Cullen nodded. "A young girl called Demi Baird. They were engaged."

"But they didn't live together?"

"No. Apparently because he was religious." Cullen finished his coffee. "Nothing in their flat suggested Aitken was particularly zealous. She might be a beard."

Cargill tutted. "I warned you about the homophobia."

Wilkinson frowned. "What's a bloody beard?"

Cullen grinned. "Certain men marry to hide the fact they're gay. Like Elton John?"

"He's married to a bloke, though."

"He married a woman in the eighties." Methven laughed. "What do you suggest we do?"

"Speak to her again." Cargill wrote Demi on the board. "See what we can glean from her."

Methven nodded. "I'll get Angela and Buxton to do it."

"DI Wilkinson and I will speak to DI Bain." Cargill looked at Cullen and Methven. "In the meantime, can you two interview Richardson about Smith? See if you can get him to link Smith to these killings."

"Will do."

"Try speaking to Gavin Tait again." Cargill led Wilkinson away.

Cullen got out his phone and dialled the number Tait had given him. Straight to voicemail. "Bastard. He's killed that phone number."

"Try again after the interview."

51

"We've caught the ringleader of your group, Mr Richardson." Methven folded his arms. "Craig Smith."

Richardson glanced at his lawyer, Alistair Reynolds. "Really?"

"What, do you think it's someone else?"

Richardson grinned. "No, Craig's a respectable business man. I'm surprised he was the ringleader of a bunch of football hooligans."

"Don't play that game with us. We know you were there. We know you're involved. Mr Smith will be going away for a very long time."

Richardson didn't say anything.

Cullen opened his notebook. "Mr Richardson, did you know Kenny Souness and Alexander Aitken were lovers?"

Richardson looked away. "I don't know anything about that."

"What about if we were to drop the charges against you?"

"The phone charges?"

"Aye."

Richardson sniffed. "I might know something, but I'd want to speak to my solicitor."

"Well, he's here."

Reynolds smiled. "In private."

Methven paused the interview. "We'll be back in a few minutes, we expect you to be singing by the time we're back."

Outside into the corridor, Methven gave a deep groan. "I think I need to go to the doctor. My balls are still absolute sodding agony."

"I'd get them checked out. Not something you want to mess about with."

"No." Methven screwed his face up.

Cullen's phone rang — Angela. "Hi."

"We've just spoken to Demi, Scott."

"And?"

"When we spoke to her the first time, she was going on about Aitken being religious, right?"

"Yes."

"Well, she said it again. Seems to have already deified Aitken. He's an angel now, according to her. Anyway, turns out that they were saving themselves for marriage."

"They'd never had sex?"

Methven raised a bushy eyebrow.

Cullen nodded at him.

"That's right."

Cullen swapped hands. "Could he have been using her as a beard?"

"She's not going to know if she was, is she? Unless there was some bloody contract between them, which I seriously doubt."

"Yeah, I think you're right. Thanks for heading out there." Cullen ended the call and glanced over at Methven. "Never had sex."

Methven grinned. "More evidence."

"Right." Cullen redialled Gavin Tait.

"Hello?"

"Gavin, it's Scott Cullen of Lothian & Borders. I need to ask you some questions. When would be a convenient time to get you into the station for a statement?"

"I've given my statement. When you didn't call me back, I thought you didn't want me any more."

Cullen ignored the innuendo, glad he didn't have it on speaker. "I need to know about your relationship with Kenny Souness."

"I told you."

"We've reason to believe Kenny was homosexual."

"It's no longer a crime."

"I'm not saying it is. I just need to know if you can confirm it for me. Did anything happen between the pair of you?"

"I think I told you I tried it on with him."

"That's right." Cullen flipped through his notebook, finding the notes from the last time he'd spoken to Tait. "He punched you and ran off."

Tait sighed down the line. "That's right."

"Are you sure?"

There was a long pause. "Maybe not."

"What happened, Gavin?"

"I think I told you I tried to kiss him. It was more than that. He kissed me back. It was a real Brokeback Mountain moment. Kenny was strong, he took control of me."

"What happened? Did you have sex?"

"Not quite. Xander caught us."

"What did he do?"

"He ran off. Kenny shouted after him, then he turned back to me and called me a poof. I said it takes one to know one. He punched me and said if I told anyone he'd kill me. Then he ran after Xander."

"You knew that they were an item?"

"An item?" Tait exhaled down the line. "I thought Kenny was worried Xander would tell people. Are you saying they were both gay?"

"It appears that way. Why didn't you tell anyone?"

"When Kenny said he'd kill me, I believed him."

"Why didn't I hear any of this on Friday?"

"I've got to keep some things in my back pocket."

"What about the second time you saw him? In the pub toilets?"

"He thanked me for not telling anyone. I was pretty pissed so I said I might mention it. He came right over and pushed me against the wall. He grabbed me by the balls and said if anyone found out I'd lose them. He called me a cheap rent boy and said I'd lose my biggest assets."

"What did you do?"

"I think I cried and pissed all over my shoes. There's only so long you can keep up the hard man act when a psychopath has your balls in his hands. He punched me and left."

Cullen stayed silent for a few seconds, thinking. "I need you to go to a police station and give a statement covering everything we've said. It's important. Otherwise, I'll come and see you myself."

"Still haven't recovered from the last time."

"I'm serious. I need you to do it right away. There's a station just up from where you live. Remember, it's Scott Cullen in A Division of Lothian & Borders."

"Fine, I'll do it."

"Thanks." Cullen ended the call. "Tait just told me Souness was gay. Kissed him back. Xander saw them at it."

Methven grinned and motioned towards the interview room door. "Let's get back in."

They returned to their seats.

Methven recommenced the interview. "Have you had your chat?"

Richardson nodded. "Aye, we have."

"And?"

"What's the deal here?"

"The charges will be dropped relating to the theft of one Samsung Galaxy S3."

Reynolds shook his head. "I'd love to know how you can arrange that."

Cullen folded his arms. "I can, because your client nicked it off my flatmate."

"Fine." Reynolds waved with his fingers.

"The charges will be dropped if it leads to a useful piece of information which helps secure the conviction of Mr Smith."

Richardson creased his forehead. "Go on, then."

Methven got the interview going again. "Mr Richardson, can you confirm what you know about the relationship between Mr Alexander Aitken and Mr Kenneth Souness?"

Richardson took a deep breath. "They were poofs."

Cullen swallowed. "You mean homosexual?"

"Aye, that."

"How do you know?"

"Saw them. Just after that Kenny boy got slotted at the quarry."

"What were they doing?"

"They were all smoochy, kissing and cuddling. Aitken was saying 'I'll protect you,' shite like that."

"And this was before you saw Mr Aitken stab Gordon Beveridge?"

"Aye, it was. He grabbed the knife and stabbed him. Then he took Souness away, back to their love nest, I'd wager."

Cullen looked round at Methven and spoke in a deliberately loud whisper. "What do you reckon? It's not much, is it?"

Methven returned it. "I can't see us getting away with dropping those other charges."

Richardson leaned forward, his eyes dancing all over the place. "I can tell you more."

Cullen echoed the posture, leaning across the table. "Oh aye?"

"Aye. I told Craig Smith about it."

"And did Mr Smith do anything with that information?"

Richardson raised his hands. "That's as far as my part of the story goes."

52

"This is from Dean Richardson." Cargill tossed the written and signed statement in front of Craig Smith and Campbell McLintock, his lawyer.

Smith swallowed hard, nibbling his bottom lip. His hands were cuffed together and he lay them on the desk.

McLintock picked up the statement and started reading.

Cullen stood off to the side, avoiding looking at anyone in particular, just listening in.

Cargill flattened her hands on the table. "Mr McLintock, what I've presented to you will stand up in court. We've a signed statement showing Mr Smith had knowledge of a homosexual relationship amongst members of the football hooligan outfit he led." She tossed over a transcript of an interview with Derek Miller. "We have it from a separate source that Mr Smith wasn't pleased with this news."

"You think this will stand up in court?"

Cargill smiled. "I know it will."

"This is all hearsay, Inspector."

"We've enough to send Mr Smith away for a long time. This is your chance to make good on all your public proclamations and save taxpayers money."

Smith hugged his arms tight to his torso. "I'm saying nothing."

"Fine, then it's a matter for the courts." Cargill smiled at McLintock. "Do you have faith your client's version of events will stand up? We've checked and he has no alibis for the nights in question. We do have statements pointing to his guilt. That's a risk to your reputation, Campbell, as much as anything."

McLintock nodded slowly. "It is up to my client to listen to my advice and then act accordingly."

Smith drummed his fingers on the table. "I'm saying nothing."

Cullen rubbed the back of his neck. "Why did you run?"

Smith turned to look at him. "Come again?"

"We came to arrest you at your car showroom and you fled. That's pretty guilty behaviour."

"Let's just say I've got a healthy dislike of police officers."

"So you're denying any involvement in the deaths of Alexander Aitken and Kenneth Souness?"

"No comment."

"You're responsible for the deaths of two young men. It might help us understand if you could tell us why."

Smith sat and glowered. "I'm not standing for it."

Cullen frowned. "For what?"

"Nothing." Smith looked away.

"For getting beaten by Hibs and Celtic fans?"

Smith laughed it off. "No comment."

"Having homosexuals in your outfit?"

Smith glared at him. "I'm not having my firm infested with poofters."

"You're referring to Mr Aitken and Mr Souness?"

"Aye. I'm not having a pair of bufties in my team. Don't want the rest of the lads to catch it."

"Catch what?"

"Being gay. The pair of them will try to suck all my lads' cocks. I'm not standing for it."

"We've reason to believe they were in a relationship since their teens."

Smith scowled. "That's shite. Aitken was engaged to be married. Souness must've turned him into a poof."

Cullen smirked. "As far as I'm aware, homosexuality isn't like vampirism, it's not something that can be caught."

"Fucking AIDS is, though." Spittle formed at the side of Smith's mouth. "They're all at it, fucking each other all the fucking time. Makes me fucking sick. Fucking poofs. What if we got cut in the same fight, eh? I'd have fucking AIDs."

"Neither victim was HIV positive." Cullen folded his arms. "It happens to heterosexuals as well."

Smith got to his feet and pointed a finger at Cullen. "Are you one? If you are, I want some proper officers in here."

The PCSO stood to attention, readying himself to jump in.

McLintock reached over and grabbed hold of Smith's arm. "Sit down."

Smith stabbed the digit at McLintock. "I'll stand if I fucking like. This prick here's trying to tell me it's okay for a bunch of Scottish hard men to have a pair of nancy boys in their number."

Cullen cleared his throat. "Sit down."

Smith complied, shaking his head as he did so. "Fucking poofs."

"Is that enough reason to have them killed?"

"They made the rest of us look weak. All over the message boards across Scotland, people are talking about how the Ravencraig Rangers firm let a pair of jessies in. I'm the fucking laughing stock of this great nation."

"You had them killed because of their sexuality?"

"Aye, I did. That little bastard Kieron Bain told you about it, didn't he? I knew I shouldn't have trusted him. Shouldn't have got the little toerag to drive it off the edge of that fucking bing."

"So Kieron killed him?"

"Aye. We gave him a good pasting beforehand, but it was Kieron who started the engine and let him go." Smith shook his head. "After all I did for him over the years. Fuck's sake. That's gratitude for you."

"Why did you have Aitken killed in your car?"

"To throw you dickheads off the trail. I'm hardly likely to have used my pride and joy to kill that little arsehole. I could've done with the money as well."

"It almost worked."

Cargill leaned forward and terminated the interview. "Mr McLintock, I think we both appreciate your client's candour in the last ten minutes. I sincerely hope it'll avoid going to a lengthy trial in the courts."

"I bet you're a fucking dyke." Smith spat at her.

Cargill brushed at her blouse, her face screwed up. "I beg your pardon?"

"You're a fucking clam jouster, right? A lesbian. You make me sick."

"My sexuality is my own business." Cargill got to her feet and squared up to him across the desk.

Smith launched his head at her. He caught her on the chin, sending her sprawling. She collapsed on her chair and spun backwards, pushing Cullen over.

Smith shoulder-barged the PCSO into the wall and headed towards the door.

McLintock kicked Smith's feet from under him.

The PCSO stumbled to his feet and grabbed hold of Smith's arm, forcing it behind his back.

McLintock helped Cargill up. "I don't think I'll be representing him any more."

53

"Here you go, Scott." Cargill handed him a large measure of Glenmorangie. "I thought you'd be a Dunpender man?"

"I'm keeping well away from it." Cullen took a sip, savouring the burn. "How's the chin?"

"I'll survive. I got worse in my rugby days."

Methven and Wilkinson entered the Incident Room, busier and noisier than it had been for days.

"The Procurator Fiscal's happy to progress with the case against Craig Smith." Cargill handed them both shots of Dunpender.

Methven knocked his back in one go. "I imagine we'll need a bit more information to make it concrete."

Wilkinson topped his glass up. "Feels like as good a time as any to celebrate."

"How do we get DI Bain to confess?" Cargill sipped her whisky. "It's clear as day he hid the knife. We just have to get him to let it out."

Cullen refilled his glass. "How are the Complaints handling it?"

"Muir's back at Fettes briefing Fletcher. He spoke to DI Bain at his house. He still vehemently denies it."

"Do you believe him?"

Cargill threw up her hands. "Who knows?"

Sharon and Angela wandered over, carrying cups of wine.

Cargill raised her glass. "Thanks for your efforts this week, ladies."

Sharon avoided eye contact with Cullen. "What are the plans for this evening?"

"Wait till this lot dries up then head across the road."

Methven pushed Cullen aside. "I want to apologise for taking the piss earlier."

Cullen frowned. "About what?"

"The rising star stuff. I was a bit disparaging about it. I'm sorry."

"Apology accepted. I'm sorry for turning up pissed. Thanks for covering for me."

"That's okay." Methven winced before clutching his balls. "Need to go and check if they've progressed from golf balls to baseballs." He waddled away.

Sharon was next to him, drinking a glass of red. "What's up with Crystal?"

"Someone kicked him in the balls."

"Nice."

Cullen lifted his glass before moving off to a seat at the opposite end of the room. He sat down, stretching his feet out on a table. He sipped the whisky and stared out of the window, continually glancing at Sharon.

He'd been a total shit.

She'd not told the truth, but she hadn't gone out of her way to lie. He'd never asked her if she'd had a lesbian affair with Cargill. She'd never had to deny it.

Like he was a paragon of virtue himself.

He looked Sharon up and down. She was wearing a dark skirt and white blouse. He wanted to cuddle up alongside her, talk to her, get all of the shit out of his head. He wanted to apologise.

She caught his gaze. He looked away.

Focus on the work.

Bain had clearly hidden the knife, that was the avenue they were going down. What if it wasn't Bain that helped his son?

He sat upright, thinking other possibilities, trying to remember all the times he'd seen Kieron.

At the crime scene, Cullen had seen him talking to Irvine.

Irvine had also been in the Scene of Crime lab with Bain earlier.

Irvine lived in Dalkeith, same as Kieron Bain.

54

"Could you please describe your relationship with DS Alan Irvine?" Cullen sat in the interview room, chewing on extra strong mints to hide the stench of whisky.

Kieron frowned. "He's a good mate. He's helped me a few times with advice and that. How to be a good copper."

"So you're friends?"

Kieron paused for a few seconds. "I'd say so."

"How do you know each other?"

"We both live in Dalkeith."

"Quite a lot of people live in Dalkeith, Kieron. Did you just bump into him in the chip shop and become mates?"

Kieron smiled. "We're both Jambos."

"Now we're getting somewhere. I take it you mean Heart of Midlothian supporters?"

"Aye."

Cullen frowned. "I thought you'd be a Rangers fan."

"Cos of my old man?" Kieron laughed. "Mum's old boy played for Hearts in the sixties. He got in there before Dad did."

"Were there any formal means by which you and Mr Irvine were acquainted?"

"We were both in the Midlothian of Hearts Supporters Club."

Straight on the money. "Would that be a front for hooliganism?"

"No. It's a genuine supporters club. It covers all of Midlothian — Dalkeith, Lasswade, Bonnyrigg, Penicuik, Gorebridge."

"Did Mr Irvine steal the knife for you?"

"I've no idea." Kieron opened his eyes wide. "No idea at all."

~

"CAN YOU HURRY UP, MATE?" Cullen shivered as he leaned against Irvine's black sporty Astra, parked in the station's rear garage.

The specialist forensic officer looked up from the lock. "This will take precisely as long as it takes."

Cullen sighed. "My whisky's getting warm."

Methven chuckled then winced. "My sodding balls."

"Not getting any better?"

"Almost bloody basketballs." Methven closed his eyes and groaned. "I want to see this through."

"You could just get a taxi home."

"I've half a mind to take the rest of the Dunpender with me."

"You're welcome to it."

"Why is that one left?" Methven scowled. "All the Likely Laddie is gone first."

"It's a long story."

The driver door lock eventually popped up, triggering the central locking.

"Here we go." Cullen sprang into action, opening the passenger door.

His gloved hands search the footwells.

He checked the glove box.

He rooted around in the CD caddy.

He checked the back seat.

The door pockets.

Nothing.

"Got it."

Cullen got out of the car and raced round to the boot.

Methven pointed in. "There you go."

Sitting in the middle, wrapped in a Tesco carrier bag, was the knife.

~

AN HOUR LATER, Cullen and Methven stood in the observation room, watching Cargill and Fletcher interview Irvine with the usual coterie of lawyer and Scottish Police Federation rep.

The interview boomed through the large speakers, almost too bassy. Fletcher's voice was so deep it was difficult to make out, but Cullen was there to hear Irvine.

Tears flooded down Irvine's cheeks. "I thought he was innocent."

"You thought Kieron Bain was innocent?"

Irvine nodded. "Aye, I did."

"You admit to stealing the knife from the Scene of Crime lab?"

Irvine nodded again. "Aye."

"You know how serious that is?"

Irvine didn't answer.

"DS Irvine, you're going to lose your pension. You are going to go to prison."

"I know." Irvine slumped down on the table top with his head resting in his arms. "He was a mate. He was innocent. We knew each other from the Hearts supporters club. He can't have done it."

"DS Irvine. Mr Bain has admitted to the crime. He is going to trial for murder. You are going to be charged with accessory to murder, amongst other things. You'll be lucky to be out of prison in five years."

Irvine looked up and screamed, the primal noise filling the small room. Cullen slammed his hand against the mute button, killing it dead.

He watched Irvine for a few minutes. He thought back to all the dealings they'd had, mainly to Irvine abusing him or to the time Cullen grabbed him by the throat. He'd wanted to see him suffer so many times.

Seeing it now didn't give him much joy.

55

"I'm off for a slash." Wilkinson put his latest empty pint glass on the bar. "Get us another Stella, lad."

Cullen sank another gulp of Staropramen — he was getting his money's worth from Turnbull's credit card. He ordered a brace of pints.

Wilkinson returned, drying his hands on his trousers. He took a big dent out of the pint. "Cheers."

Cullen held up his glass. "Cheers."

"Penny for them."

"It's nothing."

"Doesn't look like nothing."

Cullen sighed. "All right, I was thinking back to just over a year ago. We were in here celebrating getting the Schoolbook Killer."

"Aye, before you proved Bain wrong."

Cullen shrugged. "Feels different tonight. It's my collar this time and it's airtight. I've worked hard to get this."

"Aye, it's a proper result."

Cullen looked across at the officers celebrating. "Buxton's off his head already."

"Aye, he's not been interviewing suspects or finding bloody knives."

"He's going to fire into Chantal Jain. Just you watch."

Wilkinson shook his head. "Remember what I said?"

"Never shit where you eat?"

"Right."

Cullen sank the rest of his previous drink and started on the next. "What'll happen with Irvine?"

"That's him proper fucked." Wilkinson took a deep pull of his drink. "You don't fancy a detachment to a hooligan unit, do you?"

"Is there a DS position in it?"

"Not likely."

"Forget it." Cullen glanced over and caught Sharon, sat with Cargill and Turnbull over by the door, looking at him.

Wilkinson patted a damp hand on Cullen's shoulder. "I'm off for a tab." He grabbed the pint and headed outside.

Cullen caught Turnbull's look as he watched Wilkinson stagger outside.

Turnbull got to his feet and made his way over to Cullen. They clinked glasses. "Bit of an odd drinking partner for you."

"I didn't used to think much of him but we've worked pretty well together on this case. He's not that bad."

"Better not be trying to poach my rising star."

"He might be."

Turnbull chuckled. "I'm glad to be rid of him." He fixed a stare on Cullen. "You've done well on this. Again. You're going places, Cullen."

"Thanks." Cullen blushed.

"I mean it. This isn't a fluke. Your tenacity and determination is a testament to us all. I know you like to bend the rules slightly, which is something you need to document on your personal development plan. I'll make sure you're looked after."

Cullen held Turnbull's gaze, feeling sweat trickle down his back. "Remember what I said earlier, I want to be a DS."

Turnbull slowly nodded. "Let me think about it. We've got a situation with DS Irvine. Let's see what we can do about that."

Cullen didn't get a chance to thank him — there was a commotion from the front, Wilkinson trying to push someone out of the door.

"Let me at him!"

Turnbull and Cullen jostled their way to the front.

Bain.

"Get yourself back home!" Wilkinson grabbed Bain by the collar of his polo shirt. "You shouldn't bloody be here!"

"That fat bastard is getting his fuckin' arse handed to him!" Bain spotted Turnbull. "You!" He pointed his finger. "You fucked me over here! I'm going to kick your fat fuckin' arse!"

"Stay here." Cullen pushed Turnbull back to the far side of the bar before going over to help, grabbing Buxton and a couple of uniformed officers on the way.

Wilkinson manhandled Bain out to the street, locking him in a wrestling hold.

Cullen squared up to him. "What are you playing at?"

Bain's eyes were almost bulging out of his head. "That fat bastard's fucked my career up!"

Cullen pointed a finger at him. "The only one make an arse of your career up is you. Get a cab home. Now."

"He's trying to frame me for what my idiot son did!"

"Irvine stole that knife."

"What?"

"It was in the boot of his car." Cullen looked around at Wilkinson. "Come on, back me up here."

Wilkinson stepped in. "He's right. You're in the clear. I suspect your little show here won't do you any favours."

Bain looked at the ground. He didn't say anything.

Wilkinson flagged a black cab down. "Come on, I'm taking you home." He bundled Bain into the taxi.

Cullen watched the taxi head off up Leith Walk, towards Bathgate and Bain's home. He looked at Buxton and shook his head. "Come on, Britpop, let's get you back to Chantal."

"There's bugger all happening there."

A FEW HOURS LATER, Cullen couldn't remember how many, he sat in a corner of the pub on his own, the room starting to spin.

Sharon sat down next to him. She was bleary-eyed as well. "Well done."

He smiled at her. "Thanks. Been a nightmare of a case."

"Hasn't it just."

"I spoke to Turnbull."

"Finally." Sharon rolled her eyes. "What did he say?"

"Said he'd think about it." He swallowed a burp. "Shite."

Sharon laughed. "I want to talk."

"I'm struggling on that front."

"I miss you, Scott."

Cullen looked into her dark brown eyes. "I've missed you, too."

"I'm sorry about what happened."

"Not as sorry as me. I've been a dickhead."

"I want you to know something. When I went out with Cargill, I was confused about who I was. We didn't really do anything, but she latched onto me and I couldn't get rid of her. I thought I might have been gay — I even came out to my parents. It turns out I wasn't."

"Christ."

"I'm sorry I didn't tell you. After all the shit I put you through with Alison. Believe me, I wanted to tell you when Cargill started working with us but I just felt so guilty."

Cullen bit his lip. "I understand."

"You do?"

"I do. Sorry for being a wanker."

"Not sure I can accept your apology, Scott."

"What?"

"I'm joking."

They looked at each other and, for the first time in days, neither of them looked away.

Sharon stroked a hand through his hair. "What do you want to do?"

"I want to see that mole again."

SCOTT CULLEN WILL RETURN IN

"BOTTLENECK"

(Scott Cullen Book 5)

Available now

Subscribe to the Ed James newsletter to keep on top of upcoming releases —
http://eepurl.com/pyjv9

AFTERWORD

AFTERWORD

Revised edition notes —

Since going full-time in January 2014, I decided to edit all four Cullen novels at the same time as writing book five and also starting a new series. Not a great idea in terms of sanity but, now I'm the other side of it, I can really appreciate how much my style has come on in that time.

This book took a hell of an editing — started out with 111,000 words and ended up with 84,000ish. It's a LOT better for it. Tighter, more focused and less fuckin' from Bain.

Now, on with something new.

Ed James

East Lothian, July 2014

Original Afterword —

When I clicked submit for GHOST IN THE MACHINE to be released on Amazon last April, I didn't expect to have four full novels published in fifteen months. That's pretty freaky.

Anyway, that's DYED IN THE WOOL finally done and out of my system.

Thinking back, this one had a bloody ridiculous gestation like all of the others. Back when DEVIL IN THE DETAIL was just going to be a stopgap novella (instead of the longest — well, second longest now — Cullen book), this was going to be the second full novel. It started out as a terrorist bombing Edinburgh, then became about the EDL and then about Neil Lennon being attacked on the football pitch. I finally settled on this plot when I remembered a discarded plot line from an early draft of GHOST IN THE MACHINE (if you must know, Caroline Adamson's friend Steve Allen was killed, and there was some weird gay revenge motive thing going on — glad I sorted that one out) — there's something in that which I've not used and will be in the next Cullen book.

It's been pretty difficult this one. It was the first one I wrote with my amazing new method on my amazing new MacBook Air (coming up to a year old now), so I got the plot nailed down really early. I plotted it in November, between chaotic drafts of FIRE IN THE BLOOD and before I plotted a non-Cullen book out at Christmas (more on that later). I wrote the first draft in February to mid-March. I got it reviewed by a couple of people, edited it and then did something I've seen on the net — get some fans to read it through and comment.

A huge thanks, therefore, go to Jon, Mags, Zoe, Andrew, Pat and Rhona. The comments I got back strengthened the book immeasurably.

I then did something that a shambling amateur like me just doesn't do — I got a professional editor. Rhona (the same one) did an incredible job in May/June, going through the lines of stuff I'd churned out and helped me turn them into something a bit more professional. Thanks go to Rhona for the editing and also, along with Claudia, for the proofing. I feel like a proper author now, and that's not something I ever expected to say.

Oh, and a couple of other mentions: Peter, I hope the sex scene meets your expectations; Rich, I doubt you'll ever read this but that wee ned trying to nick your phone was wild; the Rick Astley fanclub, I got a mention in there; and an anonymous Twitter follower (only anonymous because I can't remember), for the mole thing.

In all, I'd say that it's the best book I've done and I hope you agree.

As ever, I made some shit up. Ravencraig (the eagle-eyed among you will remember a mention in FIRE IN THE BLOOD) does not exist, of course. And to the real 'Crystal' Methven — I just couldn't resist.

What's next, you wonder?

Well, followers of my blog will know that I've moved job and I'm now based in London four days a week, so my writing pattern is certainly different. I'm trying to keep it up and I've managed to get a load of editing done in the last few weeks. The next big project is finishing off SHOT THROUGH THE HEART — my vampire thriller that has nothing to do with Scott Cullen or any of those clowns — which is about 75% through a fairly tight first draft, but is a lot shorter than this beast so should be out in late August or so.

I've already plotted out much of Cullen five (BOTTLENECK). I've got Cullen six pretty straight in my head.

Thanks again for buying and reading this — do let me know what you think of my books. And I'd really appreciate it if you would leave a review where you bought this — it seriously helps indie authors like me.

Ed James
London, July 2013

Subscribe to my newsletter at http://eepurl.com/pyjv9 (news on new releases and miscellany).

Visit edjamesauthor.com for my blog and news on forthcoming books.

Speak to me — I don't bite!

- Twitter is at twitter.com/edjamesauthor
- Facebook is at facebook.com/edjamesauthor
- Email me at ed@edjames.co.uk

34581293R00174

Printed in Great Britain
by Amazon